Praise for

RACING THE LIGHT

"*Racing The Light* is another grand slam for the master storyteller Robert Crais. If there's a better dynamic duo than Elvis Cole and Joe Pike in all of crime fiction, I'm not aware of it."   —David Baldacci, author of *Long Shadows*

"I devoured Robert Crais's *Racing the Light*, starring his iconic duo PI Elvis Cole and ex-cop Joe Pike. This time, Cole and Pike search for a missing son at the behest of the boy's mother, and *Racing the Light* packs plenty of twists and turns to keep the pages turning. What makes Crais's writing stand out is the deft humor, warmth, and heart on every page. Crais does the impossible in this thriller: moves the story at a breakneck pace while creating characters you absolutely adore."

—Lisa Scottoline, author of *What Happened to the Bennetts*

"Elvis and Joe return in *Racing the Light*, a novel as deeply human as it is compelling. If you want to understand why Robert Crais is considered a modern master of crime fiction, crack this book open now. His trademark humor and insight drive every page."

—Gregg Hurwitz, author of *Dark Horse*

"Crais' affection for his characters, masterful pacing, and dry wit make this one of his better efforts. . . . [Crais] keeps the traditional detective novel alive and well."

—*Kirkus Reviews*

"Crais is a meticulous plotter. This story is dazzling."
—*Dayton Daily News*

"Everything builds toward a smash-up ending, which author Crais delivers."
—*St. Louis Post-Dispatch*

Praise for

A DANGEROUS MAN

"[Crais is] an enlightened crime writer."
—*The New York Times Book Review*

"If you've always wished Lee Child's Jack Reacher had a little more balance in his life—but the same formidable talents—you'll love Joe Pike and the latest book in this long, superb series. . . . A taut, exceptional thriller."
—*Kirkus Reviews* (starred review)

"Crais is a whip-smart writer. Cole and Pike are carefully drawn, multilayered characters who've grown more complex through the years. This is one of the very best entries in a long-running and still first-rate series."
—*Booklist* (starred review)

"Outstanding . . . Crais begins the story with deceptive simplicity but slowly ratchets up both the tension and the action with surgical precision. . . . This one's sure to hit the bestseller charts."
—*Publishers Weekly* (starred review)

RACING THE LIGHT

—

A NOVEL

ROBERT CRAIS

G. P. PUTNAM'S SONS
New York

PUTNAM
— EST. 1838 —

G. P. PUTNAM'S SONS
Publishers Since 1838
An imprint of Penguin Random House LLC
penguinrandomhouse.com

The Library of Congress has catalogued the G. P. Putnam's Sons hardcover edition as follows:

Names: Crais, Robert, author.
Title: Racing the light: a novel / Robert Crais.
Description: New York: G. P. Putnam's Sons, [2022]
Identifiers: LCCN 2022026950 (print) | LCCN 2022026951 (ebook) |
ISBN 9780525535720 (hardcover) | ISBN 9780525535751 (ebook)
Subjects: LCGFT: Detective and mystery fiction. | Thrillers (Fiction).
Classification: LCC PS3553.R264 R33 2022 (print) | LCC PS3553.R264 (ebook) |
DDC 813/.54—dc23/eng/20220609
LC record available at https://lccn.loc.gov/2022026950
LC ebook record available at https://lccn.loc.gov/2022026951

First G. P. Putnam's Sons hardcover edition / November 2022
First G. P. Putnam's Sons trade paperback edition / May 2023
First G. P. Putnam's Sons premium edition / September 2023
G. P. Putnam's Sons premium edition ISBN: 9780525535744

Printed in the United States of America
1 3 5 7 9 10 8 6 4 2

For Martha De Laurentiis,

a light in the sky

Acknowledgments

Lauren Crais, Carol Topping, and Pat Crais: Guardian angels during perilous times. Gary Tanouye, the Elvis Cole of physicians. Alfredo Trento, Dominick Megna, and PK Shah. Diane Friedman, Max Sherman, Gregg Hurwitz, and Kim Dower: Thanks for the love, the encouragement, and the miles. Randy Sherman flew cover and had my six: Five-One-Charlie, thanks for the help. Aaron Priest and Lucy Childs: The long detour is behind us. My editor, Mark Tavani, whose ideas, questions, insights, and thoughtful collaboration made this novel immeasurably better: Thank you.

RACING
THE LIGHT

Josh Shoe

J osh agreed to meet her at the Coffee Club, which was where they'd met the first time he interviewed her. The Coffee Club wasn't actually a club, a misnomer Josh found annoying, though he was a regular customer. The Coffee Club was a short drive from his bungalow and open late enough to abide his schedule. Most of the tables that night were filled. People in their twenties. Like Josh.

"Didn't show, huh? I get stiffed, that's it. I swear."

This was Bren, barista-cum-waitress, who appeared out of nowhere. Josh hunched across the table to cover his phone.

"This isn't a date, not that it's your business."

"Whatever. Want another soy mocha cap?"

Josh still nursed his second. A soy mocha cappuccino at the Coffee Club cost six bucks.

"Just the check. *Thank you.*"

The "thank you" was firm and pointed, saying, *Leave me alone.*

"You're such a crab."

"*Thank you.*"

"Crab."

Bren flipped him off, returned to the coffee bar, and let Josh return to his waiting. Bren acted all flirty, but she didn't really like him. She wanted to be on his show.

Josh was large, heavy, and felt like a giant seated at the annoying micro-table in the rear. He glanced at his phone and tapped out another text.

Is there a problem? Should we reschedule?

None of his earlier three texts had been answered. Their agreement had been to meet at half past midnight, this being after *she* called *him*, and told him she had something for him and wanted to see him, tonight, *now*. And *now*, two large soy mocha caps after he arrived, she was forty-six minutes late.

Josh hissed through his teeth, which was something he did when he was annoyed.

Obviously you got hung up or forgot or something. Whatever. I'm leaving. Hope you're not dead in a morgue. Please let me know.

Josh stood to go as Skylar stepped through the door, slender and gorgeous, wearing a black moto jacket over a short black dress, black tights, and black ankle boots. Her hair was different. Burnished auburn, long on one side, short on the other, with a single blonde streak. Even with Josh being all the way in the back, their eyes locked, and she smiled, a crooked smile he found charming. Josh had never decided if the smile made her seem knowing or bored. Josh liked her. He was even impressed by her, but he was also put off. She was smart—maybe, in a way, brilliant—but she was dumb as a rock in other ways, and deeply flawed. She was one of the most self-destructive people he knew.

Josh said, "I was leaving."

"Sit. Leave three minutes from now. I have something for you."

"I was worried. And now I'm annoyed. You couldn't text?"

Her eyes crinkled with lines almost too faint to see.

"I'm sorry. I'm a horrible person. Now sit."

Josh made a big sigh to show his annoyance. But he sat.

"This is me, sitting. I'm still mad, but I'm sitting. Want a coffee?"

"Can't. My car's waiting, but I had to see you."

Josh rolled his eyes.

"Tonight. Now, as I recall."

She placed her phone on the table near his, and her hands over the phone.

"I have something special for you."

"Lucky me. I wait for an hour, and I get thirty seconds with your royal highness?"

"You get this."

She turned over a hand to reveal a silver flash drive. Under the table, she toed his shoe. Josh moved his foot, but she toed him again.

"You're kicking me."

"I'm kicking you because you'll be impressed."

She wiggled the flash drive back and forth—tick tock, tick tock—like a metronome.

Josh frowned.

"I don't get it."

"It's a flash drive."

"I know what it is. I can see it. And?"

"Ah. But you can't see what it contains."

"I was already annoyed. Now I'm *really* annoyed."

"Take it. See what's on it. You'll have questions, which I will answer."

Josh scowled at the flash drive.

"I hate games like this."

"This isn't a game."

The crooked smile had vanished, and now she seemed watchful.

"Is it your new work?"

"No. Not me."

"Then what?"

She nudged the flash drive toward him.

"Secrets. Dangerous secrets."

"You're annoying. You're amazing and beautiful and talented, but you're a very annoying person."

She touched the flash drive closer.

"Only when I respect someone."

"You could talk to me like a real person and spare the drama."

"I don't have time tonight or I would. Once you see, you'll understand."

"What am I supposed to do with these dangerous secrets?"

Her watchful eyes darkened.

"Talk to me and we'll decide. Until then, don't tell anyone unless you tell everyone. You see?"

"No. I don't."

Josh felt nervous. He was afraid she had gotten herself involved with something shady, and wondered why she wanted to involve him. He pushed the drive with his finger.

"Where did you get this, whatever it is?"

"I'll fill in the blanks when we talk. You'll have questions, Josh Shoe. I'll have answers."

Her phone chimed. Skylar glanced at the screen, and stood.

"Gotta jet. My driver."

Josh stopped her with a touch. She was serious, and being as real as she had ever been, which worried him even more.

"Sky? What's going on?"

"You're a good dude, Josh. We'll talk."

She turned and hurried toward the door.

Josh quickly left money on the table and tried to catch up, but two other couples rose to leave at the same time, and Josh fell behind. When he finally reached the sidewalk, Skylar stood at the open door of a black Uber car.

The crooked smile touched her lips when she saw him, but now her smile seemed sad.

Skylar slid into the Uber's backseat and Josh watched her glide away.

A light-colored sedan slowly passed and fell in behind her. Josh glanced at the passing car, but thought nothing of it. He would, later, but on this night, the sedan was simply a car within a school of cars, no different from any other.

PART ONE

The Damage
They Do

1

Elvis Cole

My office occupied a two-room suite four floors above Santa Monica Boulevard on the western edge of Hollywood. Most of my business came by referral from Attorneys or satisfied clients, but do-it-yourself parties often found me online. Prospective clients usually reached out by phone or email, most to inquire about price or learn whether I could help with their problem. Some only wanted to vent. Making an appointment was encouraged. Venters were not. Walk-in business was rare.

On the day she came to my office, the sky was unnaturally clear, a clarity so abnormal the City of Angels seemed bathed in a nuclear glow. The French doors to my balcony offered an unobstructed view to the sea, but the glare was so bright I found myself squinting. The French doors were usually open, but that day they were closed. The heat.

By ten-oh-seven, I had filed two reports and returned three calls. Another backbreaking day at the office.

I said, "How about we grab a sandwich and fight crime tomorrow? Sound good?"

The Pinocchio clock on the wall beside the door to my partner's office had a long nose, a jaunty yellow cap, and bulging eyes. The eyes slid side to side, but Pinocchio didn't answer. He never answered, but he always listened.

I said, "Okay, then, let's do it. I'm starving."

At ten-oh-nine, I was packing up when the outer door opened and a woman in a tailored navy pantsuit stepped in from the hall. She was tall and square-shouldered, and her sleek black hair was pulled into a short ponytail. A man in an expensive summer-weight gray suit followed her. The man was maybe six-three, broad, and sported hands the size of catchers' mitts. They wore their suits like uniforms.

The woman eyed me with a casual curiosity.

"Elvis Cole?"

I leaned back and considered her.

"He's downtown with the mayor. Was he expecting you?"

The woman drifted closer as her friend circled to the French doors. He looked outside, opened the doors, stepped out, and raised a hand to shield his eyes. He peered over the rail, then checked overhead as if he expected Spider-Man to swing down from above. When he looked up, his jacket opened and a holster peeked out. I made them for federal agents or bill collectors.

"If you guys aren't building inspectors, I charge for my time."

The man stepped inside and went to my partner's office. The door was closed.

The man said, "Anyone home?"

I leaned farther back until my chair squeaked.

"Marines. Go in. Say hi."

The big man peeked inside and glanced at the woman.

"He's alone."

I leaned forward and touched the edge of my desk. A Dan Wesson .38 Special revolver waited in the drawer, but the drawer and the pistol were a mile away.

"Are you going to tell me what you want, or do I have to guess?"

They turned without a word, returned to the outer office, and the big woman opened the door. A small, older woman clutching an enormous brown purse entered. She wore no makeup or jewelry, and looked to be in her seventies. Her wispy hair was more gray than not, and her thin flower-print dress looked shabby. She glanced at me, glanced quickly away, and turned to the woman in the blue suit. She appeared uncomfortable.

The woman in the blue suit gave her a gentle smile.

"We'll be right outside, Ms. S. Take as much time as you like."

"Thanks so much, Wendy."

Wendy and her partner left, and Ms. S finally looked at me. She raked threads of hair behind an ear, but they floated free and drifted toward the ceiling.

"You're Mr. Cole? The detective?"

I stood, hoping she couldn't hear my stomach grumble.

"I am. And you?"

She came to my desk and held out a weathered hand. She was one of those people who should've avoided the sun, but hadn't. Faint spots and fine creases covered her skin.

"My name is Adele Schumacher. Forgive me for not phoning first. I don't care for phones."

I glanced toward the hall.

"And them?"

"Wendy and Kurt?"

She frowned as if my question was odd.

"They're my helpers."

I nodded. Helpers.

"I apologize for showing up without an appointment. If now isn't a good time, I could wait or come back later if you'd—"

I held up a hand, stopping her.

"I think I can fit you in. Please, sit."

She sat in one of the leather director's chairs across from my desk. I took my seat again, facing her.

"All right, Ms. Schumacher, how can I help?"

"You find missing persons."

A statement of fact.

"Among other things, yes. We offer a wide array of services."

We. This was the detective presenting himself as a multinational corporation.

"My son was kidnapped. I'd like you to find him."

I pulled a yellow legal pad close.

"Are we talking about a minor child?"

"Josh is twenty-six. Joshua Albert Schumacher."

She spelled his first and last names. She probably figured I was smart enough to spell Albert.

"If you believe he was kidnapped, you should call the police."

"I filed a missing persons report four days ago. The first detective referred me to a second detective, but I haven't heard from her since."

I nodded. She probably filed the report at her local division station, but division dicks don't look for missing people. The division dick would have passed the case downtown to a detective at the Missing Persons Unit.

"Uh-huh. Have you received a ransom demand?"

"I have not and don't expect to. I believe Josh was kidnapped to silence him."

"Silence him?"

"Yes."

She drew a 9x12 manila envelope from her purse and placed it on my desk.

"I have pictures of Josh here, and information you'll need. Address and phone, a key to his home, and so forth. The second detective's card is here, too. She was smug."

I made another note. Smug.

"Why would someone want to silence him?"

"He's an investigative journalist. He was going to expose them."

"Expose who?"

"You may have heard of his show. *In Your Face with Josh Shoe*. It's a very popular podcast."

"Sorry. I'll look it up."

"He's becoming quite famous."

"I'll give it a listen."

I tapped the pad with the pen, encouraging her to continue.

"So who is it Josh was going to expose who kidnapped him but hasn't demanded a ransom?"

She raked the hair behind her ear again, but it still didn't stay.

"He's likely being held at a secret facility. If so, your job will not be easy."

"Secret facility?"

"In Nevada. They might be holding him at Site 4 or Area 6, but he definitely went to Area 51. He's been there several times."

Pinocchio's eyes slid from side to side. Their unchanging precision was reassuring. I cleared my throat.

"Area 51. Where the government develops stealth aircraft."

Her eyes grew bright, like bits of mica catching the sun.

"Stealth technology is the least of their projects."

I jotted another note. Aliens.

I wondered if Wendy and Kurt were outside laughing.

"Uh-huh. And did you explain this to the police?"

Adele Schumacher sat a bit taller.

"They dismissed me just as you have. The difference between them and you is you work for hire. You are my last best hope, Mr. Cole. I need you."

She fished a white envelope from her purse. The envelope was thick and held closed by pink rubber bands. She peeled off the bands and showed me the contents. The envelope was fat with hundred-dollar bills.

She said, "How much would you like?"

I wet my lips.

"You shouldn't carry so much cash, Ms. Schumacher. You could lose it."

"Electronic transactions are not secure. Cash is secure. How much?"

She pushed the envelope toward me.

"I don't want your money. Please put it away."

She didn't.

"I don't expect you to find him for free, Mr. Cole. How much?"

"Have Wendy and Kurt tried to find him?"

"They did what they could before we went to the police. Joshua has not been admitted to a hospital in Los Angeles County, nor has he been arrested."

The envelope was heavy with cash, but she didn't seem to be tiring.

"Have you asked his friends? His friends might know."

She glanced at the manila envelope.

"I have. They don't. But I've included a list of Joshua's three dearest friends, so please follow up. Ryan has known Josh the longest, and even Ryan can't reach him. I assume you'll want to see Josh's home? He rents a bungalow in Los Feliz."

"Maybe."

The big-time detective laid out his game plan: Maybe.

"Ryan is there now, waiting to help however he can."

I wrote Ryan on the pad and drew a box around it.

"Have these people all tried to reach your son?"

"Yes, and he hasn't responded. I've also left messages. I can't know if the calls have been blocked or his phone was taken, but Josh would have responded. If he hasn't, he can't. Quod erat demonstrandum."

"Q.E.D.?"

"Yes. It means the proof is—"

"I know what it means, Ms. Schumacher."

She lowered the cash. Adele Schumacher seemed like a nice person. She was a delusional conspiracy theorist at worst or a gullible eccentric at best, but her fear was genuine. I chose my words carefully.

"Does Josh have a girlfriend or boyfriend?"

Her eyes grew vague and she didn't respond. I hadn't accepted her money. She was afraid I wouldn't. I tried to sound reassuring.

"He's twenty-six, Ms. Schumacher. He's single and self-employed, which means he's mobile. I go to the Sierras each year. There's no cell service, my phone doesn't work, and nobody can reach me. Josh probably left with a friend and didn't think to tell you. It happens."

"Josh hates the outdoors."

"It was only an example."

Her eyes focused, and she placed her palm on my desk.

"Josh and I meet for lunch every two weeks. If Josh can't make it, he lets me know, and we meet the following day. Always. Joshua never misses our lunch."

"But this week he did. Things like this happen."

Ms. Schumacher leaned forward, and her mica eyes grew sharp.

"Mr. Cole, my son makes very little money. When he moved out to live on his own, we began meeting for lunch. At those lunches I give him cash. It's what he lives on. So when I tell you Josh has never, not once, missed our lunch without calling, he hasn't. But this past week, he did. He did not call, nor reschedule, and he has not responded. Therefore, he cannot."

"Q.E.D.?"

"Q.E.D."

We stared at each other.

"Is his father in the picture?"

"His father—my ex-husband—refuses to support him. They barely speak."

She leaned so far forward she gripped my desk for support.

"Josh was working on an exposé. He had an inside source, he said, and proof, but he wouldn't say more. Josh has done shows about classified programs before. I'm certain the two are connected."

"An exposé about aliens."

She sat back.

"Does it matter? My son is missing. I want you to find him."

She counted out twenty one-hundred-dollar bills, hesitated, and counted another ten. She pushed the stack toward me.

"Three thousand dollars. If he's with a friend as you say, finding him should be easy. Find him, and I'll double this amount."

I told myself it couldn't hurt. I could swing by his

bungalow and maybe have a line on her son by the end of the day. And even if I didn't, Adele would feel better knowing I was looking.

I picked up the bills, kept ten, and pushed the rest back.

"Let's start with this."

"I'd like a receipt, please."

"Of course."

She tucked the receipt into her purse, stood, and offered her hand.

"Please find him."

"Try not to worry. I'm sure he wasn't abducted."

She looked at me as if I were slow.

"Are you, Mr. Cole? I'm not. I've seen things you can't imagine."

Adele Schumacher went to the door and let herself out. Wendy stepped in a moment later, and came to my desk.

"You'll do it?"

I nodded.

"This is me, twenty-four-seven."

Wendy gave me a plain, cream-colored card bearing her name, phone number, and email. Gwendolyn Vann.

I raised my eyebrows.

"I went with a Sherlock Holmes motif, myself. The magnifying glass. The deerstalker cap. People seem to like it."

Wendy tipped her head at the Mickey Mouse phone perched at the end of my desk.

"Sit tight. Mickey will ring in three minutes."

"Who's calling? Aliens?"

Wendy ignored me.

"When the mouse rings, answer."

Wendy walked out and closed the door. I waited. Three minutes later, the phone rang.

I answered.

2

lvis Cole Detective Agency. If we can't find it, it can't be found. To whom am I speaking?"

The man's voice was cultured and reasonable. He did not introduce himself nor greet me. He began as if we were in the middle of a conversation.

"So you agreed to help. Good, I'm pleased, but I'm surprised a man with your credentials took the job."

People who didn't introduce themselves were usually top-tier corporate executives or self-absorbed celebrities. I went with corporate.

"Surprises are my business. To whom am I speaking?"

He went on as if I hadn't spoken.

"So tell me, I'm curious why this nonsense about aliens and secret projects didn't put you off."

I carried the phone out to the balcony. The Mickey phone didn't have a remote, so I'd bought a twenty-five-foot extension. The line was tight as a bowstring when I reached the rail, and tighter when I peered down at the street.

I said, "Pretend I just answered and let's begin again. Elvis Cole Detective Agency, this is Elvis Cole. To whom am I speaking?"

He muttered so softly I barely heard him.

"Good Lord."

"No, not the Lord. Elvis. Who is this?"

Four floors below, Wendy, Kurt, and Adele crossed the sidewalk to a cream-colored Mercedes sedan. A red-haired man by the Mercedes opened the rear passenger-side door for Adele, helped her inside, and climbed in behind the wheel. Wendy saddled up in the front passenger seat. Kurt slipped into a white Lincoln SUV waiting behind the Mercedes. The Mercedes pulled away. The Lincoln pulled out behind the Mercedes. Trail car. The shabby housedress and wispy hair didn't go with a top-of-the-line Mercedes and personal security detail, but people were often surprising.

They drove away as the caller responded.

"This is Corbin Schumacher. Adele is my ex-wife."

I watched the Mercedes disappear and returned to my desk.

"Making you Joshua Schumacher's father?"

"As much as it pains me, yes. I'm also the person who suggested Adele contact you."

"Do we know each other?"

"We do not, but I had you vetted. Your reputation for this kind of thing is excellent."

"Uh-huh. This kind of thing being?"

"Finding people. When I hire someone, I hire the best."

"Let me stop you, Mr. Schumacher. Adele hired me, not you, so everything she and I discussed is confidential."

"Adele knows I'm calling. Please confirm this with her. I'm not snooping behind her back."

"Then why the call?"

"First, to make sure you don't take advantage of her."

"I thought you had me vetted."

"Let's be frank. The woman came to you with an outlandish story and a bag of cash. Her claims would make most people doubt her sanity, yet you took the job. One type of man might refuse. Another might see an opportunity to take advantage."

I made my hand into a gun and fired at Pinocchio's nose. The puppet didn't flinch. He was a helluva puppet.

"Luckily for Adele, I'm a third type. Is there a second reason you called?"

"Yes. To explain the true reason you were hired."

"You don't believe the Men in Black kidnapped your son?"

Corbin Schumacher hesitated. When he spoke again his voice was softer, but somehow more threatening.

"I'm speaking difficult truths, Mr. Cole, but let's be clear. I will not allow you to take advantage of her. I also will not allow you to demean her."

The pain in his voice left me embarrassed.

"I apologize. I was trying to lighten what's clearly a painful subject, and I made a mess of it. I'm sorry."

He sounded tired when he continued.

"Josh hasn't been kidnapped. This is Josh being Josh, ignoring her."

"Why would Josh ignore her?"

"Because he can. He's self-absorbed, arrogant, irresponsible, and rotten with privilege."

"Oh. The usual reasons."

"He's probably in his hobbit hole right now, playing video games or wasting his life with one of his degenerate friends. If he's out of town, well, since he has no job and lives off his mother, he might be gone for days."

"His mother told me he's a journalist. With a successful podcast."

Schumacher laughed.

"If you call pandering to fools on a homemade talk show no one has heard of journalism. I don't. He isn't. Period."

Period.

"Regardless, Adele has spun herself into a frenzy with this kidnap business. The stress isn't good for her."

"Hence, me."

"Correct. I expect you'll find him in a day or two, and end this nightmare."

"And if it takes longer?"

"If you need help, call Wendy. If Wendy can't help, I have other resources."

Resources was an interesting word.

"What do you do for a living, Mr. Schumacher?"

"As little as possible. I was a teacher once at the college level. I'm retired."

"What if I find your son but he won't contact his mother?"

"Your mission is complete when you locate my son."

Mission was another interesting word.

"Then, if you would, call Wendy. Wendy will take over."

"Do Wendy and Kurt work for you or Adele?"

"They work for Adele. Like you."

"Why would Adele need bodyguards?"

"Is that what she called them?"

"She called them helpers."

"So they are. They drive, run errands, whatever Adele wants."

I didn't respond, and after a while he sounded tired again.

"Mr. Cole. Adele and I were married a long time. We worked under strenuous conditions for almost as long, and these conditions took a toll. Especially on her. When our marriage ended, I didn't stop caring for her."

He paused, but only for a moment.

"Adele believes our son is being held by the government in Area 51. She actually believes this. She believes our phone calls are monitored by artificial intelligence, corporations manipulate our biometrics, and half a hundred other ludicrous notions. If Adele watches the news, she can't sleep because murderers creep past her window. Do you understand what I'm saying?"

"Wendy and Kurt keep the monsters away."

"Yes. A last point, and I'll let you get on with it. As I said, I'm pleased you agreed to help."

His voice firmed up again.

"But I don't know you. Don't be tempted to run up the bill. I'm not Adele."

Corbin Schumacher stopped. He was waiting for a response, so I let him wait before I answered.

"A gentleman came to see me about ten years ago. Nice man. A retired physician. He was frantic. His grandchildren—a boy and a girl—had been abducted by their mother—his daughter-in-law was a foreign national—and taken out of the country. Mom refused to bring them back to the U.S., and wouldn't let their father or grandparents see them or speak to them. I agreed to find them and arrange for their return."

"What does this have to do with Adele?"

"The doctor gave me a check for eight thousand dollars. The check cleared and the money was in my account that afternoon. Four days later, I returned the full amount."

"Why are you telling me this?"

"His daughter-in-law and grandchildren died in an auto accident the year before. The poor guy couldn't accept the loss, I guess, so he found a way to explain their absence."

I waited for Corbin Schumacher to say something, but he didn't.

"It's the same with every client, Mr. Schumacher. A stranger comes to me with a problem. I can't know what's real until I see for myself."

"Of course."

"Whatever Adele believes, no matter why she believes

it, has nothing to do with her problem. She can't reach her child, and wants to know he's safe. I'll find him, and report what I find."

Corbin Schumacher was silent for several more seconds.

"Looks like Adele hired the right man."

"One more thing, Mr. Schumacher."

"Yes?"

"In the future, any conversation I have about this case or Joshua will be with Adele, until or unless Adele tells me otherwise. Not Wendy. Not you. Are we clear?"

Corbin Schumacher went silent again. I thought Wendy and Kurt might crash through the door and grab the thousand dollars, but they didn't.

I asked him again.

"Are we clear?"

The line went dead. The call was over. We were clear.

3

I tucked two of the hundreds into my wallet, filled out a deposit slip for the remaining eight, and opened the manila envelope.

Adele had seemed disheveled with her flyaway hair and frumpy dress, but the information she left was presented with PowerPoint precision.

The first page showed four photographs of a heavy, unsmiling young man with a round, clean-shaven face, a double chin, and dark red hair.

Detective-2 Veronica Largo's LAPD business card was clipped to the second page. The card identified Largo as a Missing Persons Unit detective. The case number and date of filing were written on the back of the card. I put Largo's card aside and flipped to the third page.

The third page looked like a dossier.

Joshua Albert Schumacher's name, current address, email, and cell number led off. His height (6'3"), weight (280 lb), hair and eye color (rd, bl), blood type (O-neg), and date of birth followed. His social security, driver's license, and passport numbers came next, then a description of his car (a ten-year-old black-on-black MINI Cooper) and the Cooper's license number. A highlighted note at the bottom of the page read: FINGERPRINTS AND DNA PROFILE PROVIDED UPON REQUEST. Including his blood type was odd, but the DNA profile stopped me. Who kept their son's DNA profile lying around and why would they have it?

I studied Josh's phone number, pulled Mickey close, and punched in his number. Corbin thought Josh was ignoring his mother, but maybe I'd get lucky.

A flat computer voice answered.

"The message box is full."

So much for luck.

The last page was labeled FRIENDS. Adele had listed three names, notes about each, and their contact information. She'd already told me about Ryan Seborg, who she described as Josh's oldest and closest friend. Traci Tanner and Josh had been friends since high school, where they were active in the school's math, science, astronomy, and film clubs. Davis Kleimann and Josh had met during Josh's one and only year at Caltech. According to the notes, Adele had spoken with all three, and all three denied having knowledge of Josh's whereabouts. This made me wonder why Adele suggested I speak to them. Since all three claimed to know nothing, maybe she believed they were lying. Maybe she thought I would pistol-whip them into coming clean.

I called Largo first and got the inevitable voice mail. I

left a message with the case number and asked her to call back as soon as possible. Sometimes, they do. Most of the time, they don't.

I phoned Tanner and Kleimann next. Traci Tanner explained she wasn't as close to Josh as she once was, and the two hadn't spoken in more than a year. Davis Kleimann sounded wary. When I told him Adele Schumacher had given me his number, his voice turned hostile.

"I don't know you. You could be after anything."

"I'm after Josh. Didn't his mother speak to you?"

"These people mean nothing to me. Don't call again. I mean it."

Kleimann hung up. I glanced at the heading on the page and shook my head. Friends.

I pushed the pages aside, got up, and wandered out onto the balcony. A woman named Cindy runs a beauty supply business in the office next door. Some days, she would sit on her balcony, reading. Other days, she would lay out in a bikini so small it appeared to be made of dental floss. She wasn't outside. I peeked across the divider separating our balconies and found her at her desk. She saw me and raised a hand. I motioned her to come out. She shook her head and mouthed, "Too hot." Then she pointed at me, touched her temple, and made you're-out-of-your-mind circles. I laughed and returned to my desk.

It was six minutes after eleven. I began thinking more about the deli downstairs, and less about the Schumachers. The deli served a very nice turkey baguette with Chinese hot mustard. The Schumachers probably didn't. On the other hand, Adele had given me one thousand Schumacher dollars. I girded myself and called Ryan Seborg.

"Hullo."

"Ryan? Elvis Cole. Has Adele Schumacher spoken to you about me?"

After Tanner and Kleimann, I expected the worst.

"Uh-huh. You're going to find Josh."

Progress. At least Seborg was in the loop.

"I'm going to try. Are you at his residence now?"

"Yeah. It's our studio. We do a podcast together."

"*In Your Face*."

His voice perked up.

"Yeah. You've heard the show?"

"Adele told me."

"Oh."

"She also gave me permission to look through Josh's things. Are you willing to answer a few questions?"

"What are you looking for?"

"Clues."

"Okay."

Seborg didn't laugh.

I said, "That was levity."

"Okay. When will you be here?"

"Noon sound good?"

"Okay."

"Ryan?"

"Yeah?"

"Adele believes Josh was kidnapped. Why would she think someone kidnapped him?"

"His mom—"

Ryan hesitated, as if deciding how to answer.

"His mom's kinda weird. I love her, but—"

"She's weird."

"Uh-huh."

"So you don't think the Men in Black grabbed him?"

"Nope. Not this time."

"Okay, Ryan. I'll see you soon."

Nope. Not this time.

I was wondering what he meant when my cell phone rang. The caller ID read CITY LAPD.

"Elvis Cole Detective Agency. Brand-name detection at cut-rate prices. Discounts available."

A woman said, "You always answer like a cheap ad?"

"Sometimes I do impressions. Want to hear my Tom Cruise?"

"This is Detective Largo returning your call. What do you want?"

"Adele Schumacher filed an MPR regarding her son—"

She interrupted. Impatient and rushed.

"Yeah, yeah, you left the case number. What's the word? Her boy turn up?"

Largo wasn't out of line for asking. Eighty percent of adults reported as missing returned voluntarily within three days, and most returned in two.

"He hasn't, which is why I called."

"Okay. What do you want?"

"Leads. Got anything?"

"Sure. Fourteen missing women and eleven missing men. Six of these women were likely taken south against their will, two are pregnant, and one of the pregnant girls has the mental capacity of a four-year-old. The other has a history of suicide attempts, so she'll probably try again if I don't find her fast enough. Three of the remaining six have dementia, and, oh, by the way, half the dicks in my unit were pulled to work hate crimes. Want to hear about the men?"

Largo didn't sound smug. She sounded fried.

"I get it, Detective. You're swamped. I just want to know if you have anything I can use."

She cleared her throat.

"As of this morning, Schumacher hasn't been arrested in the past two weeks, he isn't in jail, he hasn't been admitted to a hospital in L.A. County, and he's not in the morgue. I issued a BOLO on him and his vehicle, which, by the way, this case does not warrant, but we haven't gotten a hit. Anything else?"

These were standard due diligence checks she could do at her office.

"Yeah. Have you interviewed anyone besides his mother?"

"Cole. If she gets a ransom demand, our priorities will shift, but this report should not have been taken. The guy's a voluntary. Trust me. He isn't impaired and there's no evidence of foul play. An adult is free to disappear without telling anyone, no matter how much pain it causes. They're a shit if they do, but it isn't illegal. So, excuse me, but finding three old ladies with Alzheimer's and a pregnant suicide seems more urgent than chasing a guy who split to get away from his mother."

"His mother believes he was kidnapped."

Largo groaned.

"C'mon, Cole, the Men in Black? Area 51? You should be ashamed of yourself, taking money from this woman."

"The Area 51 stuff is beside the point. He's missing. She hired me to find him."

"Then look in Area 51. That's where you'll find him."

"Thanks for nothing, Largo. Sorry I bothered you."

"I mean it. Did she mention his arrest record?"

I hesitated.

"No."

"Two pops for misdemeanor trespassing, the first twenty-six months ago, the second nineteen months ago. Want to guess where?"

"Area 51."

"How about that? One mile on the wrong side of Rachel, Nevada, which is as close as the military lets anyone get."

"You think he went back?"

Largo laughed.

"His mother does. Anything else I can help with?"

I tried to think of something.

"Does his record show other arrests?"

"Nope. Only the two trespasses."

"Was he arrested with anyone else?"

"Hang on."

I heard background noises, but couldn't make out what they were. Then she returned.

"The first arrest, a Ryan Seborg was with him. His mother probably mentioned him."

"She did."

"Her boy flew solo the second time. The record doesn't name anyone else."

I said, "Damn."

"Cole—"

She hesitated.

"For what it's worth, I extended the BOLO to Arizona and Nevada, and looped in Vegas PD and the Nevada sheriffs. Maybe they'll spot him."

I nodded, but she probably didn't see it.

"Okay, Detective. Thanks."

I hung up, gathered the pages, and slipped them into the envelope. The elevator was silent as I rode down to the lobby. I picked up a turkey baguette, and took it to my car.

As soon as I pulled out from beneath my building, the temperature climbed. Maybe the heat was a warning. Maybe I should've listened. I didn't.

4

The low hills between Los Feliz and the Silver Lake Reservoir were crowded with small, working-class homes, slapped-together apartment houses, and discount transmission shops. Joshua Schumacher's address led to an unlikely village of six stucco bungalows, each of the six painted a different color. The bungalows stepped uphill in two columns of three, facing each other across a central concrete stair that zigzagged between them like a deflated S. Pink, yellow, and blue were on the left. Red, mauve, and peach were on the right. Nobody was outside watering plants and no voices or music came from the windows. Everyone was probably at work. Or abducted. Schumacher lived in the middle bungalow on the left. The yellow.

I parked downhill by a fire hydrant and climbed to the yellow. The front door was open. A thin kid with limp sandy hair sat outside the door. He stood when he saw me.

"Mr. Cole?"

"Elvis. You must be Ryan."

Ryan Seborg wore cargo shorts and a green T-shirt, and looked to be in his early twenties. The limp hair curtained his eyes, but he pushed it aside.

"I don't know how I can help, but I'll try. Where do we start?"

"We'll start with you. Where do you think he went?"

Seborg shrugged and stepped into the bungalow.

"I dunno. He didn't tell me he was going away. He just left."

I followed him into a stuffy living room crowded with tired furniture and cardboard boxes stacked along a wall. A mound of bedding was heaped at the foot of the couch and open soda cans and takeout cups dotted the room like dead flies. A small dining area with a casement window was separated from a tiny kitchen by a counter loaded with takeout food containers. A short hall directly ahead led to a bathroom and a bedroom, but the living room walls stopped me. Dozens of photos of UFOs printed from the internet were pinned to the walls. Scattered among them were images of the Pyramids, the Nazca Lines, pre-Aztec temples, Stonehenge, and hand-drawn sketches of aliens. So many photos covered the walls they overlapped like fish scales.

I looked at Ryan.

"Adele believes he went to Area 51. Maybe she's right."

Seborg dropped onto the couch, and crossed his arms.

"I know what she thinks, but she's wrong. Josh doesn't

want to do Area 51 anymore. He wants to rebrand the show. He wants to go mainstream."

Ryan didn't look happy about going mainstream.

I tipped my head toward the hall.

"What's back there, his bedroom?"

"Our studio and the bathroom. We turned his bedroom into a studio, so now he sleeps out here. He keeps his clothes and stuff in the boxes."

He shrugged toward the boxes lining the wall.

I took a quick tour through the bungalow. The studio was a small, dim room split by a narrow table. Swivel chairs and microphones faced each other across the near end of the table. A desktop computer cabled to two oversized monitors filled the opposite end. Acoustic foam panels covered the ceiling and half of the walls. The remaining half was covered by even more photos. A large poster showed a glowing UFO hovering above the desert. Two words stood tall beneath the spacecraft. THEY'RE HERE.

I wandered back to the living room.

"Your podcast is about UFOs?"

"Sometimes. But our show wasn't *about* UFOs."

He made air quotes when he said "about" and seemed irritated.

"We explored subjects the mainstream media suppresses. Government programs, corporate conspiracies, whatever. And, yeah, UFOs. We did crashed and captured vehicles, reverse-engineering alien tech, the Roswell Grays—"

My head was beginning to hurt.

"The Roswell Grays?"

"The aliens recovered at Roswell. Big heads, big eyes, gray skin. The Grays."

He showed me how big by raising his hands above the sides of his head.

I changed the subject.

"Josh told Adele he was on a new story."

Ryan shook his head before I finished.

"This is bullshit. He took his laptop. He took his toothbrush, and he didn't even tell me he was going. Asshole."

He sounded hurt.

"He probably told someone, Ryan."

I asked the same questions I'd asked Adele.

"Does he have a girlfriend?"

Ryan snorted.

"Please."

"A boyfriend?"

"He's straight."

"Other friends? Traci Tanner? Davis Kleimann?"

Ryan glanced up, sneering.

"Kleimann's a dick. Traci's okay, but she hasn't been around for years. Who gave you their names? Adele?"

"If not them, who else?"

"Besides me?"

"Yeah. Anyone."

Ryan's brow furrowed, but he came up empty.

"Not really."

"Okay, if friends are out, can you get us into his email?"

Ryan blinked.

"His *personal* email?"

"Yes. Can you access his account?"

"We have a show account, but I can't get into his personal. I don't know his password."

"Then check the show account. Do it tonight and let me know. Where does he keep his financial records?"

Ryan stared as if I'd spoken Urdu.

He said, "What?"

"Receipts for payments. Bank statements. Adele gives him cash, so he probably deposits the cash into a checking account. Where does he keep his bills?"

"How would I know?"

If Josh deposited the cash into a checking account, most of his banking was likely done online, but we still had to check.

"Okay. We'll start in this room, and take it room by room."

"Start what?"

"Detecting. Digging through these boxes and going through his things. You asked how we find him. We snoop."

Ryan didn't complain. We divided the boxes and quickly went through them. Many were taped and hadn't been opened in years. Most contained clothes or books, and one held Josh's high school yearbooks. He looked glum in his ninth-grade photo. Ryan's picture was on the same page. Ryan's chin was fierce with zits, but his eyes were happy. When we'd gone through most of the boxes, I stood.

"I'll check the kitchen. You finish the boxes, okay?"

"It's just clothes and stuff."

"It's clothes and stuff until it's something else. Keep looking."

I moved into the kitchen and went to work. No notes were taped to the fridge saying *Gone to Tahoe*. The drawers and cupboards contained nothing helpful. All I found were takeout cups and crumpled soda cans spilling from a plastic bin and a mountain of bloated garbage bags piled against the kitchen door.

I moved to the dining table. The table sat in the corner beneath the casement window. The mauve bungalow sat directly across the zigzag concrete courtyard. It had a maroon door with what looked like vines across its face, and a curtained casement window beside the door. When I looked, the curtains swayed, as if someone had closed the curtains when they saw me.

I said, "Ryan?"

Ryan looked up from a box.

"Huh?"

"Who lives in the mauve?"

Ryan came up beside me and studied the mauve.

"Some old dude. He's a jerk."

I turned from the window and faced him.

"Does Josh use drugs?"

Ryan frowned.

"What are you talking about?"

"I'm not talking about weed. Does Josh use illegal drugs?"

He squinted and shrugged and looked uncomfortable.

"Maybe some weed every once in a while, but nothing illegal."

I thought about Josh rebranding their show. I thought about Ryan's enthusiasm when he told me about the Grays. "Did you and Josh argue about changing the show?"

Ryan stepped back.

"Not like you mean. Yeah, there's give and take, but the show is our baby. We were having a blast."

"Were you? Best friends and partners, having a blast, and Josh left without telling you. He must've had a reason."

Ryan Seborg blinked and wet his lips. He glanced away, and glanced back. I could see wheels spinning in his head without gaining traction.

I said, "You're the person he would have told, Ryan. I agree. But he didn't. So maybe he thought you wouldn't approve or you wouldn't want to be involved. Why wouldn't he tell you?"

The wheels spun faster and Ryan dug deep for an answer. Then his eyes lost focus and I sensed he saw someone or something he hadn't seen before. He suddenly turned and hurried down the hall to their studio.

"I think I know how to find him."

5

RYAN POINTED AT a poster of a red-haired woman wearing eight-inch stripper heels and red lingerie. It was pinned to the studio wall along with the UFOs and aliens. A banner at the top of the poster read: *MEET XXX STAR SKYLAR LAWLESS—live and in person—one day only!*

Ryan said, "Her."

An inscription was scrawled across her legs in looping red script. *Josh, I luv you! Thanks for the best O ever! Luv, SkyXXX!*

I looked at Ryan.

"A pornstar?"

Ryan dropped into a swivel chair as if he hadn't heard me and tapped at the computer's keyboard.

"Skylar Lawless. We've had her on the show twice, but the last time was like five months ago. Then, two weeks ago, she called. She probably called four or five times. They were talking a lot."

I studied the poster.

"About what?"

Ryan suddenly stopped typing.

"Josh was kinda vague. I thought she wanted back on the show, and he didn't want to tell me."

I reread the inscription she'd written. *Thanks for the best O ever!*

"Maybe she wanted something else."

Ryan swiveled around to frown at me.

"Please. Josh didn't have sex with her. We're journalists. You get involved with a guest, you lose credibility."

I glanced at Skylar Lawless in her sexy red lingerie. Her back was arched and the tip of her tongue gleamed between unnaturally white teeth.

I said, "Oh."

"I'm serious. Standards matter."

He pulled a cell phone from his shorts, tapped at the screen, and held it to his ear.

"You said Josh probably told someone where he was going, so maybe she knows."

"What are you doing?"

"Calling her."

He suddenly scowled and held up a finger, the finger telling me not to speak.

"Skylar, this is Ryan Seborg, Josh's producer. Call me as soon as you get this, please. It's important."

He left his number, ended the call, and scowled even harder.

"Bitch."

He swiveled back to the keyboard.

"If she doesn't call back, maybe she'll talk to you. Here. Look."

I moved closer and peered at the monitor.

"What is this?"

"Our website."

The *In Your Face with Josh Shoe* home page showed a picture of Josh in headphones beside the show's logo. A nav bar with a row of buttons ran below it.

"The index guide lists our episodes. Just scroll through the list and pick the show you want. We're looking for Skylar."

Ryan clicked a button, and a numbered list of the episodes appeared. Their most recent episode topped the list.

#66: CELL TOWERS OR SPYCRAFT?

Is your local cell tower spying on you?
Dr. Adrian Reece, Ph.D., offers proof
of a Silicon Valley conspiracy.

He scrolled past titles like "Alien-Human Hybrids," "Big Pharma's Hidden Nanobots," and "Is LSD the Key to Other Dimensions?"

I said, "Catchy."

"Subversive. Here, this is her."

#51: TRIPLE X STAR SKYLAR LAWLESS PAINTS NAKED!

Josh gets In Your Face with
the pornstar taking the art
world by storm!

Ryan clicked the title. A page opened, revealing a photo of Josh and Skylar Lawless at what appeared to be a crowded, upscale party. Skylar had traded the red lingerie for a black jacket over a black sequined dress, and looked better for the change.

I saw nothing sexual in the photo. They were standing together, but not as a couple. They weren't touching, or hanging on to each other, or mugging the way people mug when they're being silly or flirty. Skylar Lawless came across as a very attractive professional woman with a bright smile and intelligent eyes. Josh loomed beside her like a giant. He was the largest person in the room.

"Where was this?"

"An art gallery downtown. She was just a porn actress the first time we had her on the show, then she got into art, and Josh wanted her back. He loved the idea of her reinventing herself as a painter. Look at this stuff—"

He clicked again and photos of Skylar posing beside what appeared to be tall, rectangular posters lined with typed sentences appeared. Then I looked closer, and realized the upright rectangles were cell phones.

I said, "She paints phones?"

Ryan snorted.

"Text exchanges, like when people text each other. She says her paintings examine how men and women relate. It's bullshit."

Ryan glared at the image as if having Skylar Lawless as a guest had left a sour taste in his mouth.

"Anyway, you can listen to her interview, see more pictures, whatever. Maybe she knows where he is."

"This was five months ago?"

"Uh-huh."

A five-month-old interview was probably worthless, but her recent calls with Josh might lead to his whereabouts.

"Give me her number."

Ryan scooped up his phone and sent her contact card. The card showed a San Fernando Valley area code and an address in Studio City.

I put away my phone and circled their studio. Folders, articles, printouts, and bent soda cans spotted the table and floor. Post-it Notes sprouted from the monitors and lamps like pink and blue leaves. A white marker board bearing names and more Post-its was propped against the wall, and wadded papers spilled from a basket beneath the table.

I said, "Don't you guys ever clean?"

Ryan didn't answer. He was staring at the poster of Skylar Lawless.

I said, "Ryan."

He didn't look at me. He stared at the poster.

Ryan said, "I had a bad feeling when he told me he wanted to go mainstream. It was like everything we've been doing didn't matter. Then she called, and I got really scared."

I didn't say anything.

"I thought maybe he wanted to stop doing the show."

Ryan finally looked at me. His eyes glimmered.

"I love our show. It matters."

Ryan was frightened. Maybe of losing Josh. Maybe of losing himself.

I said, "We don't know if Josh is with her. He could be anywhere doing anything."

Ryan chewed his lip. He didn't believe me.

I said, "Either way, we need to look through the things in here."

I picked up a stack of articles about homeless encampments.

"We might find a note he left, or a name. A clue."

I began stacking the articles and folders together.

Ryan pushed to his feet as if he'd been tasered and clutched at the pages.

"Dude! This is our research. If you mix it up, I'll have to sort it out again. Please. I'll go through it."

"It's a lot to look through, Ryan."

"Please."

His eyes seemed desperate.

"This is my work."

I let go of the papers and watched Ryan put them in their proper places. When everything was as he wanted it, we left their studio and walked down the hall through the living room. A large flat-screen TV filled the wall opposite the couch. A reproduction of the *In Your Face* logo was pinned above the TV. Past the TV at the end of the wall where it opened to the dining room was a smaller sign. It looked homemade, like Josh or Ryan had printed it. The sign read: MATTER. I wanted to ask which of them had made it, but I didn't.

Ryan followed me to the door. Outside, the concrete steps were blindingly bright. Across the courtyard, the curtains hung still on the mauve bungalow.

I dug out a card and gave it to Ryan.

"If you find anything, let me know. If you hear from Josh or Skylar, call."

Ryan studied the card.

"He should have told me he was leaving."

I nodded.

Ryan flexed the card back and forth.

"Even if he wants to stop doing the show, it would've been okay. He's my best friend."

I nodded again.

"You're a good friend, Ryan. You and Josh should talk about this when he gets back."

Ryan glanced up.

"He didn't go to Nevada."

I didn't say anything.

Ryan turned and walked down the hall to their studio.

I put on my sunglasses, stepped out into the searing light, and called Wendy Vann.

Standards mattered.

Everything mattered.

Always.

6

A calico cat had appeared at the top of the steps. Two emerald hummingbirds circled a bright red feeder like angry fairies and window-mounted air conditioners thrummed against the heat. The cat noticed the hummingbirds, yawned, then fell onto his side. Otherwise, the courtyard slept.

Wendy Vann answered on the second ring.

"Wendy Vann."

"Elvis Cole. Can you talk?"

"Man, you're fast. Find him already?"

Humor.

"Adele gives Josh a biweekly cash allowance, correct?"

"That's correct."

"Does he pay monthly expenses like his phone and utilities with the allowance, or are they billed to Adele?"

"I don't know. Why?"

"I searched his bungalow, but I didn't find any billing or account records. It's possible he pays through an online service, but if the statements go to Adele, I'd like to see his call log."

"I'll get back to you."

"Same for credit and debit cards."

"Adele doesn't trust credit cards. If Josh has plastic, I doubt she'd pay for it."

"Can you find out?"

"Will do. Anything else?"

"Couple of things."

I snuck a glance at the mauve bungalow. The curtains rippled, but the ripple might mean nothing. Maybe the air conditioner disturbed the air. Maybe a cat slipped behind the curtains, chasing a bug. I turned away, and continued with Wendy.

"The day Josh missed lunch with Adele, did you or Kurt enter his home?"

"The bungalow? Sure. That afternoon. Adele was concerned."

"Did you check the windows and door locks?"

Wendy hesitated.

"What are you saying, Cole? We had no reason to expect foul play."

"Just asking. I'm coming into this late."

"No, we didn't check, but everything looked fine. Besides, Ryan was there. He hadn't been able to reach Josh, either, and they had plans."

I wanted to check the mauve, but pretended to watch the cat.

"Did you talk to the neighbors?"

"A couple of days later, but only two of his neighbors

were home, an older woman in the pink house and two kids in the peach. The kids moved in the week before, and didn't know who we were talking about. The woman wasn't much better."

I studied the pink and the peach, and snuck a peek at the mauve. The curtains did not move.

I said, "Okay, last thing."

"Go for it."

"Did Ryan mention a woman named Skylar Lawless?"

"Negative. Who is she?"

"She's a porn actress."

"Okay. And?"

"She and Josh are friends."

Wendy Vann hesitated.

"Friends friends, or *friends*?"

"It's only a possibility, but I'll run it down."

"Josh and a pornstar?"

"Let me know about the phone. Tell Adele I'm on it."

"I'm not telling her about the pornstar."

I put away my phone and climbed to the blue bungalow. It was a pretty sky blue with a dark blue door, but nobody answered. I peered through a gap in the curtains and saw rooms without furniture. The blue bungalow was vacant. The peach was across from the blue, but Wendy had spoken with the two people who lived in the peach, so I walked downhill past the mauve to the red. The red bungalow appeared lived in, but nobody was home. Which left the mauve.

I climbed the steps to the cracked maroon door. A long time ago, the cracks had been filled with liquid wood and someone had painted the door. But over time, a relentless sun had shriveled the putty. The cracks had opened, and the paint had bubbled and flaked. Now the cracks looked like varicose veins.

I knocked three times. Nobody answered, so I knocked again.

"Sorry to bother you. I'm looking for Josh Schumacher, your neighbor across the courtyard here. Could I speak with you for a second, please?"

The peeker didn't answer and the curtains didn't move.

An air conditioner jutting from the bungalow's side thumped as the compressor kicked off. Maybe the AC had drowned out my voice, and the peeker hadn't heard me. I knocked harder and spoke louder.

"We haven't been able to reach him, and we're concerned. Have you seen him recently?"

Something creaked on the far side of the door.

I said, "It's important."

Silence.

I stepped back and glimpsed the curtains ripple.

People.

I stepped into a bed of ivy and followed the ivy around the side of the bungalow past the air conditioner and gas meter to the electric meter and the breaker panel. The breaker box was old, corroded, and cocooned with cobwebs. I opened the panel and cut the power. The air conditioner stopped with a heavy thump.

I hurried back to the door, and stood to the side. Forty seconds later the door cracked open and a thin man in his sixties shouted from the crack.

"I know you're hiding, you prick! The cops are coming. I called'm!"

I stepped out fast and wedged my toe into the crack before he could close the door.

"Thanks for your help, sir. This won't take long."

He put his shoulder into the door and made unh-unh-unh sounds as he pushed.

"You prick! I'm warning ya! I got a gun!"

Unh-unh-unh.

I said, "Josh Schumacher, the guy who lives in the yellow house? Have you seen him recently?"

"This is breaking and entering. This is assault."

Unh.

I said, "Josh disappeared. His mother believes he was kidnapped."

The man stopped pushing and peered through the crack.

"You're lying. Kidnapped?"

"Tall guy, redhead, heavy—"

"I know who you mean. The lardass. You police?"

"Private."

I slipped a card into the crack. He squinted at the card, then peered at me.

"No shit. A private eye?"

"Awesome, isn't it?"

He read the card again.

"Elvis. People give you grief?"

"Not more than once."

He stared for a moment, then burst out laughing.

"Good one."

Good one.

I said, "Getting back to Josh, have you seen him?"

Leon Karsey stepped out and introduced himself. His hair was long, slicked back, and mostly gray. A stained white T-shirt hung from his shriveled shoulders, and legs as skinny as chopsticks stuck out of plaid shorts. He was barefoot.

Karsey sneered, and waved toward Josh's bungalow.

"How could I miss the bloated blimp? He lives right in front of me. I can hock a loogie on his doorknob from here."

He hocked a loogie, let fly at Josh's bungalow, and admired his work.

"The thicker they are, the farther they go. It's a gift."

You meet amazing people in my line of work.

I said, "Did Josh say where he was going?"

"Didn't say we'd spoken. We haven't traded six words since blubberboy moved in."

Amazing and sensitive.

Mr. Charm waved at the surrounding bungalows.

"I keep an eye on these people, but I don't socialize. You socialize, they end up taking advantage."

Karsey hocked another loogie, looked for a target, and let fly at the hummingbirds. Missed.

I said, "Socializing aside, have you seen him in the past week or so?"

He thought about it.

"Nope. The other kid's been around, his friend, but not the hog."

"Ryan."

"Whatever. I knew something was up. The cops been here a lot."

He probably meant Wendy and Kurt.

"A big woman with a short ponytail and a bigger man? Nice suits."

He nodded before I finished.

"Yeah, yeah, the cow and her cuck. Them, and the other two."

I said, "The other two?"

"A scarecrow and a meatball. Sniffing around fatso's place."

"A man and a woman?"

"Yeah, yeah. A skinny chick and a round guy, looked like a meatball with legs."

"How were they sniffing around?"

Karsey seemed annoyed.

"You know, *sniffing*. Banging on his door. Peeking in his windows. Cramping my ass. Like you."

The woman might be Largo, but a second possibility occurred.

I pulled out my phone, opened the *In Your Face* link, and showed him the picture of Josh and Skylar Lawless at her opening.

Karsey leaned close and grabbed his crotch.

"Holy crap on a Twinkie! How did Jabba the Hutt score a honey like her?"

"Is this the scarecrow?"

"Nah, you kiddin'? This girl has a body. The scarecrow was skinny. Her hair was darker and a lot longer. Hung straight down, ya know?"

"Sure."

"Dressed nice, though, like the cow."

"And the meatball? Taller than me? Shorter?"

"Shorter, but wide. Not fat like El Blimpo, but burly."

"They were here at night?"

"Once or twice. Hey, if you find the oinker, you get a reward?"

I put away my phone, thinking the scarecrow might be Largo and the meatball her partner.

"Nope. Flat fee. His mother hired me."

"Too bad. If they paid by the pound, you'd be set."

Karsey scratched his neck.

"The cow brought an old lady a couple of times. I guess she'd be the butterball's mother."

"Yep. Her name is Adele."

Karsey made a grunt.

"A walking wrinkle. Well, good luck to her."

He offered back my card, but I waved it away.

"Keep it. If you see Josh, I'd appreciate a call."

"I'd appreciate having my damned power turned on. Think you can hook me up?"

I turned on his power, and left. I felt pretty good. I had a lead. Her name was Skylar Lawless.

Two gardeners in a dusty red pickup truck watched me come down the steps. The driver wore a wide straw hat and wraparound shades. His partner sported a long black ponytail and three-day stubble. They watched from the safety of their truck with the windows up and the AC blasting cold air, but they scowled like men trapped in an oven. I nodded, one potential heatstroke victim acknowledging another, but the driver turned away. Heat made people sour.

I started my car, hit the AC, and phoned Skylar Lawless.

A pleasant female voice answered.

"Hey, this is Sky. Let's talk later, okay?"

The same voice mail as Ryan.

"Ms. Lawless, hi, my name is Jeremy Floyd. I own a gallery in Tucson, and I'd love to discuss showing your work. Perhaps we can meet for drinks? If you're interested, and I hope you are, I can be reached at the following number."

I recited my cell, plugged her address into my map, and waved at the gardeners as I left. Neither waved back. Sour.

Skylar Lawless lived in a lovely French Normandy apartment building two blocks south of Ventura Boulevard in an enclave of older upscale homes and boutique prewar apartment houses. Apartment #3.

I slowed when I reached her address and idled past.

Set well back from the curb behind a sycamore tree, the building with its corner turrets and black slate roof looked more like a manor home than an apartment house. A matching mailbox sat beside an entry gate. A gray tile walk led through the gate past the sycamore and a small green lawn to a courtyard. Built in the twenties when the Valley was a weekend getaway, it looked like a place where studio bosses kept mistresses and dipso screenwriters earned two grand a week slugging it out with deadline demons.

I checked the street for Schumacher's car as I passed, but his black-on-black MINI was not observed.

I parked and went to the mailbox. Five brass doors were set in its face, each showing a nameplate and an apartment number. One, two, four, and five showed names, but not three. The nameplate was blank. I checked to see if anyone was watching, then used a Kwick Pick to open three. Three was empty. Ryan's contact info was five months old, so Skylar might have moved. Someone else might be living in number three, or maybe the unit was empty. Then again, maybe she didn't want her name on the plate.

I shut the mailbox and walked up the flagstone path.

Two young women wearing large oval sunglasses were

sprawled on the lawn, surrounded by bottles of water and sunscreen. The one with short auburn hair wore a pale green bikini. Her braided blonde friend sported a bright pink bikini top and tiny white shorts. They watched me from a beach towel island in a rectangle of sun.

The blonde pushed herself up on an elbow.

"Nice shirt."

"Yours, too."

"I'm not wearing a shirt."

"Exactly."

They laughed, and I laughed with them.

Ever the charming detective.

Each of the five apartments had a discreet entrance shielded from prying eyes by alcoves designed for privacy. I crossed the courtyard to unit three and stepped into the alcove. The apartment was quiet, but this didn't mean it was empty. I took out my phone, called Skylar's number again, and put my ear to the door. Skylar's phone rang in my phone, but not inside the apartment. When her voice mail answered, I pushed her doorbell. A buzzer inside buzzed, but nobody answered. I pushed the button again and knocked. Nothing.

I was deciding whether to kick down the door or climb through a window when I peeked at the women on the lawn. The blonde waved. So much for being stealthy.

I walked back to the women, and the blonde flashed another big smile.

"She's not home."

"Know when she'll be back?"

The auburn blocked the sun with a hand.

"She's been gone a couple of days."

I glanced back at Skylar's apartment and tried to look confused. Confusion was one of my better expressions.

"That can't be. We had an appointment."

The blonde sat up.

"I haven't seen you before, have I? Are you and Rachel friends?"

Rachel. Rachel might be Skylar's actual name, or Skylar had, in fact, moved out, and Rachel had, in fact, moved in.

"I write about art for the *Times*."

The blonde cocked her head.

"Are you writing about Rachel?"

"Depends. Has Josh been around?"

They glanced at each other. The auburn answered.

"Which one is he?"

The blonde giggled.

"She's very social."

The auburn smirked.

"Slut."

These two were killing themselves.

"Her manager or agent maybe? I'm not clear how they're connected, but Josh was supposed to be here."

I took out my phone and showed them the picture of Josh and Skylar at her opening.

"Here. This guy."

The auburn lifted her shades to examine the picture.

"Did she really wear sequins?"

The blonde made a face.

"She's gonna get brain damage with all the spray paint.

She wears one of those masks, but I don't care. She's gonna get brain damage."

Rachel was, in fact, Skylar. This was professional detection at its finest.

I said, "Getting back to Josh."

The auburn lowered her shades and sat up.

"We've seen him but we haven't met him."

The blonde nodded along.

"They had a fight. It got kinda loud."

I felt dangerously close to a clue and prompted her for more.

"No way! When was this?"

The blonde shrugged, saying she wasn't certain.

"Four or five days ago?"

The auburn said, "Four. What an asshole. He got really loud."

The blonde nodded.

"*Really* loud. I bet this is why they blew off your meeting. She probably fired him."

The auburn ran a hand down one calf and up the other.

"Creep. She should've crushed his balls."

I put away my phone.

"So Skylar left after they fought?"

The blonde said, "Uh-huh."

"Maybe they made up and went together."

The auburn said, "Ha."

The blonde said, "No, definitely not. He came back yesterday, being all weird."

Yesterday.

I said, "Weird how?"

"Driving back and forth out front. He parked across the street and sat there all stalkery."

The auburn said, "I should've called the police."

The blonde said, "Right? Me, too!"

I studied the street.

I said, "So what happened? Did they hook up?"

The auburn peered at me over her glasses.

"What's with all the questions?"

"I'm a writer. Questions are my business."

The auburn gave me a nasty grin.

"I think you like talking to us."

The blonde elbowed past with an answer.

"She was gone. He finally came up and knocked, but he was only here for a minute."

"This was yesterday?"

"Uh-huh."

"And the last time you saw her was four days ago?"

"Uh-huh."

Josh hadn't returned to his bungalow in a week, yet these two had seen him four days ago and again yesterday. It was possible he hooked up with Skylar at another location, but it sounded as if they were on the outs. If Josh wasn't with Skylar, I wondered why he hadn't returned to his bungalow.

The auburn said, "I'm bored."

She pushed to her feet, gathered her towel, and walked away. Just like that.

The blonde rolled her eyes.

"Always the drama."

"Must be difficult."

The blonde gathered her towel and sunscreen, stood, and rolled her eyes again.

"You wouldn't believe."

I lowered my voice.

"Has Josh been here much in the past couple of weeks?"

"Yeah. He was here a few times. Why?"

"Just curious."

I thanked her and walked past the sycamore to my car.

Ryan Seborg's best friend Josh had been keeping secrets. He kept secrets about Skylar Lawless, and his trips to see her in Studio City, and the nature of their relationship. These didn't seem like large secrets to keep, or worth the drama of abandoning his life and the people who loved him, but I wasn't Josh.

I wondered what other secrets he kept, and if those secrets had driven him away from his home and his family and Ryan.

Ryan probably wouldn't like the answer.

Adele probably wouldn't like the answer, either.

The people who hired me to find someone they love almost never wanted the truth.

And when I found the truth, I often wished I hadn't found it.

8

A Thai place I liked in Sherman Oaks served excellent dry curry squid and duck spring rolls, so I phoned ahead, added an order of ginger rice, and picked up the food a few minutes later. I headed for home.

Home was a redwood A-frame on a woodsy street off Woodrow Wilson Drive in Laurel Canyon. My house sat perched on the downhill side of the street, overlooking the canyon below. A wide deck jutted from the rear, offering a peaceful view of the canyon, the surrounding hills, and the city beyond the ridges. I liked my little house a lot.

I parked in the carport, let myself into the kitchen, and set the Thai food next to the sink. I grabbed a bottle of water from the fridge and carried my gun and the water up to my bedroom loft. I showered, pulled on cargo shorts and a T-shirt, and returned to the kitchen.

A large black cat waited by the takeout bag. He had a fine flat head striped with scars, ragged ears, and he held his head cocked to the side from the time someone shot him with a .22. He licked his lips when he saw me.

"We're having Thai. Sound good?"

He said, "Naow."

"Coming up."

People who lived with a cat talked to the cat. It was inevitable.

I found a Modelo beer in the fridge, drank some, and set out a plate and utensils for me and a clean dish for the cat. I lifted the takeout containers from the bag, opened them, and forked out four large pieces of squid. The Thai food was generously spiced with bird's eye peppers, so I rinsed each piece, minced the pieces, and mixed the squid with kibble in his dish. When he saw the food in his dish, he leaped off the counter, raced to his eating place, and growled. This cat was something.

With the cat squared away, I made a plate for myself and carried the food and the beer to the dining table. I ate a duck roll and some rice, then opened my laptop. The ginger rice was superb.

Adult film performers often used stage names for the same reasons as mainstream actors. Their true names were dull or difficult to pronounce or had poor marketing appeal. Other adult performers hoped to hide their Triple X work from families or future employers, but the internet made hiding next to impossible. I googled "Skylar Lawless real name" and learned her true name with a single click.

Rachel Belle Bohlen had been born in Visalia, California, up in the San Joaquin Valley. She was twenty-nine years old, the oldest of two girls, and enjoyed riding horses. I ate another duck roll, helped myself to the squid, and opened the *In Your Face* episode page Ryan had showed me.

Beneath the photo of Skylar and Josh was a button for listening to her interview. Buttons labeled *Her Opening*, *Her Studio*, and *Her Art* were beside it.

Her Opening led to a photo album from Skylar's show at ClaudeSpace Gallery and a link to the gallery's website. The album showed photos of Josh interviewing Skylar and a couple of dozen pix of Skylar posing with friends or admirers. Most of her friends were young, attractive people with names like Cherry Glaze, Sindi Wett, Jock Slammer, and David Q. Bones. You didn't need a deer-stalker hat to know they worked in porn. A note at the bottom of the page credited the photos to Ryan Seborg.

Her Art led to images of six paintings and information for prospective buyers. Each painting looked like a cell phone screen with a text exchange between couples who seemed to be having trouble.

Stephi: i SAW u!!

                         Rick: her locker ws stuck

Stephi: i h8 u
Stephi: i hope u die

                         Rick: i luv u
                         Rick: pleez steph
                         Rick: steph

Stephi: call

I clicked the *Her Studio* button and pushed on.

As Josh had repurposed his bedroom into a recording studio, Skylar had repurposed her living room into an art studio. Large windows covered by bright, airy drapes filled the room with light. A straight flight of stairs with a wrought iron rail climbed to a second-floor landing and a curved corner in the background matched with a turret I'd seen at her apartment. Canvases leaned against the walls in uneven rows. Action shots showed Skylar cutting a stencil or adjusting a vertical projector or sipping coffee as she stared pensively at something we couldn't see. Skylar didn't look like a pornstar in her studio. She wore stained sweatpants, a paint-streaked tank top, and a backward Dodgers cap smudged with paint. A respirator mask with large pink filters made her look like a bug as she sprayed paint across a stencil. The studio photos were interesting, but offered no clues.

I got up, stretched, and wandered into the kitchen. The cat had finished his food and left. Off hunting coyotes for dessert.

I ate the last duck roll and wandered out onto the deck. The eastern sky had darkened to midnight blue and hazy shadows pooled in the deeper parts of the canyon. It was still warm, but not terrible.

My nearest neighbors lived across from me on the far side of a bend in our street. Grace Gonzalez was a stuntwoman, her husband was a stunt coordinator, and their two grown sons were stunt performers as well. I heard laughter, and saw their entire family out on their deck,

Grace, her husband, the sons and their wives and a couple of grandkids, poking at something on their grill and laughing. Grace saw me and waved. I waved back. Grace cupped her mouth and shouted.

"Burgers and links! You're welcome to join us."

I shouted back.

"Thanks. Another time."

Her husband hoisted his beer and they returned to their grill.

The quality and warmth of their lives was as real as the grill and the mountain we lived on. I waved again, but none of them noticed.

I went inside and listened to Josh's podcast with Skylar Lawless.

The outlandish subjects favored by Josh and Ryan left me expecting an amateurish geekfest, with Josh firing off sex jokes and snickering like an eighth-grade dweeb. I hit the play button and expected the worst. After two seconds of silence, Skylar Lawless quietly opened the show.

"When people recognize me, they see a woman who was photographed having sex with strangers. What they don't see—and don't know—are the insights I gained into ordinary human relationships. These insights inform my art. They free me to tell the truth without shame."

Skylar sounded nothing like I expected and neither did Josh. She spoke with a warm contralto voice, and described her career as a sex worker in terms of empowerment and growth. The few times she laughed, her laughter was quiet. Josh spoke too quickly, sometimes talking over himself, but his questions were thoughtful and his comments were never salacious or lewd. His questions focused on her art and what she hoped to achieve with it. I found myself interested and wondered if Corbin Schumacher had ever heard his son's show. I doubted it.

The interview ran for one hour and twenty-eight minutes. The production quality was stellar.

When it ended, I thought about the blonde- and auburn-haired women I'd met at Skylar's apartment and about Josh being loud and stalkery. The podcast left me feeling Josh and Skylar were friends, but not friends with benefits. He had sounded interested and obviously enjoyed their conversation, but he hadn't been flirty. A lot could change in five months and probably did.

I put my laptop aside and went to the sliding glass door. Darkness had filled the canyon. Golden lights specked the far ridges, each light marking a home. The Gonzalez family still laughed.

I was trying to decide what to do next when the phone rang. I thought it might be Ryan or Wendy Vann, but a woman with a soft southern voice spoke.

"Hey, Studly. Are you busy?"

Lucy Chenier always made me smile.

"I'm sorry. Who's calling, please?"

It was a silly joke Lucy and I had traded a hundred times, me pretending I didn't know her or her pretending she didn't know me. It was a play on our familiarity and fondness, but this time Lucy did not respond. Her slight hesitation was a gaping chasm.

I said, "Lucy?"

"This is sudden, so if you can't, we'll understand."

Her words came out as if she was nervous and trying to hide it.

"Can't what? Luce, what's wrong?"

"Nothing's wrong."

Something was wrong.

"Oh, well, good. I feel much better now."

"We're coming to L.A. tomorrow. We'd like to stay with you."

"We?"

"If you don't mind. If it's okay."

Something was wrong. Lucy Chenier was my closest female friend. Once upon a time, I would have married her, but she left. Lucy had not slept under my roof in years.

This was her choice.

Not mine.

I would have married her, but the choice wasn't mine.

9

An actress named Jodi Taylor had hired me to help with a problem in Louisiana, so I flew to Baton Rouge and met her Attorney, a woman named Lucille Chenier. Lucy and I fell in love. Lucy and her son, Ben, who was eight when we met, eventually moved west to be with me. Lucy's ex-husband decided to drive a wedge between us and in many ways did. Bad things happened to Ben, and before it was over people had died. Lucy's ex went to prison, but the damage was done. Lucy and Ben returned to Louisiana. Better for Ben to heal, Lucy said. Safer from the violence I seemed to attract. I couldn't blame her. She was his mother.

I said, "Luce?"

"I'm with Ben. Here, let me put him on."

Ben Chenier was a junior in high school now, but he sounded as excited as his nine-year-old self the first time I took him to Disneyland.

"We're coming to L.A."

The abrupt way Lucy had shoved the phone into his hands left me irritated.

"Great."

"Right? The UCLA law school has a program called Law and Law Enforcement for High School Students. They offer it next month during my spring break, so we're coming to check it out."

"Tomorrow?"

"Mom only found out about it yesterday."

"Tomorrow."

Lucy Chenier was a meticulous Attorney and thorough planner. She was not a spur-of-the-moment person.

"Mom wants to see the dorm and meet the administrator. You know Mom. Can we stay with you?"

"You know it, buddy. What a great surprise."

"This is so cool. Here's Mom."

Lucy took the phone.

"He's very excited."

"And you'll stay here."

"I thought we would. If you don't mind."

After Lucy moved back to Louisiana, things between us were strained, but we remained close. I flew down once or twice a year to see them, and sometimes Lucy and Ben would come to L.A. When they came to L.A., Lucy would let Ben stay with me, but she would not. Too awkward, I guess. Too uncomfortable.

"I don't mind."

"It's such short notice and you have a life."

"I'm surprised is all."

"I know. I understand."

"But I have to warn you, I'm on a job. I won't be around much during the day."

"We could stay at a hotel."

If she wanted to stay in a hotel, she would have booked a room.

"Only, you want to stay here."

She paused.

"Ben loves you."

"What's going on, Luce?"

"We'll talk tomorrow. Is it okay if we talk tomorrow?"

"Sure."

"Elvis?"

"Yes?"

I thought she wanted to say more, but maybe this was only me wanting to hear more.

She said, "I'll see you tomorrow."

I put aside the phone and walked into the kitchen. I drank a glass of tap water. I washed the glass and put it in the drain. The cat was gone. I wondered what he was doing and hoped he was safe. If I had gotten him as a kitten I would've raised him as an inside cat and never installed his door. But he showed up full-grown one day and he'd been with me ever since. I worried, but I couldn't bring myself to trap him inside and make him a prisoner, so I'd put in his door. The house felt empty without him.

I returned to the living room, stretched out on the couch, and stared up at the A-frame's peaked ceiling high overhead. Shadows lived at the peak even though the room was filled with light. I held up my right hand, flexed it,

and studied the front. A thick scar etched a line across
the four fingers. The scar was an angry violet color for a
long time, but it had paled to a grayish white. Three of
the fingers had required reconstructive surgeries. I was
cut when a man named Mazi Ibo held a long, curved
knife to Ben Chenier's throat. I grabbed the blade to stop
Ibo from cutting Ben. Ibo had been a large man and a
professional soldier. I shouldn't have been able to beat a
man as large and strong as Ibo, but I beat him and killed
him with the knife.

Richard Chenier had hired Ibo and two other men to
kidnap Ben so Lucy would blame me and Richard could
look like a hero when he recovered his son. This was
Richard's plan, but his plan went sideways and terrible.
The men Richard hired buried Ben Chenier in a box.

Richard's own son.

Buried.

In a box.

I flexed the hand and remembered the night Joe Pike
and I fought and killed three men to save Ben. My fingers ached from time to time, but I had learned to live
with it.

We saved him.

We found Ben and saved him and brought him home
to his mother.

I lowered my hand and stared at the darkness above.

10

Jared Walker Philburn

The twilight sky deepened to a rich bloody orange as Jared Walker Philburn made his way home. Time was short as darkness approached, so Jared picked up his pace, striding past the mansions along Los Feliz Boulevard. Jared avoided looking at the mansions. To look was to be seen, and he did not wish to be seen. Jared, who was homeless, wore grimy wool pants split at the knee, a threadbare brown jacket, and cast-off running shoes he'd found in a dumpster. His appearance drew attention in lovely neighborhoods, and Jared did not want more, especially when he was heading for home. So, head down, elbows swinging, knapsack bouncing with every step, Jared left the beautiful homes and coral trees of lower Los Feliz, and climbed into the deepening hills of Griffith Park.

Traffic leaving the park was heavy, but once Jared passed the Greek Theatre, the number of cars thinned. Most were day hikers up to enjoy the trails or families who had visited the observatory. Jared stayed well off the road to avoid the cars, and braced himself in case someone threw a bottle or can. He tried not to think about being hit by a bottle (which had happened, twice). Instead, Jared walked faster. The sooner he reached home, the sooner he would be safe, and the sooner he could enjoy the treasures in his pack.

Earlier that day, Jared had found two discarded paperback novels, an unopened bottle of Diet Coke, a small pocket mirror, and a bright blue spiral notebook. With money earned collecting recyclables, he had bought toothpaste, a disposable razor, two rolls of toilet paper, and a machaca burrito. But most exciting of all, near the end of his day, Jared had stopped at a small Italian restaurant near the park and offered to sweep their parking area. The sous-chef, a burly woman with enormous tattooed forearms, sent Jared away with a white paper bag containing takeout containers of bread and food. Jared's mouth had been watering ever since. He was anxious to get home, where, in the safety that came with quiet solitude, he could enjoy the chef's generosity.

Jared preferred quiet, which was why he chose the park as his residence. Quiet brought calm, calm brought peace, and peace softened the whispers he heard. *Loser, freak, failure.* Sometimes, when the world was kind, the whispers were so faint, they vanished. Jared might not hear them for days, but he knew they were only sleeping. *You're disgusting, you're worthless, you're garbage.* Then they'd grow louder, more damning, and hateful. *You're sick, schizophrenic, defective.* Spinning faster into a maelstrom around him. *Kill yourself, kill yourself, die!* But quiet brought calm, and calm brought peace, which was why Jared was so careful to guard his secret sanctuary in the park.

Residing in the park was illegal, of course, which was why his little home was his most carefully guarded secret, and why Jared raced the night. Once the sun went down, park rangers and police were more likely to ask why he was in the park and where he was going. So Jared raced the sun each day, hurrying to avoid their scrutiny.

The road grew steeper, but the day's last light was fading fast. The old art deco streetlamps along the road floated in a dim ochre glow. Jared walked so fast he was almost hopping as he rounded a curve and saw the black maw of the Mount Hollywood Tunnel ahead. A road to the observatory branched to his left, but Jared took neither.

Two cars passed from behind him and disappeared into the tunnel. A single car emerged as they passed, its lights washing over Jared as it headed downhill. Jared quickly hustled across the road and scrambled up an erosion cut around a tall steep shoulder rising above the road. He followed the cut between two scrub oaks, around a slender pine, and behind a stunted oak shaped like an igloo. The little trail abruptly widened into a flat depression, and Jared was home. The remains of the sun disappeared in a bright orange wink as Jared lowered his pack.

Jared stood for a time, motionless, staring at the ground. The clean scents of wild rosemary, pinesap, and garlic were comforting. A flock of doves, roosting on a water tank farther up the slope, cooed softly as they bedded for the evening. Jared's secret home was only ten yards above the road, but behind his little scrub oak igloo, the tension he carried down in the world grew lighter, and less, and floated away like a rising mist.

Jared drew a deep breath. He sighed.

The world felt peaceful and safe.

Jared rubbed his face, and grinned.

"Well. All right then. Yum, yum, yum, let's boogie."

Jared dragged a tattered green sleeping bag and faded blue duffel from beneath the oak's prickly branches. He sat on the sleeping bag, took his eating utensils from the duffel, and opened his daypack. The wonderful smell of Italian food enveloped him. Jared rolled his eyes with heavenly pleasure and licked his lips.

"Good golly Miss Molly, what has she done?"

Working without a flashlight or lamp, Jared lifted the takeout containers from their bag and carefully opened them. The rising three-quarter moon and the city provided his light.

Jared made a soft whistle.

"Thank you, Chef. May God bless you for your kindness."

Dinner was capellini with meatballs, sautéed spinach, a lemon tart, and three large pieces of garlic toast.

Jared set aside one meatball and two pieces of bread for breakfast, and feasted on the rest. The occasional car passed as he ate, emerging from or disappearing into the tunnel. A ranger passed, her headlights sweeping the road below, and then she was gone.

Finished with dinner, Jared tucked the empty containers into his daypack, then picked his way across the moonlit slope to the far side of the knoll. He often saw coyotes trot along the road, but they had never bothered him and he enjoyed their singing. He'd been told a mountain lion roamed the park. He had never seen the lion, but sharing his home with a lion didn't frighten him. Jared felt perfectly safe being alone in the dark in the canyons. Only people frightened him. And doctors.

After his bowels moved, Jared washed his hands and utensils with a bit of bottled water, brushed his teeth, and took a blanket and poncho from the duffel. He wrapped the blanket and poncho around his shoulders, wiggled into the sleeping bag, and settled back against the duffel.

The glittering lights of Los Angeles spread before him to the horizon. Red and green lights marked helicopters crisscrossing the star-field city. Moving stars were jets carving long gentle descents into LAX.

Jared watched the moving lights, and grew sleepy. He dozed, woke with a start, and dozed again. Sleep came easily, but never lasted. Each time he woke, Jared noted the moon. The moon and the stars were Jared's clock, giving him a measure of the night's passage.

Jared judged he was awake at approximately two in the morning when a flash of light in the tunnel startled him. The tunnel grew brighter, abruptly went dark, and a car emerged.

Jared sat up.

The car's headlights had been on in the tunnel, but now they were off.

The car's brake lights flared. The car stopped in the dim ochre light from the streetlamp, and its brake lights died.

This wasn't a police car or a ranger's SUV. Jared couldn't make out the color, but it was dark. A small sedan, Jared thought. Then the driver's and passenger's doors opened, and two men stepped out.

Fear flashed through Jared like a lightning bolt. He threw off the blanket and poncho, and scrambled up the hill. He tried to move quietly, but his frantic heart thundered. They might be gangbangers or kids who'd seen him earlier and had returned to have their fun. It had happened before when Jared lived by the beach. He scrambled higher, thinking he could hide above the old water tank, and that's when he stopped and saw they were still by their car.

They opened the trunk and lifted out something large and heavy. Then an arm dangled free, and Jared realized they were lifting a body.

The men carried their burden to the edge of the slope and heaved it over the side. Jared heard one of the men grunt with their effort, and the snapping of brush as the heavy weight rolled downhill. The two men immediately returned to their car. They did not turn on their headlights. Their taillights did not glow. Their dark car disappeared into the shadows of the canyon, and they were gone.

Jared stood motionless. His heart slammed and he did not breathe. His head buzzed with a high-pitched whine. He wondered if the person they'd thrown into the brush was still alive. He wanted to see and help if he could. They might need help. They might be dying.

Jared did not move.

Jared spoke aloud.

"Go see. Help."

He tried to move, but his body was filled by the whine.

"Jared. Do something. Find a ranger. Get help."

The whine became a maelstrom of rushing thoughts.

The police might blame him. They might think he was responsible and lock him in a hospital and fill his head with chips and chemicals.

Above him, the water tank creaked.

Jared lurched sideways, and shouted.

"Leave me alone! I didn't do it. I didn't see it. I'm not even here."

Jared stumbled back to his camp, and peered down at the empty road.

A whisper came from beside him.

I imagined it. There's no car, no men, no body. It's all in my head.

Jared nodded, agreeing.

"That's right. I imagined it."

The whisper was behind him.

Doesn't matter. You're sick. You're a head case. You'll be in trouble.

Jared clenched his eyes and pressed his palms to his temples.

"But I didn't hurt anyone. I didn't."

Tell the police.

"I can't! I'm scared!"

Do what's right. You know what's right.

Jared sat in the rocks and wrapped his arms over his head.

"Stop talking. Stop shouting. I can't think."

You're pathetic. You're worthless. You're psycho.

"I'm scared!"

You saw what happened. You're a witness.

"They'll drug me. They'll blame me and lock me up."

The dead need you, Jared. Are you going to help?

Help?

Help?

"I need quiet. A quiet moment, is all. Please."

The voices grew silent. Across the park, coyotes sang and yipped and yodeled.

Jared fell asleep again, but his sleep was plagued by terrible dreams and did not last.

PART TWO

The Boy in the Box

11
—
Elvis Cole

A thin mist filled the canyon the next morning. The cat was in the kitchen when I went down. He was lying on his side in the middle of the floor with the hindquarters of a gopher nearby. He often brought home bits of squirrels, birds, and snakes. Once he showed up with an eighteen-inch rattlesnake. The snake's head was missing, but the body coiled and uncoiled as it died. The cat dropped it at my feet and seemed proud. He was a generous cat.

I got a couple of paper towels and picked up the gopher.

"Yum. Thank you."

The cat rolled onto his back and looked at me upside down.

I said, "Listen. Lucy and Ben are coming. I want you on good behavior, okay? No growling or hissing."

He rolled right-side up and stretched.

"No body parts."

I tossed the gopher, cleaned the floor, and went onto the deck. I warmed myself with twelve sun salutes, then knocked out a hundred push-ups, two hundred crunches, and two sets of sixty dips. The deck's corners where the rails met were perfect dip bars. The PT left me tight, so I stretched again and worked through a series of tae kwon do katas, kicking and punching and spinning from one end of the deck to the other, back and forth until my muscles burned and sweat speckled the deck. The physical effort was intense, focused, and left me rippling with energy. The endorphin rush was excellent.

I showered and dressed, put on a pot of coffee, and inspected the guest room. After my last guest, I had stripped the bed, vacuumed the room, and put fresh sheets and pillowcases on the bed. The bed had not been touched since, but I stripped it again. When I was in Ranger School, a sergeant named Zim inspected our area with microscope eyes. If he found a thread out of place, he upended our bunks, raked our belongings out of our lockers, and screamed like a maniac as we scrambled to make our area Ranger Ready and Good to Go. I put on fresh linen, squared the corners, and tightened the spread. The spread was so taut when I finished an ant could have used it as a trampoline. Sergeant Zim would have been proud.

I tackled their bathroom next. When the bath was good to go, I shut the light and checked the guest room again. The room didn't need to be checked, but I found myself in the doorway. A framed photo of Ben and me at Lake Arrowhead stood on a chest. I used to keep it on a shelf in the living room, but I had moved it. In the picture, Ben was still small. We were standing in shallow water at the edge of the lake with me holding Ben overhead, both of us laughing. Lucy had taken the photograph. I wondered if the picture would make her uncomfortable. I thought about moving it back to the living room, but after a while I told myself I was being silly and left it.

I needed to tell Joe. Joe and Lucy and Ben were close. I wandered back to the kitchen, poured a fresh coffee, and called him.

Pike answered on the first ring. I've never called Joe Pike when he didn't answer the first ring. Pike would have to be dead in a ditch not to answer the first ring, and then he'd probably answer the second ring.

I said, "Guess what?"

Pike didn't respond. If you asked Pike "guess what?", this was what you got.

I said, "Lucy and Ben are coming. They'll be here tonight."

"I know."

"How do you know?"

"She told me."

"When did she tell you?"

"Last night."

Amazing.

"In other headlines, we have a job. Or did you know this, too?"

"Need help?"

"Not yet."

"Whenever."

Pike hung up. Didn't ask what. Didn't ask who. Hung up.

Breakfast was the last of the squid and ginger rice. I ate standing in the kitchen and opened the *In Your Face* site on my phone. Josh had included a link to ClaudeSpace Gallery, along with a photo of Skylar and the gallery's owner, a tall, thin woman named E. Claude Sidney, and a pitch for purchasing Skylar's work. If Skylar maintained an ongoing business relationship with the gallery, it stood to reason Ms. Sidney might be able to reach her. I headed downtown to find out.

ClaudeSpace occupied the ground floor of a renovated industrial space south of the 101 between Little Tokyo and the river. The gallery's glass front let people see the art on the walls before they entered. E. Claude Sidney and a younger man were talking in front of an enormous red painting. The painting had to be eight feet on a side, and was solid red except for a single black dot in the upper right corner. E. Claude looked exactly like her photograph, only taller.

I pushed through the door and tried to look like a customer. The paintings were all squares of various sizes, each square painted a single color. A yellow square, a pale green square, a luminous green square, a black square, a lavender square. Ten or twelve squares filled the walls, and each square had a black dot in the upper right corner except the black square. The black square's dot was red. I was staring at the red dot when E. Claude Sidney joined me.

"Are you drawn to the dot?"

"I am."

"I find this fascinating. Everyone watches the dot as if it might move. Are you interested?"

"I'd like to get in touch with Skylar Lawless."

She made a wide, toothy smile.

"Isn't her work fabulous? The originals are sold, but I do have a series of signed prints."

"If I wanted to commission an original, could you arrange it?"

She smiled even wider.

"I'm sure I could. What did you have in mind?"

I held out my license. The moment she saw it she frowned.

"I'm sorry?"

"Do you recall a Josh Schumacher?"

"I do. Of course. He interviewed her on his podcast."

"Then you know Josh and Skylar are close."

"What is this about?"

"Josh is missing. I've been hired by his mother to find him. Skylar might be able to help."

She frowned again.

"What does missing mean? Is he all right?"

"We don't know. I've called, but his message box is full. As I said, Skylar might be helpful. It's even possible he and Skylar are together."

She looked uneasy.

"I don't think so."

"May I ask why?"

The younger man lingered at the red painting. E. Claude glanced his way, motioned me to a small desk in the corner, and lowered her voice.

"Josh phoned last week, asking if I'd heard from her. He was trying to find her."

"Did he leave a message, or say where he was?"

"I'm sorry. He didn't."

"So what did you tell him?"

E. Claude Sidney looked nervous.

"Sometimes, she's away."

"She's out of town?"

E. Claude looked even more uncomfortable.

"I don't know, but she'll be in touch. She has more prints to sign, and I'm holding money from sales. I can't guarantee she'll call, or when, but I'll certainly give her a message."

"I've left messages, Ms. Sidney. It would help if you called her for me, and asked her to speak with me."

"Mr. Cole. There are times when she won't return anyone's calls. Even mine."

"If you can reach her for a commission, please try to reach her for this. Josh promoted the hell out of her work."

Ms. Sidney looked straight up at the ceiling. She touched her throat with the tips of two fingers, looked down at the floor, and took a breath.

"Well, it's nothing she hasn't said in the interviews."

"What?"

She went behind the little desk and took a card album from the drawer.

"Skylar's income as an artist doesn't yet cover her expenses, so she makes other arrangements."

"Are we talking about sex?"

"When she's engaged this way, she turns off her phone. I doubt she even checks her messages."

She found a business card, took it from the album, and placed it in front of me.

"Speak with her. If Skylar returns anyone's calls, they would be hers."

The card showed a woman's name in a classic font, an address in Canoga Park, and the usual contact info.

MEREDITH BIRCH

The Birch Agency
Talent Management

I looked from the card to E. Claude Sidney.

"Her agent?"

"In Skylar's former career, yes. My understanding is they still have business."

E. Claude touched her throat again. Embarrassed. The careers of actors and actresses in the adult film trade were uncertain. Most performers made next to nothing, and most careers had the shelf life of a fish in the sun. More than a few gigged on the side as escorts.

I said, "I see."

Meredith Birch was a pimp.

"And you know this for a fact?"

She nodded.

"Skylar is, perhaps, too open about such things."

The name looked familiar, but I couldn't place it.

"Could I ask you to call? As an introduction?"

"I'd rather not."

"I understand."

I tucked away the card, stood, and offered my hand.

"Thank you, Ms. Sidney. Josh's mom thanks you, too."

I left and drove to the Valley.

The Birch Agency was located in an upscale business park in Chatsworth at the western end of the Valley. Other tenants included personal injury Attorneys, family practice Attorneys, a couple of insurance brokers, and a marriage and family therapist. The therapist was probably slumming. Traffic moved well, but driving to the far end of the Valley was like driving to Mars.

The two-story black glass building was shaped like a U around a courtyard. The Birch Agency occupied a ground-level suite at the back of the courtyard with raised aluminum letters spelling out the agency's name. I tried to enter, but the knob wouldn't turn. A buzzer and a little speaker were beside the door, so I pressed the buzzer. A male voice answered.

"Birch Agency."

"Elvis Cole to see Meredith Birch."

"Who?"

"Cole. First name rhymes with pelvis."

"Do you have an appointment?"

"No, sir, I don't. I'd like to speak with Ms. Birch about a client."

"We don't see anyone without an appointment."

"I'm here. Could I make an appointment for now?"

"Gimme your number. We'll get back to you."

"Getting back to me implies you might not get back to me until some unknown time in the future, which means I would have to leave. Since I'm here, and we're talking, let's make the appointment now."

"Getting back to you means we'll get back to you whenever the fuck we get back to you."

"This won't take more than a couple of minutes."

"Fuck off, asshole. Beat it."

I pressed the buzzer again. This time he didn't answer.

I pressed the buzzer again and held it.

"The fuck, dude? Knock it off."

I pressed the buzzer over and over, bz-bz-bz-bz-bz.

The door flew open and a large guy with a square jaw and overdeveloped pecs filled the frame. He was three inches taller than me, thirty pounds heavier, and did his best to scare me. Too much spray tan made him look like a tangerine.

He said, "Beat it, or I'll—"

I stepped close fast, hooked my right arm under his left shoulder, planted my right foot between his feet, and spun hard. He fell over my foot and stumbled into the courtyard. I stepped inside, shut the door, and locked it.

A woman said, "That's enough."

We were in a well-appointed outer office with pale blue wallpaper, a tufted leather couch for waiting clients, and an impressive desk for the lox in the courtyard, who was probably Meredith Birch's assistant. Meredith Birch stood in the door to her office, pointing a slick little Ruger .380 at me. It was one of their fancy subcompact models with a bright pink nylon grip and satin aluminum slide. Ideal for purse or pocket.

I raised my hands and knew why her name was familiar. Skylar and Meredith Birch had been photographed together at Skylar's opening. I'd seen the photo and her name on Josh's website.

I said, "I give up. Also, I apologize."

Outside, the big guy twisted and yanked the knob, and pounded on the door.

Meredith didn't move. Neither did the gun.

"Accepted. Now get out. If you don't, I will shoot you and call the police."

"Five months ago, ClaudeSpace Gallery hosted a showing for Skylar Lawless. You attended. Do you recall Josh Schumacher?"

Outside, the big guy pressed the buzzer.

Meredith Birch cocked her head. A vertical line appeared between her eyebrows, but not because of the buzzer.

She said, "Skylar's friend. With the podcast."

"That's right. He interviewed her before the show and promoted her work."

The tiny pink gun dipped, but only a little.

"We spoke. A bit intense, but I appreciated the respect with which he treated her. I know Skylar did as well."

The buzzer buzzed. The big guy pounded.

"Josh is missing. My name is Elvis Cole. I'm a private investigator. His family hired me to find him."

"And you're here why?"

"It's possible you can help."

She suddenly lowered the gun, went to the big guy's desk, and spoke into a call box.

"Everything's fine, Randall. You can come in."

She pressed a button to unlock the door, and Randall rushed inside. He glowered like a bull about to charge.

"Meredith, are you okay? Want me to throw his punk ass out?"

I said, "It didn't work out so well the first time, Randall, did it?"

"I wasn't expecting it!"

Meredith said, "Shush. We'll be in my office."

I followed her into a larger, more spacious version of the outer office, with the same blue wallpaper and tufted leather couch. A wall-to-wall tinted window gave her a view of the parking lot, but it wasn't an unattractive view. Neither was my view of Meredith Birch. She looked to be in her fifties, with good arms, a trim build, and the tight calves of someone who worked at it. She closed the door behind us, offered me a seat on the couch, and leaned against her desk.

She said, "All right. I met Mr. Schumacher the one time at Skylar's showing. How could I possibly help?"

"I have reason to believe Skylar has knowledge of his whereabouts."

"If so, I'm sure she'd be happy to help. Why come to me?"

"She hasn't returned my calls. Her friends tell me she might be away on business. They suggested you might be able to reach her."

Meredith Birch shifted against the desk.

"I'm simply her friend now, Mr. Cole. I have nothing to do with art."

"I'm not talking about art. A different business. Possibly business arranged by you."

Meredith Birch raised her eyebrows.

"I have no idea what you're talking about."

"Forgive me for being direct, but you do. You've arranged such business in the past."

She smiled. It was a pretty smile, but sharp at the edges.

"I represent actors and actresses in the adult entertainment industry. My business is legal and licensed by the state of California. I have no other business."

"My mistake. Thing is, Skylar herself has described your relationship. In detail, and to more than one person."

Meredith Birch crossed her arms.

"I'm not here to make trouble, Ms. Birch. My only interest is finding Schumacher."

"Hence, you want to speak with Skylar."

"Yes, ma'am."

Her gaze was cool, as if she was deciding what to say.

"I do arrange personal appearances for certain clients, but if they choose to break the law, I am not party to it. I certainly don't condone it."

"Of course not. I wouldn't assume otherwise."

"Having said this, I don't know where she is. I haven't spoken to Skylar in weeks."

"Is it possible Skylar arranged an appearance for herself?"

Meredith Birch pursed her lips.

"Possible, but I would know. She's always told me where she would be, and with whom, even if I were not part of the transaction."

"Always?"

"Mr. Cole, women—and men, mind you—who place themselves in such positions require what we call a safety, even when their clients are well-to-do people. I am her safety."

"A safety?"

"A person who knows where she's going, who she's with, and when she expects to return. In case."

In case.

She uncrossed her arms and went behind her desk.

"You say you've left several messages?"

"I have."

"She doesn't know you. Perhaps she's ignoring you."

"An all too common response."

Meredith scooped up her phone and punched in a number she knew by heart. A moment later, she left a message.

"Hey, hon. Please call. It's important."

She put down the phone and came from behind the desk.

"Leave your number. When she calls, I'll ask about Mr. Schumacher."

I stood and gave her a card.

"Please let me know either way."

"Of course."

She walked me out through the outer office to the door. Randall sat at his desk, sulking. He glared as we passed. I glanced at him, and leaned close to Meredith Birch.

"About Randall?"

She glanced at Randall, too.

"What about him?"

"You could do better."

Randall said, "You suck."

"A lot better."

Randall was still sulking when I left.

13

Facing tiny pink guns required sustenance. I stopped for tacos in Winnetka at a taqueria the size of a closet. The pollo proved best, but the asada and carnitas were excellent. I ate in a parking lot crowded with firemen, construction workers, and Ukrainian plumbers. The little taqueria was making a mint.

Josh and Skylar were either with each other or not, and, together or singly, somewhere on the planet. Skylar being away didn't mean she was away with a client. She might be in Vegas with friends or at Disneyland. My lack of hard information was impressive, second only to my lack of clues.

Skylar might be anywhere, but Josh had been seen at her apartment twice in the prior week, and the most recent time had been after Skylar had left. Maybe I'd find a clue at her apartment. Maybe I'd even find Josh.

I bought two tacos for the road and drove to Studio City.

Skylar's neighborhood was as peaceful as before. A woman with curly black hair walked a German shepherd.

A jogging man in his sixties braved the heat in a UCLA T-shirt darkened with sweat. I parked up the block, walked back, and checked the property for people and movement. The lawn and courtyard were empty. No braided blondes or women in green bikinis. I went up the sidewalk and crossed the courtyard to Skylar's alcove. I pressed the buzzer one time, listened, and checked the courtyard. Nobody screamed for the police. I used a pick gun and opened the dead bolt in forty seconds. The knob lock turned in twenty. I readied to run if an alarm went off, but when I opened the door nothing happened. The alarm panel on the wall was dead. I stood very still. I pushed the door closed with my foot, pulled on a pair of gray nitrile gloves, and locked the door.

The organized workspace of Skylar's studio in the photos had been upended. Her tables and drawing boards lay on their sides, and the vertical projectors and enlargers were floor junk. Paint thinner fumes burned my nose. I wanted to leave, but I didn't.

I slipped the Dan Wesson from its holster, held it along my leg, and picked my way through the rubble.

I saw no streaks or splatter patterns on the walls or floor or on the paintings. The paintings stacked on the floor and those on the walls were mostly undisturbed. A few had fallen or been knocked over, but not many. I found no body or body parts or blood smears indicating a body had been dragged. A small couch and two lounge chairs at the turret corner were overturned and the bottoms were slashed. This wasn't vandalism. Her apartment had been searched.

I could see the kitchen from the living room. The drawers had been dumped and the cabinets left open, but I went to the kitchen anyway. I opened the fridge and the dishwasher and the oven and the large cabinet beneath the sink. These spaces were large enough to hide a body. I checked. Clear.

I checked a small bathroom beneath the wrought iron stair, and moved up the stairs. I found no blood on the steps or the rail and none on the landing. The stairs led to a large master bedroom with windows overlooking the courtyard and a master bath and three closets, two in the bedroom and one at the end of the landing. They had been searched. Clothes had been dumped from drawers and thrown from the closets. The bed and dresser had been pulled from the wall, and the mattress pulled from the box spring. I heard a voice below and peeked out the window.

The braided blonde crossed the courtyard toward the street. She was on her phone. I watched until she disappeared, took two photographs of the bedroom, a shot of the landing, and three shots looking down at the living room. I hurried downstairs, checked to be sure the blonde was gone, and let myself out. I wiped the outside knob, peeled off the gloves, and walked away.

Nobody shouted and no one tried to stop me. Nobody saw me. I walked directly to my car, but I didn't leave. I didn't even start the engine. I sat in my car and thought about Joshua Schumacher.

I wondered if he had done this.

If he hadn't, I wondered who did, and why.

14

was thinking through the timeline when Leon Karsey called. He shouted through the phone.

"Who's this? Hello? This is Leon Karsey. I'm calling the detective."

Karsey was so loud I moved the phone.

"This is the detective."

"I guess you haven't found Mr. Beevo, huh?"

Josh.

"Not yet. You calling to tell me he's home?"

One could only hope.

"Nah. Listen, the old lady offer up some cash yet?"

"Still no reward. Why?"

"What a cheapskate. Can you imagine what she spent on Gerbers?"

"I'm in the middle of something."

"They came back."

I didn't understand.

"The cow and her cuck?"

It was like speaking in code. Like we were Cold War spies in a John le Carré novel.

"Nah, nah. The scarecrow and the meatball."

"They're at the bungalow?"

"Not now. This morning. Three-thirty, maybe, a quarter of four. I don't sleep so good, and here they come, sneaking around, cramping my ass."

"Like before? Sneaking around Josh's bungalow?"

I wondered if they worked with Wendy and Kurt. Maybe Wendy and Kurt pulled the day shift, and the scarecrow and the meatball worked nights.

"Nah, uh-uh. They went in this time. Right through the front. I saw'm."

"They entered his bungalow."

"And get this, they were wearing those bug-eye goggles let you see in the dark. How about that, huh? Looked like a couple of spacemen."

Probably weren't working with Wendy.

"How long were they inside?"

"Nineteen minutes on the dot. I clocked'm."

Nineteen minutes was long enough to ransack an apartment.

"Could you see what they were doing?"

"It was dark."

"They didn't turn on the lights?"

"Not even a flashlight. Place was as black as my butt crack."

Another delightful image.

"Did they take anything when they left?"

"If they did, I didn't see it, and you can bet your weenie I was looking."

"Will you be home for a while, Mr. Karsey?"

"I'm always here and I'm always watching. Tell the old lady. She might wanna pass me some green."

I started the car, drove to Ventura Boulevard, and pulled over to call Wendy Vann.

"Were you and Kurt at Josh's bungalow last night?"

"No. Why?"

"A man and a woman entered his bungalow between three-thirty and four this morning. Were they yours?"

Wendy hesitated.

"They were not. What did they look like?"

I repeated Leon Karsey's description and told her about his call.

Wendy stopped me.

"Hang on. They wore night vision goggles?"

"That's what he said."

"The guy's a crank. He's half a loon, Cole. Josh has told me stories about him."

"I'm going to check the bungalow. How about you check with Corbin? See if they work for him."

"I'll ask, but if they worked for Corbin they wouldn't have to sneak inside in the middle of the night. That it?"

"Josh's phone. Can Adele access his account?"

"I'm working on it."

"Either she can or she can't. What's to work on?"

"There are issues."

"Did you ask her?"

"It's complicated. These things take time."

"Put her on. I'll ask her myself."

"I'm on it, Cole. Do you have anything new to report?"

"As of two days ago, Josh is in Los Angeles. He was seen twice in the past week."

"Wait. Josh is here, and he's ignoring her?"

"He isn't in Nevada and he hasn't been abducted."

"Stop it. Where's he staying?"

"I'm working on it."

"Don't be smart, Cole. This isn't funny."

"I don't know where he's staying."

"With the porn girl?"

"He's been seen with her, but I have reason to believe they're not together. I'm not positive, but it's shaping up this way."

"Adele will ask. Why is he doing this?"

"I don't know."

"Is he in love? Is that it? He fell in love with a porno actress and he's embarrassed?"

"I don't know, Wendy. Maybe he doesn't want to give his father another reason to shit on him."

Wendy sighed.

"I hear you. Anything else?"

"The call log."

"Jesus, Cole, I'm on it."

Wendy hung up.

Her being on it wasn't getting anywhere, so I called a friend named Terri Grafino. Terri worked for a company that owned twenty thousand signal towers throughout the United States. The company leased antenna space and signal repeaters to hundreds of cell service providers, whose billions of signals flowed through Terri's system.

Terri sounded excited when she answered.

"This is so crazy! I was just thinking of you!"

"You're always thinking of me. Who can blame you?"

Terri laughed.

"Nicky, for one, but let's not tell him."

Nicky was Terri's husband. A week after they married, one of Terri's former boyfriends started calling her, sending emails, and showing up at Terri's office. Terri and Nicky got a restraining order, but the boyfriend ignored it. Then they hired me, and the harassment stopped. Terri and Nicky and I remained friends.

She said, "We are *way* overdue for a dinner. Pick a night, and it's yours."

"Can we put it off a couple of weeks? Lucy and Ben are coming."

"I'm pouting. Can you see my pouty lips?"

"Flawless."

"Ha. So this job. What do you need?"

"Call log on a blind number. I don't know the service provider."

She thought for a moment.

"Identifying the current provider is doable. As for the rest, I dunno. If one of our contract companies provides service, maybe. If not, I might not be able to help."

"Whatever you can do, Terr."

I read off the number twice, thanked her, and drove to Los Feliz.

Twenty-two minutes later, I crept up Josh's street. Cars, trucks, garbage cans, and dumpsters lined the sides, reducing the street to a single grudging lane. Parking was the usual hillside nightmare. I was six houses away when I passed a woman climbing into a Volvo. I hit the brakes and backed up, feeling as if I'd won the lottery.

I was walking uphill when a white SUV parked across from the red bungalow pulled from the curb and rolled toward me. I moved to the side and the SUV picked up speed. The SUV was dirty. A thick pelt of dust coated the windshield and hood, and dried mud caked the bumper as if the two men inside had been off-roading in a pigsty.

The SUV came faster.

I stepped to the side even farther.

The driver punched the gas and the SUV swerved toward me.

I jumped onto a Chevy's hood and shouted.

The SUV flashed past.

The driver tried to mask his face with a hand, but the wraparound sunglasses gave him away. The ponytailed man in the passenger seat didn't bother. He grinned as they passed, as if he was sorry they missed me.

I tried to get their license number, but dried mud caked the plate.

I watched the SUV disappear.

I sat on the Chevy in the very hot sun for a long time. Then I returned to my car, put on my gun and my jacket, and went to check Josh's bungalow.

15

Leon Karsey stepped outside as I climbed the steps. He wore the same shorts and T-shirt as yesterday.

"You gonna see what they did?"

"I am."

"Can I come?"

I changed the subject.

"Two men were down below in a white SUV. They were in a red pickup yesterday, pretending to be gardeners. Today they were in the SUV. They're watching for Josh."

Karsey stood on his tiptoes and craned to see the street.

"You're shittin' me. Where?"

"They're gone. Males around forty. The driver had a round face and wraparound sunglasses."

"The meatball?"

"Didn't look burly, but his head was roundish. The other man has a thin face and a long black ponytail."

"You sure he's a man? The scarecrow's a woman."

"He's a male."

Karsey craned for the street.

"I'll keep an eye out."

"Don't get involved. Please. These people are danger-ous."

Karsey stopped craning and leered.

"I got a little something something inside for danger-ous people. Wanna see?"

"Not today. Thanks."

I left Karsey at his door, crossed to Josh's bungalow, and examined the locks. Both the knob and dead bolt keyholes showed the bright golden scrapes of a pick gun. I let myself in with the key.

I had expected Josh's bungalow to look like Skylar's apartment, but it didn't. The living room looked the same, only neater. The soda cans, takeout cups, and fast-food debris were gone. The kitchen counter had been cleared. It was possible the meatball and the scarecrow worked as midnight janitors, but the odds were against it.

I circled through the kitchen and down the hall to the studio. Yesterday's clutter of printouts and folders stood in a single neat stack. The Post-it Notes sprouting from the monitors and lamps like pink and blue fins had been removed and clipped together. The floor was free of clut-ter and the table had been straightened. Skylar Lawless still smiled from the poster, licking her gleaming teeth, but something felt off. I studied the studio from the door, trying to figure out what, and finally saw it. The big mon-itors and audio equipment remained, but the desktop computer and keyboard were missing.

I dug out my phone and called Ryan.

Ryan said, "Yeah, I know. I took it. Easier to go through it here."

"Did you take anything else?"

"A hard drive. Why, what else is missing?"

I told him about the meatball and the scarecrow.

He said, "No shit? Why didn't he call the police?"

"Let's do a video call. I want you to see."

We hung up and I video-called him back. Ryan held his phone low when he answered, so I saw him from below. He was shirtless and appeared to be in his childhood bedroom. The image instantly jerked sideways to show the computer tower and keyboard connected to a monitor on a small desk.

"See? I brought it home."

The image jerked back to Ryan.

I said, "I believed you. I'll pan around the room. Tell me if anything looks different."

I flip-flopped the camera and gave him a slow tour. I walked him around the table and walls and neatly stacked articles and notes.

He said, "Looks the way I left it."

I walked him down the hall and slowly around the living room. I lingered over the boxes and furniture and walls and the big flat-screen, and then around the kitchen.

Ryan said, "Dude. Nothing's missing that I can see. Nothing's even disturbed. That guy Karsey's a jerk. He made it up."

I considered the room and wondered why nothing had been disturbed. The meatball and the scarecrow hadn't broken in at three in the morning to use the bathroom. I flip-flopped the image so Ryan and I could see each other.

I said, "They were here. Them and at least two others. They're watching the bungalow, Ryan. Don't come back, okay? It isn't safe."

Ryan squinted.

"What others?"

"I don't know, but I've seen them twice."

"Why would they watch Josh's place?"

"Maybe they're looking for Josh. Maybe for Skylar. I don't know."

"This is bullshit."

Ryan seemed irritated.

I glanced around the room again, seeing the meatball and his friend slipping through the darkness with night vision goggles. It seemed absurd, but two guys in an SUV had tried to kill me. Or scare me.

"How well do you know Josh's dad?"

"Corbin?"

"Does he have more than one?"

"He's kind of a dick. Josh hates him."

"Wendy and Kurt work for Adele. Maybe Corbin hired people to watch the bungalow. Maybe the people from last night work for him."

"It's possible, I guess. Corbin has people like Wendy and Kurt."

"Guards?"

Ryan made an uncertain shrug.

"I guess so. Josh's folks are kinda rich."

"I thought they were retired teachers."

Ryan smirked.

"Uh-huh. Right."

I gazed down the hall toward the studio. The bungalow hadn't been ransacked, but this didn't mean it hadn't
been searched. If the meatball and his partner were looking for Josh, they had probably been looking for clues.

I said, "Did you find anything helpful?"

Ryan's mouth tightened and he looked unhappy.

"I don't know how helpful, but it pissed me off. Josh
was working on something he didn't tell me about."

"What are you talking about, Ryan?"

He shifted, and I saw the computer behind him.

"A folder on the drive. Looks like research for a show."

"On the computer?"

"Yeah. On the drive. It's stuff he downloaded after
Skylar called. All these downloads about real estate stuff."

"What kind of real estate stuff?"

"Like from the news. Articles and stories and stuff.
Looks boring as hell."

"Is there anything about Skylar or Josh or his plans?"

"It isn't about them. It could be a coincidence, I
guess, but the download dates start when Skylar called.
Remember what I said? I was right. Josh was working on
something with this bitch and cutting me out."

Ryan looked hurt and angry.

"We don't know what he was up to, Ryan."

"Screw him and screw her. I know I'm screwed."

I sighed.

"Can you send me the folder?"

"It's only articles. All public stuff."

"Send it anyway."

"Okay."

"Anything else?"

"Isn't this enough?"

Ryan looked sullen and miserable. I tried to think of something encouraging to say, but my best efforts felt maudlin and false.

I said, "Is there anything you need or want from here? I'll bring it to you."

"I don't need shit."

Sullen.

"Okay. Just remember. Don't come back. Not until we know what's going on."

Ryan smirked.

"I'm never going back. And I'm keeping the computer. Fuck'm."

Ryan hung up.

I let myself out, locked Josh's bungalow, and headed for home. No red pickup trucks or dirty SUVs appeared in my mirror, but every vehicle was suspect. The Dan Wesson rode shotgun.

16

I phoned Joe Pike as I worked my way across Holly-wood.

"This thing's heating up. Two guys in an SUV tried to run me down."

"Get the plate?"

"It was covered. You free tomorrow?"

"I'm anxious to meet them."

"Come early tonight. I'll fill you in before Lucy and Ben arrive."

"Lucy asked me to take Ben after dinner."

"She did?"

"So you can talk."

"About what?"

"Didn't say."

"You didn't ask?"

"No."

Typical.

I picked up skirt steak, chicken thighs, and handmade nixtamal tortillas from a Mexican market on Franklin. The women at the little market made the tortillas in the traditional way, and made them to order. I ordered two dozen and watched them shape and pat the masa dough into taco-sized tortillas and flip them onto a hot comal. They didn't use a tortilla press or a rolling pin. They worked the dough by hand the way they'd seen their grandmothers and great-grandmothers do it back in Cozumel, and they made the best tortillas I've eaten.

I stopped for salad stuff and veggies at a market closer to home and pulled into my carport a few minutes later. Nobody tried to kill me on the way.

The salad and veggies went in the fridge, then I set to work prepping the skirt steak and chicken. Skirt steak was my fave for carne asada. Thighs were great for tacos because they stayed moist. The prep work didn't take long.

I skinned and trimmed the thighs, then laid them out on a sheet of foil. I seasoned them with chili powder, garlic powder, a little oregano, and salt. When the seasoning looked good, I dropped the pieces into a plastic bag, added a little olive oil and a couple of squeezes of lime, sealed the bag, massaged it to bring everything together, and tucked the bag in the fridge. I cleaned up the chicken gunk, laid out a fresh piece of foil, and repeated the prep with the beef. When the beef and chicken were marinating, I went out onto the deck and prepped the grill. When the grill was good to go, I showered, dressed, and returned to the living room with my laptop. I brought up the *In Your Face* website.

Skylar's original appearance on *In Your Face* bore their typical snappy episode title.

#29: WANNA GET PAID FOR NASTY SEX?: PREPARE TO BE SCREWED!

*Josh gets the hot and heavy down-low
from Skylar Lawless, Jasmine Juggs,
and superstud Mario Root!*

The extras available for the episode were minimal. *Behind the Scenes* led to a few photos of Josh, Skylar, and the other guests in his tiny studio. *Curriculum Vitae* listed their video credits, and *Raw Talent* led to nude PR shots and stills from their videos.

I clicked back to the podcast page, carried the laptop into the kitchen, and listened to the interview while I washed and sliced the vegetables. Portrait of the detective at work.

Despite the episode's outlandish title, Josh was neither salacious nor vulgar. He introduced each actor, asked funny warm-up questions, and guided the conversation into the serious topics of their working conditions, health concerns, and security. The performers shared stories about being misled, lied to, or cheated, and how they had supplemented their fluctuating incomes. Jasmine earned more as an exotic dancer than she earned making porn, but the celebrity she derived from Triple X videos allowed her to demand higher rates as a dancer. She viewed porn as advertising. Skylar had begun as a dancer, but hated the night-to-night grind. Mario confessed he had worked as an escort during lulls in his career, and Jasmine and Skylar admitted they and many of the girls they knew had also worked as paid escorts. Josh followed up.

JOSH: I wanna make sure the audience understands. Escorting means outcall, right? Somebody pays to have sex with you.

JASMINE: (laughing) Guys'll pay just to be *seen* with these titties, and if they want more, I'm down! You want the ass, bring on the cash!

JOSH: How's that work?

MARIO: You never had sex? You stick your weenie in'm.

(laughter)

JOSH: Seriously. Wait. I'd be scared. You go to a house or hotel alone. You're meeting a total stranger who could be a psycho killer. I'd be terrified. Isn't it dangerous?

JASMINE: Tell me about it!

SKYLAR: Yeah, kinda, so you need a safety.

JOSH: What's—

MARIO: (interrupting) You tell someone. Here's where I'm going, here's how long I'll be. You call'm. Okay, I'm going in. Okay, I'm out. Everything's cool.

SKYLAR: Yeah. It's like, if you are even *one second* late . . .

MARIO: Come running. So you gotta have someone you trust, someone dependable.

SKYLAR: My homegirl Kimmie. Shoutout to *YOU*, Kaykay! I love this girl so much! She takes care of me. We go back, man. For*ever*!

JOSH: She's your safety?

SKYLAR: And more! My absolute bestie. I totally love this girl.

I hit the pause button. Meredith Birch had claimed she was Skylar's safety, but Skylar was saying her safety was someone named Kimmie. I wondered if "forever" meant Visalia. I hit play.

JOSH: Is she hot like you?

SKYLAR: (laughing) Hotter!

JOSH: Give us a couple of titles. How can the listeners check her out?

SKYLAR: No, no, no—she's not in the business. She's a good girl. I was the bad girl. Ohmygosh, we're the Odd Couple.

The interview lasted another nine minutes. I set the veggies aside, took the laptop back to the couch, and reread the articles about Skylar I'd bookmarked.

Besides having a sister and riding horses, details about Skylar's family and childhood were scarce. She was bored, dyed her face green to freak people out, and everyone thought she was crazy. She had quit school halfway through the eleventh grade, hitchhiked to L.A., and lied about her age to get a job stripping. None of the articles mentioned someone named Kimmie or the names of her family.

I pulled up the Visalia directory, and found six Bohlens: Anna P., Emma L., Gene R., George A., Kandace, and Richard L. The directory didn't list cell numbers, so thousands of Bohlens might live in Visalia, but they wouldn't be listed unless they had a hard line.

I called Anna P. first. Her phone rang so long I was about to hang up when she answered.

"Yes, hello?"

Her voice was strong and breathy, as if she'd run in from outside to answer. She sounded like someone in her fifties, which meant she could be Skylar's mother.

"My name is Cole. I'm calling from Los Angeles regarding a Rachel Belle Bohlen."

"Uh-huh. That isn't me. My name is Anna."

"Yes, ma'am. Thank you. Would you happen to know of a Rachel Belle?"

"Well, let's see—"

She made little mumbly sounds, somewhere between humming and talking to herself.

"No. I don't think so. What is this regarding?"

"She's applied for a position with the Los Angeles Police Department, so we do a little background check."

"Oh, uh-huh, well, I don't know her."

"If Bohlen is your married name, maybe your husband knows her."

"He's dead."

"Sorry, Ms. Bohlen."

"I'm not. He was an awful man."

Emma L. didn't answer.

Gene R. sent me to voice mail. I didn't leave a message.

I dialed George A. next. George answered on the third ring, and stopped me when I mentioned her name.

"Not interested. I got nothing to say."

George A. hung up. I debated whether to call back, and decided against it. At least I'd found someone who knew her.

Kandace Bohlen's number led to another voice mail. This time, I left my name and number, and told her I'd like to speak with her about Rachel Belle Bohlen. She would call back, or she wouldn't.

Richard L. was last. A young woman answered on the second ring, yelping out a hello in a cheery voice. She sounded like a teenager. I heard background voices, but they were probably on television.

I said, "Hey. Don't hang up, okay? Picture me begging."

This was me, laying on the charm.

She giggled.

"Who is this?"

"Every Bohlen I've called hangs up. Be a rebel. Resist the urge. Pretty please?"

"Who is this? Did Ronnie put you up to this?"

"Actually, no. I'm calling from Los Angeles. I need information about a Rachel Belle Bohlen."

She didn't respond. In her silence, the background voices were loud.

I said, "I take it you know her?"

Her voice was completely different when she answered. Hushed and low, like she didn't want anyone to hear.

"Is she okay?"

"So far as I know. May I ask your name?"

"I can't really talk."

Her voice was so muffled she might have had a blanket over her head.

"My name is Elvis Cole. I'm a private investigator."

"April."

A whisper.

"Are you her sister?"

She didn't respond.

"Did Rachel have a friend named Kim or Kimmie? Maybe went by Kaykay?"

"Can't talk."

The line went dead, and April was gone.

Can't talk didn't mean won't talk. Can't talk was promising.

I put the laptop aside and checked the time. Lucy and Ben were due to land and Joe would arrive in minutes. Dinner was prepped and ready to go. The house was clean, the guest room was squared away, and I had showered and shaved. Nothing left to do except wonder what Lucy wanted to talk about. I was deciding whether to check the guest room again when Terri Grafino called. Terri didn't sound like her usual friendly self. She sounded subdued.

Terri said, "This number."

That was it.

I said, "Couldn't find the account?"

"I found it. I couldn't get into it, but I found it."

Her voice trailed away to silence.

I said, "Terri?"

"Be careful, Elvis. Don't get stupid on me."

I'd never heard Terri sound empty.

"I don't understand. Is this about the phone?"

"The number, not the phone. It's the account. Whose number is this?"

"Just a guy. Nobody special. I'm trying to find him."

"The number's account is caged. When I tried to access the account, which I did, a message appeared. Please contact the Defense Advanced Research Projects Agency, Department of Defense, Washington, D.C."

I felt a dull throb behind my eyes.

"The Department of Defense."

"I'll probably be investigated."

"Maybe you transposed a digit."

"It's the number you gave me. A DARPA number. It's caged."

DARPA handled research for the military.

"At least they said please."

"These people don't joke."

"No. I guess they don't."

Terri Grafino hung up without saying good-bye. I went to the glass doors and stared across the canyon without seeing it. I felt angry and a little scared. Maybe more than a little. I called Wendy Vann.

"Did you get his call log yet?"

"Give me a break, Cole. I'm working on it."

"Might be faster if you didn't need to ask the Defense Department."

"Take it easy."

"Why does Josh Shumacher have a DARPA phone number?"

"Take it easy."

"Who are you people?"

"His parents used to work for the government. That's all. The phone's a perk. That's all it is."

"How about you and Kurt? Are you a perk?"

"Forget the phone, Cole. You were hired to find her son, so find him. Do your job."

"Answer my question. Who are you people?"

Wendy paused.

"Here's my answer."

She smiled. I sensed it. I didn't like the smile or the reasons behind it or what she said next.

"Enjoy your tacos."

17

Joe Pike and I had been partners since the day we bought the agency from old George Feider, my former boss. He'd been my friend even longer. Pike's uniform du jour was jeans, a gray sweatshirt with the sleeves cut off, and military-issue sunglasses, which was pretty much what he wore every day. He leaned against the counter in my kitchen with his arms crossed. Pike stood as still as a tree. Arrows tattooed on the outsides of his shoulders wrapped forward across his deltoids as if pointing at me. The arrows were red.

I said, "It was a threat. They want me to find Josh, but they didn't expect me to discover the DoD connection. Wendy was warning me to stay clear."

"Think they're feds?"

Wendy and Kurt.

"The government doesn't provide free phones and security to retired academics."

I had googled the Schumachers after Wendy hung up. Adele Schumacher, under her maiden name Adele Raisa Voight, had received a Ph.D. in Computer Theory & Mathematics from MIT, after which she joined the faculty at Stanford. Corbin Schumacher was on the faculty when she arrived, having received a doctorate in Materials Science the year before. During the next eight years, they married, published sixty research articles, and registered as an LLC called Applied Thought, through which they worked as consultants to the aerospace industry. They left Stanford the following year, after which I could find no further information about them or their company.

Pike said, "Maybe they aren't retired."

I set out bowls of chips and salsa as we talked, and took the bags of marinating beef and chicken from the fridge. Lucy had called. They had landed, picked up a rental car, and were on their way.

"I got fake chicken cutlets for you. Figured we'd grill them with a little lime and cilantro."

Pike faced the window and studied the canyon.

"A spotter couldn't tell you're making tacos. They must've followed you to the market."

"Adele hired me to find her son. Why would her people follow me?"

"To see if you pad the bill."

"Is your name Corbin?"

Pike turned from the window.

"Spooks spook. It's what they do."

The world according to Pike.

"I'm not the only person trying to find her son."

I told him about the men in the SUV and the night crew.

"I don't know if they play on the same team or we have two sets of two. It's a crowded field."

"What did Wendy say?"

"Corbin's people wouldn't need to sneak into Josh's place in the dead of night."

Pike's head moved.

"The dead of night."

"Sorry. I've got a lot on my mind."

"Lucy."

I stopped. I nodded, but the nod was for me. I looked at Joe, but the blank lenses were empty.

"Want a beer?"

"Sure."

I broke out two bottles. We twisted the caps.

I said, "I don't like the suddenness of this."

"Their trip."

"I'm glad for the chance to see them. I love seeing them. I don't see them enough."

Pike nodded, a move so slight most people wouldn't notice.

He said, "But."

"I'm concerned. Her wanting to talk but not saying why is not Lucy. She isn't coy."

"No."

I glanced at him again.

"They're staying here. With me. Lucy is staying here, too."

"Sounds good."

"I'm fine with it, but you know how it's been."

"Yes."

"We've had boundaries."

"I know."

"For a long time. She drew lines and I respected them. Never liked them, but I accepted her limits."

"Maybe you're making too much of this."

"I'm concerned."

"They'll be here soon and I'll take Ben. Ask her."

"It'll be strange, knowing she's down in the guest room. It'll be strange in the morning."

"Ask her."

"I'll ask her."

I stared at the fridge, and wondered if I'd forgotten anything.

Pike interrupted my staring.

"These people after Adele's son."

"What about them?"

"Maybe they're not after her son."

"I'm listening."

"How many people were with Adele when she came to the office?"

"Wendy and Kurt, a driver below, and a second driver in a trail car. Two vehicles. Four suits."

"A security detail. And her husband?"

"Ryan told me Corbin has a crew."

"Having security implies you feel threatened. Maybe her son's disappearance is connected to the threat. Maybe the people watching his place are the threat."

I had considered it and considered it again.

"It's possible, but Josh and Skylar were into something. Way it looks, they argued, she left, and he's trying to find her."

"These are maybes."

I thought it through. Bending the narrative away from Skylar was as difficult as bending sheet metal, but thinking about it gave me an idea.

"If the gardeners watched Josh's place yesterday and again today, they'll probably watch it tomorrow. They might even be watching it now."

Pike sipped his beer and nodded.

"Might be worth a look."

He sipped again.

"Unless you scared them off."

I grinned.

"Did you make a joke?"

Pike checked his watch, giving me nothing.

"I'll take a look after dinner."

"One more thing."

Pike waited.

"The nineteen minutes. They were in his bungalow for nineteen minutes, but nothing was disturbed or missing. Nineteen minutes is a long time to stand around doing nothing."

"The meatball and the scarecrow?"

"Yes."

"If they took nothing, maybe they left something."

It made sense.

"If they planted a listening device or a camera, they'd know if Josh went home."

"Josh. You. His mother. Whoever entered."

I didn't like it, but Pike was right.

"Be nice to know if they left something."

"I'll take care of it."

"Can you do it without them knowing?"

To find a surveillance device, Pike would have to enter the premises. But when he entered, he'd trigger the device.

"Not me. But I know someone who can."

We heard a car pull up outside my house and Pike tipped his head toward the street.

"They're here."

18

We met them outside as Lucy and Ben climbed from a dark green rental car. Ben flashed a huge smile and threw his arms around me.

"Elvis, oh, man, this is great. I miss you."

"Me, too, bud. Look at how big you are."

Even as I hugged him, I watched his mother. Lucy Chenier was as beautiful as the day we met. She had played collegiate tennis at LSU and moved with natural grace. Smile lines fanned from the corners of her amber eyes and soft lines bracketed her mouth. The lines had deepened, but they added a richness that made her even more attractive. Her auburn hair was streaked with highlights.

Ben went to Joe, and Lucy and I traded smiles. If something was wrong, I didn't see it.

I said, "Hey."

"Hey."

"Your hair is shorter."

"A little."

"Looks good. It's good to see you."

We shared a polite kiss and hugged, and she turned to Joe. Ben returned to their car.

"Mom! Open the trunk. Let's get our stuff."

Ben and I wheeled their bags into the guest room. He noticed the picture.

"Think you can still press me over your head?"

"With a crane."

He grinned and turned back to the photo.

"Arrowhead was fun. We should go."

"How long does the program at UCLA last?"

"Only a week. But maybe I can come back this summer."

I squeezed his shoulder.

"I'm happy you and your mom are here."

I let go and nodded toward the kitchen.

"C'mon. I'll bet you're starving."

"What's for dinner?"

"Tacos."

"Tacos!"

Lucy and Joe were in the kitchen. They'd been talking, but stopped when they heard us coming. Ben dove on the chips and salsa like a starving hawk.

Lucy said, "I heard the magic T-word."

"You did. Carne asada, pollo, and fake pollo. All we need to do is fire the coals and put the salad together."

I took a bag of sliced zucchini and squash from the fridge.

Pike said, "Hold off the coals. Ben and I are making a beer run."

"We have beer."

"Not the right beer. C'mon, bud. Grab some chips for the road."

Ben scooped a mound of chips into a paper towel and shot me a look as he followed Pike out the carport door.

"Mom wants alone time so you can talk."

Ben pulled the door as they left. The house suddenly felt like a deserted island with only the two of us onshore.

Lucy said, "He reads minds."

"He reads signs. Want to talk in the living room?"

"I couldn't sit."

Lucy went to the counter and crossed her arms. She wet her lips, and glanced away. She was nervous and her being nervous made me fearful.

"If you tell me you're dying, I'll kill you."

She blinked.

"Oh, no. It's Richard."

The ex.

"Fine. Richard is better than dying."

"Not by much."

Her eyes hardened the way they did when she charged the net.

"I am mad. I've been mad since that despicable man did what he did and I hate this."

She closed her eyes and raised a hand, stopping herself.

"How about some water?"

"Gin."

I poured two on the rocks. She held her glass with both hands.

"Richard is writing to Ben. Did he tell you?"

"He has not."

"A letter came to the house last year. Thank God I saw it first. Here's the return address, prison. I was beside myself. I wanted to shred it, then and there, but, honestly, I didn't know what to do. I hid it. In a shoebox."

I didn't know what to say so I nodded. Lucy hadn't mentioned the letters, either, but Lucy had tried to keep Richard out of our relationship since the beginning.

She said, "Then a second letter came. And a third."

"The shoebox?"

"The shoebox. I finally told Ward and he suggested I read them."

Dr. Ward Berteau was Ben's shrink. Ben began suffering from nightmares and anxiety attacks after they went home, and Berteau helped mitigate his PTSD. Ben seemed fine now, but I only saw him two or three weeks each year. I didn't live with them.

"Has Ben seen them?"

She took one breath and sighed it out.

"After I read them, we read them together with Berteau, there in his office."

"Ben seems fine to me and he hasn't mentioned the letters or his father."

"He never mentions his father."

"It must be painful."

"He didn't seem interested. It was very mechanical, as if he was detached."

I didn't know what she wanted from me.

"Are you looking for my opinion?"

"I'm just telling you. I'm concerned. Every few weeks, another letter arrived and we'd read it with Berteau. Ben finally refused to read them. He said if I made him read the letters he'd stop going to therapy."

"Okay."

"Okay, what?"

"Okay, he didn't want to read the letters. They probably make him sad or unhappy or angry. They probably hurt. I don't blame him. He'll read the letters if he chooses to read them or he won't. He's growing up. He's almost grown."

I ran out of gas and felt embarrassed.

Lucy did not move or react. She seemed to be watching me. She watched for a very long while. The right corner of her lips curved into a gentle smile.

She spoke so softly I barely heard her.

"Do you know what scares me?"

"Clowns?"

"What frightens me is the power Richard still has over Ben."

"The father."

"Ben put Richard into a box just as he was put in a box, and buried him so deeply he can't even talk about him. Because he's afraid. And now Richard is trying to wheedle his way back into Ben's life. Ben needs to be stronger."

"So you dug up this program at UCLA so you could ask me to help with Richard?"

"No. No. I dug up this program so Ben could spend more time with you. He loves you."

"I love him, too."

"I know you do. You're a good, decent, wonderful man, and you're good for him."

Her eyes grew pink and blinked.

"Luce."

She raised a finger, the finger saying she needed to keep going.

"The decisions I've made about Ben and myself and you and our moving back to Baton Rouge were made with good reason. What happened with Richard, yes, but there was Sobek and that time you were shot and almost died."

This was old ground. The one time, a lunatic named David Reinneke tried to kill me with a shotgun. He came pretty close. Another time, the police found Lucy's name and address at the home of a killer I was trying to find named Lawrence Sobek. We had talked these things to death.

"A miss is as good as a mile."

"It was a nightmare."

"Close, but no cigar?"

"Don't joke. That's what you do. You joke. These things happened."

"You didn't need to concoct a reason for us to be together. I'm here. I've always been here."

She blinked faster, but the blinking didn't stop her eyes from filling.

"Yes. Other men would've moved on."

Lucy studied the ice in her glass, then set the glass on the counter.

She said, "I love you, you know. I've never stopped loving you."

I nodded.

"I know. Me, too."

We stood there in the kitchen, neither looking at the other, and did not move until Joe and Ben pulled up with beer we did not need.

19

We settled into a friendly, familiar rhythm as we cooked. The beer probably helped.

I grilled the meats and veggies, brought them inside to chop, and set out the chopped meats in separate bowls. Lucy and Ben added the veggies to the salad and made the dressing. Pike sliced limes, diced onions, and minced cilantro to top the tacos. Pike's knife skills were impressive. Each slice of lime was identical. He transformed the onion into precise, uniform cubes.

I said, "Le Cordon Bleu–quality work."

Pike said, "Yes."

The cat came through his cat door, saw Lucy and Ben, and jumped sideways as if he'd been shot. He spat, his hair stood up, and he let out a deep, guttering yowl.

I said, "Stop that!"

He flashed through his cat door at a dead sprint, but stayed on the slope below. Growling.

Lucy said, "Well, he hasn't changed."

We built our own tacos in the kitchen, served ourselves salad, and ate on the deck in the deepening twilight. Lucy relaxed still more. She told funny stories about the partners at her firm and bragged about Ben's skill at tennis. Ben laughed and told funny stories of his own. He seemed fine. Lucy seemed fine, too. I tried to seem fine, but probably didn't.

After dinner, we cleaned the dishes, put away the leftovers, and returned to the deck. The evening was winding down. It was two hours ahead for Lucy and Ben, and Lucy dropped hints about the hour.

Pike said, "How long will you be here?"

"Two nights, tonight and tomorrow."

She glanced at me.

"Though we could stretch it to three."

She went back to Pike.

"I hope we'll see you before we leave."

Ben said, "Yeah."

"You will."

Pike checked his watch and looked at me.

"I'd better get moving."

Pike said his good-nights and let himself out. Lucy and Ben assumed he was going home. He wasn't.

Lucy said, "We'd better hit the sack, young man. Early start tomorrow."

Ben suddenly pointed up.

"Is that a helicopter?"

A tiny gold speck floated above the canyon, but without the telltale red or green of a helicopter or an airplane.

I said, "I don't think so. No running lights."

The speck crossed overhead like a drifting balloon.

Lucy said, "It's Tinker Bell."

"Stop it, Mom."

Ben pointed to a different part of the sky.

"Check it out! There's another."

A second gold speck appeared from the opposite direction, drifting toward the first. They were high, but I couldn't tell how high. They appeared tiny, but the dark sky offered no reference.

Lucy suddenly pointed behind us.

"Look! Another! There's three."

Ben and I twisted to see.

The third speck moved faster. It arced directly to the first and circled it.

I said, "Drones. Gotta be."

Ben said, "This is really cool."

The second speck reached the third and the first, and the three specks froze in a perfect equilateral triangle.

Lucy leaned back to watch.

"Someone's giving us a show."

Ben turned fast and pointed again.

"Wow!"

A fourth and a fifth speck came fast from the east, barely clearing the trees. They dropped beneath the ridgeline, streaked through the canyon, turned ninety degrees, and shot straight up. They joined with the first three, forming a perfect pentagon.

I said, "Listen."

Lucy and Ben looked at me.

"Hear anything?"

They traded a look and shook their heads.

"We should. Drones sound like bees and they're loud."

The five specks drifted toward us like balloons in a gentle breeze. They moved as one, retaining their perfect pentagonal formation, and stopped directly above.

Lucy pushed me with her foot.

"Did you arrange this?"

"No."

"You're lying."

"I'm not."

We tipped back in our chairs, watching. The five gold specks hung motionless, almost as if they were watching us.

They vanished.

Ben yelped.

"Hey! Where'd they go?"

I studied the area where the lights had vanished, but saw no glints or movement. I listened, but still heard nothing.

"Maybe they didn't leave."

He looked from me to the sky.

"They turned off the lights?"

"That, or they're aliens."

Lucy said, "I vote for E.T."

She stood.

"Show's over, buddy boy. Gotta be fresh for the Bruins."

Lucy hooked an arm around his waist and I followed them into the house. Ben hugged me and the three of us said our good-nights.

I watched them disappear into the guest room, closed

the sliders, locked the house, and set the alarm. I put out dry food for the cat, filled his water bowl, and climbed the steps to my loft.

The cat was crouched on the top step. Sullen.

"They're going to bed. You're safe."

He did not acknowledge me and did not move. I had to step over him.

When I came out of the bath a few minutes later, he was curled on the foot of my bed.

I shut the lights, climbed into bed, and looked out at the canyon. I saw house lights on the far ridge and hillsides, and the glittering city beyond the ridge, and the brilliant black sky. The drones had been invisible once their lights went out. They could have left and they could have stayed. I didn't know. We often couldn't see the things in front of us, no matter how hard we tried.

Sleep did not come quickly. I thought about Lucy and Ben. I tried to see us together the way I had once seen us together. I wondered how Lucy saw us and whether we saw the same thing.

20

Jon Stone

Jon Stone, rock god.

Now up on his rotation: "Play That Funky Music" by Wild Cherry.

Jon jerked and whirled to the beat pounding his home above the Sunset Strip like a one-man boy band wrecking crew, every cell in his body a pulsing celebration. Jon Stone, naked as a jaybird, sixteen days back from a security stint in Turkmenistan on the northern Iranian border, had banked so much cash in the past twenty-four hours he buzzed with a burning energy.

And play that funky music
'Til you die!

Jon Stone sold death. Jon, who had spent thirteen years with the U.S. Army's Special Forces, six of which as a Delta Force officer, was a private military contractor. As such, he sold the services of those who could deliver death and those who could defend against death. Business was booming.

Rotation change: "Money" by Pink Floyd.

Jon rolled with it, and sang with the band.

Money
It's a gas

The pullout from Afghanistan had created a security panic. Corporations with vulnerable assets in nearby countries were offering contracts at mind-blowing rates faster than a minigun sprayed bullets. Think of Jon Stone as an agent for mercenaries. For every contract he filled, he got a piece of the action. He had filled twenty-six security contracts in the past thirty hours, all from the safety and comfort of his black-and-steel home. No risk to life and limb required.

Jon's home was a sleek contemporary above the Sunset Strip, resplendent with floor-to-ceiling sliding glass doors, Carrara marble floors, and a glittering pool. The house overlooked the broad expanse of the Los Angeles Basin and was totally private. Jon preferred to be naked when he was home. Currently, his only adornment was a headset Bluetoothed to his computer. If someone phoned, his computer instantly muted the music, allowing him to conduct business. And dance.

Rotation change: "Thank You" by Sly and the Family Stone.

Hell yeah!

Lookin' at the devil, grinnin' at his gun

Jon caught reflections of himself in glass and polished steel. He had the hard build of a surfer with spikey blond hair and a stud in his ear. The stud was an equilateral triangle, also known as a delta triangle, the delta for his time in the Unit. Jon spun, twisted, and belted along with Sly. Damned if he didn't look like a rock star in the mirror behind his bar. Kinda like Sting. Only better.

The music abruptly stopped. Jon's earpiece chirped simultaneously, indicating an incoming call. Jon was expecting a call from a former British SAS operator named Rafael Highgarten.

"Jon Stone."

A low male voice whispered.

"Turn."

Jon Stone stood absolutely still. Five cocked-and-locked .45-caliber Kimber pistols were hidden in discreet but accessible locations throughout his home. Had Jon been in his bedroom, kitchen, entry, or next to the bar, he would have broken left or right without hesitation. But Jon currently stood well away from guns or cover on a white Carrara plain. He raised his hands slowly out to the sides, and turned.

Joe Pike stood on the far side of the pool, phone to his ear.

Stone dropped his hands.

"No."

He cupped his mouth and said it louder.

"No."

Pike said, "Gear up. I need you."

Pike lowered his phone, and Sly and the Family returned.

Thank you . . . for letting me . . . be myself . . . again

Jon pulled off his headset and geared up.

21

Joe Pike

They needed two vehicles, so Pike drove his red Jeep Cherokee and Stone took his black Range Rover. The Rover was turbocharged and a beast of a vehicle.

A half mile past the Hollywood/Sunset split, they left Pike's Jeep outside a Cuban restaurant. Pike wanted to make a fly-by. If people were watching Schumacher's bungalow, Pike didn't want them to see his Jeep twice.

Stone guided them toward the target, slumped against the door as he drove, looking all gloomy and sour.

"This guy Cole is really something. How much he paying you?"

Pike ignored him. Jon knew he wouldn't be paid. At the end of the day, he was doing this as a favor for Pike.

Jon scowled.

"Yeah, that's what I thought. Kinda like you, not paying me."

"Coming up. Right turn."

"If a friend of mine took advantage like that, I'd cut his ass off."

"Around this curve, a left, then a right."

Jon put on a phony look of surprise.

"Oh, wait! I thought I was talking about you and Cole, but it sounds exactly like you and me."

"Jon."

Jon looked over. Scowling.

Pike touched his lips. Be quiet.

Jon raised his hands, and drove on in silence.

Jon Stone was a deadly superb operator, but he could be annoying. Especially about money.

Pike said, "Slow five. Coming out of the next curve, it'll be on our left."

Jon eased off the gas, and they lowered their sun visors. Pike had chosen the route so the address would pass on Jon's side of the vehicle. Jon would have to enter and exit the bungalow. Pike would be in his Jeep.

Prior to departing Jon's house, they had studied satellite imagery to locate Schumacher's bungalow, the surrounding structures, and possible routes to enter and exit the property. They discussed the locations where Cole had seen watchers, additional locations where a surveillance team might hide, and Leon Karsey, who lived directly across from Schumacher.

Jon had smirked.

"Old dude doesn't sleep. I should bring him a fifth. Feed him booze until he passes out."

They reached the far side of the curve, and the bungalow village was ahead on the left. Neither of them looked at it. Two people were crossing the street directly ahead.

Jon said, "Holy shit."

Pike said, "Slow five."

"Is that—?"

"Yes."

The scarecrow and the meatball shielded their eyes from the oncoming lights as anyone would, but otherwise seemed unconcerned. They continued across the street, mounted the concrete steps, and disappeared between the bungalows.

When Pike glanced at Jon, Jon Stone was grinning.

"The scarecrow and the meatball. I just like saying it."

They continued past without looking at the bungalows. Pike considered the woman and the man to be high-value targets. If there was a bug, they had planted it, so he didn't want to risk losing them. Their presence required a change of plans, so Pike dug out his keys and passed them to Jon.

"No time to drive down for the Jeep. I need the Rover."

"I know, I know. I'm still a go for the bungalow?"

"Yes."

"Groovy. Let's do it."

Jon maintained their steady pace until they rounded the next curve, and hit the brakes. They threw open the doors, bailed, and Pike slid in behind the wheel. Jon went to the rear, popped the Rover's hatch, and slung a go-bag over his shoulder. Pike watched him come forward in the driver's-side window. Jon had an ear-to-ear grin. The grin made him look like a cruising shark.

"Know what I like saying even more? The cow and her cuck. Isn't it mah-velous?"

"You don't do this for money, Jon. You enjoy it."

"The cow and her cuck. How'd you like to be that fuckin' guy?"

Jon tapped the Rover and started away.

"Good hunting, brother. Stay groovy."

Pike punched the gas. The scarecrow and her friend had crossed from right to left, which suggested they had parked on the right side of the street or come from a house on the same side. Pike had an image of a light-colored sedan, but it was possible they'd stepped around the sedan if they emerged from a house. Either way, he needed to be in position before they returned. He had two options: set up below the bungalows, hoping the targets went south, or above, hoping they went north. Driving south was the fastest and most direct route to Sunset Boulevard, but the street branched several times, and many of those branches led to Sunset. Driving north led to a meandering array of streets branching through the surrounding area, some looping south again to Sunset, and others leading as far north as the I-5 freeway. If Pike guessed wrong, he would lose them. He needed an eyes-on view to eliminate the guesswork, and this meant he had to set up on foot.

Pike turned east at the first turn, hammered the Rover north until he was above the bungalows, then hooked south again in a broken loop and approached the bungalows from above exactly as he had with Jon. Pike parked as close as possible while remaining hidden, and moved closer on foot. When the bungalows were in view, he found a place to wait behind the shadowed stalks of a yucca tree. Pike fit a headset connected with his phone into his ear, and positioned a military-grade Flexmike as thin as a toothpick to his lips. He surveyed the scene.

Ahead on the right were a small pickup, a couple of compacts, and the light sedan. The sedan faced away from him, and was parked almost directly across from the bungalows. Pike found this odd, and wondered what it meant.

Pike settled in to wait, and visualized possible scenarios. If the man and the woman drove away from him, he would run to the Rover, and drive like hell to catch up. If they turned around and came toward him, he would hide beside the house until they passed. Then he'd have to run for the Rover.

His cell phone vibrated.

He touched a button to answer. Stone, speaking soft. Pike said, "Go."

"I'm hanging out in some weeds up here. Smells like rats."

Pike didn't respond.

"They're inside. Guess what? The windows look like three kinds of green hell. They got it lit with IR."

Elvis had mentioned their night vision equipment. They were using infrared illuminators as a light source, and NVG to see. Jon was wearing his own night vision goggles, or he wouldn't have been able to see the glow. The old man who lived in the mauve wouldn't be seeing anything.

Jon said, "Stand by."

A second passed.

"Lights out. The party's over."

Ten or twelve seconds passed before Jon spoke again.

"Early night, bro. Elvis is leaving the building."

Another pause.

"Not your Elvis. The real Elvis."

Another pause, and Jon's tone changed.

"Dude."

Pike waited.

"Their goggles are crazy, bro. Really small. Kinda flat. I don't see any tubes. No shit. This is wild."

A tube was a cylindrical image intensifier used to intensify available light in night vision equipment. Jon Stone had enormous experience with night vision gear, yet didn't recognize these.

Pike said, "Shop later."

"They're on the steps. Check'm out."

The woman and man emerged between the bungalows. They weren't wearing the goggles now, but Pike noticed a bag slung on the man's shoulder, which probably held their equipment.

Jon said, "You got'm?"

"Got'm."

"Have you seen goggles like this?"

"Gear's off. You good?"

"The old man came out. I'll move in when he settles."

"Rog."

The woman and her round friend didn't hurry. They went to the sedan, and the woman got in behind the wheel. When she opened the door, the interior lights did not come on. The man climbed into the shotgun seat. A moment later, the brake lights flared, the lights came on, and the sedan pulled away. Pike waited to see if they turned around, and kept waiting until he was sure they weren't.

Pike raced to the Rover at a dead sprint, fired the engine, and powered away on five hundred thirty-five turbocharged horses.

Jon's Rover truly was a helluva beast.

Pike saw their taillights ahead twenty-two seconds later and eased off the gas. He dropped back, dropped back a little more, and followed.

22

Jon Stone

The old man was a double-royal pain in the ass. He poked around outside Schumacher's dump for a good twenty minutes, just dicking around. He peeked in the front windows and tried the front door, then crept down to the street, screwed around down there doing God knew what, finally came back, and peeked in the windows again. When he returned, he shined a little light through the window, so Jon figured he'd gotten the light from his car. Jon made the guy for a Peeping Tom and figured he was a regular outside his neighbors' windows. Creep.

Jon waited him out in the empty blue bungalow. Pike had told him the blue was uninhabited, but Pike hadn't told him it reeked like a cat box. The instant Jon entered, the sharp stench of ammonia burned his eyes. And for this, for standing around in a piss-soaked-carpet ammonia hell, Jon Stone was being paid exactly *nothing*. The only thing keeping him from obsessing about the money he wasn't making was the funky night vision goggles the scarecrow and the meatball had worn. These were the stuff of Jon Stone's trade, and he had never seen goggles like these. He was, officially, fascinated, which left him equally curious to see what they'd left in Schumacher's bungalow.

Assuming they'd left something. Since they'd spent only a few minutes inside tonight, tonight might have been a retrieval mission. They could have planted something earlier and returned tonight to retrieve it. Jon had planted such bugs himself. Rather than transmitting motion alerts or conversations or images in real time, which made detection easier, recordings were made on SIM cards. The recordings could be transmitted at a later time or the SIM card could be retrieved by hand. The downside being someone had to physically retrieve the card, said someones possibly being the scarecrow and the meatball.

The peeper finally returned to his bungalow. Jon waited for another ten minutes before letting himself out. He crept uphill away from the old man's bungalow, circled behind the blue, and crept downhill toward the yellow. He checked the old man's bungalow again. Jon's night vision gear amplified ambient light and read infrared thermal energy. Jon saw the old man's heat signature lying on what appeared to be a couch. Jon couldn't tell if he was sleeping, but at least the dude wasn't at the window.

Jon worked his way behind the yellow to the kitchen door. Pike had shown him a sketch of the interior Cole drew, so Jon knew what to expect. Assuming Cole hadn't gotten it wrong. With a loser like Cole, you never knew.

Jon did not attack the door. He shined a needle-thin laser through a window and listened. Sounds within the bungalow would cause micro-vibrations in the glass, which his laser listening device could read and magnify. Jon heard nothing. The bungalow was quiet.

Jon still did not move to the door. If the scarecrow and the meatball were running a bug, they would know someone had entered. He stowed the laser and took out a high-speed drill the size of a tube of toothpaste. The drill had a unique diamond bit designed and built by a woman in Grand Rapids, Michigan, under an exclusive contract for the United States Army. Jon knew for a fact the bits were also used by the CIA, the DIA, and the Navy SEAL teams. The woman did not know this and did not need to know. The drill cut a small hole in the glass in less than a second with the sound of a single breath.

The device couldn't be killed until it was found, so the next best thing was to jam its signal. Most bugs transmitted RF signals similar to a TV remote, so Jon inserted a short microwave antenna through the hole. The antenna was mated to a signal generator Jon wore on his equipment vest. The generator broadcast a white noise signal across the entire RF spectrum, which included VHF, UHF, cell signals, and Wi-Fi. This effectively garbled the bug's signal. The generator, like most of Jon's equipment, bore no manufacturer's name. It had been developed in the black, manufactured in the black, and remained in the black. Jon did not own the generator, but the generator was his. The DIA had given it to him. Jon often worked for the DIA, though they would never admit it. He worked for many alphabet companies.

Jon unlocked the kitchen door in twenty-two seconds and shouldered the door open through a mountain of garbage bags. He fired up a second signal jammer, moved into the living room, and set about hunting the bug.

The interior of the bungalow was dark as a cave to the naked eye, but not to his NVG and countersurveillance scanner. The scanner revealed walls lit by pockets of thermal shadows, some brighter than others and some larger than others. All electrical devices produced RF signals, whether they were active or sleeping. The TV and cable box pulsed with sleepy heat. The TV remote did the same. The junction boxes in the walls and the light switches produced a soft glow. A box of spare batteries, a second remote, the video game controllers and game box all glowed with ghostly shadows.

Forty-two minutes into the search, Jon Stone found the first device in a receptacle box beneath the dining room table. He pulled the table aside, slipped out of his vest, and fired up an IR illuminator for more light. Jon unscrewed the faceplate and saw the little monster peeking out like a weasel in a hole.

Then Jon frowned and leaned closer.

Weird.

Jon took a red penlight from his vest, removed his NVG, and cupped the red light. He let his eyes adjust, then painted the bug with red light and leaned in for an eyeball-to-eyeball look.

Jon's frown slowly split into a grin.

"No. Effin'. Way."

He gripped the device with a pair of needle-nose pliers and pulled the bug and a miniature battery pack free.

Jon laid the device on the floor.

He studied it, turned it over, studied it some more, then picked it up with his fingers and looked even closer. Jon Stone had seen these devices at training facilities, but he had never seen them in the actual US of A.

Jon Stone tingled the way he tingled when he choppered into the shit.

He grinned at the little device the way a tiger shark grinned at a seal and murmured a little song.

"Thank you. For letting me be myself. Again."

Jon placed the device on the floor. He photographed both sides, the top, and the bottom. He photographed the battery pack and the batteries, put the device back into the outlet box, replaced the cover, and continued searching the bungalow.

Jon found a second device eighteen minutes later.

Thirty-two minutes after finding the second device, Jon exfilled the premises but did not leave the premises as he had found them.

Jon Stone left something special behind.

23

Ryan Seborg

Ryan was still awake when his sister came home. He was up in his room, lying in bed with his feet on the wall and headset on, listening to a podcast about the Lonnie Zamora UFO encounter in New Mexico. Back in junior high, Ryan and Josh had listened to old radio shows all night, streaming one show after another about UFOs, alien encounters, and how the government misled the public with lies and misinformation. Other kids were obsessed with rock bands or sports. Ryan and Josh were obsessed with learning the truth. They scoured the internet for leads, filed Freedom of Information Act requests, and posted to hundreds of message boards. The truth was out there, as real as a white light on a dark horizon. They devoted themselves to catching it, but the light had remained out of reach. It was like a race they vowed not to quit. If they could reach the light, the truth would be revealed.

The overhead light flicked off and on, off and on, and off. Ryan angrily pulled off the headset.

"Turn it on."

The light came on.

His sister, Bethany, smirked from the doorway. Ryan lived at home with his mom and dad, his younger sister Bethany, who was twenty-two, and their baby sister, Clare, who was nineteen. His brother, Robert Anson, was twenty-four and the lone Seborg sibling to leave the nest. Robert Anson had joined the Navy. Ryan, being twenty-six, was the oldest.

Bethany said, "Loser. Why are you still up?"

"Shut up and get out. You're gonna wake Mom."

"I'm not in your room, stupid. I'm in the hall. I have not transgressed your precious door space."

Bethany suddenly frowned, leaned toward him as if for a better look, and touched her chin.

"What's on your face?"

Ryan touched his face and checked his fingers. White.

"Powdered donuts."

"You're disgusting."

"Go to bed."

Bethany continued to stare, but after a moment her expression softened.

"Seriously. You've been in that exact same spot all day. Are you okay?"

"I'm fine."

"You look depressed."

"You're depressing me. Go away."

"Do you get up to pee or do you just wet yourself?"

Ryan threw a package of powdered donuts at her.

"Go!"

Bethany stalked away.

Ryan listened until she entered her room, then swung his feet from the wall and sat up. He slapped his laptop closed, shoved it aside, and glared at Josh's computer. The desktop's tower stood tall on Ryan's desk. Ryan had been glaring at it since he'd found the secret file with the boring crap Josh downloaded for that bimbo Skylar Lawless. He felt like peeing all over it.

Ryan said, "Like she'd ever screw *you*, you moron."

Ryan was livid.

"Get real, dude. What were you thinking?"

The computer didn't answer.

Ryan wadded up an empty powdered donuts package and threw it at the computer.

"*Asshole.*"

Ryan's eyes fluttered and the computer blurred. Josh had abandoned him. He had cut Ryan out, gutted their dreams, and disappeared without so much as a kiss my ass. Ryan ached so badly he thought he might die.

"You were my friend."

Ryan clenched his eyes. He rubbed his face and smeared powdered sugar.

The cell phone on the bed by his leg buzzed.

Ryan wiped his eyes and nose and checked his phone. He didn't recognize the number. Some idiot dialing a wrong number, maybe, or Russian scammers. Ryan sent the call to voice mail and tossed the phone aside.

His phone buzzed again and Ryan snatched it up.

"What the fuck?"

Same number.

He sent the call to voice mail.

"Idiot."

Buzz.

Ryan jabbed the phone to answer.

"Wrong number, dipshit! Stop calling."

"It's me. Ryan, it's me. Can you hear me?"

"Josh?"

It was Josh, but he was speaking more quietly than Josh ever spoke and he sounded hoarse.

"Yeah. Ryan, listen—"

"Fuck you!"

Ryan jabbed his phone to kill the call. He jabbed his phone hard two more times, killing it dead.

Buzz.

Buzz.

Buzz.

Ryan answered in a blind fury.

"*What?*"

Josh was crying and trying to speak through the sobs.

"Please, Ryan, save this number. You gotta. This is the number I'm using. *Please.*"

The rage Ryan felt vanished. Josh was crying and gasping and his voice was shaky. He sounded afraid.

Ryan glanced at the door, checking for Bethany.

"Dude. Where are you? What's going on?"

"I'm in trouble."

"What's going on?"

Josh sobbed.

"It's bad."

Ryan closed his eyes and listened and loved his friend more than ever.

PART THREE

Hidden Truths

24

Elvis Cole

was making coffee when Ben Chenier appeared. He still wore the gym shorts and T-shirt he'd slept in.

"Mornin'."

"Hey. How was the futon?"

"Great. What's for breakfast?"

A teenage male calorie furnace.

"Eggs, bacon, whatever you want. Let's check with Mom."

"We could do tacos."

We had tons of leftovers.

"Sure. We could also do chilaquiles. Let's check with Mom."

Lucy appeared in the door.

"Mom would like coffee, please."

I smiled and reached for a mug. Lucy was dressed for their day and looked terrific in light gray pants, a sleeveless white shirt, and a thin gold necklace. Polished agate dangles hung from her ears. The earrings were a gift from me.

I said, "One coffee coming up. Sleep okay?"

"Very well, thank you. I vote for chilaquiles."

I filled the mug and held it out. Lucy smiled and brushed my fingers when she took it. I felt odd. I wasn't sure why, but I did.

I turned away and busied myself making breakfast. I used the leftovers, and the chilaquiles were good to go in twenty minutes.

We enjoyed a leisurely breakfast as Lucy outlined their day.

"After we finish on campus, we'll walk around Westwood Village and drive to the beach. We may not be back until late afternoon or so."

"Take your time. I won't be home until later."

Ben said, "I wish you could come."

He looked hopeful when he said it.

"Know what, buddy? I do, too."

Lucy patted my arm.

They left exactly at eight-thirty. I gave Lucy the alarm code and a key to the house, and walked them out to their car. I was back inside and washing the dishes when Pike called.

"You alone?"

Asking whether I could talk.

"Yeah. What's going on?"

"Sending pictures."

I dried my hands and wandered into the living room.

A photograph of the rear end of a gold or tan Ford

sedan appeared in my message window. Pike had enlarged its license plate, which left it pixelated but readable.

"Is this the gardeners?"

"No gardeners. The scarecrow and the meatball were in the street when we arrived."

I dropped onto the couch.

"Excellent. Did you get their pictures?"

"Nothing usable. They were kitted out with NVG and IR illuminators, like your friend there reported, and they entered the bungalow."

"What were they doing?"

"Dunno. I was below on the street. Jon saw them exit, but couldn't see what they were doing."

"Did you guys enter after they cleared?"

"I stayed with them. Jon entered. He found two devices. No way to tell how long they've been there."

"I hope he didn't take them or kill them."

"They're in place and active, plus Jon left one of his. Now the surveillance goes both ways."

"Okay. Good."

"You should know, Jon's trying to identify their equipment. He's concerned. This is Jon we're talking about and Jon has never seen goggles like theirs."

I tried to picture Jon Stone looking concerned and couldn't.

"Why concerned? What's he concerned about other than, you know, someone bugged Josh's house?"

"The source. I followed them to Ontario Airport."

Ontario was forty miles east of L.A., straight out the I-10 freeway. The airport began life as a military facility, but was released to the public and converted to a twenty-four-hour international airport. Most of its heavy jet traffic were cargo flights.

"They entered a security gate on the south side of the airport. Lot of private jets and charter jets on the south. They had a key card, but this was as far as I could go. Next picture."

The next picture showed the tan sedan beside an open, brightly lit hangar. The area outside the hangar's mouth was flooded with light. Two men in what appeared to be work clothes were walking toward the empty maw of the hangar. They looked like maintenance guys. I could make out two heads in the sedan, but no details.

Pike said, "I took this from across the street through a chain-link fence. My guess, it's a private hangar. This is them."

Two headshots arrived. The meatball showed a hazy profile. The scarecrow had been walking when Pike got the shot. Part of her face was masked by her hair and part by the shadow her hair cast.

"This is them in the car?"

"Yes."

"What are they doing?"

"Waiting."

"Oh."

"They waited for one hour and sixteen minutes. Then this happened."

In the next picture, a large white private jet sat in the light outside the hangar. A door on its side was open and its stairway was down. A black limo sat by the aircraft's nose with its driver nearby. A thin female figure and a burly male figure appeared to be greeting a balding man in slacks and a short-sleeved shirt who had just emerged from the jet. Another female waited in the background with what appeared to be a briefcase and a purple wheelie travel bag.

Pike said, "They were waiting for this guy."

The next photo showed a round-faced man with a wide jaw and thinning hair. The image was hazy from poor light and distance, and slightly pixelated, but much better than the shots of the scarecrow and the meatball.

Pike said, "He huddled up with the meatball for a few minutes, then he left with the thin woman and the woman with the bags."

"The meatball didn't go?"

"Stayed at the hangar. I followed the limo."

A new photo arrived, showing the limo outside the sleek front entrance of a hotel. It was probably three-thirty in the morning, so the street and the sidewalk were deserted. The boss and the two women were entering.

Pike said, "The Crystal Emperor Hotel."

"This is downtown."

"Yes."

"We have to figure out who this guy is."

"We will. Look at the plane again."

I scrolled back to the photo of the jet.

"I'm looking at it."

"Enlarge the tail number."

I expanded the tail number until it was readable.

All civil aircraft operating anywhere in the world were

required to display a registration number. A unique alphanumeric code was assigned to each airplane, same as a license plate number was unique to a specific car. These numbers were almost always painted on the tail, so people called them tail numbers. Since airplanes could pretty much fly all over the world, each number began with a code indicating the aircraft's country of origin. In the U.S., tail numbers began with the letter N. In the UK, a G. In Mexico, an XA. I had never seen a tail number like this and I didn't know what it meant.

"It begins with a B."

Pike said, "China."

"China?"

"The People's Republic of China."

I studied the number. I went back to the wider shot and studied the jet.

"The plane came from China."

"It bears a Chinese registration."

It seemed silly. A jet from China.

"Wait. What you're saying is, the people who bugged Josh Schumacher's little bungalow—the same Josh with a podcast about aliens and pornstars who gets an allowance from his mother—the people bugging his bungalow came all the way from China?"

"The People's Republic. Jon has questions about Josh."

"Because the jet came from China?"

"Because of the equipment they use. The jet came later."

"You know what I know. Tell him."

"May I tell him who hired you?"

Jon Stone's concern bothered me.

"Yes. Tell him. He can call me if he wants, and I'll tell him."

"I'll get back to you."

"What's Jon going to do?"

"Spooks spook."

The line went dead.

"Joe?"

Dead.

I lowered the phone and thought about Josh and Adele and a jet from the far side of the world delivering a balding gentleman to the Crystal Emperor Hotel. The Crystal Emperor was an excellent hotel. I'd been there for drinks. It was new and very, very expensive.

I scrolled through Pike's photos and copied the license numbers from the limo and the sedan. I phoned a guy I know at the DMV.

Spooks spook.

Detectives detect.

25

J erry Leff traded DMV information for Dodgers tickets. A former client I helped in a big way had primo tickets in the Dodgers Dugout Club and sent a few my way each season. When I told him I used them to buy information, he sent more.

Jerry said, "Hey, man! I hope you need something!"

They were excellent seats.

"As a matter of fact, I do."

I read off the plates.

Jerry always told me to hang on and I've never known why. I assumed he had to leave his office to find a free terminal, but I didn't know. Maybe he was so happy to get the tickets he danced in circles, throwing fist pumps.

Jerry returned a few minutes later.

The limo was registered to the Crystal Emperor Hotel. Something called LWL Development Inc. in San Gabriel, California, owned the sedan. I googled LWL Development and learned it was a midsize commercial real estate development firm. Their largest project to date was the Crystal Emperor Hotel, which they'd built in partnership with the Crystal Future Hospitality Group.

Real estate.

The file Ryan discovered on Josh's computer contained downloads about real estate. Boring, he'd said. Dull. Downloaded on dates that coincided with Skylar's calls. Ryan had sent the file, but I hadn't opened it. I called him. His phone rang four times before his voice mail picked up.

I said, "Ryan, it's Elvis Cole. Call me."

I hung up and googled the Chinese jet's tail number.

The jet was a twin-engine Gulfstream G500 registered to the Crystal Future Hospitality Group headquartered in Shanghai, China. A flight tracker site showed the G500 had departed Shanghai for Sapporo, Japan, then crossed the Bering Sea to Anchorage, hopped to Vancouver and turned south to Ontario. Six thousand, seven hundred, ninety-nine miles. The balding man had gone to a lot of trouble to get here.

I googled Crystal Future Hospitality Group next.

The CFHG website was written in Chinese, but an English language option was available. Crystal Future appeared to be in the hotel business. The company's mission statement claimed CFHG was committed to "aggressively expanding" their network of "crown jewel hotel and resort properties offering unparalleled luxury accommodations" throughout the global market. Photos of sleek,

modern hotels in Shanghai, Ho Chi Minh City, and Bue-
nos Aires accompanied the statement. They looked expensive. I checked to see if the Crystal Emperor Hotel
was part of their aggressively expanding network. Big
surprise. It was.

I was reading about Crystal Future when Ryan called
back.

He said, "Hey, this is Ryan Seborg."

"Does the name LWL Development ring a bell?"

"What are you talking about?"

"Did Josh ever mention it?"

"I dunno. I don't think so."

"It's a real estate development firm in San Gabriel.
You said Josh downloaded articles about real estate after
Skylar called."

Ryan hesitated.

"Yeah, well, I've been thinking. I was wrong."

"About what?"

"I dunno. Josh was talking about real estate stuff last
year. I just forgot, I guess. It wasn't new."

"Don't the dates match up with Skylar?"

"You get new dates when you re-save files. I was just
pissed, but now I remember him talking about this crap
last year, so I thought you should know."

Ryan Seborg was lying.

I said, "Uh-huh."

"Yeah, well, you know."

I could see him scuffing his feet and hanging his head.

"What's going on, Ryan?"

"I just remembered!"

"That Josh was interested in real estate long before Skylar."

"He wanted to go mainstream. I told you. I should've kept my mouth shut."

He sounded like a six-year-old trying to sell a lie.

"Okay, Ryan. Thanks for sending the file. I'll check it out."

"Fine."

"Don't go back to his bungalow. I mean it."

"Eat me."

Ryan hung up.

I moved to my laptop and downloaded the file.

Josh's secret stash contained twenty-seven PDFs of articles taken from the *Los Angeles Times*, the *Daily News*, *LAist*, three local television stations, two real estate gossip blogs, and a handful of business journals.

I was about to open the first when my phone rang.

The caller ID read APRIL BOHLEN.

26

April Bohlen called from her cell phone, which was why her name appeared in the caller ID. She probably wasn't calling from home and she had gone to the trouble of finding my number. These were good signs. They suggested she was willing to talk about Rachel.

"Um, hi, I couldn't talk. My mom was there."

April sounded nervous.

"No worries, April. I'm really glad you called. You sounded a little tense yesterday."

"We don't talk about Rachel. My mother goes off. Rachel's like, I dunno, the family Satan."

"You and Rachel are cousins?"

"Uh-huh. My dad and her dad are brothers. Her dad is my dad's big brother."

"So you must be younger than Rachel."

"Uh-huh. I'm seventeen. Rachel is like twenty-nine? I'm not really sure."

Twelve years was a large gap.

"So you were pretty young when she left Visalia."

"Yeah."

"Did you know her much when you were little?"

"Um, yeah, Rachel was fun. She was older, but we all got together. NFL game day every Sunday. Barbecues and family stuff. Rachel used to babysit for me 'til she started acting out."

Acting out.

"Have you stayed in touch with her?"

"Um, not really, no. She went to Los Angeles. I guess you know that."

"Yeah."

"Staying in touch has not been encouraged. Not in *my* house."

"What about her mom and dad? Do they keep in touch with her?"

"Her mom passed. They got divorced, and, I dunno, her mom got real depressed or sick or something? She up and left. Nobody talked about it, at least not to us, but, I dunno, a couple of years later maybe—I was in ninth grade, so maybe three years—Uncle George called one day and told Daddy she passed. My mother, of course, the saint of Visalia, says it's on Rachel."

"I understand Rachel was older, but do you know if she had a friend named Kimmie?"

"Yes! I *love* Kimmie! OhmyGod, she was my babysitter!"

My shoulders tightened. If I could reach Kimmie, Kimmie might know how to reach Skylar.

"Kimmie and Rachel were tight?"

"The bestest of besties, which was kinda crazy, them being so different. They didn't seem different to me, but you should hear my mom. Even my mother loved Kimmie."

"Is Kimmie her actual name?"

"She's a Kimberly. Everyone calls her Kimmie."

"Okay. I understand she's here in Los Angeles."

"She is! She comes up all the time to visit, though. They're different that way. Rachel never comes home."

"Are they still close?"

"Um, I don't really know. When Kimmie's here, she never talks about Rachel, not to anyone in our family."

"I need to talk to her, April. It's really important. Do you have her phone number?"

"Um, I don't, no, but I know where she works. Or used to work. I don't know if she's still there."

"Terrific, April. Where?"

April sounded thrilled to help.

"A place called Stennis. She does hair, you know? I don't know what Stennis means, but it's a salon in Santa Monica."

"One more thing. What's her last name?"

"Laird. L-a-i-r-d. Kimberly Laird. She's really sweet. You'll like her."

"If she's anything like you, I will."

April Bohlen giggled.

"Bye, Mr. Cole."

"Bye, Ms. Bohlen."

I hustled out to my car and left to find Kimmie Laird.

27

Stennis was a small salon on Wilshire Boulevard between a vegan cupcake shop and a children's store with a FOR LEASE sign in its window. A stylish black entrance fronted the salon with a large window so private eyes could see inside. The window revealed a receptionist's desk and three salon chairs facing three mirrors. A middle-aged woman with bits of foil in her hair occupied the chair nearest the window. She was watching a tall male stylist paint the foil like an angry school principal watches a class clown. A thirtysomething man in the last chair watched a younger female stylist run an electric trimmer over his scalp. The stylist sported a shaved pixie cut with a subtle magenta streak. I phoned the salon as I watched.

A woman I didn't see answered.

"Stennis Salon."

"Hey. Is Kimmie Laird in today?"

"She is, but, um, she doesn't have anything available."

"I'm calling for a friend. We're driving down this afternoon and she'd love if Kimmie could squeeze her in. Kimmie knows her really well. Would you please ask?"

"Of course. What's her name?"

"Rachel Bohlen."

"Lemme ask."

The invisible receptionist appeared with a handset phone and went to the pixie cut stylist. They traded a word and the pixie cut snatched the phone and stepped away from her client.

"Wherehaveyoubeen? OhmyGodwhydidn'tyoucall? Iwassoworried!"

Rachel was missing for everyone.

"I'm trying to find her, too. I believe Rachel is in danger. Will you help?"

Kimberly Laird stiffened the way a sparrow stiffens as a snake glides toward its nest.

"April Bohlen gave me your name. She said you'd help. Call her. She'll confirm what I'm saying."

Kimberly moved farther away from her client. The client tracked her in the mirror.

"Who is this?"

"Rachel was interviewed on a podcast, *In Your Face with Josh Shoe.* Remember?"

"She's been on with Josh twice. Where's Rachel? Who are you?"

"Josh is missing, too. His parents hired me to find him."

"Is Rachel with Josh?"

"I don't know. It's possible, but I don't know. I need

to talk to you, Kimberly. I believe you know something that could help."

"I don't know where she is. I've been going crazy trying to find her. I don't know anything."

"Kimberly, you do. You know things no one else knows. You were her safety."

Kimberly stepped farther away and spoke in a smaller voice.

"I'm at work."

"I know. I see you."

Kimberly slowly turned toward the window. I raised a hand.

"Finish his hair. I'll wait."

She came out six minutes later and we talked in front of the cupcake shop.

"When was the last time you spoke with her?"

"A week? I was gonna do her hair. It's a thing. She comes over, we try out different looks, we hang, but she never showed up. She didn't answer my calls or texts, and I didn't know what to think, like, is she mad at me? But her other friends haven't heard from her, either."

She pulled at her fingers as she spoke. Nervous.

"Was she having her hair done for an escort job?"

Little dimples appeared on her chin. Kimberly seemed uneasy, as if she didn't want to discuss Rachel's escort work.

"She likes trying new looks. She wasn't seeing a client."

"Would she see a client without telling you?"

"I really don't want to talk about this."

"She would or she wouldn't, Kimberly. Would she risk seeing a stranger without telling you?"

Kimberly glanced into the cupcake shop and twisted her fingers.

"She tells me everything."

"Did she mention seeing Josh?"

Kimberly looked confused.

"The podcast Josh?"

"Maybe something about real estate."

She shook her head before I finished asking.

"I don't know what you're talking about. Rachel and I talk all the time. We tell each other everything."

"Funny. The past few weeks, she spoke with Josh all the time, too. She didn't mention it?"

Kimberly stared for a moment and stopped pulling her fingers.

"About what?"

"I was hoping you'd know. Do you?"

"She didn't mention Josh."

"She started calling him about three weeks ago. He's been seen at her apartment. Were they involved?"

A smile kissed the edge of her lips.

"Hardly. She definitely would have told me *that*."

She studied me for a moment, and cocked her head.

"Besides, he isn't her type."

"Because he's heavy?"

"Because he isn't me."

I nodded.

She said, "Gotcha, didn't I?"

I nodded again, but I wasn't thinking about her and Rachel. I was working through the timeline.

"If Rachel didn't want to tell you she was seeing Josh, maybe she didn't want to tell you she was seeing a client. Maybe she told Meredith Birch."

Kimberly shook her head a single sharp time.

"She didn't tell Meredith. That part of their relationship ended."

"Meredith told me she's still Rachel's safety."

Kimberly's eyes turned cool.

"She can think what she wants. Rachel doesn't trust her. Meredith is more concerned with her clients than her escorts."

"So who sets up Rachel's dates now, you?"

"Are you nuts? I hate this escort thing. I've been after her to quit for years."

"Then who sets up her dates?"

Kimberly pursed her lips.

"Rachel doesn't escort much anymore. When she does, she usually dates one of her regulars. They're safe. It's less stressful."

"How safe?"

"Safe. She's dated some of these men for years. They're regular customers."

"How recent was her last escort date?"

The uneasy eyes returned.

"She would've told me if she went on that kind of date."

"I believe you. When was her last date you know of?"

She thought for a moment, figuring it out.

"A month ago. Maybe more. It was a long time."

"This was a date with a regular?"

"I'm not going to tell you who she saw. She'd kill me."

"Her date might be the reason she's gone."

Kimberly Laird stepped back and shook her head.

"You don't understand how it works. She called me that night after. She was fine. We got together the next day. Everything was fine."

"Who'd she see?"

She stepped back again.

"None of your business. She's dated this guy dozens of times. It's been almost a month."

I stepped closer.

"Then where is she, Kimberly? Can you tell me, right now, Rachel is safe?"

Kimberly took another step back and bumped against the cupcake shop. She pulled and twisted her fingers so hard I thought she would pull them off.

"These are substantial people she sees. Important people. They wouldn't hurt anyone."

"Is this what Meredith says? When she cares more about her clients than the escorts?"

Kimberly's breathing was fast and shallow. I took her nervous hands in mine.

"Help me find her, Kimberly. If I'm wrong, this man will never know I was nosing around. Rachel won't know, either."

I thought she might break her own fingers, but she suddenly took a single deep breath and told me.

"Grady Locke."

The name meant nothing.

"Who is he?"

"He's in city government. For a councilman. He's very important."

"Locke was her most recent date?"

"Yes."

"Do you remember her other recent dates?"

"I remember them all."

Kimberly Laird gave me two names. I recognized one, but not the other. The name I recognized belonged to a Superior Court judge. I noted the names and Kimberly's number in my phone.

"Please don't tell. Rachel will kill me if you tell. She'll never speak to me again."

"I'm not going to tell. I'm going to find her."

I left Kimberly Laird twisting her fingers outside the cupcake shop and drove to my office.

28

The twenty-seven PDFs in Josh's secret stash didn't take long to read. Most were only three or four paragraphs. I skimmed through them for a general sense, then read them more slowly and took notes. The name Grady Locke did not appear, but LWL Development Inc., the Crystal Emperor Hotel, and the Crystal Future Hospitality Group were prominent.

I read all twenty-seven articles and had no idea why Josh had researched these subjects. No crimes were reported or alleged. No criminal activity was suggested. Most of the articles simply described upcoming civic development projects, the movers and shakers behind those projects, and the usual quotes from rah-rah supporters and outraged opponents. The only thread between them was LWL Development Inc., Crystal Future Hospitality Group, and Sanford L. Richter, the council member representing Council District 16 on the Los Angeles City Council. LWL was mentioned in eighteen of the twenty-seven articles, Crystal Future was mentioned in thirteen, and Richter was mentioned in nine. This suggested they were the focus of Josh's attention, but nothing in the articles suggested why.

I read the articles a third time and listed every person and developer mentioned. I ended up with a list of twenty-three individuals and businesses. I leaned back and studied Pinocchio. I got up, took a bottle of water from the little fridge, drank some, replaced the cap, and returned to my desk.

I put the list aside and googled Grady Locke. The facts thereafter should have been surprising, but left me with a sort of jaded irritation. Grady Locke was Sanford Richter's chief of staff.

I tipped back again and considered Pinocchio.

"Well?"

Pinocchio didn't have an opinion.

I scrolled through the photos Pike had taken at the airport and studied the balding man from the PRC. This time he looked familiar. I opened the CFHG website and went to the company's mission statement page. Above the statement was a stodgy corporate portrait of a balding man in his late fifties or early sixties wearing a conservative gray suit, white shirt, and dark red tie. Determined eyes made him appear commanding, responsible, and fiscally conservative. I compared the portrait to the pixelated picture Pike had taken. If I squinted, they could pass for the same person. The website's English version translated his title as "leader." His name was translated to Chow Wan Li.

I pulled the Mickey phone close and called Joe.

I said, "The man who got off the jet is named Chow Wan Li. He runs the Crystal Future Hospitality Group. His job title is 'leader.'"

Pike said, "Zongtong."

I said, "Okay. I give."

"It's the word for president in Standard Chinese."

"You don't speak Chinese."

"Jon Stone."

Of course. Stone was multilingual. He was fluent in Spanish, Korean, Arabic, Russian, and now, apparently, Chinese. And these were only the languages I had personally heard him speak. Some guys were born annoying.

"What did Jon learn from the bugs?"

"They're of Chinese origin, but the PRC tech he's seen is usually cloned from our stuff or EU gear. These aren't. He's checking with people who know."

"More spooks."

"If they know, they know."

"Are you still watching the bungalow?"

"Yes."

"No gardeners?"

"No."

"Has Jon learned anything about the Schumachers?"

"No."

"Heard any good jokes lately?"

Pike hung up. Mr. Conversation.

I leaned back and reread my list. Then I opened my email account, wrote a note to Eddie Ditko, attached the list and folder of articles to the email, and sent it.

Eddie was a reporter for most of his eighty-plus years. He'd covered the city beat for every major news organization in town and had been hired and fired a hundred times. When the newspaper business shriveled at the cold hand of the internet, Eddie jumped online and cranked out more copy than ever. He also smoked three packs a day and didn't care who liked it or not.

I was looking up his number to call, but Eddie beat me to it.

"Why'd you send this email? What is this?"

"I'm not sure."

"Hang on."

Eddie made a long hacking cough, then gurgled and hawked again.

I said, "You okay?"

"That one damn near got me."

"Anyway, I'm not sure. They're all tied in with downtown development."

"Sure. Sanford 'the Sandman' Richter. You know why they call him the Sandman?"

I didn't know they called him anything.

"He puts people to sleep?"

"What the hell? I thought you didn't know."

"Lucky guess."

"Ya got Wilson Torres, ya got Zelman from Planning, fucking Robbie Early, man, talk about a douche."

Eddie was going through the list.

"Know anything about Grady Locke?"

"I know everything about everyone. Best you remember."

Eddie suddenly snorted, coughed, and spit.

He said, "Allergies. The crap they sell over the counter is bullshit."

"Grady Locke."

"Is this blood?"

"Eddie?"

"Hang on."

He blew his nose.

"Locke. Yeah, bright kid. Richter's chief of staff. Started in communications for ol' Liz Meretta, the one had the stroke. Constituent services for Able Dean, economic development for that nutcase Willamena Lemley, thank God that bitch cancered out, then Richter. Been around, well liked."

Maybe Eddie did know everything about everyone.

"How about Chow Wan Li?"

Eddie thought about it.

"How ya spell it, c-h-o-w or c-h-o-u?"

I tried to remember how the translator spelled it.

"I don't know. C-h-o-w."

Eddie said, "Mm. Anyway, no. Who is he?"

"Owns the Crystal Emperor Hotel."

"Yeah, yeah, sure. Downtown. The new place."

"Runs a firm in Shanghai called the Crystal Future Hospitality Group. It's on the list."

"I see it."

"See LWL Development Inc.?"

"Yeah. Them, I've heard of."

"Crystal Future partnered up with LWL to build the Crystal Emperor."

"Uh-huh."

"It's possible—and this is what I need to know—at least some of the people and companies on the list are into something."

"Something rotten?"

"Yeah."

"They're developers and politicians. Everything they do is rotten."

"Criminally rotten."

"Believe it or not, I understood you."

"Whatever it is, Crystal Future is scared. They're hiding something and they're trying hard to contain it."

"A hint might help."

"Grady Locke and Crystal Future. Probably LWL."

"In other words, you don't know and you're hoping I'll save you."

"Something like that, yes."

The door in the outer office banged open. A homicide dick I'd seen around named Leifertz and a second dick in a green plaid sport coat slammed in hard. They were holding guns. Two uniforms entered behind them, but hung back. The senior officer was a tall, bony guy with parched skin, a thirty-year pin on his collar, and angry eyes. He barely looked at me. He was glaring at Leifertz.

I knew better than to stand. I kept the phone to my ear and my hands in plain view.

"What the hell?"

Eddie said, "What was that, a gunshot?"

Leifertz and his partner beaded up and separated as they entered my office. Leifertz shouted.

"Elvis Cole!"

I did not move. I held perfectly still and spoke softly to Eddie.

"Call Charlie Bauman. Tell him I'll be at Hollywood Station. I'm being arrested."

Bauman was my lawyer.

Eddie said, "Didn't Charlie get disbarred?"

"Call Lou Poitras. Call him now."

Leifertz came around my desk and twisted the phone from my hand.

"Get off that silly phone and stand up."

Leifertz pulled me up, spun me around, and shoved me against the desk. His partner twisted my hands behind my back and snapped on the cuffs.

I didn't resist. I watched the uniforms. The tall cop met my eyes and grimaced. He seemed embarrassed. He looked like a good man who was caught in something wrong and wanted no part of it.

29

The dick who cuffed me was Bud Leifertz. His partner was a dud named Vince Osch. They walked me into the Hollywood Police Station through the back door, led me up to the second floor, and cuffed me to a little table in a small yellow interview room. Then they walked out, closed the door, and left me alone.

The yellow walls were originally a pleasant pastel, but years of sweat and spit and splashed coffee nobody bothered to clean had changed the once pretty yellow into the color of pus. I'd been in this very room twice before. It came equipped with a gray plastic table and two gray plastic chairs. There were no windows or two-way mirrors, but a camera mount without a camera hung from a corner of the ceiling like a dead spider on a frayed web. By cuffing me they had technically arrested me. They had frisked me and taken my wallet, my phone, my keys, and my watch, but they had not booked me nor told me why they had arrested me nor read the Miranda warning. I wondered why. I was still wondering about it forty minutes later when Leifertz and Osch returned.

I said, "Did you guys know the camera was missing?"

Leifertz took the chair across from me. Osch leaned against the door with his arms crossed. Leifertz leaned forward and rested his forearms on the table.

"Lemme start by saying we can get this cleared up here and now. You're in control, man. How this plays out is up to you."

Every bullshit interrogation began the same way. Word for word.

I gestured at his arms.

"The booger."

Leifertz hesitated, not understanding.

"What did you say?"

"Your sleeve."

I gestured toward his arms again.

"On the table. Somebody left a big booger. You're on it."

Leifertz flushed, but moved his arms. He looked into my eyes and spoke softly.

"Vince? Did you hear Mr. Funny?"

Osch spoke from the door.

"They're all the same."

Leifertz leaned closer.

"People like you end up dead."

"Everyone ends up dead, Leifertz. What matters is how we live."

Osch spoke from the door again.

"Have you ever had sexual relations with the young

woman known as Skylar Lawless, whose actual legal name is Rachel Belle Bohlen?"

His saying her name surprised me. I shouldn't have looked at him, but I looked. Osch had the calm, quiet voice of a pastor and the empty eyes of a carp.

I said, "Who?"

Leifertz made a nasty slash of a grin.

"Bet you watch her movies over and over."

I forced myself to look at the camera mount. It was still empty.

"Whatever you guys are doing, bag it until my lawyer gets here."

Osch never changed his expression or tone.

"How long have you been stalking her?"

I shook my head.

"Lawyer."

Leifertz made the nasty grin even nastier. He looked like a deranged jack-o'-lantern.

"I watched a couple of her vids this morning. Hot little freak like her, yeah, dude, I can see how you'd get obsessed."

"Lawyer."

Osch smiled.

"Stalker."

Leifertz rapped the table.

"We have you at her apartment. We have you tracking her all over town. You're good for it."

Osch said, "That, or he's covering for someone."

Leifertz slapped the table.

"Are you covering for someone?"

Osch said, "He's covering."

Leifertz slapped the table harder.

"We own you, Cole. Who hired you? Who are you working for?"

I looked from Leifertz to Osch. Osch shifted a little as if his knees were beginning to ache. They were playing off each other too quickly. They were rushing the interview and rushing meant they were in a hurry.

I settled back as best one could when handcuffed to a table.

"You guys look nervous."

Leifertz wet the corner of his mouth. It was a bush-league tell.

Osch was better. He showed no expression at first, then shoved from the door, charged toward me like an attack dog, and pulled up short beside Leifertz.

"Why did you trash her studio? What were you looking for, Cole? What did you find?"

Leifertz tried to look fierce, but wet his lips again.

"We've got witnesses, you sonofabitch. Who's nervous now?"

"You guys are embarrassing yourselves. Talk to my lawyer."

Leifertz said, "Tell us, you bastard. We'll cut you a deal. What do you know about Rachel Bohlen?"

"Lawyer."

Osch stepped back. He took an envelope from his jacket.

"Here's what he knows."

Osch fingered a photograph from the envelope and placed it on the table.

The photograph had been taken in an autopsy suite at the medical examiner's office downtown. I knew this because Rachel Bohlen's head was resting on a steel autopsy table. The close shot showed her face and head. Her body was not visible. Rachel Belle Bohlen was dead. Her face showed contusions and multiple lacerations. Her tongue peeked between her lips like a swollen frog and a coarse black line crossed her throat beneath her jaw like a ligature mark. I felt bad for Kimmie Laird and April Bohlen and for Rachel Belle. I wondered where Josh Schumacher was and if he was dead and whether he had strangled Skylar Lawless. I didn't think he had, but I didn't know.

I looked at Osch and Leifertz, and wondered what they knew and how they knew it. They hadn't asked about Josh. If they had interviewed Meredith Birch or E. Claude Sidney, they would have known I was looking for Josh. Josh would have been on their suspect list, yet they hadn't asked about him. It was as if they didn't know or were keeping him out of it.

I said, "You know I'm lousy for it. You have no evidence, no DNA, no proof I've ever met or even been in the same room with this poor woman, but now this, and I'm asking myself what's in it for these two assholes?"

Leifertz shoved to his feet.

"I'll show you, you sonofabitch."

Leifertz didn't have time to show me.

The door opened so hard it knocked Osch sideways and Lou Poitras filled the room. Lou tipped the scales at two hundred and sixty pounds, and a lifetime of lifting heavy weights had left him wide, thick, and strong as a backhoe. I'd once seen Lou Poitras deadlift the back end of a Volkswagen and walk the little car in a circle. Lou was also a Captain of Detectives at the LAPD's West Bureau. I was godfather to one of his children.

He looked from Osch to Leifertz.

"You two, the watch commander's office. I'll be along."

Leifertz visibly paled but tried to cover it.

"Cole's a person of interest, Cap. We need to question him."

"Yeah? And I need to ensure compliance with the department's policies, procedures, regulations, and standards. So get your asses into that office."

When Lou stepped aside to let them pass, I saw Charlie Bauman and the senior uniform from my office outside. The uniform snake-eyed Leifertz as he left and Charlie Bauman shoved between them as he entered.

Charlie spoke loudly as they left.

"We'll expect an official letter of apology, thank you."

Charlie slammed the door.

"Shitbirds."

Charlie Bauman had been a federal prosecutor until alimony and child support for three ex-wives and eight children forced him to defend the criminals he once put in prison. Charlie was small, thin, and moved like a ferret.

"You didn't admit to anything, did you?"

"Of course not."

"Good. Tell me what happened."

I told him. By the time I finished, he was licking his teeth like a wolverine.

"We've got these schmucks by the ass. I see two rights

violations off the top and at least four procedure violations."

He leaned closer and glanced around like someone sharing juicy gossip.

"The uni, the one in the hall with the stripes?"

"Yeah. He doesn't like it."

"No, he does not. He was huddled up with Lou when I got here and whatever he said—I don't know what— Lou didn't like it, either. You know that look he gets?"

"I've seen it."

"Yeah, I guess you have."

The door opened again and Poitras was alone. He held a large manila envelope.

I nodded.

"Thanks for coming."

He held out the envelope.

"Your stuff. Make sure everything's here."

I emptied the contents and pocketed my things.

Charlie said, "Count your cash. These guys steal."

"It's fine."

Poitras grunted.

"Certain irregularities regarding this incident have been brought to my attention. So you know, I will look into it."

"What irregularities, Lou?"

He ignored me.

"If department regulations or policies were violated, an appropriate action will be taken."

Charlie said, "Damn right it will."

Lou didn't bother to acknowledge him.

"So let's get back to the vic. Do you know who murdered her?"

Charlie spoke fast.

"Don't answer."

I touched his arm.

"I didn't know she was murdered until ten minutes ago. I was looking for her, but I hadn't found her. None of the people I interviewed were able to tell me where she was or with whom."

Lou crossed his arms. His upper arms looked like bowling balls.

"You didn't answer my question."

"No, I don't know who killed her. What about you? Do you have a suspect?"

He stared at me and I stared back, hoping he wouldn't describe Josh. He finally answered.

"Not at this time. Do you?"

"Not at this time."

"Maybe the person who hired you killed her."

I did my best to look unconcerned. I didn't want to bring Josh Schumacher into this unless I believed he was involved.

"I'm working for a seventy-two-year-old woman who hired me to find a relative. I had hoped Ms. Bohlen could help locate this person, as they once worked together. That's it."

I spread my hands, leaving the rest unsaid.

Poitras said, "Yeah?"

"Yeah."

If Poitras believed I was leaving things out, he let it

ride. Maybe he knew I wouldn't lie unless I had good cause. Or maybe he wanted to give me enough rope to hang myself.

He unfolded the massive arms.

"If you happen across the murderer, give us a call."

"Absolutely."

"They pull you out of your office?"

"They did."

"Charlie?"

"I'll give him a lift. And bet your ass I'll bill the city."

Lou gripped my shoulder. His fingers were steel.

"So you know, I don't like what happened here. We'll talk."

"Sure, Lou. Whenever you want."

He gave me a squeeze.

"Take off. You're free."

I didn't feel free. I wanted to know who killed Skylar Lawless and I wanted to find Josh. I rode back to my office in silence. My phone rang as we drove, but I saw the caller ID and sent it to voice mail.

Charlie said, "Get it, you want. I'm your lawyer. You can talk in front of me."

"I'll get it later."

I checked the message as soon as Charlie dropped me off.

Joe Pike had called.

Jon Stone had answers.

30

We met in a parking lot at the southwest corner of Fairfax and Sunset, two miles and a lifetime west of Hollywood Station. Pike's red Cherokee sat by the entrance. Stone's black Rover idled at a meter on Fairfax. I was waiting to turn onto Fairfax when Pike called.

I said, "I see you."

"Don't enter the parking lot. After you turn, take the second right, then another right, and pull over."

I checked my rearview.

"Is someone following me?"

"Jon wants it this way."

I could see the back of Jon's head in his Rover. He stared straight down Fairfax without looking around.

I said, "Will do."

I made the turn and the Rover pulled out after I passed. Pike pulled out after the Rover. I took the second right, turned again at the first cross street, and pulled into a red zone outside a white, three-story apartment building. The entire block was lined with three- or four-story apartment buildings, and they all looked pretty much the same. Jon Stone pulled up behind me, blocking a drive. He remained in the Rover. Pike passed, pulled over a few spots ahead, and walked back along the sidewalk. I got out and met him.

"Jon's car."

I climbed into the shotgun seat, and Pike got in back behind me. Stone had the AC maxed. Frigid air screamed from the vents like an arctic gale. He cut the fans when I pulled the door.

"I don't know how you do it, Cole. You must be an honest-to-God shit magnet."

Pike said, "Stop."

I frowned at Pike.

"What does he mean?"

Stone said, "Here's what he means."

He held out his phone, showing me a photograph of the device. The photo was red, as if it had been taken in a photographer's darkroom. He held the phone too close.

"See this?"

I slapped the phone away.

"Keep it up, you'll eat it."

Pike said, "Jon."

Stone flicked his finger across the screen, showing the device from a different angle.

"What we have here is an audio surveillance device. I removed it from an outlet in your boy's bungalow."

I let him keep going.

"It's what we call a passive listener, meaning it constantly listens, but only transmits when it hears non-ambient, atypical sounds, like someone knocking or someone speaking."

"How does it know what's ambient?"

"It's smart. Plant this baby in an office, it figures out the air conditioner and freeway noise don't matter."

He flicked to a red photo of a larger device connected to a small rectangular box by a wire.

"Found this one hidden in the door buzzer at the end of the hall, up near the ceiling above the bathroom door. It's a digital camera and motion sensor tied to a digital transmitter."

Stone lowered his phone.

"This isn't off-the-shelf technology. Not here, in China, or anywhere else."

"Okay. So what?"

Pike said, "Jon's source believes these devices are used by ChiCom intelligence agencies."

I looked from Pike to Stone.

"Spies?"

Jon Stone muttered in Chinese before shifting to English.

"Likely the Ministry of State Security or the Military Intelligence Department, not that there's much difference. This gear—"

He jiggled his phone, meaning the pictures.

"—is their version of *my* gear, which means we may have a serious problem."

I didn't like it. I didn't like Rachel Belle Bohlen being

beaten to death, or her apartment being ripped apart, or Joshua Schumacher being missing, but Jon Stone was talking nonsense.

"The guy owns hotels. Are you saying the Chinese government sent spies to hunt down a kid with a podcast nobody listens to all to protect a hotel magnate?"

Stone gave me wide, innocent eyes.

"Unless they want his mommy."

It didn't take Sherlock Holmes to know where he was going.

"They're after Adele?"

Stone glanced at Pike, then made the big eyes again.

"I have access to certain sources. You understand this, right?"

"Is this about his parents?"

"Cole, listen. I don't know. But once upon a time these cats lived under so many layers of black they ceased to exist. Whatever you read online after they left Stanford is bullshit. Even my source, and my source knows everything, only knows rumors. And you know why those rumors exist?"

Jon didn't expect an answer, so I didn't interrupt.

"His mother worked on projects so black even my guys can't find out, and, brother, these dudes are top of the food chain. When you're that deep, you are working on dangerously secret shit."

"Adele."

"Applied Thought. Adele and the husband, but she was the money. Legend."

"Adele and Corbin worked for the government."

"Your mailman works for the government."

"The military."

Jon shrugged.

"Maybe. Who knows? People like this work in little compartments only two or three other people know about. They're funded with untraceable money nobody has to explain or account for, not even to the president or the Joint Chiefs. Nobody knows what these people did."

"They're retired. They're not even together anymore."

"They still did what they did and know what they know."

He stared at me with the big eyes again, watching. Pike was watching, too.

"You think the spooks want their son for leverage?"

He jiggled his phone again. The pictures.

"I want to know who the meatball is, is what I think. I need nice, clear pictures of him and whoever the hell else is involved. My sources will try to identify them."

"Tell them to identify Chow Wan Li."

"They're working on it."

"Have them work faster."

I told them about Rachel Bohlen.

"I want to know if these people killed Rachel."

Pike's dark glasses seemed blacker than before.

"Josh will be a suspect."

"Yes, eventually. Which means the police will go to his bungalow, so you'd best stay clear."

Stone smirked.

"The bungalow's covered. Don't sweat it."

"I'm not sweating it, Jon. I'm sweating the meatball

and Josh and whether he's alive or dead. I don't want the same thing to happen to Josh."

Pike reached forward and squeezed my shoulder.

"We'll find them and stop them."

"The sedan they used is owned by LWL."

"We're on it."

Pike got out without another word and returned to his Jeep.

Jon Stone frowned.

"We?"

I climbed out, went to my car, and called Wendy Vann. I told her we had a problem. I needed to see Adele and I needed to see her now.

31

The sky was too bright when I reached Adele Schumacher's home in Toluca Lake. She lived not far from Universal Studios in a single-story ranch-style home with batten board sides, a stone entry, and a diamond glass front door. The street was nice and the house was nice, but I was surprised by its modesty. With its shake roof, stone chimney, and orange trees bearing Day-Glo fruit, her home might've been clipped from *Life* magazine in 1958, maybe from an article showing Lucy and Desi and little Ricky splashing in their pool, an idyllic family enjoying an idyllic Southern California day. Lucy and Desi probably wouldn't enjoy Kurt in his gray suit and earbud standing post in their drive, but Lucy and Desi hadn't worked on secret government projects.

The cream Mercedes sedan crouched nose-out in the drive and the white Lincoln SUV hunkered out front on the street. The red-haired driver chatted with a beefy bald man by the Lincoln and both wore earpieces like

Kurt's. A black Cadillac Escalade and a gleaming red Tesla were parked across the street. A man and a woman who looked like Wendy&Kurt 2.0 stood by the Tesla watching me pass. After speaking with Jon, so much obvious security creeped me out. Whatever Adele and Corbin knew, whatever they had seen or been part of was not in the past, and realizing this creeped me out even more.

I parked behind the Tesla and walked up the drive. Wendy came out of the house to meet me.

Wendy said, "Adele's in back. Are you allergic to bee-stings?"

"Are you with the Secret Service?"

Wendy started up the drive.

"I'll take that as a no. C'mon. Corbin's here, too. She invited him."

We passed four high-end security cameras before Wendy opened an ivy-twined chain-link gate and led me into a garden. Kurt trailed behind, head swiveling as if he thought we might be jumped.

The yard was large and lush with colorful flowers, more citrus trees, and more security cameras. The flowers drew bees and the air was filled with them, circling and swirling between bursts of red and yellow and purple and pink. We followed a gravel path past what appeared to be a guesthouse but probably wasn't. Shiny white antenna domes dotted the roof.

We came to a square plot of lawn at the rear of the property. Five short white beehive boxes stood at the end and Adele stood with them. She was leaning over an open box as a cloud of bees swarmed around her. She wasn't wearing gloves or a veil or the protective gear beekeepers wear. All she wore were sandals and the same thin dress she'd worn at my office.

I sidled close to Wendy.

"Shouldn't she be wearing a net or something?"

"They won't hurt her."

"What about us?"

"You, no promises. Come meet Corbin."

Corbin Schumacher was smaller and older than I would've guessed from his voice. He sat in a folding chair under a canopy umbrella at the edge of the lawn, wearing baggy tan slacks, a retro bowling shirt, and well-worn loafers with no socks. He grimaced when he stood, as if he'd felt a sharp pain, but his grip was firm.

His words of greeting were "Well? Have you found the useless moron?"

Adele noticed me and waved me to join her.

"Mr. Cole! Come see. You'll enjoy this."

Corbin grumbled.

"Adele, he doesn't have time. For God's sake."

She waved me over again.

"Come look!"

Wendy and Corbin followed along behind me, but stopped well away. Adele leaned over the open hive and tugged me closer.

"The girls won't hurt you. Look here. Tell me what you see."

The box contained what looked like three or four thousand bees crawling over each other in an undulating brown mass.

I said, "May I show off?"

She looked amused.

"I hope so."

"Western honey bees. Also known as *Apis mellifera*."

She beamed and slapped my arm.

"Well done! I'm impressed."

"Don't be. A friend used to keep a hive in Santa Clarita. An apiculturist, like you."

Adele peered into the hive again.

"Oh, I'm not an apiculturist. I don't care for honey. I study how they make decisions."

I glanced at Wendy and Corbin.

"We should talk about Josh. I've learned things you should know."

Corbin seemed unsteady. He did a little sidestep stagger, as if he'd lost his balance, and clutched Wendy's arm.

"He doesn't care about the damned bees, Adele. Come away from there."

Adele tugged me closer to better see, or maybe to avoid the news about her son.

"Singly, a bee responds to pheromones, temperature, what have you, with behaviors preset in her neural net, like commands in a software program, yes? When she encounters new stimuli, she can learn, but her software limits the complexity of her responses. Make sense?"

She was the professor at Stanford again and I was her student.

"Sure."

Corbin said, "Adele, did you take your medication? Wendy, did she take it?"

Adele stared into the hive.

"But when the girls and the drones and the queen come together, something changes. A swarm intelligence emerges and the swarm is capable of much more complex behavior."

She covered the hive and considered me.

"Think of them as tiny machines. Imagine if we could alter their software so the swarm could carry out even more complicated tasks. Drones wouldn't have to be built, would they? We could grow them."

I looked from Adele to Corbin and back to Adele. I wondered if the tasks she imagined included millions of wasps swarming a battlefield. *Here they come, bro, pass the Raid.*

I said, "Josh was involved with a woman named Rachel Bohlen. Ms. Bohlen is dead. She was murdered."

Corbin's face shriveled into something lined as a walnut.

"Did Josh kill her? Is he a murderer now?"

"I don't know. It's possible, but I don't think so."

Adele showed no reaction, as if we were discussing his shoe size.

"Joshua hasn't killed anyone. Where is he?"

"He was in Los Angeles two days ago. I don't know where he is now."

Adele seemed surprised.

"He didn't go to Nevada?"

Corbin's nostrils flared and he gripped Wendy's arm again.

"Of course he did, Adele. He's with the damned aliens."

She painted him with an icy glare.

"You would know."

I interrupted.

"Adele, listen. Bohlen's neighbors saw Josh at her apartment and heard them argue. Her apartment was ransacked. As soon as the police identify Josh, he'll be named as a suspect. You need to prepare yourself."

I looked at Corbin and Wendy.

"All of you."

Wendy said, "Why did Josh search her apartment?"

"I don't believe he did. Other people are looking for him besides me."

Corbin glared at Adele.

"My lord, how many people did you hire?"

I pushed ahead over them.

"Do you know the name Chow Wan Li?"

Corbin flicked his hand, like waving away a bee.

"Why should I?"

"He's a Chinese national from the People's Republic. He runs a company called the Crystal Future Hospitality Group. They own hotels."

"What does this have to do with Josh? Did he leave without paying his bill?"

"People in his employ have been watching Josh's bungalow. They've entered his bungalow at least twice and planted surveillance equipment known to be used by Chinese intelligence agencies."

Kurt immediately turned away, touched his earpiece, and spoke in low tones.

Wendy said, "How do you know this, Cole?"

I ignored her and spoke to the Schumachers.

"You were involved with classified projects for the government."

Corbin flicked his hand again and shook his head.

"Absurd. Absolutely untrue. Wendy!"

I talked over him.

"If they were spying on Josh, is it possible they learned something they shouldn't know? About you or your work?"

The color drained from Adele's face. Her skin grew splotchy and her eyelids fluttered.

Wendy said, "That's it, Cole. We're done."

"If they have Josh, they'll use him. If you know anything that will help me find him, tell me now."

Corbin shouted, "Wendy!"

Corbin threw an arm around Adele and staggered toward the house.

Wendy stepped between us like a blocking back.

"Cole, we have to take care of her. Go."

Wendy herded me toward the gate.

"Who are these people?"

"His parents. Do your job. Find their son."

She muscled me harder.

"How'd you know I was making tacos?"

Wendy said, "Kurt!"

Kurt trampled through a bed of gladioli and added his weight. They shoved me past the guesthouse.

"Did you send drones to my home?"

Wendy said, "Find him."

"To my home?"

"Find him."

"Were those your drones?"

Wendy and Kurt shoved me through the gate into the driveway. We stood there, me on the drive, them in the yard, sucking gas as we stared at each other.

Wendy's eyes turned sad.

"Find him."

Kurt closed the gate.

32

walked down the drive to my car. Nobody tried to stop me. Black helicopters didn't suddenly appear. The red-haired driver and the bald guy watched me, but didn't seem interested. I didn't know what to do and wasn't sure I wanted to do anything. I sat in my car. I considered Adele's house and decided I liked it. I saw myself walking back up the drive, ringing the bell, and telling Wendy I quit. I wanted to quit but I didn't. Being unable to quit was probably a character flaw, but sometimes not quitting was all you had left.

I was wondering what to do when the front door opened. Wendy stared at me for a few seconds, then came across the lawn and the street to my car. She stopped four feet away.

"Josh's phone can't be located or tracked so he's probably removed the SIM card. He hasn't used it since he disappeared. The only calls made or received during the days prior were with his mother and Ryan Seborg."

I said, "Okay."

She didn't move, so I said it again.

"Okay. Thanks."

"He's probably using a burner. It's clear he didn't want anyone to know who he was talking to."

It was clear Josh understood people could access his phone and probably would. And probably had since his parents gave him the phone. I wondered if all the rest of it was clear to Josh and decided it was.

I nodded.

"Yep. Clear."

Wendy glanced up the street, but still didn't move.

"He didn't turn off his phone and use burners because he was involved with a pornstar. He anticipated trouble and planned for it. He didn't want anyone to interfere."

I said, "Not anyone. His family. He didn't want his family to interfere."

Wendy glanced toward the house. She took a breath and the tension in her shoulders eased.

She said, "It hasn't been easy."

"For him or for you?"

Her eyes flashed with something hard.

"I feel for the kid, all right? Josh has never been allowed to be Josh."

She meant it. I liked her for meaning it.

"How long have you been with them?"

"Long enough."

She considered the house again.

"These people are genius smart, Cole. Truly genius. So is Josh, by the way."

"But are they happy?"

The hardness flashed, but a little grin replaced it. The grin looked lonely.

"No comment."

"I hear you."

"Whatever they are, they don't understand their son. She smothers him and Corbin does nothing but criticize and demean. Seems to me Josh wants to grow up, but he's never been given the chance."

"So this is him, making the chance?"

She thought for a moment.

"What do I know? I only work here. How about you? You still on the job?"

I nodded.

Wendy Vann said, "Good."

She turned to go.

I said, "Wendy."

She stopped.

"Chow Wan Li."

The corner of her mouth curled with a tiny smile.

"I hear you."

I watched her cross the lawn, then started my car and idled away. I meandered around Toluca Lake, thinking about Josh and his parents and the guards and a phrase Jon Stone used. *These cats lived under so many layers of black they ceased to exist.* Yet here they were in Toluca Lake. Maintaining an outwardly normal life must have been stressful when their true lives were hidden by lies. Spies and criminals thrived on lies, but Adele and Corbin had been college professors. Not to say professors couldn't be liars, but once the Schumachers entered the black, they'd been forced to lie to their parents, their siblings, their oldest and dearest friends, and their child. I wondered if all the lying had driven them apart. I wondered if Adele's paranoia was the result and the strain had caused Corbin to focus his frustration on Josh. I couldn't know these things and never would. None of it mattered. Maybe I was just giving myself a reason to continue.

I was heading west on Ventura toward Laurel when Eddie Ditko called. I cringed when I saw his name on the caller ID. I didn't want to answer. I was tired. I wanted to go home, wash off the day, and sleep. I pulled over and answered.

First thing he said was "Can you hear me? Hello? Goddamnit."

"Eddie, I'm here."

"They let you out already?"

"I'm out."

"Sue'm. A cop farts sideways these days, whiny scumbags bank a fortune."

"I'm good. What did you find out?"

"Okay, listen. The Sandman helped the Crystal Emperor get built. They had problems out the ass with the planning commission, but once the Sandman stepped in, the problems disappeared."

"Business as usual. So what?"

"So LWL and Crystal Future have five *more* projects up for approval and all five are sailing through committee faster than a goose shits buttered bullets. Wanna guess who's paving the way?"

"Richter."

"I heard this from two different sources."

"Meaning what, he's on the take? They're all on the take."

"Damn. You must be having a bad day."

"Nothing eight or nine beers won't fix."

"Maybe this will help. You have these other firms on your list, Dieder-Scotti, Mendez-Warren, Block Sixteen, these other developers."

I had listed them, but only a few of the articles focused on them and their projects.

"Are they paying the Sandman, too?"

Eddie made the heh-heh laugh.

"Nah, but maybe they should. They all had projects killed in committee by the Sandman or his friends. What I'm hearing is, if a developer won't play ball, his project doesn't get approved."

"Hang on. Are you saying Richter shakes down developers?"

"Do the math. Which brings us back to Crystal Future's partner, LWL. A guy named Horton Tarly owns LWL. Ever heard of him before now?"

Tarly was mentioned in several of the articles, but otherwise I'd never heard of him.

"No."

"Me neither, and I hear everything."

"Is this important?"

Eddie made the snide *heh.*

"Tarly started out building car washes over in San Gabriel and worked his way up to low-rent strip malls. So ask yourself, here's this international hotel chain from China, got all the money in the world, they wanna build hundred-million-dollar projects here in L.A., why in hell would they partner with a car wash guy from San Gabriel?"

"Should I break out the Ouija board or guess?"

"Horton Tarly is married to Grady Locke's sister."

And just like that, I saw it. Rachel and Grady Locke, Grady Locke and Richter, Richter and Chow Wan Li. Rachel and Josh.

I said, "Chow Wan Li used Tarly to get in bed with Locke and Richter. They're partners by marriage."

Eddie cackled.

"See? You're not stupid."

"Neither are they."

"It's a smart play. Tarly's local, which looks good to members who don't like all this foreign money buying up the city. Tarly and his little car wash business plays the front. Chow's the wizard behind the curtain, paying off Richter. Richter green-lights their projects and—I promise you—he does not work cheap. We just gotta find it."

Eddie was so pleased with himself he cackled with glee, but the cackling erupted into the wet, hacking cough.

"Eddie, c'mon. Quit the smokes."

"Lemme get lit up."

I heard him light up.

"Eddie, c'mon."

He inhaled between coughs and the coughing settled.

"Now listen, I'm waiting to hear on a couple of things. I'll get back to you."

"Quit smoking. I'm begging you."

"Beg some woman for a piece of ass."

Eddie hung up.

If Rachel Bohlen had learned about shady dealings from Grady Locke, she might have told Josh. Josh wanted to go mainstream, so maybe he began researching the rest of it and Locke found out. This part of it bothered me. Even if Locke told Richter a kid with a podcast was onto them, and even if Crystal Future was a PRC Intelligence front, their reaction seemed over the top. Josh was an unknown with almost no audience. The smart play would've been to deny Josh's charges, write off his allegations as coincidence or misunderstanding, and dismiss him as a crank. Yet they had ripped apart Rachel Bohlen's apartment, murdered her, and were hunting for Josh. None of this made sense unless Josh and Rachel had come by evidence they couldn't dismiss. Maybe some physical thing Rachel had taken from Grady Locke, so they'd brought in professional operators to get it back. Maybe Josh had it now, which was why they were hunting him hard.

My job was simple.

Find him first.

33

I let myself in through the carport and found Lucy in the kitchen. She was at the counter near the sink, chopping. A large pot on the stove smelled terrific.

She said, "I'm making jambalaya."

Her back was ramrod straight and her jaw was tight. I knew something was wrong the moment I saw her.

"Where's Ben?"

"Went for a run. He'll be back soon."

I joined her at the counter. Neat mounds of chopped onions and bell pepper were pushed to the side. A small mound of skillet-fried andouille sausage was draining on paper towels.

"How'd it go today?"

"Tense."

I wanted to eat a piece of the sausage but didn't.

"He didn't like it?"

She stopped chopping and sighed with a soul-deep exhaustion.

"I don't know, I think it was me."

"You pushed."

Her eyes closed. She nodded.

"I tried to be encouraging. I was enthusiastic and positive and I don't know what I was thinking. He *loved* it. He's excited about it, he wants to do it, but I kept pushing."

"Cut yourself some slack, Lucille. He'll be fine."

She opened her eyes but didn't look at me.

"He told me if I wanted to get rid of him so badly I should bury him in a box like his father."

We stood there silently for a time and I put my arms around her.

"I'm sorry."

"I feel awful."

"I'm sure you do."

"It's been a really bad day."

"The worst."

Lucy said, "Crap."

I hugged her tight and stepped away.

"So how's Ben?"

"Quiet."

She turned back to the chopping board and continued chopping.

"Cooking helps."

"Always. Mind your fingers."

I left her to it, changed into gym shorts and a T-shirt, and lugged some workout gear onto the deck. I was setting it up when Ben got home. He saw me from the living room and came outside. His T-shirt was wet and sweat trickled from his hair. Lucy was still in the kitchen, frying her anxiety in bacon grease.

I said, "Good run?"

"Really good. Ran to Coldwater. Gonna work out?"

"That's the plan. Want to join me?"

"Sure."

Ben had enrolled at a karate dojo in Baton Rouge and had gotten pretty good. Lucy believed Ben's interest in martial arts stemmed from me. I liked knowing it had. He watched me rope my old heavy bag to the rail. The bag was a beast. Sixty inches tall, its leather was cracked and patched with duct tape, and it weighed a solid one hundred ten pounds. Heavy bags were usually hung so they moved when they were hit, but I didn't want it to move. I roped the old bag tight to create an immovable object.

I set up facing the bag and waved Ben away with a finger flick.

"Stand back. I don't want you getting hurt."

Ben said, "Ha ha."

I attacked the old bag with aggression and purpose. Right front kick, right roundhouse kick, left front kick, left roundhouse kick, right reverse spin kick, left reverse spin kick. The wraparound gardener, the ponytail gardener, the meatball, Leifertz and Osch. The strikes hit fast and sounded like muffled explosions.

I looked at Ben and wiggled my eyebrows.

"Wanna see it again?"

"Bring it!"

I did it again. Faster. This was male bonding at its finest.

I stepped aside so he could square up.

"Don't try the combos yet. We'll work into it. Give me a right front rolling to the right roundhouse, okay?"

He did it. He was awkward rolling into the round-house, but he had good power.

I said, "Now from the left."

He kicked from the left. I gave him a small adjustment as he rolled, and this time he was smoother.

I said, "I heard you and your mom had a moment."

His expression immediately closed.

"I guess."

He kicked from the left again but kicked too quickly. He immediately kicked from the right, but didn't square up.

My voice was even and quiet.

"Breathe. Always breathe. Stay within yourself."

He kicked. He kicked again. They were sloppy. He kicked hard, but they landed weak. He kicked twice more before he spoke.

"She's driving me crazy."

"She's worried. Not saying it shouldn't bother you. Just saying."

"She told you about the letters."

"Uh-huh. You mind?"

He kicked.

"You should hear them, Mom and Berteau. They act like there's something wrong with me and if I don't feel what they think I should feel I'm gonna go psycho."

"About your father?"

"All of it. Him, the box, those guys, what happened.

I don't want to talk about it all the time. Mom wants to talk about it. All. The. Time. Maybe Mom should be in therapy instead of me."

"You think they're projecting?"

He kicked hard again. He launched a beast of a spin kick and barely brushed the bag with his toe.

"I'm sick of it."

"Don't blame you. I'm sick just hearing about it."

Ben stared and suddenly laughed.

I said, "Buddy, feel what's true to you. If you want to talk about this stuff, or anything, twenty-four-seven, I'm yours. If not, then not, but I'm here."

I wondered if Corbin Schumacher had ever said such a thing to Joshua. He probably hadn't.

Ben rested a hand on the bag. The air was cooling. Being out on the deck felt good. He picked at a patch.

"They expect me to care. I don't."

"Their expectations are another box."

"Yeah."

"You went through some pretty heinous stuff."

"Not that. The letters. Him."

Richard.

Ben stopped worrying the tape and tapped the bag with a soft rhythmic tap-tap-tap as light as water dripping from a faucet.

"I hardly ever think about him. I don't love him or hate him or miss him. I don't feel sorry for him. I feel sorry for Mom. He'd get in her face, all red and shouting, and scare her so bad. Mom's tough, but he was awful."

I couldn't think of anything to say. I nodded and felt

I should've been able to offer more. Ben was small back then, a little boy.

He said, "Like now, when I remember him, you know what I feel?"

"Tell me."

"Nothing. He's something that happened a long time ago and he's gone."

I touched his head.

"I need to ask you something."

He made a small smile.

"Sure. Twenty-four-seven."

"You and me. Are you okay with my role in putting Richard away?"

Ben seemed surprised.

"Are you serious?"

"I wonder, sometimes. I want us to be good."

Ben shook his head as if he didn't understand what I had asked or why I asked it.

He said, "I love you. We're way more than good."

I nodded.

"Good."

I nodded again.

"That's good."

Ben suddenly hugged me and held tight. I hugged him back and saw Lucy at the sliding glass door. She didn't come out. She watched us and traced a heart on the glass.

34

The jambalaya was excellent. After dinner we put away the leftovers, loaded the dishwasher, and settled in front of the television. We were deciding what to watch when Lou Poitras called.

I said, "Lucy and Ben are here."

Lucy spoke loudly.

"Hi, Lou!"

Poitras said, "They're in town?"

"For a couple days."

"Lemme speak to her."

I handed Lucy the phone. They only spoke for a minute, but Lucy laughed at something he said. Probably about me. She and Lou had hit it off the moment they met, and Lou and his wife and Lucy and I had enjoyed getting together. She passed the phone to Ben and Ben eventually passed it back to me.

Lou said, "We need to talk."

"Yeah. Hang on."

I took the phone into the kitchen.

"Go."

"Leifertz told me a CI tipped him you were involved in the Bohlen murder, so he and Osch decided to bounce you."

"He's lying."

"I know he's lying. Micky Scanlon heard Leifertz and Osch before they hit you."

"Scanlon the tall uni?"

"Yeah. Leifertz told Osch a friend downtown wanted to know what you're doing so Osch should play along. Mick didn't like it."

"Did Leifertz name the friend?"

"He's denying it. I was hoping you'd suggest a name."

"I can't prove what I'm about to say."

"Never stopped you before."

"Sanford Richter or someone associated with Richter."

"The Sandman?"

"More likely Richter's chief of staff, Grady Locke, but it could be someone associated with Locke."

Lou was silent, so I filled the silence.

"Rachel Bohlen was a call girl. Grady Locke was a regular. She may have learned about or come into possession of evidence connecting Richter with a pay-to-play real estate scheme."

"What's your interest here?"

"Finding Josh Schumacher."

I told him about Rachel and Josh and Josh's disappearance. I told him pretty much everything except what

I'd learned about the Schumachers. I'm not sure why I didn't tell him, but I didn't.

Lou said, "A council member."

"The Sandman."

He was silent again and I let the silence ride. I knew he was thinking it through. Lucy came to the door and gave me a questioning look. I held up a finger saying we were almost finished. She smiled and left me to it.

Lou's voice was low.

"The U.S. Attorney and the FBI take on councilmen. A cop takes on a council member, he'd be crazy. He'd need an airtight bulletproof case before City Hall caught wind. Leave a little wiggle room, even a sliver, they'd gut the poor bastard. Isn't this true?"

"True."

"You hear what I'm saying?"

"I do."

Lou was letting me run with it. He wouldn't sit it out, but he needed to move slowly so Richter and Locke wouldn't suspect they were the subjects of an investigation.

He said, "I would, of course, appreciate any further information you happen upon."

"It's yours. And anything you can tell me about Bohlen's murder would help. Suspects, witnesses, time and place. Whatever you have."

"She was up in Griffith, so Central Bureau has the case. I'll find out and catch you tomorrow."

I hung up, returned to the living room, and flopped on the couch.

"What're we watching?"

We watched a baking show from Britain and enjoyed it so much we watched two more. Midway through the third, Ben nodded out spread-eagle on the floor.

Lucy said, "I guess it's bedtime."

"What's on the sched for tomorrow?"

Tomorrow would be their last day.

"We hadn't decided. I feel like I haven't seen you."

She suddenly looked embarrassed.

"I shouldn't have said it. I am so sorry."

"It's okay. Next time we'll plan."

She nodded.

"We'll plan."

She hesitated, as if about to say more, but I guess she changed her mind. She called it a night, nudged Ben awake, and the two of them went to bed. I watched them go.

A little bit later, I locked the house and climbed the stairs to my loft. Still later, I was in bed when Lucy came up the stairs. She stopped at the landing.

"May I come in?"

She had changed into a loose LSU T-shirt and baggy purple shorts. Ready for bed.

"Absolutely."

I scooted upright. Lucy perched at the foot of the bed and raked her hair behind an ear.

"You believe I'm projecting my fears onto Ben?"

She didn't seem angry or defensive. She seemed thoughtful. I tried to give a thoughtful answer.

"Ben believes you do. I used the word, but his feelings were clear. So, yes."

She nodded.

"What are his feelings?"

"You don't hear him."

"He said this?"

"My words. He isn't in denial about what happened. He doesn't feel helpless before Richard's fatherly power. He's tired of talking about it. He doesn't want to be the boy in the box anymore."

"I'm keeping him in the box."

"You're using his therapy to work through your own feelings."

"Your words again."

"Yes. He escaped, Luce. A long time ago."

She thought. She nodded, but the nod was more to herself.

"I see. I'll think about this."

"May I offer something else?"

"Why stop now?"

"I don't believe you flew here at the last minute to talk about Ben or ask me to be a larger part of his life. I think you do want those things, but he's grown. We've missed those years, Luce. You're here for me."

"I'm not. I can't go through it again."

"I'm not trying to convince you. I wish you'd never left and we'd lived happily ever after, but this is who I am. I'm a detective. Like a cop, but better dressed."

"Don't joke."

I took a breath.

"I'm scared. I'm scared if we get back together you'll dump me again. I don't want to go through it again, but I'm willing to risk it."

"What are you talking about?"

"Decide. We were great. We can be great again. It's what I want and I think you want it, too. But I don't want to be just friends anymore."

She sat on the bed for a very long time. I felt hollow and sick. I was sorry I had said these things. I wished I had said them a lifetime ago.

After a while she got up and left. I wanted to follow after her and take it all back, but words, like actions, were with us forever.

I shut the lights and stood at the edge of my loft. I searched the night sky and the black well of the canyon for tiny hovering lights. I saw none, but I suspected they were there.

I slept, but it was ugly and fitful.

I dreamed about Rachel Belle Bohlen. Her face was battered and bruised and she was naked, but she wasn't dead. In my dream, she ran across a field. She ran as fast as any sprinter, knees high, long strides, fine legs churning, but she didn't run fast enough. Thousands and thousands of bees swarmed and swirled around her like an angry black cloud. Rachel ran. She ran for her life. But she couldn't outrun the bees.

35

woke in a panicked sweat well before dawn. The sky was still black. I sat up and checked my phone, but found no messages. I texted Joe Pike.

What's going on? Call if able.

Pike called thirty seconds later.

"The sedan is at the hotel."

"Did you get his picture?"

"Didn't see him. Checked the bungalow and the airport, and came here. Found the car on the B4 parking level."

"Where's the meatball?"

"Don't know. Didn't see who drove it. Might be the scarecrow or one of the others. No valet ticket, so we can't check the room."

"So what are you doing?"

"Waiting. Jon stuck a transponder on it. When the car moves, we'll intercept and get the shots."

I thought about them waiting for a dot on Jon's laptop to move and didn't like it. The meatball could leave in the limo or another car. The scarecrow or the gardeners or a driver might pick him up.

"Has anyone returned to the bungalow?"

"No."

"Is anyone watching it?"

"No."

Nobody watching for Josh bothered me even more.

"I don't like this. If they're not watching his home, maybe they already have him."

"No way to know."

I didn't like not knowing.

Pike said, "The battle space is changing. The girl's body was found. The police are involved. You're involved. They're making adjustments."

"So they've pulled back to figure it out."

"I would. Their bugs will tell them if Josh goes home, so they're waiting to see what happens."

Pike made sense, but I still didn't like it.

"Maybe I can wake the dragon."

"What?"

"The device Jon left in the bungalow. Does he have eyes?"

"Yes."

"I'll be in touch."

I dressed and crept down to the kitchen. I didn't like leaving in the middle of the night and I didn't like leav-

ing the way we'd left things, but I didn't know what else
to do. I wrote a note.

Leaving to meet Joe. Sorry. I didn't want to wake you.
Back later. Please be here.

I read it over and hated it, but I left it on the floor
outside their door and let myself out.

The drive to Josh Schumacher's bungalow was easy
that time of night. Traffic was light. Few cars were parked
along his street. The phony gardeners weren't lurking
in the weeds and the meatball and his skinny partner
weren't peering over a steering wheel. I parked at the
steps leading up to the bungalows and texted Pike.

Bungalow still deserted?

A few seconds later, Pike responded.

Yes

A man of few words.

I climbed the steps to Josh's door, opened it with
Adele's key, and turned on the lights. The sudden glare
made me squint. I shut the door, locked it, and turned to
face the living room. According to Jon Stone, the meatball's camera was above the bathroom door and looked
directly down the hall past the flat-screen to the front
door. I stayed at the door long enough to give them a
good look. Then I coughed loudly three times and made
a face as if I smelled something sour.

"Man, could it stink any worse? Wow."

Atypical, non-ambient sounds.

I moved toward the camera, looking around at the living room walls as if I was searching for something. I drifted to the left far enough to be out of their view, then returned and stood by the sign Josh had pushpinned beside the flat-screen. MATTER. I recalled what Ryan had told me. *Josh pretends he doesn't care, but the only thing he cares about is showing his father he matters.*

My phone buzzed with an incoming text. I glanced at it. Jon Stone.

Cole u asshole! What r u doing?

I slipped the phone into my pocket and moved closer to the poster. This put me dead center in their field of view. I pulled the pushpin from the lower right corner, lifted the paper, and peered underneath. Then I pretended to remove something tiny from the wall. I took out my handkerchief with my free hand, pretended to wrap the tiny thing in my handkerchief, and stuffed the handkerchief into my pocket. Then I took a card from my wallet, placed the card beneath the poster, and pushpinned the poster into place. My phone buzzed again.

I took out my phone and glanced at the text. More Stone.

r u high?

I pretended to dial and pretended to leave a message.

I did not whisper and I did not shout. My voice level was appropriate.

"Got it, man. You were right. They didn't find it. I left the Crystal Future info. And, Josh, thank you, man. Later."

I pretended to end the pretend call, turned off the lights, and let myself out.

Jon Stone texted again.

Then again.

hats off, bro. #respect

When I looked up, Leon Karsey opened his door.

"It's the middle of the damn night. You robbing the place?"

"Working."

"Work someplace else. A man needs his beauty sleep."

"Some men more than others."

"Hey. Was that a crack?"

"It was."

He considered the crack and nodded.

"Not bad, kid."

Karsey hocked a loogie, let fly, and disappeared into his bungalow.

Pike called as I reached my car.

Pike said, "He's rolling."

36

Jared Walker Philburn

Jared Walker Philburn lay beneath the beautiful night sky and knew himself to be truly blessed. He pointed out his friends above and called aloud their names.

"Andromeda, Pegasus, Pisces, Cassiopeia, Perseus."

The stars overhead were old and dear friends. Stars closer to the horizon were lost in the city's glow, but Jared knew them as well from time spent beneath darker skies. Jared found peace in the stars and their unchanging courses. Mighty Orion would rise shortly, anchored by Rigel and Betelgeuse. Castor and Pollux would follow, marking the rise of Gemini. The stars never changed. They sailed across the sky in dependable patterns and were always where they were supposed to be.

Jared was glad to be home. The officers had been very kind and the lady at the shelter meant well, but Jared could not abide sleeping indoors surrounded by ceilings and walls and hapless strangers. Fresh air was scant, he'd grown anxious, and felt as if he'd suffocate. So Jared

Walker Philburn had slipped away and returned to the freedom of home.

Lying on his sleeping bag in the open air beneath the infinite stars was so much better.

Jared said, "Thank you, Lord. Bless this world."

The Lord said, "You are my blessing, Jared."

"That's very kind. Thank you."

"Of course."

Jared startled awake, surprised and confused.

"Lord?"

The Lord didn't answer.

Jared realized he'd been dreaming and chuckled.

Then he heard others' voices and knew they weren't the voice of the Lord or the voices in his head. These voices were below. Sounded like two men, but Jared wasn't sure. He didn't understand what they were saying.

Jared rolled to his knees, gathered his sleeping bag, and crept to the edge of the overlook.

A man with a ponytail and another man stood by a small red truck in almost the exact spot where the poor girl's body had been heaved over the side. These men weren't heaving a body. They held powerful flashlights and swept their beams from side to side as they peered down the hill. Then the men turned and their lightsabers flashed toward Jared.

He ducked.

Jared clenched his eyes, held his breath, and prayed to the Lord God above.

Doors slammed.

An engine started. Gravel crunched.

Jared slowly raised his head.

The little red truck pulled away. Jared watched its lights until they disappeared.

Jared gave a big sigh and stood.

"How 'bout *them* apples, Genghis Khan?"

Jared spread his sleeping bag, settled himself, and felt the slow touch of sleep.

Jared said, "Thank you, Lord."

The Lord said, "Anytime."

Jared lurched awake. His heart pounded and he thought for sure the men were back, but he heard no voices. Jared scrambled to his feet and peeked at the road, but the truck and the men were gone.

"False alarm, Red Ryder."

Jared made an exaggerated sigh and returned to his sleeping bag. Sleep did not come easy this time. These weren't the same people who disposed of the girl's body, but they shouldn't have been here in the dead of night and Jared didn't like the way they'd been searching the slope. It was as if they were searching for him.

Jared closed his eyes.

"Dearest Lord, please don't let them return."

This time the Lord did not answer.

PART FOUR

"They tell me you are
a man with true grit."
—MATTIE ROSS

from the novel
True Grit *by Charles Portis*

37

Elvis Cole

I drove away as the first kiss of dawn purpled the eastern horizon. I wasn't sure what to do with myself. Joe and Jon Stone were on it. They would follow the sedan, position themselves for clear and revealing pictures, and see where the meatball led them. If he led them to China they'd be gone a long time.

I wanted to go home. Lucy was probably still asleep. I didn't like the idea of her waking to the note I'd left. Better she should wake to me. Better we should deal with this square up and face-to-face.

I headed toward Laurel Canyon but ended up circling through Hollywood. Portrait of the tough guy detective, sick to his stomach.

Canter's Deli on Fairfax was open twenty-four hours and made the best New York cheesecake in Los Angeles. I parked out front and bought a small cup of coffee, a cheesecake, a dozen plain bagels, and cream cheese. Anxiety made one hungry. I ordered a pound of hand-sliced lox and sipped the coffee while I waited.

It was still early but full-on day when I reached home. Lucy's rental car was gone.

Maybe she ran out for Starbucks.

Maybe she had a craving for donuts.

Maybe they were heading back to LAX and I'd never see Lucy and Ben again.

The maybes rained down like hellfire.

I let myself in and called from the kitchen.

"Hello? Ben? You home?"

If Lucy ran out for coffee, Ben might be home, but nobody answered. The note I'd left was on the counter. It was not crumpled, torn, or defaced, and she hadn't written anything on it. The note was simply there.

I placed the bagels and cheesecake beside it and hurried to the guest room. I expected to find their bags gone, but their clothes still hung in the closet and their bags stood against the wall.

I wandered back to the kitchen, put away the food, and checked for a note. Nothing was stuck to the fridge or oven or microwave. I wandered through the living room to the guest room, but found nothing. I checked my bedroom, thinking she might have left a note on my mirror or bed or the stairs, but she hadn't. No "be back later." No "we need to talk." No "you're an asshole." Nothing.

I wandered back to the kitchen and looked in the freezer. Nothing.

I took out my phone and called. Voice mail.

"Hey, Luce, it's me. I'm home for a bit, but I don't know how long I'll be here. Call."

I cradled the phone in my hands. Thinking.

I decided to text. I tapped out the first word of a message, told myself I was being stupid, and deleted it. She would call or she wouldn't. I put away the phone and ate a bagel with lox and cream cheese. I was still eating when Lou Poitras called.

He said, "Can you talk?"

"Yes."

"Here's what we have."

I took the phone to the couch as I listened.

Bonnie Newberg and Dana Ito caught the case. They were both Detective-2s at Central Bureau. Lou knew Ito well and considered her a fine detective.

Rachel Bohlen's body had been wrapped in black sixty-five-gallon trash bags made from one-point-five millinear low-density resin. This was a heavy-duty, stretchable plastic ideal for heavy trash, yard waste, sticks, and sharp objects. Each bag measured fifty inches by forty-eight inches. Ms. Bohlen could have easily fit inside a single bag, but the killer or persons associated with the killer had wrapped her body using five bags, and secured the wrapping with a common black plastic duct tape. They had not taped the wrapping well. At some point, her right arm slipped free. She was found in an area of coastal sage scrub and chaparral on a south-facing slope thirty-two feet downhill from a street in Griffith Park.

Lou spoke as if reading from notes.

"She was murdered elsewhere and left in repose between twenty-four and thirty-six hours before she was moved. No indications of rape. No semen. Multiple DNA and fibers, but so far they're nothing. No suspects as yet, but a wit claims he saw the dump."

"He saw her being dumped, or murdered?"

"Dumped. A homeless dude. He flagged a black-and-white and led them to the body. Ito has her doubts."

"She thinks he's trying to insert himself?"

Murderers often approached the police.

"Nah. Mental issues. They questioned him on and off for most of a day, but he didn't offer much. Two men wearing jackets and hats in a light-colored vehicle shaped like a box."

"A box."

"Lemme see—"

Lou checked his notes.

"Unable to provide make, model, characteristics, or color beyond 'light.' Jackets and hats described as dark. Described subjects as two males, one large, one smaller. No face, hair, race, or skin tone. On and on. Maybe he saw it. Maybe he didn't."

"But he reported the body."

"He did, though it's unclear whether he reported it the following day or two days later. He didn't seem sure."

"He lives up in the park?"

"Says he was camped up there when he saw the dump. If he actually saw it. Otherwise he found her body when he was screwing around and imagined the rest. Some of these poor folks can't tell the difference."

Two men, one large, one smaller, could describe the

meatball and a partner. One of the gardeners maybe or even the scarecrow.

"How'd she die?"

"Asphyxiation following prior strangulation. Perp closed the deal with a plastic bag."

I saw the image of her battered and swollen face.

"She was beaten."

"I don't want to go through this stuff. You want, I'll send the M.E. notes."

"She was beaten bad."

Lou sighed.

"It was bad. Ligature abrasions on her wrists and ankles. The M.E. thinks the killer tied her and dragged it out."

"He wanted something from her, Lou. It fits what I told you."

"Listen. Go down this road and you'll be finding fantasy clues. We don't know what the killer was thinking or why he or she did this. We'll find out, but for now we don't know. Maybe the freak's just an animal."

Rachel's face floated before me. A bee landed on her cheek. A second bee settled on her nose. I pushed off the couch and clenched my eyes. Rachel and the bees vanished.

"What happened to him?"

"Who?"

"The wit. I want to talk to him."

Poitras hesitated and I wondered what he was thinking.

"I'll call Dana. Give me ten minutes."

38

The phone buzzed thirty seconds later with an incoming video call, but it wasn't Lou Poitras. Joe Pike and Jon Stone were on the call together in what looked like a mausoleum.

Stone grinned like a shark and gestured behind himself.

"Check out my digs. If you made more money, you could upgrade."

"It looks like a mausoleum."

"Don't hate me because I'm beautiful."

I ignored him and focused on Pike.

"Are these people spies?"

"They are not known operatives of the Ministry of State Security or the Military Intelligence Department. They're criminals."

"Criminals with top secret PRC spy gear."

Jon Stone tapped his phone.

"Sending picture one."

A close shot of the meatball's face appeared.

"Meatball Man is Donghai An Bo, formerly of the People's Armed Police Falcon Commando Unit. He probably stole the gear when they dumped him."

Pike said, "The Falcons are their version of a Special Forces Antiterrorist Unit. Like Delta."

Stone smirked.

"These clowns aren't close to Delta. We'd eat them for snacks and shit their toenails for fun."

Pike and I both looked at him.

Stone said, "It's an expression."

Pike said, "Tell him the rest."

"The PAP court-martialed him for theft of the People's property. His record shows two later arrests, one for aggravated assault and one for murder. Did time in prison and currently works for Crystal Future as what they call a foreign security advisor."

"What about Chow?"

"The ChiCom version of an all-American corporate shit-heel success story. Multiple indictments for shady business practices. Always skates, likely due to connections within the Communist Party. No known connection to PRC Intelligence."

"So they're not foreign agents?"

"They are not foreign agents."

"So it's all about Josh and Skylar. They're not interested in Adele."

Stone shrugged, like he didn't care either way.

"Who's to say?"

I looked at Pike.

"Where is he now?"

"San Gabriel. He found your card and drove direct to the LWL Development building."

Reporting to Tarly. I wondered if Chow had been there as well and what they were planning.

My phone buzzed with an incoming call.

"Poitras. I have to get this."

Pike said, "Go."

I picked up the call.

Poitras said, "The individual's name is Jared Walker Philburn, spelled with a p-h. They set him up at the Bright Day Shelter, let him get something to eat, clean up, whatnot. No guarantee he stayed. You can't force these people."

"I understand. Now I have something for you."

I sent him the full-face photo of the meatball.

"This is Donghai An Bo, also known as the meatball. He works for Chow Wan Li. He's also a convicted criminal from the People's Republic."

I sent the photo of his sedan showing the license plate.

"He uses this car, which is leased to LWL Development Inc. in San Gabriel."

Poitras said, "A light-color sedan."

"The car may be there now."

"What are you going to do?"

"Show Mr. Philburn. I'll call after I talk to him."

I killed the call and googled Bright Day Shelter. It was located in a repurposed bus terminal not far from Union Station. Like most shelters, they cooperated with police and other law enforcement agencies, which they viewed as community partners. But shelters usually weren't so cooperative with private citizens or paid snoops. Private citizens often turned out to be drug dealers, debt collectors, or long-lost associates looking to settle old scores. I needed an introduction, so I called a social worker friend named Carole Hilegas. Carole's practice focused on domestic abuse and sexually abused children, and she had shelter contacts all over town.

"Hey, Carole. Elvis Cole. Are you familiar with the Bright Day Shelter downtown?"

"I am. What do you need?"

"An introduction."

Carole was great. She offered to call the director, and forty-two minutes later I parked in a pay lot three blocks away.

39

The sidewalks surrounding the old redbrick building were crowded with lingering men and women and more than a few children. I made my way to the entrance, introduced myself to a woman seated behind a flimsy desk, and asked to speak with Beth Lawrence. The woman eyed me as if I'd come to shut them down and didn't like me any better when I told her Ms. Lawrence was expecting me.

She said, "Wait here at this desk. Don't go wandering off."

"Ixnay on the wandering."

A burly man with a large gut and a pockmarked chin was leaning against the wall a few feet behind the desk. He wore a faded green vest with SECURITY stenciled on the flap and didn't seem to like me any more than the woman.

I gave him a nod.

"Hey. How's it going?"

If he moved I didn't see it.

"Can't bring in weapons. No guns or knives, no screw-drivers or ice picks, no hammers or clubs."

"Left them in the car. Thanks."

"No brass knucks, saps, broken glass, or sharp objects."

"Flamethrower okay?"

"No fires."

"Got it. Thanks."

He went back to staring and I went back to waiting.

Beth Lawrence introduced herself two minutes later. She was a round, sturdy woman with a firm grip and cheery eyes. She led me through an empty dining room the size of an airplane hangar, along a short hall, and into her office. Her office was half the size of Josh's studio, but painted a pale blue as cheery as her eyes.

"Carole says you'd like to speak with one of our residents?"

"Yes, ma'am. Jared Walker Philburn. Officers from Northeast Station brought him here the day before yesterday. He'd witnessed a crime."

She nodded before I finished.

"Griffith Park."

"Yes, ma'am. That's him."

"He was quite the celebrity for a day."

She unlocked a desk drawer, took out a small tablet computer, and tapped at the screen. A few seconds later, an inexpensive printer on a small metal shelf behind her spit out a page.

"I'm sorry, but he declined to stay."

She placed the page in front of me as she continued.

"It's a shame, but we can't force people to accept services. So many of these folks, like Mr. Philburn, could truly benefit by using services, but if they refuse, they refuse."

The page was an intake form for registering persons who received services, assistance, or medical care. They had photographed him, and entered whatever personal information he provided, which wasn't much, or they observed. Jared Walker Philburn was described as being an Anglo male, five feet eight, one hundred forty pounds, with no visible scars, tattoos, or missing limbs. He had given his age as fifty-nine, but the man in the photo appeared twenty years older. His face was dark from years of unending sun, his cheeks were hollow crevices, and the skin beneath his eyes and jaw sagged like furled sails.

"I understand he has a certain degree of impairment."

She leaned back until the little chair squeaked.

"Schizophrenia. Paranoid ideation with an aversion to closed spaces. It's classic, in its way. He doesn't trust doctors and refuses medication. He had agreed to see one of our medical partners, but they all agree until their anxiety builds. Then it becomes untenable."

"So he left."

"Early the following morning, I believe. One of our security staff saw him."

I stared at the intake form. No entries had been made for a spouse, siblings, or children. No current or former addresses were listed. He'd given his place of birth as Sunbeam, Oklahoma, which may have been true but probably wasn't.

"Did he have any sort of identification? An old driver's license, maybe? A V.A. or Medicaid card?"

She shook her head.

"No, but this isn't unusual. People in Mr. Philburn's situation typically hide their things because they're robbed so often. He had very little with him. The clothes he was wearing, a faded purple cap, but no personal photographs or keepsakes. It's likely he hid his belongings before he went to the police."

"You spoke with him?"

"Oh, yes. I handled the intake. He was very pleasant. He was looking forward to a shower and a meal. He wanted to know if we were having Italian food. Italian food is his favorite."

Maybe I should look for him in Italy.

"Did he say anything to suggest where he might have gone?"

She thought for a moment.

"Not that I recall."

She thought a moment longer.

"The officers told me he'd been living in Griffith Park. You might find him there."

Returning to the park made no sense.

"You understand he found a murder victim in the park. He claimed he saw people hide the body."

"I understand. But if his belongings were there, he'd return. He might not stay, but people like Mr. Philburn are comfortable with what's familiar."

The park.

I didn't like it. Sooner or later the people who killed

Rachel Bohlen would learn a homeless man who lived at the park had seen them. Then they would return to kill him.

I said, "He'd go home."

She smiled.

"Like anyone else."

"You mentioned a purple cap. Like a ball cap or a beanie?"

She gestured up by her head, as if she were wearing it.

"A ball cap with something embroidered above the bill. It was faded, almost white in places, like he'd been wearing it for years. He didn't want to take it off."

I touched the intake form.

"May I take this?"

"Of course, Mr. Cole. I printed it for you."

Beth Lawrence walked me out. Forty-three hundred acres of steep slopes, canyons, and tourist attractions was a lot to search, but I had a good idea where to find him.

The coroner investigator's notes contained a hand-drawn map of the park. A tiny "x" marked the exact location where Rachel Belle Bohlen's body was found. The killers knew where to look, but I needed the map.

I hoped he didn't go back.

I hoped he was still alive.

I called Joe as I drove.

40

Jared Walker Philburn

Jared was walking up Hillhurst Avenue on his usual route, collecting plastic bottles and aluminum cans from refuse bins, when a man called out behind him.

"Sir! Wait up!"

Jared turned and was horrified to see a young gentleman running toward him. Jared lurched sideways and prepared for the blow, but the young man stopped and offered a large white paper bag.

"For you. Enjoy it."

Jared took the bag suspecting a ploy, a snake inside or poop, but the young gentleman seemed pleasant enough. He smiled and walked away.

Jared carefully opened the bag and peeked at the contents.

"Holy moly rockin' rolly!"

The bag was filled with food. Six tacos, two burritos, and six plastic containers of salsa. Too much to eat in a single sitting and far too delicate to brave the day's heat,

Jared opted for home. He could store the young man's generosity in the cool confines of the shade and feast at his leisure.

Jared cashed his recyclables at the nearest purveyor and hurried up Hillhurst and into the park. He passed the golf course and the theatre and didn't notice the dusty red pickup parked beside the filthy white SUV facing the road. He did not see the driver with the ponytail or the driver with the wraparound sunglasses, but the drivers saw Jared.

They started their vehicles.

41

Elvis Cole

Rachel's body had been found below one of the two streets leading to the observatory. The observatory's parking lots were crowded when I arrived. Drivers had parked along the road, forcing walkers and joggers to dodge tourists who'd come for the views. I parked a quarter mile away and walked back. Rachel Bohlen's final resting place was easy to find. Removing her body had left an obvious path of broken chaparral, flattened sage, and disturbed soil from the chaparral below to the top of the slope.

The light-colored vehicle would have been parked nearby. The killers had lifted her body over a guardrail, carried her to the edge of the slope, and heaved her over. One of the park's old streetlights was only a few feet away, so either the lamp didn't work or the people who dumped her believed the park was deserted. They had fallen for the illusion. Venture into a canyon and you could forget you were surrounded by millions of people.

Her body had been dumped on a short stretch of street bracketed by sharp curves at either end. Jared couldn't have seen them if he'd been in the canyon below or beyond the curves. He needed to be in a line-of-sight view and he needed to be close. This left a small stand of trees near a turnoff to the observatory and a steep upslope shoulder directly across the street. The shoulder was too steep to climb, but appeared to flatten about twenty feet above the road.

I walked east searching for a path up, but the slope only grew steeper. When I reached the far curve I turned back and found a weathered erosion cut. The cut climbed a dip in the slope and wound behind the shoulder.

The path was a slippery mix of crumbling soil and dislodged rocks between hulking balls of coastal sage. I passed between gnarly oaks, pushed through some sage, and reached a flat area crowning the shoulder. I went to the edge. Rachel Belle Bohlen had been found in the brush directly below me.

Scattered footprints dotted the clearing, but no fires had been built and the area was free of litter and trash. It might be a place where hikers admired the view, but it didn't look like a campsite.

I called out.

"Mr. Philburn? Are you here?"

Maybe he'd never been here. Or maybe he returned for his things as Beth Lawrence believed and would never return.

I called louder.

"I come in peace."

I didn't expect an answer. I just wanted to say it.

I circled the clearing and spotted the faded remains of a rusted water tank beyond the ridge above me. A narrow path led up to the tank, so I followed it, circled the tank, and peered inside. The rusted metal was layered with faded graffiti, but I saw no evidence of habitation, recent or otherwise.

I spotted a pop of blue between the branches of a gnarled scrub oak on my way down. The change of angle was revealing. A tightly rolled sleeping bag and faded blue duffel were hidden beneath the oak. I did not want to search his belongings, but I did. A thin billfold beneath his clothes held three worn photographs, his teenage driver's license, seven library cards from seven cities, and forty-two dollars. The driver's license had been issued to Jared W. Philburn. The billfold was folded around a page torn from a small spiral notebook. The page bore a note written in square block letters.

> *I AM JARED WALKER PHILBURN*
> *IN THE EVENT OF MY DETH*
> *PLESE DONATE MY BELONGINGS*
> *TO THEM WHO NEED HELP*

An uneven signature was scrawled across the bottom.

I stood and looked around.

"Mr. Philburn? If you're here, I would very much like to speak with you."

Philburn didn't answer and neither did the brush.

I put forty dollars into the billfold and the billfold

into the duffel. I put everything back as I'd found it, walked to the lip of the shoulder, and studied the people below. I studied everybody I saw for as far as I could see, but I did not see Jared Philburn or anyone wearing a faded purple cap.

I took out my phone and called Joe.

"I found it. His things are here, so he'll be back."

"Say location."

"The top of the shoulder across from the dump. He was right on top of them. He saw it."

"On my way."

Pike was cruising the western side of the park.

"He's probably down in Los Feliz making his rounds. I'll call Lou. Lou can have the area cops look for him."

I was saying it when I saw the red truck. It was far away and small and moving very slow, coming up the eastside road with a line of cars bunched behind it. I could not see the driver, but it was the gardener's truck. A tiny figure darted across the truck's path and the truck swung hard past oncoming cars.

"Joe! This side! They're here!"

I scrambled and slid and ran as hard as I could.

42

Jared Walker Philburn

Jared yearned to smile at the walkers and joggers and dogs he passed. The world held too little joy and comfort to turn one's back on a smile, but Jared's smiles were rarely welcomed and almost never returned. This left him sad. He did not wish to impose on others, so he kept his eyes down and shared a smile with himself.

Almost home and his mouth was watering.

Jared was imagining the joys to come when horns startled him so badly he stumbled.

A red pickup truck crept behind him a mere twenty feet away. The cars behind it passed when they could, but were otherwise trapped by oncoming vehicles.

Jared was well out of the street at the far side of the shoulder. He posed no obstruction. The truck could have easily passed, but idled along behind him.

Jared moved farther to the side and glanced back again. The truck didn't pass. Horns blew. Cars roared past when able. Drivers cursed.

The red truck seemed familiar.

Jared tucked the white bag under his arm like a foot-ball and increased his pace. He glanced back again.

The driver's face was a threatening mask. His mouth was a slash with down-turned corners and angular sun-glasses masked his eyes. When Jared looked at the man, a sharp-eyed demon looked back.

Familiar.

Jared lowered his head and strode forward, waving his arm for the truck to pass. *Go, go around, please.*

The truck stayed behind him.

Jared walked faster. His legs moved faster than they'd ever moved before and his arm windmilled. *Pass me, please, the street is yours!*

The truck stayed with him like a shadow.

Get out of the street, fool!

Jared abruptly stepped off the shoulder onto the sandy dirt well off the road and stopped in a clump of weeds. He was completely off the pavement.

The truck stopped.

Jared stared.

The truck idled.

And then Jared knew. This was the truck with the men who had come in the deep of night, the men who had flashed and slashed with their lights to find him.

The driver raised a cell phone to his lips and Jared knew he was doomed. A terrible grief for the young gen-tleman's kindness filled his heart and the bag of tacos fell to the earth.

Jared said, "My only friend, the end."

He bolted across the street. Horns blared and tires

screamed. The red truck swerved after him. Jared plunged downhill into the chaparral, fell, and slid to his feet. He glimpsed the driver, gun in hand, plunging after him.

The slope was steep but flattened quickly. Jared pushed past grasping oaks and prickly balls of sage. He tripped, stumbled, and saw the man gaining.

"Gracious Lord, help me!"

Jared knew trails were ahead, though he'd never been on them. He clawed and fought his way down, but the man steadily drew closer. The crashing behind him grew louder like a wave thundering ashore and when Jared glanced again the man was almost upon him.

"Lord, please!"

Jared pushed blindly through a thick wall of brush and fell forward onto a trail. The man broke out behind him and pinned Jared with a knee. He pressed the gun hard into Jared's neck.

Jared clenched his eyes and shrieked.

"Mercy!"

Jared braced for death, but did not die.

The painful knee vanished. The steel at his neck disappeared. The world was suddenly quiet.

Jared opened an eye.

A fearsome man with bright red arrow tattoos on his arms stood over Jared's pursuer, who lay still as a rock and might well have been dead. The arrowed man held his gun.

Jared said, "Did the Lord send you?"

The arrowed man stepped close and extended a hand.

"Let me help."

Jared accepted the hand and felt himself rise.

43

Elvis Cole

Two Northeast Station area cars arrived code three to pick up the gardener and secure his vehicle. Lou sent a third to transport Mr. Philburn.

I said, "He saw them, Lou. Maybe he couldn't describe them, but he saw them dump her body."

"Two guys in hats and a car box."

"Show him the sedan. The pictures might help order his memory."

"You think Donghai An Bo was one of them?"

"If Philburn IDs the car, it gives you something to work with, doesn't it?"

"It gives me plenty. The People's Police want him for murder."

"In China?"

"We don't have a People's Police in America."

"Keep going."

"I reached out this morning about Bo and Chow Wan Li. Took a while for them to confirm I was who I said I was, but once they were satisfied they were very cooperative."

"The People's Police."

"He's good for a double homicide in Shanghai. They've been looking for him for the better part of a year, so they were thrilled to learn his whereabouts."

"Crystal Future is headquartered in Shanghai."

"Correct. So they were doubly surprised when I told them Donghai is here in L.A. working for Chow Wan Li. They didn't like it. Offered to help on their side if we needed it."

"What kind of help were they offering?"

"Didn't ask."

"Probably best you didn't."

"I'll let you know what we get from your gardener. Maybe he'll put the meatball in prison."

"Maybe he'll finger the Sandman."

"Hold your breath."

I still hadn't heard from Lucy. I wanted to call but didn't. She and Ben were probably back at the house. I felt anxious and irritated. I wanted to go home. When Philburn rolled away I turned to Joe.

"Have you heard from Lucy?"

"No."

"I thought she might call."

"Why?"

"I don't know. You guys talk so much."

Pike said, "Mm."

"I'm going home. You're welcome to come. We have plenty of bagels."

Pike said, "Maybe later."

I drove home and felt even worse when I rounded the curve and didn't find Lucy's car. I let myself in and checked their room. Seeing their bags made me feel better. At least they hadn't shipped off to LAX while I was gone.

I made a lox and bagel sandwich. I really piled it on. Heavy cream cheese. Six slices of lox. Sliced jalapeños for a little kick. I ate it at the sink.

The cat walked in and looked at me stuffing my face.

I said, "What of it?"

He left.

I washed cream cheese off my fingers, wiped my mouth, and went upstairs to shower. I dressed and sat on the couch. I didn't know what to do. I looked at my phone as if a voice mail might magically appear. It didn't. I felt listless and even more irritable. I toyed with the idea of another sandwich. Maybe add bacon this time. I was ravenous. The phone rang. I checked the caller ID so fast I almost sprained my neck. Wendy Vann. I answered with a snarl.

"What is it?"

"Corbin's on the way. He's two minutes out."

"He's coming here?"

"One minute."

"How'd he know I'm home?"

"Please."

Wendy hung up as gravel crunched out front. The same crunch Lucy would make when she arrived, only this wasn't Lucy. I opened the door as Corbin Schumacher struggled to stand from the beautiful red Tesla. He had driven himself. I checked up and down the street and saw no one.

I said, "No helpers?"

He waved toward the door. Walking was difficult. He hunched over his cane and his balance seemed tenuous.

"Let's go in."

I held the door and followed him into the living room. He pivoted in an unsteady circle as he took in the room. He looked at the loft and up at the high peaked crest and out at the canyon and back to me. He was smiling. I had not seen him smile.

"Very nice. A very nice home."

"Thanks."

"Adele and I lived in a house like this when we married. Outside Stanford in the hills. We had a loft like this. We had a deck. Very nice."

His fondness for the house outside Stanford was obvious. But maybe his true fondness was for the time they'd shared before their lives changed.

I said, "Would you like a bagel?"

The fond smile vanished.

"No, I do not want a bagel. I didn't come here to eat. Where's my son?"

"I haven't found him."

"Are you looking or are you too busy eating bagels?"

He had me there.

"Josh and Skylar Lawless discovered a payoff scheme involving a city councilman and multiple real estate developers. I believe they took it upon themselves to investigate, during which time Ms. Lawless was murdered."

"The tramp? This whore he was with?"

"Her name was Rachel Belle Bohlen."

"Fine. Whatever. Where's Josh?"

"Hiding. He knows she was murdered. It's in the news. It's possible he's left town, but I don't know. It's just as possible he's still investigating."

Corbin smacked his cane into the floor.

"Stupid! A simpleton! He's no journalist."

"He considers himself a journalist."

"Magical thinking! Assuming there's anything to this, he should have taken it to the police."

I nodded, but my nod was slow.

"I guess he wanted to do it himself."

"And now this girl is dead and he may be dead, too."

"I guess it was important to him."

"Idiot."

I was tired. Lucy was gone and I hadn't slept and I didn't know if she would leave or stay or if they'd be gone from my life forever. I was tired of Corbin demeaning his son and from knowing what it must have been like for Josh growing up.

I said, "He wants to matter."

"Oh, please."

"Josh made a sign for the wall in his apartment. One word. It says 'Matter.' A reminder, I guess, to do something that matters."

"He hasn't."

"I asked about it and Ryan told me something you should know. The only thing Josh cares about is impressing you."

Corbin frowned. He shifted the cane but said nothing.

"He wants you to think he matters. I guess he feels like you don't."

Corbin shifted and the cane bore his full weight.

"You must've been a helluva father."

Corbin leaned on the cane, swaying gently. He swallowed. His face was dark and closed and he swayed. His mouth worked. The hooded eyes glistened. He blinked faster and his mouth worked and he turned for the door.

Corbin said, "Bring him home."

I watched him go, but I did not go with him. He let himself out. I felt angry and mean and small.

Some days were bad all the way around.

orbin left me thinking about Josh and the means by which Josh could investigate a seated member of the council. Josh didn't work for the *Times* or NBC. His resources and access were limited, but Josh was smart. According to Eddie Ditko, many of the articles Josh downloaded concerned developers whose projects were rumored to have been stalled or killed when they refused to pay Richter's price. If Josh was still trying to dig up dirt on Richter, he might have reached out to them. If he had, they might have a means to reach him.

I opened my laptop, googled the companies, and identified the principal owners and their contact information. Keeping busy was better than brooding.

I called Block Sixteen first. A young male voice answered.

"Paul Hanlon's office."

"Jace Evers. I'm calling from the Internet Fraud Division. May I speak with Mr. Hanlon, please?"

"Um, he's not available. What is this regarding?"

"Has Mr. Hanlon been approached by a podcaster named Josh or Joshua Schumacher, also known as Josh Shoe, anytime in the past two weeks?"

The young male voice hesitated.

"Josh who?"

"Do all Mr. Hanlon's calls go through you?"

"I'm his assistant."

"Josh or Joshua Schumacher. A podcaster, though he may have identified himself in another way. Regarding Councilman Richter's office."

"You could leave your name and a number."

"You don't recall speaking with Mr. Schumacher?"

"I'm afraid I don't."

"And if Schumacher called for Mr. Hanlon, it would've gone through you?"

"Mr. Evers, *everything* goes through me. I have no life."

I thanked him, phoned Frank Pinella of Crest Pinella Construction, and did it again.

"Jace Evers. I'm calling from the Internet Fraud Division. May I speak with Mr. Pinella, please?"

"I'll see if he's available."

She put me on hold and returned a few seconds later.

"What's this regarding?"

"A podcaster named Josh or Joshua Schumacher, also known as Josh Shoe. I'm calling to see if—"

The line went dead, so I called again.

"Crest Pinella. Mr. Pinella's office."

"We were cut off."

The line went dead again. Josh had reached out, and Pinella didn't want to talk about it.

Helene Moskavich's assistant recognized Josh's name, but asked her boss if she would like to speak with me. Her answer must've been no. Her assistant hung up.

Edward Dane's assistant also recognized Josh's name, and put me on hold to ask if Mr. Dane would speak with me. I waited on hold for almost six minutes, but Edward Dane finally picked up the line. He didn't say hello or greet me. He started right in.

"I'll tell you what I told Mr. Schumacher. I have nothing to say. That's it. If he shows up again, I'll call the police."

I was surprised.

"He came to your office?"

"Well, I didn't return his calls, so, yes, he showed up."

"When was this?"

"Who are you again?"

"Jace Evers. Internet Fraud Division."

Official-sounding names were usually best.

"Uh-huh. This was the day before yesterday. As soon as he opened his mouth I threw him out."

"But he called several times."

"He wouldn't take no for an answer."

"Would you have his number? We've been trying to reach him."

"I didn't keep it. Why would I keep it? I have no intention of speaking with him."

Edward Dane sounded nervous.

"He asked you about Councilman Richter."

"I threw him out. I have nothing but respect for Councilman Richter."

He didn't sound as if he respected Richter. He sounded afraid he was being recorded.

The day before yesterday. Josh was still in town and still chasing Richter.

George L. Rolly's assistant refused to put me through. The assistant at Daemler-Riggins hung up without asking her boss if he'd speak with me. Andrea Scotti of Dieder-Scotti took my call, but only to tell me she had nothing to say. She asked me not to call again. People were afraid.

I phoned Mendez-Warren next. Lou Warren's assistant sounded pleasant and upbeat when she answered, but when I mentioned Josh, she lowered her voice and seemed uncertain.

"I don't think he'll speak with you."

"Please ask. It's important."

"He asked Mr. Schumacher to leave."

"Because Mr. Schumacher asked about Councilman Richter?"

She hesitated.

"I'm sorry."

She was sorry, but she didn't hang up.

"Did Mr. Schumacher leave a phone number or a way to be reached?"

She hesitated, and said it again.

"I'm sorry. Hold, please."

She kept me on hold for almost three minutes, but then she returned. Her voice was even softer now.

"Who are you, really? And please don't tell me this internet fraud nonsense."

She wanted to talk, but she'd read me like a Sunset Strip billboard. I liked her for it.

"My name is Elvis Cole. I'm a private investigator. Josh Schumacher's mother hired me because Josh disappeared. I believe him to be in danger."

"Because of this business with the councilman?"

"I believe so, yes. In part."

"In part."

"Did he leave a number or way to reach him?"

"He didn't, but I referred him to a friend of Mr. Warren's. She might be able to help. I'll send her contact information, if you'd like."

I gave her my cell. Three seconds later the contact information for someone named Allie Rice arrived in a text.

"Did you get it?"

"Who's Allie Rice?"

"Hold, please."

She put me on hold again. I waited almost six minutes, but she returned with the answer.

"Someone who tried to help Mr. Warren. She was wonderful. A truly good person."

"How'd she try to help Mr. Warren?"

"She was a flight attendant then—I don't know if she still is—for one of those private jet companies. She actually saw money change hands with her own eyes, and heard what they said about Mr. Warren."

"This was Councilman Richter?"

"Him and others. I don't know who. I wasn't in the room."

"I understand."

"Whatever it was, she told Mr. Warren. She came here to warn him. He was livid, but he couldn't do anything about it. He was scared."

"Scared of confronting the councilman."

"These people control his livelihood."

"You told Josh about her?"

"I did. She saw them. She actually saw the money. He was very excited."

I was excited, too. I could feel myself gaining ground, as if Josh was just out of sight over the horizon, but I was catching up fast.

"When was this?"

"Three or four months ago."

"Not what she saw. When did you tell Josh?"

"Yesterday. People need to know. Someone needs to stop this."

"Someone does. You know my name. May I ask yours?"

"I'm Gina, Gina Freid, but please don't tell anyone I told."

"I won't, Gina. I promise."

The contact card showed an address in Marina del Rey. Allie Rice might or might not be home, and Josh might or might not be in touch with her, but I didn't want to risk scaring him off. I hustled out to my car and got on with the hunt. It was better than eating more bagels.

45

Allie Rice lived in the right half of a duplex home not far from Venice Beach. Many of the homes on her street favored nautical decor with fishing nets or surfboards on their porches. Allie Rice's porch held potted hydrangeas.

The odds were slight, but I hoped to find Allie Rice at home. If she wasn't, I planned to break in and search for more clues. Maybe a note saying "Meet Josh Schumacher at 2" or "Josh is at the Islander Palms rm 312." I never thought Josh would be with Allie Rice when I arrived, but his black-on-black MINI sat two doors away. I parked in a red zone at the corner, walked back, and confirmed the plate. Josh. Takeout food debris, crumpled soda cans, and a sleeping bag littered the interior. Josh had been living in his car.

I stood in the brilliant sunlight and placed a hand on the MINI's roof. I squinted up at the clear blue sky. The meatball might scream around the corner with blazing guns or a formation of drones might appear, but I wanted to enjoy the moment. I enjoyed it too long.

Allie Rice's front door opened and Ryan Seborg stepped out with a gear bag over his shoulder. He saw me and literally jumped. He looked like Sylvester the Cat.

"Josh! Run! It's him!"

He slammed the door and something crashed in the house.

I ran onto the porch, but the door was locked. Another crash came from the back of her house. I hopped off the porch, ran down the side of the house, and jumped a wooden gate into her backyard. Josh and Ryan were struggling to climb a fence in the rear, but a huge mound of bougainvillea blocked their way.

I said, "Josh, stop. I just want to talk."

Josh shouted, "Help! Help!"

I raised my hands.

"Ryan, c'mon. Tell him."

Josh shouted, "I'm not going back!"

Ryan shouted louder, "Stay away, asshole!"

A trim, attractive woman in black tights and a red T-shirt appeared at the back door. She put her fists on her hips and didn't look happy to see me.

"Get out of my yard. I'll call the police."

Josh made a break for the far side of the house. I beat him across and he veered to the other side. I beat him again and he cut back again.

"Josh, you're found. This is silly. Stop."

Josh was large and he wasn't in shape. He stopped and leaned over with his hands on his knees, sucking breaths like a bellows. Ryan came up beside him and glared like a guard dog.

I said, "Don't have a heart attack, okay? Breathe."

Josh nodded and sucked air.

"Did my mother actually hire you?"

Ryan said, "This is him. He's a detective."

"What did you expect? You vanished."

"I couldn't stay."

"There were three or four hundred better ways to handle this."

He looked at Ryan.

"I knew they'd come. I didn't want anyone hurt."

"Rachel Bohlen is dead."

Allie Rice called from the door.

"Who's Rachel Bohlen?"

Josh looked up.

"She was a brilliant artist and a good person. She discovered Richter's scam and here we are."

He slumped and shook his head. His eyes were bubblegum pink and swelling.

"Look what they did to her. Look what they did."

Ryan put his hand on his friend's back.

"You'll kill'm, dude. You're gonna crush'm."

Allie Rice was still at the door, listening. I edged closer to Josh and lowered my voice.

"She doesn't know Rachel was murdered?"

"She personally witnessed Grady Locke receive a cash bribe. She was willing to go on record for the podcast. That's why we're here. We recorded her statement."

Allie Rice had crossed her arms as if she was having second thoughts. She looked cold. Even in the bright California light.

I lowered my voice still more.

"Who killed her?"

"Them. I don't know. I wasn't there. Maybe Locke. I don't know. She went to see Locke at his loft. Stupid. Stupid. I tried to stop her."

The argument the blonde and the auburn heard. When Josh got loud.

"She went to see Grady Locke and she never came back."

He nodded.

"Why would she go to his loft?"

"Evidence. She thought she could get more evidence. Stupid. Maybe she threatened him. I don't know."

He wasn't breathing so deeply now. He finally stood.

I glanced at Allie Rice and moved even closer.

"More. Meaning she had evidence Richter was taking payoffs?"

He nodded.

"Yeah. He's a crook. Allie's seen it firsthand. So did Rachel."

"This was something she took from Locke?"

"Not like you mean. She took pictures. Of cash. Of his phone. It's what she does. Did. Turning pictures of text conversations into art. She photographed texts between Locke and Richter saying how Chow Wan Li was sending over cash. Locke's brother-in-law was delivering it. It's all in their texts. The whole scam. She gave it to me. She wanted to do something with it."

"Pictures of texts."

"Yes. Maybe he caught her this time. I don't know."

"They searched her apartment. They were looking for something."

"Rachel gave me the pictures. She gave statements on audio and video. We recorded everything."

"Statements."

"For the podcast. About them and what they were doing. She wanted everything on record. She wanted to stop them."

I saw Rachel's battered and beaten face.

"Whatever you have, these people think you can hurt them."

"No shit?"

Ryan laughed.

Josh said, "They're right. I'm going to hurt them. I'm going to ruin them. I'm going to make them pay for killing Rachel and all the other people they've hurt."

He looked set, determined, and unafraid. He had no idea what he was doing.

"Can I see your evidence?"

"I'll let you listen. Rachel can speak for herself."

Allie said, "Can I listen, too?"

"Of course. You're one of the heroes of the story."

Josh started for the house, then looked at me.

"One thing, though. Don't try to stop me or talk me out of it. I'm going to expose these people and destroy them. That's it. So don't try to stop me."

"I'm not here to stop you. I'm going to help."

Ryan smirked.

"The Men in Black say the same damned thing."

We went inside and listened to Rachel's story.

46

Allie Rice was a warm and personable host. She told me her story as Josh set up two small speakers and attached them to his phone.

Allie had been a flight attendant for a charter jet company in Burbank when a real estate developer named A. O. Castillo chartered a ten-passenger jet to fly himself, his wife, Sanford Richter, and Grady Locke to Phoenix for a Lakers-Suns game. As Richter and Locke boarded, Ms. Rice saw Castillo hand two thick envelopes to Richter, who passed them to Grady Locke, who then placed them in a small handbag. He held the bag for the entire flight and twice refused her offer to store it in an overhead bin. She found his attachment to the bag odd and was suspicious of the envelopes. As they began their descent, Locke insisted on securing the bag in the plane's luggage compartment. She did so, but after the party departed for the game, she opened the hatch and examined the envelopes. Ms. Rice expected to find drugs, but each envelope contained a tightly wrapped block of one-hundred-dollar bills two inches thick. She had signed a nondisclosure agreement and never expected to tell anyone until she overheard Sanford Richter tell Castillo about a developer named Lou Warren. Warren had refused to play along, so Richter was fucking him over. Richter was fucking him so good, he bragged, Warren would end up building dog kennels and then Richter would fuck him over even more just to show him.

Allie Rice shook her head at the memory.

"He was so ugly. I didn't know Lou Warren. I'd never heard of Lou Warren. But the hateful arrogance of this man, the ugly meanness in his voice made my skin crawl."

Josh and Ryan were watching her. I was watching her, too.

"So you contacted Mr. Warren."

She shrugged.

"After I changed jobs. I thought he should know, but I don't think he did anything."

Josh glanced at me.

"You see? These people are the scum of the earth. Evil, horrible people."

He looked back at Allie.

"Thank you for sharing your story."

"I hope it helps."

"It will help. I promise you this will help."

I said, "Did you photograph the cash?"

She looked surprised.

"It never occurred to me. I guess I should've."

I shrugged like it was no big deal. I wanted to ask if

the pilots or other crew had seen any of this, but I knew what she'd say and I didn't want to make her feel bad.

I said, "Nah, it's okay. I was just curious."

Allie Rice was trying to help, but without corroboration her claims carried little weight.

I turned to Josh.

"What are we going to hear?"

"How Rachel discovered the truth."

"Let's hear it."

Josh tapped his phone, and Rachel Belle Bohlen told us what happened.

47

Her Finest Performance

She'd been with Grady Locke so many times during the past five years she couldn't remember them all. Rachel usually met him at party locations like hotels or yachts where Grady wined and dined big shots. But every so often, maybe half a dozen times a year, she went to his two-bedroom loft on the seventh floor of a former factory building in downtown Los Angeles. The concrete walls and ceilings were painted various shades of gray, the polished concrete floor gleamed, and the cabinetry in the kitchen and living room was a rich mahogany, which lent warmth to the austere gray walls. Each time she arrived, Grady made a big deal of pointing out the eastern view of the Arts District and the L.A. River bridges, and the northern view across Chinatown to the glow of Dodger Stadium, as if she'd never seen them. Skylar oohed and aahed as always, but Skylar wasn't impressed and didn't care. Acting impressed was part of the gig, and, truth was, she wanted to finish him fast and get the hell out.

The tour ended in his bedroom, him framed in the window, pointing out the golden glow from Chavez Ravine as if the view were a trophy. Skylar decided to nudge him along.

She said, "Hey. Look at this instead."

He turned from the window.

"What?"

Skylar let her black leather jacket fall. She peeled the tiny black dress up from her body like a snake shedding skin, and flipped it away. She turned left, letting him see. She turned right.

"Me or Dodger Stadium? Which view do you like best?"

They did the same stupid dance every time. Yawn.

Grady grinned and moved closer.

"You win. Want a drink?"

"If you're drinking, sure. A drink would be nice."

"I have some pot. We could four-twenty?"

He seemed hopeful, so she gave him the answer he wanted.

"Spark up, dude. Let's party."

Skylar followed him back into the living room, which, like every loft space she'd ever seen, was an enormous industrial cavern—exposed ducts along the ceiling, exposed electrical conduits running down the walls—divided into areas: here's the kitchen area, here's the dining and bar area, here's the living room area with the monster big-screen. He kept his joints in a small inlaid box behind the bar. She went to the dining table for her briefcase, which was slim and professional. The briefcase gave her an air of legitimate purpose when she entered buildings for work, as if the people who saw her might think she was a woman entering their building for some appropriate, legal reason.

He saw her opening the briefcase and smiled again.

"Bring your movies?"

She lifted out her iPad, teasing him.

"I know you dig watching, but I don't know if I should show you these. They're nasty. You might be disgusted. You might want to spank me."

He was grinning like a doof. He had paid eight hundred dollars for three hours of her time. Drool was already dripping down his shirt.

He said, "Damn, you're hot. Let's do this."

Grady, like many of her johns, dug her past as a pornstar. Watching the girl in the video *with* the girl in the video turned them on. They watched the girl in the video even when the girl who had been in the video was under them. Skylar preferred this. When they focused on the video girl, they were not with Skylar, and Skylar was not with them. Skylar could be absent.

He scooped up the joint box, tucked a bottle of gin under his arm, and followed her back into the bedroom. She was booting up the iPad when his cell phone rang.

"Shit. I gotta take this."

He scrambled for his cell, and went to the window.

"Uh-huh, uh-huh, okay."

He glanced back at Skylar, and held up a finger. Won't be long. Only a minute.

"How much?"

He turned toward the view and listened some more.

"I'm in the middle of something. A friend."

More listening. He glanced at her again and shrugged.

"Couple of hours, maybe. Less."

Skylar gave him a thumbs-up. Grady returned it, but suddenly frowned.

"Here? Can I bring it over later?"

His frown deepened.

"Boss, I'm running out of room. It's piling up, and I don't like keeping it here. It's yours. What if my building burns down?"

His frown became a scowl, and Skylar knew Grady Locke was not happy.

"I guess I could, but—I know, okay. Yes, sir. Yes. You're the boss."

Grady held his phone at arm's length and gave it the finger.

Skylar laughed.

Grady said, "Yes, sir. Okay. We'll talk tomorrow."

He ended the call and flipped off his phone again.

"Asshole."

Grady came back to bed, put his phone on the nightstand, and pulled off his pants.

"Fucking dick."

"The Sandman?"

"You wouldn't believe the guy. The shit I put up with."

He pulled off his underwear, swung onto the bed, and patted a spot beside him.

"C'mon. A double feature might help."

Skylar took a spot next to him and played one of her

scenes. The scene had taken three hours to shoot and was cut to fourteen minutes. They were six minutes into it when Grady's phone buzzed with an incoming text. He scooped his phone and immediately scowled.

"Oh, for crap's sake, my fucking brother-in-law. Pause it."

Skylar paused it.

She watched him thumb a fast reply, and a furious text exchange ensued. Grady mumbled as he tapped.

"Aw, c'mon, you *dipshit*! No way!"

Skylar said, "Is everything okay?"

Grady's landline rang.

"Idiot!"

He tossed his cell on the bed, grabbed the landline phone from the nightstand, and entered a code. Skylar knew this unlocked the lobby entrance so a guest could enter.

Grady said, "Sorry. He wasn't supposed to get here until later."

"Pretend you're not here."

"Can't. He knows I'm here. Stay out of sight, okay?"

Grady got out of bed and pulled on his pants.

Skylar said, "Don't sweat it. We can reschedule."

"No, no, no. It's cool. He's just dropping something off."

Grady pulled on a T-shirt as the doorbell rang, and hurried into the living room. Skylar slid from the bed, and watched him. It was a very long room, and the doorbell rang twice more before Grady reached the door.

His brother-in-law was a pudgy guy in a navy suit

with a bucket of fried chicken in his hands. He presented the bucket to Grady with a big smile on his face.

Skylar thought, "What the fuck?"

The brother-in-law pried the lid from the bucket to show Grady the contents. Grady reached inside and lifted out a banded pack of cash. He dug around in the bucket, and Skylar realized he was counting more packs. He kept digging and counting, and Skylar realized the bucket contained many, many packs. Then she understood why Grady was running out of room and what was piling up. Cash.

Grady's brother-in-law left a few seconds later, and Grady turned toward the bedroom.

Skylar ran to the bed, grabbed her iPad, and called out.

"Is he gone?"

"Yeah. Want something from the kitchen? A bottle of water or something?"

Grady had stopped in the kitchen to stash the bucket.

She noticed his phone on the bed, and wanted to see their texts.

She called back.

"Yes, please. Oh, wait, could I have a diet soda?"

Buying more seconds.

Grady called back.

"Sure."

"With ice, please!"

Skylar reached for his phone, and quickly read their texts. Her eyes widened, and she felt a blood-burning excitement she never felt during sex.

Skylar grabbed her iPad and snapped a pic of their

texts. She scrolled to reveal more of the exchange, snapped a second pic, and a third.

She placed his phone where he'd left it, pulled the sheet over her legs, and queued up the video.

Grady returned with a glass of soda and ice. He didn't mention the bucket, and neither did she.

He said, "Sorry about that. It won't happen again."

Skylar smiled.

"No worries. I've been thinking about your loft."

Grady beamed.

"It's fantastic, isn't it?"

"Your walls are too empty."

He looked surprised.

"No way! I love this look."

"You should have one of my paintings. I'll paint something special. Just for you."

She tossed the iPad aside and threw back the sheet.

"Now get in bed."

He attacked her like an animal, but Skylar barely noticed. She thought about the bucket and the texts. She imagined how she might use these things to make them pay for their cruelty. When she screamed, she felt a rush of incredible power.

He thought it was him, but he wasn't even there.

48

The recording lasted only eight or nine minutes. Rachel spoke well. Her voice was pleasing and she sounded genuine. Her story ended in sudden silence.

Allie Rice looked ashen. She said one word.

"Slime."

Josh leaned back.

"One bucket of Kentucky Fried cash, please. What assholes."

"She saw Horton Tarly deliver the cash."

"Yes. She was there. She saw it. The next time she went back, she found more cash. The asshole hides cash all over his loft."

I said, "How many tapes did she make?"

"Tracks. I don't record on tape."

"Tracks. How many?"

"Three. She tells about being an escort in one, how she got into it, the people she worked with, that kind of stuff. The third track is about the work she did for Grady.

Thirty-four minutes, and it is a killer. What she did, where they went, who met with who and what they talked about. How he used her."

Allie Rice murmured again.

"Slime."

Ryan said, "She names names, bro. It's awesome."

I frowned at Ryan.

"You knew he was doing this?"

"He called me."

Josh said, "I didn't want him involved. Rachel was telling me dangerous things. I thought if—"

He looked at Ryan. Sad.

"Dude."

Ryan nodded with understanding.

"Dude."

I interrupted the duding.

"Does she mention Sanford Richter or not?"

"Richter, a couple of U.S. representatives, a judge, this guy Castillo from Allie's plane, and other developers. She names them. Times, dates, and places. Want to hear it?"

"I do. But not now."

These recordings had serious problems as evidence, but I didn't want to discuss it in front of Allie Rice.

"We should let Ms. Rice get on with her life."

"I don't mind. Really."

Josh nodded, agreeing with me.

"We should go. Ryan and I have to interview more people and start cutting this thing together."

I said, "You should call your mom. Let her know you're okay."

He frowned.

"And say what, hi Mom, I'm okay, bye?"

"Tell her what's going on. Let her know you're okay. She's worried."

Allie nodded.

"You really should."

"When I finish. C'mon, Ryan. Let's roll."

I took out my phone and dialed Wendy Vann.

Josh looked alarmed.

"What are you doing?"

Wendy answered.

I said, "Let me speak to Adele."

Josh said, "Asshole!"

Wendy said, "Was that Josh?"

"Yes. He's fine. Let me speak to Adele."

Josh shook his head as Ryan packed their gear.

"This is a big mistake."

Wendy said, "Say your location. I'll come get him."

"Adele."

Adele came on a few seconds later.

"Josh?"

"Elvis Cole. Here's Josh."

I held out the phone.

Josh flipped me off with both hands.

I said, "Speak."

Allie said, "Don't be like that. She's your mother."

Josh took the phone and turned away. He mumbled to keep his conversation private, but mostly he listened. They spoke for three or four minutes before he handed back my phone.

Adele said, "Are you bringing him home?"

"No, ma'am. Not unless he wants to go."

"You were hired to find him and report his location."

"I understand. I'll refund your money."

She was silent for several seconds.

"No need. The police were here, as you warned. Is Josh in trouble?"

"Not with the police. He'll have to speak with them sooner or later, but he's fine for now."

"Will you keep him safe?"

"Yes, ma'am. So long as he doesn't do anything stupid."

I looked at Josh when I said it.

Adele said, "Mr. Cole?"

"Yes, ma'am?"

"Corbin left an odd message today."

"Yes, ma'am."

"'I'm sorry.' This was his message. 'I'm sorry.'"

"Odd."

"Yes, well, I'll be going. I don't like phones. Someone is listening."

Josh waved his hands to get my attention. He mouthed words so Adele wouldn't hear.

"Your phone. They're coming. They know where we are."

I said, "I'll call you later, Adele."

"Here's Wendy."

I hung up before Wendy came on.

Josh headed for the door. Ryan was already there.

"You have no idea. They're geolocating your phone. They're coming."

Ryan shouted.

"Dude! Take out your SIM card. What are you wait-ing for?"

I turned off my phone, took out the SIM card, and slipped it into my wallet.

Allie looked confused.

"Your mother's coming?"

"Her people. I'm sorry. I really have to go."

I said, "Wendy and Kurt. They're fine."

"You have no idea."

Allie Rice looked alarmed.

"Wait a minute. Are these people dangerous?"

I glanced at Josh, the glance saying stop.

"No, they run errands for his mother."

Josh held the door.

"Let's go. Please. Before they get here."

Allie said, "This is very weird."

We hustled to the street and I pointed at my car.

"With me."

"What about my car?"

"Ryan can take it."

Ryan said, "I'm in my car."

"Then leave it. Get in my car or I'll keep you here until Wendy or whatever Wendy sends arrives."

Josh frowned at my car.

"It's kinda small."

"In."

Ryan said, "What about me?"

"Go home."

Josh said, "I'll call."

Josh climbed into the shotgun bucket like a man stepping into boiling oil.

I pulled away and drove east.

"Can they actually locate a phone or were you being dramatic?"

"Welcome to my life."

I drove for five minutes and pulled over outside a taco stand. Prepaid burner phones and battery packs were stashed behind my seat. I got one powered up and called Pike. He didn't recognize the incoming number so he didn't answer. I left a message.

"I'm on this number now."

I dropped the burner between my legs and pulled away.

Josh said, "This is bullshit. Where are you taking me?"

"To the Batcave."

"Dude. Seriously."

I turned into the parking entrance of the first large medical building I saw, took a ticket at the gate, and circled deeper and deeper until we reached the bottom of the parking garage. Josh realized what I was doing and grinned like a kid.

"The Batcave. Brilliant."

Five levels of concrete and steel made a good cave. I put the SIM card in my phone, powered up, and transferred my contact list to the burner. When the burner was set, I pulled the card and we headed back to the surface. The exit gate wanted eighteen dollars to let us leave.

I said, "You owe me eighteen bucks."

Josh was enjoying himself.

"I'll pay you twenty if you let me drive."

"Not a chance."

We emerged from beneath the building and headed into the city.

49

Josh watched the sky with a hand shielding his eyes.

I said, "C'mon. It can't be this bad."

"It's worse."

He tried to slump low enough to rest his head, but he'd run out of room. The bright sky made him squint.

"I should've taken my sunglasses. They're in my car."

"Check the glove box. Might be an old pair."

He dug through the glove box and found a pair of Wayfarers. He cleaned the lenses with his shirt, put them on, and showed me.

"The eighties. Livin' in a river of darkness."

I laughed.

"Looking good, Sonny."

"I'm a man of the streets."

He turned to see behind us, but couldn't turn far.

"Could we put up the top?"

I pulled over, lifted the top, and latched it into place. Now he looked squished.

I said, "Better?"

"Livin' the dream. If you're helping, take me downtown."

"What's downtown?"

"Richter. I'm going to stuff his face with my mic and confront him. Cut his reaction into the show and humiliate him."

I couldn't tell if he was serious or not.

"Get real. You'll be arrested."

"This is the show. *In Your Face with Josh Shoe*. I'm going to get in his face and expose him to the entire world. That's how you beat powerful people."

"Let's deal with the evidence you have. An Attorney needs to review your recordings."

"They speak for themselves. I don't need an Attorney."

"Who was present when you recorded Rachel?"

"Me and Rachel. What's your point?"

"The D.A. will want to establish she wasn't threatened or induced to say it."

"I didn't induce her! She wanted to go on record. It was her idea."

"These aren't sworn depositions taken under oath before an officer. This is a prostitute saying she's slept with famous people. It'll play great on your podcast, but the D.A. will need corroboration. Same for Allie. Corroboration. Did the pilots see money change hands? The ground crew?"

"This is bullshit."

"It isn't bullshit. What you think is evidence and actual evidence aren't the same. I'm trying to help."

"Okay. So help. I'm waiting."

I thought about it. I wasn't sure if I could help him or not.

"How specific did she get?"

"I told you. Times, dates, and places. Specific. She knew what she was doing. She wanted to get these people."

"Why?"

Josh hesitated.

He shook his head like he didn't quite understand, but he was telling me what he knew.

"Rachel went to one of Locke's little parties. Meaning Richter, only it was Locke who paid her. She'd screw guys they wanted to be in business with or get favors from. That kind of thing."

"I know how it works."

"Richter made a deal to kill a low-cost housing project so this guy could get the property cheap and make a mint building an entertainment center. Rachel hated it. She hated them for it. They actually doomed people to live on the street."

"Is this on the tape?"

"Yeah."

"She names them? She gives the dates?"

"Yeah. Some resort out in the desert."

I saw how it might work.

"If the people she names can be placed where she claims they were on the dates she says they were there, her statements will have credibility."

"Uh-huh."

"Corroborating testimony would help. Someone else who was present or has knowledge of it."

He lapsed into silence.

I said, "Meredith Birch?"

"No way. She didn't trust Meredith. She even kinda hated Meredith. Meredith made money off Locke."

Kimberly Laird had told me the same.

"Have you met Rachel's friend Kimmie?"

"The girl from Visalia?"

"That's right. They grew up together."

Josh changed position and looked interested.

"Twice, I think. At the opening and the first time I interviewed her. We did a pornstar show. Kimmie came with her. Why?"

"What you said about Rachel not trusting Meredith. She didn't. Rachel used Kimmie as her safety."

His lips pooched as he remembered.

"Rachel mentioned this on the pornstar show."

"Not in so many words, but she did, and Kimmie confirmed it. She might be able to corroborate some of Rachel's statements."

"You heard the pornstar show?"

"I did."

"What'd you think?"

He looked hopeful.

I said, "I heard both the Skylar shows. Tell you the truth, I thought they'd be stupid. They weren't. You were better than I expected, Josh, and that's on me, not you. I enjoyed them. You made good shows."

He made a small smile and seemed pleased.

"My father was the last and only person to expect excellence of me. He gave up when I was nine."

"Must be painful."

"When people expect mediocrity, they're surprised when I prove them wrong."

He slid the Wayfarers down his nose and peered over the frames.

"And I always prove them wrong."

He slid the Wayfarers back into place, faced forward, and grinned.

"Are you hungry?"

"I could eat."

We stopped for burritos and then we went to find Kimmie Laird.

50

Kimberly had canceled her appointments for the remainder of the week. The receptionist at Stennis apologized and asked if I'd like to schedule with another stylist. I hung up, dialed Kimberly's cell, and found her at home. She sounded as lost as yesterday's kiss, but she agreed to see us.

I lowered the phone and cautioned Josh.

"So you know, they were a couple."

"A couple couple? Rachel didn't mention having a partner."

"Point is, she's in pain. Be sensitive."

Kimberly lived in a tiny courtyard apartment in Mar Vista, not far from the I10–405 interchange. The building was a featureless, two-story stucco box surrounding a concrete courtyard. A massive royal palm was centered in the courtyard, standing tall above the building on a heavy, gray trunk thicker than three elephant legs. We found Kimberly's ground-floor apartment hidden behind the palm.

Kimberly looked empty when she opened the door. Her eyes seemed lost in gray caves, and she probably hadn't slept. She wore pink tights with a beige stain at the knee and a pale blue T-shirt cropped below her breasts. Her feet were bare.

I said, "I'm sorry about Rachel."

"You warned me."

She went to the couch and pulled up her feet.

The furnishings in her tiny living room were scant. The couch was the only furniture available for seating, so I took a chair from the dining table. Josh remained by the door, as if he felt uncomfortable being with this woman and her grief.

I said, "Remember Josh Schumacher?"

Josh said, "We've met. I'm Josh Shoe."

"I remember. Hey."

"Hey."

"Those were good shows. Rach made everyone listen."

Josh seemed uncertain how to respond.

I said, "How'd you hear?"

"Online. Then people called. Now everybody's talking about it, but nobody knows what happened."

"Maybe you can help us find out."

"I don't know anything."

"You were her safety. You know things no one else knows."

Kimberly shook her head, as incredulous now as she was before.

"It can't be Grady. She hasn't seen him in almost a month and she was *fine*."

Josh came closer.

"She saw him more recently than you think."

"She would've told me. She always tells me."

Josh knelt, making himself smaller.

"She was helping me with a special podcast I'm putting together. Did she tell you about it?"

A tiny line appeared above her nose.

"What kind of podcast?"

"About her life and stuff. About Grady Locke and what she used to do for him. And his boss."

"I know what they did. They fucked."

"Besides that."

She glanced from Josh to me.

"What's going on?"

I said, "Josh has the recording. We'd like to play it. Rachel can tell you herself."

Kimberly unfolded her legs.

"Okay, sure. I'd love to hear it."

Josh took a small speaker from his pack, connected his phone, and selected the track. It was long, the track about Grady Locke.

Josh said, "Here we go."

Thirty seconds after Rachel began, Kimberly sobbed and covered her face. Josh paused the playback, and I brought her a glass of water from the kitchen. She pulled herself together and went to the bathroom. When she returned, we started from the beginning. This time Kimberly Laird didn't cry. Kimberly seemed confused at first, but when Rachel described Horton Tarly delivering a bucket of cash she took a single sharp breath. She listened intently as Rachel described the texts between Locke and Tarly, and the things she'd done after. When the track finally ended, Kimberly looked at Josh and wet her lips.

"Is this real?"

Josh sounded surprised.

"You don't believe this was Rachel?"

"No, no, it's Rachel, but—I dunno, she didn't tell me any of this. Did it even happen? Was she acting?"

Josh stared at me. I gave him a head shrug. You see? We needed more.

I said, "I believe Rachel is telling us exactly what happened. She discovered a pay-to-play bribery operation involving Sanford Richter, Grady Locke, Horton Tarly, and others."

Kimberly's eyes were turning pink. She blinked faster and faster.

"So he killed her?"

"Someone killed her, Kimberly. I can't say Grady Locke personally killed her, but Locke and his associates can't afford to be discovered. They'd lose everything."

Josh nodded, trying to encourage her.

"You've known about her escort work for a long time. You were her safety. She mentioned you on my show."

"So what? I loved that girl."

"You loved her, but right now you doubted her. You think she might be acting."

"I know, I know, I'm sorry, but it's just so crazy."

Josh edged closer, still encouraging.

"I get it. I hear you."

He nodded toward me.

"Elvis says we need to corroborate what Rachel says or the bastards who killed her will get away. This means we need people to confirm what—"

Kimberly interrupted.

"I know what corroboration means. I get it."

I said, "Josh has other recordings. Rachel names clients and the places where they met. If you remember any of these things, it would corroborate her statements."

Josh said, "Want to hear the track again?"

Kimberly Laird slashed the air. Angry.

"I don't need to hear it. I know everyone she was with. I can corroborate everything she says about the escort business."

I hesitated. She needed to understand what we were asking.

"Nobody wants you to lie. If you're caught in a lie, no one will believe Rachel."

Kimberly pushed off the couch.

"I don't need to lie. I have proof."

She stalked into her bedroom. A drawer opened, a drawer closed, and Kimberly Laird stalked angrily back to the couch.

She showed us the proof.

51

Kimberly opened a monthly planner the size of a magazine, and held it out. A month was divided between two facing pages with a square for each day. Two of the squares contained cramped, handwritten notes.

"She'd say, I'm meeting so-and-so downtown at the InterContinental at ten in room twenty-eight-fifty-two, and I'll leave by midnight. Well, c'mon. I needed to know this stuff in case something happened, so I wrote it here."

"You kept notes?"

"Not at first, but yeah."

Josh craned his head to read what she'd written.

"I'd love to interview you. This would be great for the show."

Kimberly closed the planner.

"That will absolutely never happen."

I said, "Whatever you want. May I see?"

I sat beside her and flipped through a couple of pages.

The planner covered the latest calendar year. Most of the day squares were blank. Kimberly's notes appeared only on the days Rachel escorted. Her notes filled an entire square for some dates. The entries for other dates showed only a name, a place, and times. I asked why the difference.

"When she booked a date, I needed to know who she was meeting and where and how long she expected to be there. After, she'd tell me about it, and I thought it'd be good to remember certain things, like whether she liked the guy or he smelled weird or whatever. If the guy was an asshole, she didn't want to see him again, so I wrote it down."

I found the notes she recorded for Rachel's most recent date. *Grady, his place, 9 in, 12 out, THE STUPID VIEW.*

"What's the stupid view?"

"What she said on the tape. Grady made a big deal about his view every time she went to his loft. He did it again, so I made the note. She didn't mention a bucket of money or I would've put it down. Not that I would've forgotten."

I flipped through more months. Rachel had escorted five or six times during some months, and two or three times during others. The entries all looked similar except for a two-day weekend date outlined in a starburst of angry red lines. The squares were packed with names and notes. Locke, Richter, Tarly, Castillo, and others I didn't know. Kimberly's printing was so small the notes were difficult to read. *Golf sux, JK ass, what happened?*

I said, "What happened?"

Kimberly pursed her lips and seemed unhappy.

"I put that for me, not her. Something happened. She came back weird."

Rachel had accompanied Grady Locke to a golf resort in Palm Desert fourteen weeks before she disappeared. She drove out with Grady on a Saturday morning, and returned alone Sunday night. She'd been hired as a date for an urban planner named Jackson Karch. Also in attendance were Richter, Tarly, A. O. Castillo, an environmental lobbyist named Dave Reiman, and two other female escorts.

Josh turned the book and stared at her entry.

"Palm Desert. That's where she heard Richter make the homeless deal."

Kimberly nodded.

"She hated it. I mean, who knew she even gave a damn, but she just came back angry and down. Golf sucked, Grady sucked, everyone sucked. She didn't even go home. She stayed with me for three days."

I said, "Was she scared to go home?"

"She was just—"

Josh said, "Dealing."

"We drank wine and talked about Visalia. Rach *never* talks about Visalia, but she had this whole maudlin thing on, the shit we did in high school, her family, her mother. Her mom went kinda nuts after Rachel left. She drank a lot. She left Visalia. Rachel wanted to know if she'd driven her mother crazy. It was weird."

Kimberly shrugged, like she still couldn't figure out why Rachel wanted to talk about Visalia.

"Then she felt better and went home. I drew fire around it."

"How long have you been keeping notes?"

Kimberly laughed, but it was rueful and sad.

"I have five more calendars like this."

"Six years."

Her eyes reddened again.

"I didn't do this because I enjoyed it. I hated her being an escort. I was scared something would happen."

"May I see the others?"

She left without a word and returned with five more planners.

"You can look, but you can't have them."

Josh said, "Can I photograph some of the pages?"

"No."

I said, "Looking's fine. Thank you."

Josh bugged his eyes at me.

"Pictures would be better. I could post them on my site."

"Let's start with looking."

Kimberly and I paged through the planners together. Josh looked on, but mostly fidgeted. I searched for specific names and events, made notes, and kept a running tally. Grady Locke hired Rachel thirty-two times, seventeen times as a date for himself, and the remainder for others. I copied their names, dates, and locations. A. O. Castillo's name appeared three times, including the golf resort, all arranged by Grady Locke. Dick Felt appeared as Rachel's date twice, which were also paid for by the Sandman's flunky-in-chief, Grady Locke. I wondered if Locke had charged her services to a city expense account. The city auditors would have a field day.

Rachel had not provided escort services to Sanford Richter or Chow Wan Li, but Richter was present at seven events she attended with others. Chow had been present with Richter and Tarly at three.

I said, "Why did you list people who weren't her dates?"

"'Cause she mentioned them. We always talked about her dates. Not the sex part, unless it was funny, but the fun part. Some dude took her to a party once, and she got to hang out with these rock stars and actors. They're in my notes. You'll see."

A memory book.

Horton Tarly's name appeared seven times. At the most recent three, Rachel had been someone else's date at an event where Tarly was present, like the golf resort. But the first four times his name appeared, Rachel had been his date. Grady Locke arranged their first three dates. Tarly had arranged and paid for their fourth and final date himself. The notes for each date were a curious mix. *Nice. Whiny. TTM. Scared. ughGL.*

I said, "What's TTM?"

She scrunched her face, trying to remember.

"Oh, wow. Lemme think."

I prompted her.

"Horton Tarly. Locke's brother-in-law."

"I know, I know. Talks too much. He didn't like being

in business with his brother-in-law. The way they did business made him nervous. All he did was whine about it."

"Grady Locke."

"Yeah."

Rachel had met Horton at the Biltmore Hotel for all four of their dates. They met for the fourth and final time at eight p.m. on a Tuesday night. A tiny flower was drawn in red ink beside the time-and-place details, and three notes were written in blue. *Sweet guy. Sad. 2M.*

I asked Kimberly about the notes.

"Two-M means too married. He felt guilty for cheating on his wife. He got scared Rachel might say something and his wife would find out, so he wanted to stop seeing her."

"Rachel."

"Yeah. So he booked a date to apologize and make sure they were cool."

"He bought a date to apologize."

"Rachel thought it was sweet. Kinda pathetic, but sweet. He didn't want to hurt her feelings. He didn't want to hurt his wife or his kids. See the flower I drew? He gave her a rose."

Josh leaned toward her so far I thought he might fall. His eyes were pleading.

"Kimberly, you are golden. Please. A short interview about you and Rachel would make my year."

Kimberly glanced away and shrugged.

"I'll think about it."

"If you don't want to use your name, I won't use your name. I'll change your voice, if you want."

"I'm considering it."

I thought about where we were and what we had. Nothing in the planners linked Locke or his associates to Rachel's death. None of the notes indicated Rachel had been threatened. But if established as fact, her notes showed Richter and Locke influencing city officials and others with illegal gifts and benefits. The names, dates, and locations would have to be checked. The workload would be enormous.

I said, "Kimberly."

She looked at me.

I said, "The police should have this. They need it."

Josh lumbered to his feet and waved his arms.

"Uh-uh! When I finish. I'm blowing the whistle on that sonofabitch, not them."

Kimberly didn't look at him, and neither did I. She glanced past me and pulled her fingers the way she had when I met her.

She said, "You're right. I know you're right."

Josh stalked to the door and back.

"This isn't fair. Rachel wanted *me* to do it. She could've gone to the police, but she came to *me*."

I looked at him.

"It's bigger now, Josh. It's murder."

Kimberly said, "What should I do? Just call the police?"

"You don't have to do anything. I'll set it up with a detective I know. His name is Poitras. He'll probably come see you. He's a good guy."

"Will I be arrested?"

"No."

"So I just wait?"

"Whatever you want. I'll give him your cell."

Josh said, "The least you can do is give me an interview."

Kimberly rolled her eyes.

"Okay."

I flipped back to the early dates she'd had with Horton Tarly while Josh set up his gear. The little rose she'd drawn didn't look like a rose, but it was still a rose.

Josh began the interview. His questions focused on their friendship, Kimberly's dislike of the escort business, and Kimberly's role as Rachel's safety.

Grady Locke had provided an escort to his own sister's husband. A man among men, for sure. A champion turd. This was likely Grady's way of enticing his brother-in-law to cooperate with Chow Wan Li, and Horton had, but he hadn't liked it. Just as he'd felt guilty for cheating on his wife, he came to feel guilty for signing on with Chow and Locke.

An idea nibbled at blurry shapes I couldn't quite see. The shapes became Tarly and Locke and a woman between them. The idea grew.

I said, "Kimberly."

Josh shouted.

"Please! I'm recording!"

"Would it be okay if I photographed the Tarly pages? I won't photograph anything else. Only the Tarly."

"Sure. Why not? The whole world will know."

Their interview only took eight or nine minutes, but Josh was pleased. I snapped shots of the planner pages with Tarly's entries and made sure they were in focus and readable. Then we packed up, thanked her, and went to the door. Josh stepped out, but I stopped in the door and gave her a card.

"I'll set it up with my friend. If you get nervous, or want to talk, call me."

She stared at the card.

"I don't know what to do. She was my life. She's never not been in my life."

"You're going to help catch the people who killed her."

"I hope so."

I said, "Kimberly. If anyone ever gives you trouble, anyone, about anything, call me."

She took a single step back, and her eyes grew pink.

"I miss her so much."

Kimberly Laird closed the door.

I didn't look at Josh. I didn't say anything. I walked away and went to my car. He followed, and we got in.

52

Josh squeezed into the seat and shifted to get comfortable. Buckling the belt was a wrestling match.

He talked while he struggled.

"Listen. Interpersonal people skills are not my strength. I get weird, and something about me puts people off. I can be a jackass. You've been very supportive, not telling Wendy where I was. I wanted to thank you. I appreciate it. So thanks."

"I'm going to call my cop friend about Kimberly. You should talk to him. Tell him what you know and let him hear Rachel."

He was shaking his head before I finished.

"No way. I'm not ready."

"They're investigating her murder."

"I know who murdered her. When I finish my show the whole world will know."

My head was starting to ache.

"How long will this take?"

"Not long. I need to get with Ryan, cut it together, balance the levels, mix it, make it sound pretty—"

I stopped him.

"You can't go to your bungalow."

"Why?"

"They're watching it."

"So have your cop friend arrest them. I need my equipment."

The ache was spreading to my eyes.

I took out my phone and showed him pictures of Donghai An Bo and the scarecrow.

"They work for Chow Wan Li, the president of Crystal Future Hospitality Group."

"Tarly's partner."

"The male is wanted for two homicides in Shanghai by the People's Police. I don't have a name for the woman. They planted surveillance devices in your bungalow. They'll know if you go."

Josh seemed puzzled.

"What kind of surveillance devices?"

My head was pounding.

"Chinese surveillance devices. I don't know. They're bugs. They bugged your house."

Josh said, "Interesting to know."

Interesting.

"Here's the deal. They don't know where you are or what you're doing. They want to know where you are. They want to stop you from doing whatever you're doing. So you can't go back to your bungalow."

Josh frowned. He squinted at me, worked his lips, and looked away. He finally looked back and nodded.

"You might as well take me to my mom's. I'll have Ryan bring over his stuff. We'll cut it in my old bedroom like we used to."

"And you'll share it with the police when it's finished?"

"We'll see. I need to get my car."

"Wendy can get it."

He dug out his phone to call Ryan and I called Wendy.

"Guess who."

"You jackass. What did you do with him?"

"I'm bringing him home."

She was saying something when I hung up.

It took forty-two minutes to reach Toluca Lake. Ryan was sitting on the lawn with a backpack. Josh perked up when he saw him.

"Ryan's here with his stuff."

Adele and Wendy came out of the house as we parked. Kurt appeared in the drive, as immaculate as ever. Adele put her fists on her hips and shouted so loud the neighbors could hear.

"Damnit, boy, this will not do!"

Josh muttered as we got out of the car.

"You see what she's like?"

"I'll touch base soon. The police are looking for Chow and his thugs. You won't have to sweat it much longer."

"I'm not sweating it."

Josh gestured at Wendy and Kurt and the people with earbuds.

"Look at this crew. We have more security than ten presidents."

Maybe they did.

Adele continued watching us with her fists on her hips and seemed to be getting impatient.

"What did your parents do, exactly?"

Josh seemed surprised by the question. He glanced at his mother before he answered.

"They reverse-engineered alien technology. Gravity amplifiers and phase generators, mostly. From crashed UFOs."

I stared. Josh stared back. Then he grinned.

"Dude, really? I gotta finish my show."

He and Ryan walked up the drive as I climbed into my car. I had been hired to find Joshua Schumacher. I had. My work was done. The job was finished. Mission accomplished. I should have felt a sense of closure but I felt apprehensive and tired. I looked at my phone, but the looking was wishful thinking. Lucy hadn't called. I wondered what I'd find at my home. Maybe I wouldn't go home. Starting the car was beyond me, so maybe I'd just sit outside Adele Schumacher's house for the next few years. Then I wouldn't have to deal with what I'd find at my house.

I remembered Kimmie Laird. In the time it took to bring Josh home I had totally forgotten. Maybe my brain was fried. I called Lou Poitras.

"Your boy Philburn came through. Dana hit him with a vehicle six-pack and he fingered the sedan. Good work."

"What about the people shots?"

"Meant nothing, but the vehicle hit helped. Turns out LWL filed a stolen vehicle report two days ago."

"Only two? How coincidental."

"They've begun covering their tracks, which is bad. If we could find the vehicle, we can check it for the girl's DNA."

I thought about it.

"Can I call back in a few?"

"Yeah."

I plugged the SIM back into my regular phone and called Jon Stone. He answered in his usual charming way.

"Sorry, I'm out of handouts."

"If you're able to locate the meatball's car, I need to know where it is."

"How much will you pay?"

"Could you be a bigger prick?"

"I work for money. You should try it."

"Two home plate tickets in the Dodgers Dugout Club for the Astros."

"Done. Get ready to copy and stand by."

Ninety seconds later he recited a set of GPS coordinates in the City of Industry.

I said, "Can't you just give me an address?"

"I could, but it's you."

Stone hung up. A prick to the end.

I called Lou.

"Write this down."

He stopped me when I started reading off numbers.

"What the hell?"

"Copy and read it back."

I gave him the numbers twice.

He said, "What is this?"

"The sedan."

Lou didn't respond.

I said, "Don't ask. I have more."

I told him about Kimberly Laird and sent the photos of her notes.

"Kimberly acted as Rachel's safety when Rachel worked as an escort. She kept meticulous notes of Rachel's dates for years."

"What am I looking at?"

"Her notes. Rachel's johns, when and where they met, everything. Most of this isn't connected to Locke and Richter, but Locke's name shows up again and again. Locke used her as a reward or an inducement. Richter shows up, too."

"I'm not seeing it."

"I only sent four pages. Kimberly has six years of pages."

Lou was silent for a moment.

"Is she willing to cooperate?"

"Yes."

I gave him Kimberly's address and number and told him the reason I'd sent the pages. I explained Tarly's misgivings and guilt, his growing resentment toward his brother-in-law, and his fear of their illegal schemes. Lou didn't speak until I finished.

He said, "This guy will flip."

"I think he will."

"This girl, Kimberly, will she come in?"

"Go to her. Call first. I told her you'd call. She's expecting your call now."

"I'll call. Hey—"

"You're welcome."

I let Kimmie know I'd spoken with Poitras. She sounded as if she was having second thoughts, so I told her a funny story about Poitras and me and we talked for a while. She was fine.

I successfully delayed going home for twenty-two minutes. I had stalled long enough. I started the car and drove toward my future.

53

My little house was dark when it came into view. Lucy's car was out front. I parked and touched its hood. Cold. Detectives detect. They'd been home for a while.

The kitchen door was open when I came around the corner in the carport. Lucy stood framed in the doorway. I stopped and she stood and neither of us spoke. The Corvette's hot engine creaked and popped. We looked at each other until she went back into the kitchen and I followed and closed the door.

Ben was on the couch in the living room reading something on his phone. He looked up.

"Hey. Where you been?"

I said, "Working. How about you?"

"San Diego. Traffic sucked."

I glanced at Lucy. She was leaning against the counter with her arms crossed. She looked pensive.

"There's leftover jambalaya if you'd like. I didn't know, so I didn't heat it."

I said, "San Diego."

"It was nice to drive."

Ben called from the couch.

"Kill me first next time. Mom called a guy a shithead and flipped people off."

Lucy's nostrils flared.

"We should step outside."

I followed her out and closed the slider. The air held a fresh coolness but wasn't chill. It was nice. Lucy went to the rail and gazed at the canyon. I started to make a crack about drones but didn't. I stood next to her and gazed out at the canyon like her, but we probably didn't see the same thing.

"Sorry I left in the middle of the night, with just the note. It wasn't a comment on us. It couldn't be helped."

She faced me and seemed to study me. She looked from my left eye to my right eye. She looked at my hair and my mouth and my face as if she were mapping me. Her eyes went to my chest and back up to me.

She said, "I thought about us a lot today."

She touched my arm with her fingertips.

"About us and me and how it's been. You're right. This has never been about you and how you live your life, or Ben, not really. It's been about me. About my fears and my need to control things nobody can control."

"I wasn't trying to lay blame or justify, neither one."

"You said many right things and they break my heart."

She looked at Ben, inside on the couch.

"He's grown. He'll be gone in a year."

Her eyes returned to me.

"All this time, I could have had you. We could have been together. I didn't allow it."

"Luce."

"I can't change what's done. I can't pretend I won't worry. I can't swear I won't kill you if you get hurt. I can't even promise I won't dump you."

She moved closer and placed her hands on my chest.

"But I don't want to be just friends anymore. I want to see you every day. I want to touch you every day and talk every day and know we have a future with—"

I kissed her. I held her in a way I hadn't held her in years and kissed her and felt tears leak from my eyes as I kissed her.

Ben opened the slider.

"When are we going to eat?"

Lucy said, "Go inside and close the door."

The slider slammed and Lucy stepped back.

"I mean it. If you'll risk being us, I'll risk being us. Because I want us to be us."

I tipped my head toward the house.

"Want to shack up?"

"Here's what I want."

She took a small velvet box from her right pants pocket and showed me the contents. Two thin gold bands stood side by side, one larger, one smaller.

I said, "Are you asking me to marry you?"

"I'm not asking anything. The rings express a com-

mitment. If we call them something else one day, an en-
gagement band, a wedding ring—"

She studied me carefully.

"We'll cross that bridge when we come to it."

I stared at the bands. They were simple plain rings
of yellow gold. I touched the smaller, then the larger. I
pulled the larger band from its place in the box and fit it
onto my finger.

Lucy said, "Okay. Now I want to shack up."

"How about we eat before we shack up?"

"A sure sign of age."

I fitted the smaller ring onto her finger.

"Looks good."

"I know. I've practiced wearing it."

We grinned at each other some more.

"I've missed this, me and you, like this."

She nodded.

"Yes. It's been too long. Much too long."

"Look forward, not back. Always move forward."

"Yes, Joe."

We just stood there, holding each other and grinning
at each other. It was great.

Ben tapped the glass. When we looked, he spread his
arms wide, beseeching, telling us he was starving.

Lucy laughed.

"I guess we should feed him."

"And me. I'll need fuel."

My phone buzzed as we stepped through the door.
The call window showed WVANN. I showed Lucy.

"The Schumachers."

I didn't want to answer, but I answered.

Wendy Vann said, "Here's Adele."

Lucy and Ben were watching as Adele came on the line. She was upset and shouting.

"He's gone. They took Ryan's car and their things and he left. Please! Bring him home again. Please, Mr. Cole. Before he gets himself killed."

Lucy touched my arm and whispered.

She said, "Go. If you get shot I'll kill you."

54

In Your Face with Josh Shoe

Josh and Ryan studied Rachel's apartment house from Ryan's car. The dark-haired bitch was on the lawn reading a magazine.

Ryan said, "She'll see you."

"Doesn't matter."

"What if it's gone?"

"We'll figure it out."

Josh knew Ryan was nervous. Josh was nervous, too, but Rachel had trusted him and believed in him and, in a way, made him believe he mattered. He looked at Ryan.

"I can drop you off after. You don't have to do this."

"It's my show, too."

"In your face."

"Bringing the truth—"

"—the mainstream media hides."

They'd been saying some version of this to each other since seventh grade.

Josh piled out of Ryan's car and powered up the walk,

carrying a bright green duffel rolled like a log. The girl on the lawn saw him coming and smirked. She always smirked when she saw him and made cracks about his size, so Josh knew it was coming.

"The police were here. Skylar's dead. Somebody killed her."

"Yeah, I know."

"Did you roll over and crush her?"

"Where's your friend, looking for a better roommate?"

The crime scene tape was gone. The police had finished their work and left Rachel's place to her family and the landlord. Josh knew what he wanted and hoped it hadn't been moved. He unrolled the duffel, covered the sidelight, and broke the glass. He reached through and groped around until he found the locks.

The place had been cratered like Cole said. Her art supplies and tables and cabinets had been tipped over, but her canvases remained stacked along the walls. The police probably felt they weren't relevant. Morons.

The shelves lined with cans of spray paint were intact. A bright gold key and a small paper name tag hung by a purple string from a hook on the right side of the cabinet. Josh had seen her hang the key on the hook when she told him about Locke and Richter and the cash she'd found in Grady Locke's loft. She'd also found a spare key to Locke's loft. This was the key. The card contained the entry code to Locke's building.

Josh took the key and searched through the canvases. Some were finished paintings and others were works in progress. When he found the painting he wanted, he fitted it into the supersize duffel and left.

The dark-haired girl was gone.

They loaded the canvas into Ryan's backseat and blasted off for downtown L.A. Ryan snickered as he raced the close of business hours.

Ryan said, "This is so frickin' cool."

Josh miked up and decided what he wanted to say.

"No talking."

Ryan gave a thumbs-up. Josh hit the record button.

"This is Josh Shoe. Stand back, sit down, and stick around as I get . . . In Your Face."

Ryan shook his head.

"No, *no*. Way too seventies. Do it again."

Josh thought some more and started again.

"Josh Shoe, recording on the streets of Los Angeles. Rachel Bohlen, who was also known as Skylar Lawless, was murdered while seeking the truth. The voice you're about to hear is that of Skylar herself, who will tell you how she came to be murdered. She will name the people who killed her. Listen."

Josh stopped.

"Well?"

"Not bad. A little long, but we can use it as a lead-in to her first clip."

Josh checked the time.

"Drive faster."

The Sandman's council website listed three offices, one in City Hall and two in Richter's district. Grady Locke, being Richter's chief of staff, would have offices at each location. When they were ten minutes from Grady Locke's loft, Josh phoned the City Hall office, identified himself as a segment producer for CNN, and asked to speak with Locke. Two transfers later, a deputy communications director told him Locke could be reached at their district office. This was good news. With Locke on the far side of town, they had more time.

They parked in an alley across from Locke's building. Josh miked up again as Ryan rigged his phone to a selfie stick. In a flash of inspiration, Ryan had suggested they post video clips as an extra on their website. Josh thought the idea was brilliant.

They piled out of the car and lined up a shot of Josh with the entry to Locke's building visible over his shoulder. Ryan handled the camera.

Ryan said, "Action."

Josh began.

"Grady Locke, one of the men responsible for Skylar's death, lives in the building behind me. Nice place. This is what years of corruption will buy. This is where Skylar Lawless discovered the truth. C'mon. Let's see what we find."

Cut.

Ryan beamed.

"Awesome."

"Watch for the dude. If he comes home, call fast."

Ryan would stay below watching for Locke.

Josh shouldered the duffel, hustled across the street, and entered Grady Locke's building using the code he'd gotten from Rachel. The elevator took him up to Locke's floor. He let himself in with the key and deactivated the alarm by entering the entry code. Being stupid, Locke used the same number for both. Rachel had laughed when she told him.

Rachel had told so many stories about Locke and his view, Josh went from room to room, checking the views from windows the size of walls. Josh didn't think the views were all that special. Maybe they looked better at night.

Rachel had returned to the loft at least twice after Tarly delivered the bucket of Kentucky Fried cash. Each time she returned, she found the bucket in the same place and still filled with cash. Rachel couldn't understand it, but Josh understood. These people weren't hedge fund managers and Harvard MBAs running multinational transaction scams. Richter might be an elected councilman and Locke his chief of staff, but they were as clueless as car thieves. They didn't have offshore accounts. They hid their take under kibble in their garages. They didn't know what else to do with it, which was why Richter made Locke keep his money and why Locke let it pile up. They couldn't deposit it and couldn't spend too much without drawing attention. Every cash criminal had the same problem.

Josh found the bucket exactly where Rachel told him. He photographed it in place, stacked the cash on the counter, and moved on. He found cash in the freezer and in the cabinets above the double-wide fridge. He found more cash in the pantry, in the utility closet, behind the bar, and taped beneath the dining table. He documented each location.

The mother lode was stashed in Locke's walk-in closet. Josh was so tickled by the man's small-time stupidity he set up the selfie stick, checked his mic, and gave a tour.

"I am now in Grady Locke's home, in his bedroom, and entering his closet. You have to see this."

Josh adjusted the camera to show a row of sport coats and suits and shoeboxes lining the shelf above. Holding the camera steady while using his free hand to reveal what he'd found in the jackets was difficult.

"Look at this. He's hidden cash in the pockets. Packs of cash. In the outside pockets, in the inside pockets. Look at this. And here—"

Josh lifted down a shoebox and tipped off the top.

"In the shoeboxes. The man has cash hidden everywhere. This is Josh Shoe, reporting the truth, in Grady Locke's closet."

Cut.

Time check. Bad.

Josh stripped cash from the jackets and boxes and found more with Locke's socks and underwear. He photographed the cash where he found it, carried everything to the bed, and photographed it again. He slid the painting from the duffel, filled the duffel with cash, and carried everything out to the bar.

Josh leaned Rachel's painting against the wall above the bar. He adjusted it just so, making sure Locke would see it as soon as he entered. Then he shouldered the duffel and went to the door.

Josh set the alarm and watched its digital clock count down from sixty to zero. The system allowed people sixty seconds to leave. You could open the door as much as you liked while the clock counted down, but once the clock hit zero, the alarm would go off.

Three.

Two.

One.

Zero.

Josh opened the door and hurried to the elevator.

55

Grady Locke

Grady Locke nodded with concerned understanding as the three women spoke. They had come to his office to ask for NO DOGS ALLOWED signs at the public fields used by their youth soccer league. People brought dogs to chase balls and play, the dogs shit everywhere, and nobody picked it up. So when the kids arrived for soccer, the coaches and moms had to pick up shit. It wasn't fair.

Grady nodded in thoughtful agreement.

"Well, that isn't right."

This sort of request was usually handled by a constituent services deputy. But these women ran a league fielding two hundred forty-six children, which meant four hundred ninety-two parents who lived and voted in Sanford Richter's district.

Grady pursed his lips, pretending to give the issue serious consideration.

"Tell you what, how about we start with signage saying owners must pick up the poop. There's an ordinance on the books. If they don't pick up their dogs' poop, they'll be fined. We'll give it a couple of months, see if the problem abates. If it doesn't, I'll have animal control make the rounds, and ding a few people with tickets. If all else fails, we'll ban the dogs. Sound good?"

Two of the three went along, but mostly because they found Grady charming.

Grady posed for the inevitable pictures, the women were ushered away, and he called out to his assistant.

"What's next?"

"Dentist at four. Cancel or keep it?"

The call sheet on his computer showed nine calls he still had to make.

"Is the sheet current?"

"It is. Cancel or keep? You need to leave if you're going."

"Cancel."

Grady was opening a bottle of water when his cell phone rang. The incoming caller ID surprised him. This was the first time his security company had called.

"Grady Locke speaking."

"Mr. Locke, we show an alert at your residence. Are you at the residence now, sir?"

"I'm at my office. What's going on?"

"We're seeing a breach at your front door. Would you like us to send the police?"

Locke's knees felt weak. His head buzzed and a heavy pressure filled his chest.

Maybe the system malfunctioned.

Maybe this was a false alarm.

"No. No, that's okay. Sorry. I had something delivered. My neighbor was supposed to let the guys in and set the alarm when they finished, but she probably just screwed up the code. I'll take care of it."

"So you do not want a police response?"

"No, sir. Sorry for the trouble."

Grady Locke lowered his phone. The buzzing grew until it filled his head like cotton. He touched his desk to keep his balance.

Grady grabbed his jacket and keys and staggered out of his office. He was so frightened he almost fell, but he ran past his assistant and rushed for his car.

56

Elvis Cole

Adele put Wendy Vann on the line and Wendy reported what they knew.

"He's not a prisoner, Cole. He told us they were going to Ryan's house. They didn't."

"How long have they been gone?"

"Coming up on eighty minutes."

Eighty minutes didn't seem so long.

"Maybe they stopped for a hamburger."

"They were going to Ryan's for dinner. His mother was making enchiladas. Turns out she wasn't. Ryan told her he'd be eating here. And guess what? Josh is not answering his phone and neither is Ryan."

Anyone else, two grown men going out for a couple of hours wouldn't be an issue. But this wasn't anyone else. Anyone else wouldn't have a target on his back.

Lucy and Ben were watching. Welcome back to Elvisland.

"They know not to go to the bungalow."

"Options?"

Josh had named plenty of options. They were bad.

"Whose car did they take?"

"Ryan's."

"Can you give me the make and model? Tag if you have it."

"Stand by."

I grabbed a pen, copied the information, and called Lou Poitras.

"He may be on his way to confront Richter or Locke."

Lou said, "Waitaminute. Is this kid armed? Does he intend to harm these people?"

"Not Josh. He wants to expose them."

"Like, run up behind them and pull down their pants?"

"They've been hunting him for a reason, Lou. He's been smart enough to hide, but he wants to take them on. He specifically told me he wants to confront Richter."

"Which means he's turned stupid."

"Richter's the whale."

"I can issue a BOLO to the area cars around City Hall and Richter's district offices. Best I can do tonight."

I put away the phone.

"I'd better head downtown."

Lucy lifted her hand so I'd see the ring. She smiled.

"I'll have something warm waiting."

Ben returned to the couch.

"I'm already grossed out. Just saying."

I let myself out and called Jon Stone as I drove down the hill.

"I should charge for answering your calls."

"The bungalow. Is your device still active?"

"It'll cost to find out."

"Stop it. Has anyone entered?"

"No. When the bug triggers, I receive an alert. No alerts, no entry. What's up?"

I explained about Josh.

"He didn't go home. Sorry."

"Me, too."

I called Joe Pike next.

"Meet me at City Hall. This kid is going to get himself killed."

I drove to City Hall as fast as I could, but it was over by the time I arrived.

57
—

Sanford Richter

Council member, 16th District
City Hall

Richter left his office on the fourth floor of City Hall for a statement release in Meeting Room A down the corridor. His communications director and a senior advisor tagged along, their only purpose being the appearance of power. Powerful people couldn't shit without staff.

The advisor said, "You look good. Remember to stand up straight."

"Mm."

A statement release was a photo op. Richter and the other members would basically congratulate each other for working to improve the L.A. water system in an environmentally responsible way, funding a senior meal delivery service, and leading the effort to plug the city's potholes. The members would smile, shake hands, and pose with their arms over each other's shoulders like the greatest friends in the world. Richter hated them both. Kathi Lee was a lunatic who felt everyone should go vegan and sleep under windmills, and Carlos Reed was a self-righteous roadblock who refused to cut deals. Five or six reporters would be on hand, the whole thing would last about five minutes, and Richter could return to his office.

The meeting room was ahead on the right. Four or five people waited outside the door, bullshitting with each other or checking their phones. Couple of faces looked familiar. Kathi Lee came out of her office, crossed the hall, and entered the meeting room. No staff. An airhead.

A huge, shabby young man stepped away from the others and hurried toward him. Reporter. He carried a microphone and a couple of recorders hung from his shoulder. He held out the microphone when he arrived.

"Josh Shoe. Podcast news."

Richter didn't stop.

"Save it for the room."

The kid walked with him.

"What's your reaction to the funds found in Grady Locke's home?"

Richter stopped so quickly his advisor bumped into him. He studied the kid and the microphone.

"I don't know what you're talking about."

Richter plowed forward again, wanting to get away. The kid walked with him and kept shoving the microphone at him.

"The one hundred sixty-two thousand dollars found in his home. Mr. Locke says the money belongs to you."

"Bullshit."

Richter kept moving. You had to keep moving when these assholes accosted you. Scrambled possibilities spun through his head on a panicked whirlwind. Grady had suffered a heart attack while he was screwing one of his whores. Paramedics discovered the money. The police arrived.

Richter glared at his comms director.

"Do something."

The kid shoved the microphone closer.

"Is it true you accepted bribes from the Crystal Future Hospitality Group and others to approve their development projects?"

Everyone in the hall heard him. Richter's comms director tried to push between Richter and the kid, but the kid was as large as a truck.

"Mr. Locke claims Rachel Bohlen was murdered to protect your arrangement with Chow Wan Li and others. Is it true?"

"Fuck you. This is bullshit."

His advisor shouted.

"Security!"

The kid stayed with him like a bulldog clamped to his neck.

"Mr. Locke admitted these things, Councilman. He confessed. Is he telling the truth?"

Mother*fucker*!

Sanford Richter escaped into the nearest office. His comms director and advisor clambered in behind him, slammed the door, and held it. Sanford heard them babbling but paid no attention.

Grady Locke.

Fucking Grady.

Richter clawed the phone from his pocket, shaking so badly he dropped it. He was scared to call Locke, and scared not to call. Grady could be with the police. He might be cutting a deal and fucking Richter and the rest of them.

Fucking Grady.

Fucking Chow and the simp, Tarly.

Richter had to find out.

He made the call.

58

Grady Locke

The door to his loft looked fine. It wasn't cracked, battered, or knocked off its hinges. The knob and dead bolt face appeared undamaged and the jamb wasn't split. Locke feared he might find it open, but the door was closed, locked, and perfectly normal.

Only the alarm had gone off.

Front door breach.

Grady unlocked the dead bolt, unlocked the knob, and stepped inside. He made sure the alarm was off, then closed and locked the door before turning to enter the living room.

Grady stopped, and listened for movement.

He heard nothing, so he continued. He moved deeper into the cavernous living room, listening harder, and suddenly froze in place as if struck by a bolt of cold lightning.

A painting stood against the wall above the bar. One of those things Skylar did. A graphic art painting three feet tall and a foot and a half wide filled with text messages. Grady recognized it the instant he saw it. He had seen the messages before.

Grady Locke murmured, "Holy shit."

The phone was his. Initials identified the person he'd been texting. HT. Horton Tarly.

HT: Dropping off 60K. C U in 5.

GL: WTF??? Now???

HT: SR said send it. Chow sent it. WTF?

GL: UR early.

HT: This btw SR and Chow. U want it
or not?

HT: I'm here.

HT: GRADY!! I'm standing here with a
bucket of CASH. Buzz me in.

GL: ok

They knew about the paintings. They knew about the photographs she'd taken of his texts. Grady knew the cash was gone even before he opened the cabinets. The empty chicken bucket sat upside down on the bar.

He lifted down the painting, placed it on the dining

table, and ran to his bedroom. He ran past the open night-stands and into the closet. Gone. Open shoeboxes littered the floor. The sock drawer and underwear drawers hung open. His sport coats and suit jackets were a jumbled heap. He dropped to his knees and frantically checked the pockets. Gone. His cut and Richter's cut, gone.

Grady Locke wanted to cry. He wanted to turn off the lights, curl up in the darkness, and hide in his closet forever. He wanted to run. He could hide in the Klondike. He saw himself escaping to South America or Fiji or Ireland or Pago Pago in the South Pacific. He had a few thousand in the bank. He could cash out now, drive directly to Tijuana International, buy a ticket to Belize, and figure out what to do next.

Grady got up and went to the kitchen. The storm in his head was easing. He was scared, but the worst of the panic had passed. He needed to call Sanford and Horton, but he wanted to check something first. The lofts were owned separately, but the building itself, the entry, and the pool on the roof were maintained by the company that owned the building. A feature built into the deal was security cameras in the entry. People who bought a loft were given an app and code allowing them to see who was buzzing for entry. Grady rarely used it, so it took him a couple of minutes to figure out how it worked.

He did.

He opened the entry video feed and found three different views. Two were exterior views of the call box where visitors buzzed for entry, a wide shot of the area, and a closer angle from above whoever stood at the box. The third view revealed the interior of the entry from the elevator to the entry door.

Grady played around until he found time marks allowing him to scroll back and forth in time.

He did.

Not many people came and went. Almost all of them lived in the building, so Grady recognized them.

Then Grady saw a big hulk of a man he didn't recognize. The man stepped from the elevator with a duffel slung from his shoulder and exited the building.

Grady scrolled back farther, and saw the man enter. This time he carried the duffel like a suitcase. The big green bag had a different shape now, more rectangular and sharp, as if something inside had corners.

Grady found the best view and paused the image.

This fucker was huge.

Grady had never seen him, but Chow had described him. Skylar's friend. Josh something. Chow had been trying to find him. And now the fucker had stolen their money and dropped off the painting. The painting was a threat.

Grady was staring at Josh when his cell rang. He took the call.

Richter said, "We need to talk, but not on the phone. Let's meet."

Grady said, "Her friend came by. The big guy. He took stuff. All of it. Everything."

"Jesus, Grady, what'd you do, stand by sucking your thumb?"

"Wasn't here. He left something, too. I'll tell you when I see you."

"Sonofabitch."

"Tell Chow. Chow was supposed to handle it."

"The big guy. Shit, it was him. He was here. He actually came *here*. He said things."

"Tell Chow. We have a problem, Sanford. A really big problem. And Chow has a problem, too."

"Let's meet. Come now. The usual place."

Grady ended the call. He stared at Skylar's painting and didn't know what to do with it. He carried it into his bedroom, slid it under the bed, and left to meet Richter.

He would destroy it later if the painting didn't destroy him first. The nasty bitch probably made copies.

59

—

Wendy Vann

Wendy followed Kurt into the cottage. The cottage was where Adele tinkered with her toys and projects and puzzles, which were mostly number fields generated by AI systems. The cottage also housed the secured communications gear and SatLink transceivers used by the staff, as well as their duty gear and equipment. Kurt pulled a black hard-shell Pelican case from a shelf.

"Someone was in the bug box."

The bug box held their countersurveillance equipment. They swept Adele's home, garage, property, and vehicles for listening devices every three days. If she went to a restaurant or a friend's home, they swept. If she went shopping, they swept. Packages and mail and deliveries, swept.

Kurt opened the case. Each device had its place in a thick layer of foam. One foam cutout was empty.

Wendy looked at Kurt.

"Shit."

Kurt said, "Uh-huh."

Josh.

60

Elvis Cole

The L.A. City Hall sat across from LAPD headquarters, catty-corner to the Los Angeles Times building, and surrounded by courts, jails, and credit unions. It was a three-tiered building with a wide, heavy base and a central tower topped by an aircraft beacon named for Charles Lindbergh. Counting the beacon, City Hall stood thirty-two stories tall. A seismic retrofit strengthened the structure to withstand a magnitude 8.2 earthquake. The building's strength was evident in its broad, burly stance. City Hall looked like a bulldog guarding a bone.

The surrounding streets were clogged with end-of-the-day traffic. Pike reached the scene first. He was prowling past the Spring Street entrance when I arrived and waved me over. He'd already been up to the fourth floor where Richter and Locke had offices.

"Here and gone. Made a scene with Richter outside his office."

"Was he arrested?"

"Not that kind of scene. Stuck a mic in Richter's face and shouted questions. Deps thought he was a journalist."

"So they let him go."

"First Amendment. Richter's people tried to laugh it off, but the deps are still buzzing about it."

"About Josh or the questions?"

"Stuff about cash being found in Locke's home. About pay-for-play deals and Skylar Lawless. Everyone heard. Other members. Reporters."

Josh was planting seeds. Giving the reporters something to ponder.

"When was he here?"

"An hour ago. Maybe a little more."

I thought it through and tried to decide what he'd do next. Josh had dropped his bomb and put them on notice. This was a stunt he could pull with public figures like Richter or Locke, but visiting Chow or Tarly might put him face-to-face with the meatball. Josh was smart enough to know this or maybe he wasn't. Maybe he was so invested in bringing them down he'd lost sight of the danger.

Pike said, "What do we do?"

I dialed his burner again.

Voice mail.

I shook my head.

"I don't know. I don't know what he's doing. He could be anywhere."

I was thinking up options when Jon Stone called. I signaled Pike as I answered.

"Is he at the bungalow?"

"Something weird happened."

"Is it him?"

"I don't know."

"You have eyes in there."

"I do. Did. I'm getting nothing. A blank."

"It's him."

"It's probably a system malfunction."

I lowered my phone and looked at Pike.

"Let's go."

61

Donghai An Bo

Bo was enjoying an early meal of two double-dipped lamb sandwiches at Philippe The Original. Bo was alone, seated on a stool at a communal counter and anticipating a baked apple and a large slice of lemon cream pie. Donghai An Bo was hungry. Earlier, he had lifted weights and climbed stairs for two hours at the Crystal Emperor's most excellent gym. The weights were heavy. His calorie deficit was large.

His cell phone, resting on the counter near his plate, buzzed. The woman. Mr. Chow's annoying assistant for his American operations.

Bo finished chewing and swallowed before he answered.

"Yes?"

"The devices you planted have failed."

This woman knew nothing, yet believed she knew everything.

"What do you see?"

"I see nothing. They have failed."

"Both devices have not failed."

"They have failed. They have failed at exactly the same time. This suggests they have been caused to fail. Go now. I'll send the others. Go."

Donghai An Bo immediately left the restaurant. He would eat more later. After.

62

Josh Shoe

They drove slowly past the bungalows, looking for the people who'd been watching for Josh. Ryan's head bobbed and swiveled, trying to see everywhere at once.

"I don't see anyone, but I don't know."

Josh didn't see squat. An army could be behind a car and Josh wouldn't see them. Josh wanted to drop the podcast that night while Richter and Locke were scrambling to cover their asses, but it was too dark. Josh felt queasy.

Josh said, "I don't know."

This was their third trip past the bungalows. Ryan slowed to a stop at the base of the steps.

"Maybe they're inside. I'd shit."

"Yeah."

Josh peered up the steps.

"The old man is home. I see his lights. The lady in the pink. The new kids. People are here."

"People is good."

"Yeah."

Josh turned to his friend.

"What do you want to do?"

"I don't know. I'm kinda scared."

Josh nodded.

"Yeah. This is fucked up."

"What if the jammer doesn't work?"

"It works. Everything they have works. My dad probably built it."

"Did he show you how to use it?"

Josh was getting pissed.

"It's intuitive. You power up, you're good to go. It works."

Josh pulled out the box and pressed a little switch. The box vibrated silently for half a second.

"There. Good to go."

"How do you know it's on?"

"It vibrated."

Ryan nodded. He peered up the steps into the darkness and nodded again.

"I vote yes."

"We'll work really fast. No screwing around."

"Hell yeah. In your face."

Ryan parked and they hustled up the steps with their gear. They hooked up the desktop and keyboard quickly, but powering up the equipment took forever. Josh had built most of the podcast in his car, working between his phone and laptop to piece together audio files, bumpers, and clips from Rachel's tracks. He'd even recorded intros, outros, and narrative with the windows up and his sleeping bag over his head, but the files had to be transferred and the transfers took time.

Ryan said, "We're hot."

Josh pulled on a headset and they divided the work. Ryan built the web page and Josh cut the podcast. His hands shook and sweat dripped from his scalp, but he wanted to finish and get the hell out.

First thing he did was upload the videos and pix from Grady Locke's loft and the vid of his confrontation with Sanford Richter. The Richter vid jerked and jumped, but the jumpiness gave it a gonzo cinema verité feel. Ryan copied the vids and posted them. Josh added the pix Skylar had taken of Grady Locke's phone and the art she had made of his text exchanges with Tarly. Ryan locked the page. Done. Josh split audio tracks from the vids, dropped the clips into the body of the podcast, and listened to the result. The show was rough, but coming together.

Josh took off his headset. His hair was slick and grimy with sweat.

Ryan said, "What do you think?"

"It's good."

"It's better than good, dude. It's insane. And these vids?"

"Your idea."

Ryan laughed.

"Holy crap, we're awesome."

Josh grinned. Then he laughed and they both laughed. They laughed so hard Josh didn't hear the front door open. They didn't know anyone was in the bungalow until a burly man Josh knew as Donghai An Bo stood in the doorway pointing a black pistol at them.

Ryan jumped to his feet.

"Shit!"

Josh startled as if he'd been struck by lightning.

Bo looked slowly from Josh to Ryan to Josh. He gestured with the pistol.

"Get your fat ass up. Quickly now."

Josh felt his crotch grow warm as his bladder emptied. His entire body trembled.

"No. I'm not going anywhere. Go away. I'm not going with you."

Bo seemed to consider this. Then he pointed the pistol at Ryan and fired.

Josh shrieked.

Ryan staggered and made a gulping sound. He looked down at the dark stain spreading on his shirt like a blossoming rose. He looked at Bo. He looked at Josh. He fell into the table and slipped to the floor.

Josh pushed to his feet.

"Ry!"

Donghai An Bo hit him in the face with the pistol. Bo hit him hard three times in the head and the face. Josh covered his head but Bo kept hitting him. Then Bo twisted Josh's hand behind his back and shoved him into the hall and through the bungalow and away from his dying best and only friend.

63

Elvis Cole

pulled up beside Ryan's car and left my Corvette in the street. Pike hadn't arrived, but I wasn't going to wait. The bungalows were peaceful. The street was quiet. I was at the bottom of the steps when I heard a muffled crack like a baseball bat striking cardboard. A smarter person would have waited. A wiser person would have set up an ambush at the bottom of the steps. A better person would have gotten there in time. None of those people helped.

A few windows were lit from within, but the steps were unlighted and dark. I drew my gun and ran toward the sound as Leon Karsey shouted.

"What's going on over there?"

When Karsey shouted, a man passed through the light from Karsey's window. The man was watching Karsey's and the other bungalows in case a neighbor tried to interfere. I angled to his blind side and crept through heavy shadows to the corner of Josh's bungalow. His door was open and the lights were on.

Karsey shouted again.

"I'm warnin' ya!"

Karsey's outside light snapped on, washing the space between his and Josh's bungalow with a dim ochre glow. The man outside stepped back and raised a stubby black automatic toward Karsey's door, ready to cut loose if Karsey came out. The man had a bum nose and club ears and the build of a mixed martial arts welterweight.

A shadow moved in Josh's door and the gardener with the ponytail stepped out. He carried a stubby black automatic like the welterweight. Maybe stubby black automatics were the new thing and I had missed the memo.

Josh came out next with the meatball riding his back. Josh's head drooped and dark smears striped his face like fingerpaint. The meatball seemed to be holding him up and steering. I didn't see Ryan.

The gardener started down the steps and saw me. He stopped right in front of me and dropped into a clumsy crouch. The welterweight and the meatball saw me and the welterweight ran forward three steps and covered me with his gun. The three bad guys were focused on me. They thought I might spring into action and watched for a sudden wrong move. They were looking at me, so they didn't see Joe Pike slip past the blue bungalow above. Pike was a silent shadow within the dark.

The meatball spoke quietly but firmly.

"Lower your weapon and walk away. Walk away and I'll let you leave."

Pike's shadow moved again. Coming closer.

The welterweight edged to the side.

If they wanted Josh dead they would've killed him. They wanted to know what Rachel had given him and they wanted it back. They wanted Josh to tell them what those things were, and produce them, and they wanted to destroy them. They would ask him the way they asked Rachel and they wouldn't stop asking until they believed Josh had told them the truth. He'd be dead by then.

I said, "Leave Mr. Schumacher and walk away. Walk now and I'll let you go."

Leon Karsey's shout echoed from his window.

"Meatball fuck! Last warning!"

Josh finally saw me. His drooping head came up. His eyes were vague and glassy and maybe it took him a moment to recognize me, but he met my eyes and did.

I said, "It's going to be okay."

No one else saw his face change. Veins bulged beneath the blood streaks on his forehead. His eyes shrank into furious knots. His face grew dark and large as if a volcanic pressure was building within him, and then the volcano erupted.

Josh threw himself backward into the meatball with a guttural grunt. He drove himself back, huge legs pushing and pumping, grunting as he pushed, unh-unh-unh. He slammed the meatball into the wall, then bucked and spun like a rhino trying to toss a rider so he could gore him to death.

The gardener and the welterweight hesitated, unsure what to do, then the gardener ran to help his boss and grabbed Josh. Joe Pike flashed from the shadows and hit the welterweight so hard he dropped as if he'd been shot in the head.

I slammed into the gardener's side. The meatball scrambled away, dropped to a knee, and raised his gun. Maybe Josh didn't see it. Maybe he didn't care. He charged forward as I grabbed the meatball's gun and pushed it aside. I was trying to hold on when Josh hit us like a runaway bus. The meatball and I hit the ground together and grappled for the gun. The gardener reappeared beside Josh and slammed him in the head with his pistol. Josh staggered and fell, and Leon Karsey shouted a final time.

"Fucking meatball! I warned you!"

A high-speed rip of automatic-weapon fire lit up his window and thundered across the neighborhood. The meatball flinched. I worked my fingers under the meatball's thumb and strained to pry his thumb off the pistol. I didn't know whether Karsey was firing bullets or blanks or what kind of weapon he had, but the noise was horrendous. The gardener spun toward the sound and fired three fast shots—bapbapbap. I heard the bullets hit Karsey's bungalow as Joe Pike shot the gardener.

Karsey cut loose again, a long chattering light show behind his curtain. I prayed I wouldn't get hit.

The meatball kneed me four fast times and tried to roll away, but I wrapped him up with my legs and held on tight. His thumb began to give. Golden lights swirled and gathered overhead, but I only caught glimpses.

Then Joe Pike blocked the lights. He clubbed the meatball twice with his pistol, cocked his Python, and pressed the muzzle hard into the meatball's ear.

The meatball stopped fighting. His eyes rolled as he looked up to see Pike.

Pike said, "Release your weapon."

The meatball's hand relaxed. I twisted away his pistol and scrambled to my feet. Sirens were coming.

A woman's voice echoed down from above.

"Don't move, Josh. Don't try to get up. We're coming. We're almost there."

Wendy Vann.

I looked up, but saw only lights. I stood and made my way into Josh's bungalow and found Ryan Seborg in their studio. He looked small and pale and younger than he was. He looked like a twelve-year-old.

I said, "Oh, Ryan."

I checked for a pulse. His shirt was a red mop and I knew he was dead, but I checked. I checked twice. I felt his neck and his wrist.

"Aw damn."

I went out to check Josh. Pike was kneeling beside him. His eyes opened and closed, but he seemed hazy. His temple was bleeding badly. I pulled off my shirt, wadded it, and pressed it over the wound. I was scared to press too hard. His skull might be cracked.

Leon Karsey shouted.

"Is that Porky? Porky, you all right?"

Josh's eyes fluttered. They rolled from side to side, but then they focused.

He said, "Ryan."

"I know."

"Ryan's shot."

"I know."

I didn't know what else to say.

"We gotta drop the show. We finished."

We.

"It'll drop. You and Ryan did a fine job."

I patted his shoulder.

He said, "Tonight."

I patted his shoulder again.

"You and Ryan finished."

"Rachel."

"Rachel."

Cars braked hard below. Voices and more cars rolled in. I thought the police had arrived, but Wendy and Kurt double-timed up the steps with the red-haired guy and Wendy 2.0. Kurt had an M-4 rifle slung from his shoulder. He ran to the meatball and Pike stepped away. The bald guy with the earbud ran past Wendy to join Kurt. The bald guy and Wendy 2.0 both carried MP5 submachine guns. Maybe they expected a war. Kurt quick-tied the meatball's hands behind his back, pulled him to his feet, and led him away. I didn't know if the police were down below or even coming. I didn't know where Kurt took him. I never saw the meatball, the gardener, or the welterweight again. I was never asked to testify at their trials.

Leon Karsey shouted.

"Fuck is going on out there?"

Wendy came over and knelt beside Josh. She smiled at him and rested her hand on his chest.

"Hey, Josh. Everything's fine. You're fine."

Josh said, "Ryan."

Wendy glanced up.

I shook my head.

"Inside."

She said, "Holy hell."

Wendy called to the red-haired guy and hurried into Josh's bungalow.

I patted Josh's shoulder.

"Hang in there, bud."

"Ryan."

"You hang in."

I couldn't bring myself to tell him.

Josh's eyes suddenly cleared and he gripped my arm.

"The trunk. Ryan's car. You take it. You. Not the cops. You."

"What's in Ryan's trunk?"

"Proof."

His eyes turned foggy and he moaned.

Karsey came out with a plastic bag filled with ice.

"For his head."

I patted Josh's shoulder again.

Wendy came back and touched me aside.

"You can go. We'll handle everything."

"The police will want a statement."

"We'll take care of it. Thank you. Thank you for this."

Josh said, "Ryan's hurt. Where's Ryan?"

Wendy touched my arm.

"Thank you."

I went back inside to Ryan, found his keys, and walked down the concrete steps past Josh and the others to the street. The steps seemed longer and the street seemed farther away. I transferred the large green duffel to my car and left Ryan's keys on his driver's-side floorboard.

An ambulance arrived a few minutes later. I watched them load Josh into the vehicle. Part of me wanted to follow them to the hospital to make sure he was all right, but I didn't. I drove home to Lucy and Ben. I wanted to be held. Lucy held me. She slept with me in the loft for the first time in years, but it wasn't what you'd think and it wasn't the way we had wanted. I told her about Josh and Ryan and what happened and I cried. Lucy listened and held me as I wept. She pulled me close and held my head to her breasts. I needed to be held. She held me. We held each other.

PART FIVE

The Beekeeper

64

Lucy and I stood at the rail on the deck, gazing into the mottled green bowl of the canyon. Lucy faced the canyon and I snuggled close and held her from behind. They had stayed an extra night and would fly home tomorrow.

Lucy said, "We'll be back in three weeks. Three weeks isn't so bad. It'll go by fast."

"Will you stay the week?"

"Can't. Work. But I'll fly out with him and we'll have the weekend."

I nodded into her hair. We'd have the weekend and she'd fly away.

"Three weeks isn't so bad."

"We're experienced long-distance-relationship veterans."

"Three weeks is nothing. Been there, done that."

She took a slow breath and nodded.

I said, "The rings. May I ask you something?"

"Sure."

"Did you bring them from BR?"

"La Jolla. I bought them when we went to San Diego."

I smiled, but she couldn't see it.

She said, "Do you think this is a mistake?"

"Us?"

"So many things to consider. So many changes ahead. I want to get it right."

I took her shoulders and gently turned her so we faced each other.

"The true mistake would be not trying."

Lucy gazed up at me and made the most lovely smile. Her amber eyes sparkled.

"Yes, Yoda. You are right."

"Are you mocking me?"

"Mocking you I am."

I laughed and we went inside and it was good.

65

Lucy and Ben flew back to Baton Rouge the next morning. After they left for the airport I put away the futon, then stripped the bed and carried the sheets and towels and facecloths to the washer. I got the washer going, put fresh sheets on the bed and cases on the pillows, and made the bed to Sergeant Zim's exacting standards.

Between last night and my making the bed, Josh Schumacher's podcast and episode page dropped. I found out because I had a local TV news channel on while I was washing dishes. I heard Josh's name and ran into the living room to see a shaky video clip of Sanford Richter fending off a mic as Josh's voice asked a question.

"Is it true you accepted bribes from the Crystal Future Hospitality Group and others to approve their development projects?"

The news cut to a clip of Richter on the steps of City Hall as he arrived that morning. Richter chuckled as he answered the reporter's question.

"There is absolutely no truth to these fictions. Absurd. People like this crave attention or have some darker, more sinister motive. Who knows?"

The news cut back to the anchor. A photo of Grady Locke was behind her.

"The councilman's chief of staff, Grady Locke, could not be reached for comment. Join us at noon for updates and more late-breaking news."

I muted the volume and wondered if Josh was watching. I hoped so. Josh hadn't simply dropped the podcast and launched the web page. He sent links and audio files to over one hundred local, state, and national news agencies and included Rachel Bohlen's and Kimberly Laird's unedited audio and video statements.

Mainstream journalists had risen to the bait.

Lou Poitras arrived an hour later. I knew he was coming. I had called him.

He said, "Lemme see."

I carried the bright green duffel down from my loft and opened it on the couch.

Poitras peered inside and made a little hiss.

"How much is here?"

"One hundred sixty-two thousand."

"Where'd he get it?"

"Where he said. Grady Locke's loft. Check his website. You'll see pictures, video, everything."

Poitras stared at the money as if he didn't know what to do with it.

I said, "If you don't want it, I'm happy to keep it."

"Come down later? Make a statement?"

"Sure. Whatever you want."

Over the next three days, I gave statements and answered questions for the L.A. police, the FBI, three D.A.s, and two very polite women who identified themselves as agents from the Defense Intelligence Agency. They asked if I had seen or heard anything unusual at Adele Schumacher's residence. I told them I hadn't.

Six days after the podcast dropped, the *Los Angeles Times* launched a full-scale investigation into Crystal Future Hospitality Group's L.A. building projects, Horton Tarly and LWL, and the pay-to-play allegations against Sanford Richter. Four days later, Horton Tarly cut a deal to testify against Chow Wan Li, Sanford Richter, and his brother-in-law, Grady Locke. Chow Wan Li and his jet had already returned to the PRC. To the best of my knowledge, the woman referred to as the scarecrow was never identified.

Sixteen days after Tarly cut the deal, Grady Locke flipped. In a plea agreement with the U.S. Attorney, Locke acknowledged the murder of Rachel Belle Bohlen and named as conspirators himself, Sanford Richter, and Chow Wan Li. Locke stated he found Rachel Bohlen photographing cash he'd hidden in his bedroom, after which she admitted knowing of his dealings with Richter and had photographed a text exchange between Tarly and himself. Locke stated he asked Richter what they should do and Richter had told him to get rid of her. Richter told him "the Chinaman" would do it. Later that night,

Donghai An Bo and a second Chow employee named Jeffries T. Jordan arrived and took Bohlen away. Jeffries T. Jordan was the ponytailed gardener.

Sanford Richter denied everything and refused to resign from office. He expressed outrage, disdain, and claimed Locke's allegations were vengeful fabrications. His fellow council members unanimously voted to suspend Richter from all council duties pending the ongoing criminal investigation. He was barred from his offices, not allowed to attend council meetings, and his salary was terminated. Richter vowed to fight. He vowed to clear his name and continue serving the fine people of Los Angeles. He said, "The truth is on my side."

66

—

Sanford Richter

anford and his wife, Lily, were reading by the pool at their home in Hancock Park. The home was built in 1918 on almost three-quarters of an acre for one of the most successful Attorneys in Los Angeles at the time. The forty-foot pool was a glittering aquamarine rectangle. The large flat lawn glowed green in the afternoon sun. Sanford and Lily sat side by side with their books on white chaise longues.

Lily said, "I never did like that man. There was always something funny about him, remember I said?"

"You did. I should've listened."

She was talking about Grady Locke.

"How long have you known?"

Sanford sighed and closed his book on a finger. She wasn't going to let him read.

"Three years."

"I can't believe you carried the man for three years. What were you thinking?"

He sighed again and faced her.

"I wanted to help. This business with the drugs, I don't know, it's sad. He agreed to get treatment. He begged me."

"You've always been too soft."

"Let's be honest. He was great at his job. I didn't want to lose him."

"Too soft. I would've fired him the instant I found out."

"In my defense, the erratic behavior started later. I didn't realize how often he used drugs until his behavior changed, the crazy hours, the hyperactivity, the frantic talking, yapyapyapyap. The parties with whores."

"I don't want to hear it. Enough. This will all come out and you'll be fine."

Sanford grunted.

"You think?"

"Yes! This is absurd. And the media? The trash of the earth."

Sanford checked the time.

"The lawyers are coming at one."

The best criminal defense Attorneys in California had taken his case. Chase Wylie and Debra Mitland. Killers.

"I thought it'd be nice to have a little sandwich platter. Some bagels. Some roast beef and turkey. Maybe some pickles and whatnot."

Lily said, "That would be nice."

"Would you handle it, please?"

She frowned at her watch.

"It's eleven forty-five."

"I only now thought of it. With all this on my mind."

"I could call the place over here on Larchmont. Have them put together a tray. They deliver."

"We'll be waiting 'til four and the order won't be right."

"I could run and pick it up, I suppose."

"It would be such a help if you did."

She swung her feet off the longue and stood.

"I'd better get cracking. And you'd better get dressed. Unless they're coming for a swim."

Sanford laughed.

"No swimming today. What's the old saying? Don't swim with sharks."

Lily laughed as she hurried inside to order.

Sanford dog-eared the page to mark his place, wiggled out of his robe, and dove into his pool. He swam to the far end, climbed out, and went inside to dress. He was stepping out of the shower when Lily popped in.

"I'm leaving. I'll be back before one."

"I'll be here."

"What are you going to wear?"

"I dunno. Slacks, sport coat, no tie. Casual."

"Plaid shirt, no jacket."

"No jacket?"

"You're relaxed. Confident men are relaxed men. Plaid, open collar, no tie."

"Plaid is relaxed."

"Yes, sir."

She smiled brightly and left. A helluva woman.

Sanford went with the plaid. Light gray slacks, purple

plaid shirt with the collar open and sleeves rolled. No socks. Sanford admired himself in his dressing room mirror. Lily was right. He was the very picture of relaxed confidence.

He found a white extension cord in one of Lily's dressing table drawers. He wrapped it tightly around his neck, tied it to the bedroom doorknob, and let the white cord take his weight. Lily found his body twenty-eight minutes later, four minutes before his lawyers rang the bell. Lily Richter blamed the media for his death.

67

Elvis Cole

Adele Schumacher invited me to her home for lunch on a warm fall day. We sat on lawn chairs in her backyard, surrounded by roses and zinnias and bees. Wendy was somewhere inside. Kurt sat at the far end of the guesthouse. Maybe they thought I would kidnap her and demand an unseemly ransom.

I said, "Doesn't it get old, having them around all the time?"

Adele laughed.

"I guess somebody's worried I'll spill the beans!"

I said, "Nah, you'd never do that."

She giggled.

"I might for the right price."

I think she was flirting.

Lunch was processed ham, processed American cheese, and mayo on processed white bread. Adele made the sandwiches in her kitchen while we talked and we carried them out on paper plates. I had water. She had full-sugar

Coke from the can. The bees must have smelled it. They'd circle close and she brushed them away.

Adele said, "This young woman, the dead girl, Rachel Bohlen."

"What about her?"

"Were they involved?"

Meaning Rachel and Josh.

"They were friends. If it was more than that, I don't know. You should ask him."

She pooched her lips, thinking. She thought for a while and then she looked at me.

"He blames himself."

Ryan.

"I'll talk to him."

"He's devastated. Poor Ryan. Ryan was such a sweet boy. I don't know. I don't know. I can't recall a time when we didn't have Ryan."

Adele's hands worked the can. Kneading. Twisting. Adele was grieving Ryan, too.

She said, "Now he has no one. Ryan, this girl. I wish he had someone. I worry."

"He's doing his show again. That's something. He changed the name, you know."

She nodded.

"I know! *In Your Face with Josh Shoe and Ryan Seborg.* Isn't that sweet?"

"Ryan would like it."

"Have you heard his shows? They're very good. Josh is quite the good showman."

"You should tell him."

"Oh, I do."

"Corbin should tell him."

"I don't know."

"Yes, you do. Tell Corbin. Tell him to tell Josh how proud he is."

Her eyes filled and she turned toward the bees. She reached out then and rested her hand on my arm.

"I don't think I've been a very good mother."

I covered her hand with mine.

"You're being a good mother now."

She patted my hand and stood.

"I have to see to these bees."

Adele set the plate on her chair and walked past the guesthouse and Kurt and went to the bees. They swarmed and circled around her. I wondered if the bees were making decisions. I wondered what they thought.

Kurt picked up his chair and followed her.

I let myself out and walked down the drive to my car. That afternoon, I called Josh. We made a date for the following Sunday. I picked him up and we visited Ryan Seborg's grave. I didn't say much. This was Josh's time with his friend. After a while Josh told me he was ready and stood. I drove him back to his yellow bungalow and then I went home.

Joe Pike didn't expect to rescue a woman that day. He went to the bank same as anyone goes to the bank, and returned to his Jeep. So when Isabel Roland, the lonely young teller who helped him, steps out of the bank on her way to lunch, Joe is on hand when two men abduct her. Joe chases them down, and the two men are arrested. But instead of putting the drama to rest, the arrests are only the beginning of the trouble for Joe and Izzy.

After posting bail, the two abductors are murdered and Izzy disappears. Pike calls on his friend, Elvis Cole, to help learn the truth. What Elvis uncovers is a twisted family story that involves corporate whistleblowing, huge amounts of cash, the Witness Relocation Program, and a long line of lies. But what of all that did Izzy know? Is she a perpetrator or a victim? And how far will Joe go to find out?

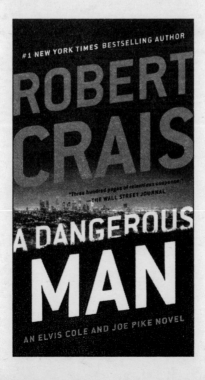

#1 NEW YORK TIMES BESTSELLING AUTHOR

ROBERT CRAIS

"Three hundred pages of relentless suspense."
THE WALL STREET JOURNAL

A DANGEROUS MAN

AN ELVIS COLE AND JOE PIKE NOVEL

Her Family

Debra Sue closed her eyes and listened with all her might. The TV was off, their modest living room was dark, and Ed was sprawled on the couch. Her husband was dead to the world, but his snores were soft as a whisper. When they bought the little house a block from Sunset Boulevard, Ed worried traffic sounds would be intrusive, but they weren't, not really. Debra Sue had grown used to the noise quickly, and found the sounds soothing. She touched her husband's shoulder.

"Let's go to bed, baby. Get up."

Ed lurched awake, eyes wide and blinking.

"What happened?"

"Bedtime. Everything's fine."

Ed's eyes flagged, and he was halfway back to sleep.

"Scared me. Sorry."

"It's late. I'll be right in."

Ed swung his legs off the couch and lumbered into

the hall. She heard him use the bathroom and settle into bed, but Debra Sue didn't move to join him.

She whispered his name.

"Ed."

She said her own name.

"Debra Sue."

She said their daughter's name.

"Isabel."

Debra Sue smiled.

"My family."

Debra Sue finally rose from the chair and moved through their quiet home. She made sure the front and back doors were locked, carefully checked the windows, and turned off the lights in each room. She set the alarm.

The warm night air was rich with the scent of night-blooming jasmine and orange blossoms, along with a trace of fresh paint. They had painted their little home with cheery colors after escrow closed—a bright lemony peach with a pale lime and burgundy trim—and joked that they'd given the place a new-car smell. Ed planted two orange trees in the backyard, but the jasmine had been there, and Debra Sue loved it. The jasmine was a sign. Their little house would be a happy and beautiful home.

Debra Sue turned on the outside lights, and made her way down the hall. She stopped outside Isabel's room when she heard her baby girl singing. Debra Sue stifled a giggle.

Isabel cracked her up.

Isabel was three years old. She was their only child,

though Debra Sue and Ed talked about having another, and an absolute sweetheart. She was sweet, good-natured, and almost always happy.

Debra Sue moved closer, and listened.

La-la-la-LA-la-la.

Debra Sue fought not to laugh. Isabel was lying in her crib, waving her arms in the air, and singing to herself.

La-LA-la-LA.

Debra Sue didn't go in. She didn't want to disturb her daughter, and have to bring Isabel into bed with her and Ed. Right now, undisturbed, Isabel was in a wonderful, beautiful dreamland, imagining whatever fanciful stories happy three-year-old girls imagined.

Debra Sue loved Isabel so much her eyes filled with tears.

"Every day, baby girl. Every day of your life will be as happy as this. Daddy and I will make sure it is."

Debra Sue eased past Isabel's door, and crept to her bedroom. Ed was out cold, and no longer snoring. She brushed her teeth, flossed, and washed her face in the dark, then sat on the edge of their bed.

Debra Sue listened, and heard only the soft, baby-girl melody.

La-la-LA-LA. La-la-LA-LA.

But now Debra Sue didn't smile. She eased open her nightstand drawer and studied the black 9mm Sig Sauer pistol. Ed's nightstand contained an identical pistol. They had bought the guns, and learned to shoot. They practiced.

Debra Sue shut the drawer, and lay down beside her

husband. She touched his hand. She sighed like a ghost in the darkness.

"Mommy and Daddy will keep you safe."

Debra Sue listened for something she prayed never to hear, and finally fell asleep.

1

Isabel Roland

hree tellers were working the morning Isabel Roland was kidnapped. Clark Davos, a sweet guy whose third baby had just been born; Dana Chin, who was funny and wore fabulous shoes; and Isabel, the youngest teller on duty. Isabel began working at the bank a little over a year ago, three months before her mother died. Five customers were in line, but more customers entered the bank every few seconds.

Mr. Ahbuti wanted bills in exchange for sixteen rolls of nickels, twelve rolls of dimes, and a bag filled with quarters. As Isabel ran coins through a counter, her cell phone buzzed with a text from her gardener. Sprinkler problems. Isabel felt sick. The little house she inherited from her mother was driving her crazy. The sprinklers, a leaky roof over the porch, roots in the pipes because of a stupid pepper tree, the ancient range that made scary popping noises every time she turned on the left front burner. Always a new problem, and problems cost money.

Isabel had grown up in the house, and loved the old place, but her modest salary wasn't enough to keep it.

Isabel closed her eyes.

Why did you have to die?

Abigail George touched her arm, startling her. Abigail was the assistant branch manager.

"I need you to take an early lunch. Break at eleven, okay?"

Isabel had punched in at nine. It was now only ten forty-one, and Izzy had eaten an Egg McMuffin and hash browns on her way into work. She felt like a bloated whale.

"But it's almost eleven now. I just ate."

Abigail smiled at Mr. Ahbuti, and lowered her voice.

"Clark has to leave early. The baby again."

They both glanced at Clark. His baby had come early, and his wife wasn't doing so well.

Abigail shrugged apologetically.

"I'm sorry. Eleven, okay? *Please?*"

Abigail squeezed her arm, and hurried away.

Isabel gave Mr. Ahbuti his cash, and called for the next customer when Dana hissed from the adjoining station.

"*Iz.*"

Dana tipped her head toward the door and mouthed the words.

"*It's him.*"

Ms. Kleinman reached Izzy's window as the man joined the line. He was tall and dark, with ropey arms, a strong neck, and lean cheeks. Every time he came in, Dana went into heat.

"*Iz.*"

Dana finished with her customer, and whispered again.

"Studburger."

"Stop."

"Double meat. Extra sauce."

"Shh!"

Ms. Kleinman made a one-hundred-dollar cash withdrawal. As Izzy processed the transaction, she snuck glances at the man. Gray sweatshirt with the sleeves cut off, faded jeans tight on his thighs, and dark glasses masking his eyes. Isabel stared at the bright red arrows tattooed high on his arms. She wanted to touch them.

Dana whispered.

"Manmeat on a stick."

Isabel counted out twenties.

As Ms. Kleinman walked away, Dana whispered again.

"Finger-lickin' good."

Izzy cut her off by calling the next customer.

"Next, please."

The man was now third in line. Dana called for a customer, and the man was now second. Clark called, and the man was hers.

"*Iz.*"

Dana.

"Ask him out."

"Sh!"

"You know you want to. Do it!"

Izzy said, "Next, please."

Dana hissed, "Do it!"

When he reached her window, Izzy smiled brightly.

"Good morning. How may I help you?"

He laid out three checks and a deposit slip. Two of the checks were made payable to Joe Pike, and the third to cash. They totaled a considerable amount.

Joe Pike said, "For deposit."

"You're Mr. Pike?"

She knew his name, and he probably knew she knew. He came in every three or four weeks.

"I've helped you before."

He nodded, but offered no other response. He didn't seem friendly or unfriendly. He didn't seem interested or uninterested. She couldn't read his expression.

Isabel fed the checks through a scanner. She wanted to say something clever, but felt stupid and awkward.

"And how's your day so far?"

"Good."

"It's such a pretty day, and here I am stuck in the bank."

Pike nodded.

"You're so tan, I'll bet you're outside a lot."

"Some."

Nods and one-word answers. He clearly wasn't interested. Isabel entered the transaction into her terminal, and gave him the deposit receipt.

The man said, "Thank you."

He walked away, and Isabel felt embarrassed, as if his lack of interest proved she was worthless.

"*Iz!*"

Dana leered across the divider.

"I saw you talking!"

"He thanked me. Saying thanks isn't talking."

"He never talks. He thinks you're *hot*."

"He didn't even see me."

"Shut *up*! He *wants* you!"

If only.

Isabel wondered if she could scrape together two hundred dollars for a new garden timer.

She glanced at her watch. Ten fifty-two. Eight minutes from a lunch she didn't want, and an event that would change her life.

2

Karbo and Bender

Karbo and Bender missed her at home by ten minutes. Materials found inside gave them her place of employment, so now they waited at a meter six blocks from a bank near the Miracle Mile.

Karbo slumped in the passenger seat, sipping a café mocha.

"Ever kidnap anyone?"

Bender glanced away. Bender was the driver. Karbo was the smile. They had worked for Hicks before, but never together. Karbo and Bender met for the first time at four that morning outside a strip mall in Burbank. They would part in approximately two hours, and never meet again.

Karbo said, "Sorry. My mistake."

No questions allowed. They knew what they were supposed to do, how they were supposed to do it, and what was expected. Hicks prepped his people.

Bender gestured behind them.

"Here he comes."

Karbo lowered his window.

Hicks was a hard, pale dude in his forties. Nice-looking, not a giant, but broader than average. Nonthreatening, if you didn't look close. A nasty edge lurked in his eyes, but he hid it well. Karbo and Bender were nice-looking, nonthreatening guys, too. Especially Karbo.

Hicks had come from the bank.

"She's a teller. Figure on making the grab at lunch."

Bender arched his eyebrows.

"Why lunch?"

"People eat lunch. Employees park in back, but with all these little cafés, no way she'll drive. She'll probably exit the front, and give you a shot. You get the shot, take it."

Bender's eyebrows kissed in a frown.

"Wouldn't it make sense to wait at her house, grab her when she gets home?"

Hicks glanced left and right, relaxed, just looking around.

"Time is an issue. You want out, say so, and I'll get someone else."

Karbo changed the subject. He didn't want out. He wanted the money.

"I have a question. What if she goes out the back?"

"If she exits the rear, you're out of the play. If she isn't alone, say she comes out with a friend, you're out of the play. Maybe she won't even come out. Maybe she brought a sandwich. No way to know, right? You have one job, and only the one."

Karbo said, "The front."

People would be watching the rear, for sure, but this was how Hicks operated. Compartmentalization. Minimum information. If an element got popped, they had nothing to give. Karbo admired the tough, precise way Hicks did business.

Hicks rested his hand on the door.

"Picture."

Hicks had given them a five-by-seven photograph of a twenty-two-year-old woman. Having changed the play, he didn't want the picture in their possession. The picture was evidence.

Bender returned the picture, and Hicks offered a final look.

"Burn her face into your brains. We can't have a mistake."

A high school photo printed off the internet showed a young woman with short dark hair, glasses, and a smile with a crooked incisor.

Karbo said, "Burned."

Bender cleared his throat. Karbo sensed the man thought they were moving too fast, but the money was huge, and their involvement would end in minutes.

Bender said, "What's she wearing?"

"Pink shirt. Kinda dull, not bright. A pink shirt over a tan skirt. I couldn't see her shoes."

Hicks tucked the picture into his jacket.

"She'll be easy to spot, but if anything looks weird, drive away. Anyone with her, drive away. Am I clear?"

Karbo and Bender nodded.

"Clear."

"Go."

Hicks walked away and Bender eased from the curb.

Their ride was a dark gray Buick SUV owned by a leasing company in La Verne, California. Late model, low miles, the full option package. They had picked up the Buick at 4:22 that morning, specifically for use in the crime. After they delivered the girl, they would hand off the Buick, pick up their cars and money, and go their separate ways.

Karbo thought Bender was having second thoughts, but Bender surprised him.

"Beautiful day, isn't it? Lovely, lovely day."

Karbo studied the man for a moment.

"Yeah."

"Gorgeous. A perfect day."

Bender hadn't said ten words all morning, even when they were searching the woman's house. Karbo figured he was nervous.

"I know we're not supposed to ask, but you've worked gigs before?"

Bender tapped the blinker and changed lanes.

"Three or four."

"This will be easy. Hicks's gigs are always easy."

"Snatching a person in front of a bank in broad daylight can't make the top of the Easy list."

"You didn't have to say yes. You should've backed out."

"Right."

"I don't want to work with someone I can't trust."

"I'm concerned, is all. He's making this up on the fly."

"A lot of these gigs, this is what happens."

"You're not concerned? You don't see the risk here?"

Karbo saw the risk. He also saw the reward.

"Look at this face."

Karbo grinned and fingered his dimples.

"I'll have her in the car in ten seconds tops. No big scene, I promise. Five minutes later, she's out of our lives. What could be easier?"

"You may be a moron."

Karbo shrugged.

"True, but you get to stay in the car. I'm the guy who gets out."

Bender finally nodded.

"You're right. And if anything looks weird, we drive away."

"Damned right we do. Fast."

Bender seemed to relax, and found a spot at a meter with an eyes-forward view of the bank.

Karbo liked the location. A commercial street lined with single-story storefronts two blocks south of Olympic. A straight shot to the freeway if needed. The girl would turn toward or away from them when she left the bank, and either was fine. A lot of people were out and about, but this shouldn't matter if Karbo did his job quickly and well.

Karbo said, "You were right."

"About?"

"The day. It's a beautiful day in the neighborhood."

My name is Percival Montmount, Jr., and I have my father's eyes. My eyes are aquamarine like his, set in a thin-boned, eagle-nosed face. But the similarity is more than a physical trait: I have my father's *eyes*. The night he died, Dad materialized at my bedside, extended a ghost arm, and opened his fingers to reveal a pair of glowing spirit eyes. He gently held the back of my head and inserted the magical orbs into my sockets.

I blinked once . . . darkness. Twice . . . light. Dad waved goodbye as he faded away.

I wept, not knowing whether the tears were mine or my father's.

TRIBES

ARTHUR SLADE

Published by
Dell Laurel-Leaf
an imprint of
Random House Children's Books
a division of Random House, Inc.
New York

Visit us on the Web! www.randomhouse.com/teens

Educators and librarians, for a variety of teaching tools, visit us at
www.randomhouse.com/teachers

ISBN: 0-440-22975-8

RL: 6.2

Reprinted by arrangement with Wendy Lamb Books

Printed in the United States of America

June 2004

10 9 8 7 6 5 4 3 2 1

OPM

For Scott Treimel, who believed from the beginning

My thanks to Brenda Baker, Vincent Sakowski and Edna
Alford for their helpful comments on earlier versions of
the manuscript; to the Saskatchewan Arts Board and
the Canada Council for financial support; to Wendy Lamb
for her insight; and to Lucy, Darwin and Rush
for their inspiration.

MY FATHER

My father, Percival Montmount, died in the Congo after lunch on a Sunday three years ago. I was fourteen. He was an anthropologist, then living with a tribe of blue-skinned pygmies who gathered fruits from the fronds of midget trees. We have a picture of Dad between a pygmy and a plastic-looking tree. Dad smiles, showing white, perfect teeth. The pygmy looks into the camera, hypnotized.

My dad died the next day. The photo was given to us by a *National Geographic* photographer, a blond hominid named Cindy Mozkowski. She called him a saint, a brilliant ethnographer, and said the pygmies had truly respected Percival of the Shining Forehead.

Ms. Mozkowski wept big tears that slid slowly down her cheeks and landed on our doorstep. Mom wouldn't let her in the house because she had brought bad news. Next it would be bad luck.

Here's how my dad ascended to the department of Heaven reserved for anthropologists. He was lying on his cot one muggy summer day, outlining an essay titled "Why a Pygmy Refers to Himself as We." A tsetse fly stole

1 ⭐

through the netting and into Dad's tent. It landed on his arm. He brushed it away. It buzzed over to his exposed toe. He wiggled, and the fly shot into the air. Undaunted, it circled around and around and compound-eyeballed Dad's neck. It touched down and bit.

That evening black Azazel sickness conquered my father. The pygmies buried him standing up. He was facing the sunrise so that he could be carried off to the next world. It was their custom.

It's what Dad wanted. It was in his will.

MY FATHER'S EYES

My name is Percival Montmount, Jr., and I have my father's eyes. My eyes are aquamarine like his, set in a thin-boned, eagle-nosed face. But the similarity is more than a physical trait: I have my father's *eyes*. The night he died, Dad materialized at my bedside, extended a ghost arm, and opened his fingers to reveal a pair of glowing spirit eyes. He gently held the back of my head and inserted the magical orbs into my sockets.

I blinked once . . . darkness. Twice . . . light. Dad waved goodbye as he faded away.

I wept, not knowing whether the tears were mine or my father's.

FIELD JOURNAL

Items to carry on the person:
Reliable pen
Backup pen
Field study notebook
Open mind

one

THE BEGINNING

Let's begin at the beginning. About 3.5 million years ago, a short, hairy hominid called *Australopithecus afarensis* walked on two legs, thus distinguishing himself from his peers. His hobbies were swinging a club and throwing stones, precursors to baseball. His offspring gave birth to taller, less hairy anthropoids, who in their turn birthed more. As the millennia passed, these hominids mutated, shed their body hair, perfected the use of their opposable thumbs and strained the boundaries of their intellect, until at last they built siege engines and sailing ships.

These creatures discovered North America. They engineered primitive cities and formed an unwieldy organization they named government. One particularly keen tribe attempted to walk across the barren Canadian prairies in search of the perfect site for a temperance colony. Confused by the wind's whistling, they wandered north. They camped near a river and named the place after the Cree word for a tasty purple berry: *Missask-quah-toomina.* Saskatoon. This camp grew especially fecund, attracting sufficient hominids to include one motivated biped who convinced the others to build a high school.

Truly, it was the first backward step in 3.5 million years. The second was the invention of football teams.

Justin, a robust member of the Jock Tribe, clutched my collar with meaty digits. His right hand was clenched in a fist.

"Don't!" *Whack.* "Ever!" *Whack.* "Call me!" *Whack. Whack.* "That!" *Whack.* "Again!" *Whack.*

His football ring flashed in and out of my vision, stamping impressions in my cheek that would likely be documented in Grad pictures next Thursday. Justin's features were Cro-Magnon: high forehead, thick skull, broad face. The color of his large gray eyes resembled that of an atomic mushroom cloud. Football season was long over, leaving him with vast reserves of simmering testosterone. I was helping burn them off.

"Got that, you little turd?" He shook me. My limbs flopped, but his grip prevented my collapse. "Don't follow me. Don't even look at me." Justin rapped Stonehenge-sized knuckles on my skull. "Got it?"

I nodded. The signal. Submission. He was Lord of the Apes, the Almighty Banana King. I was a low monkey, not worth his energy. Not worth—

Whack!

An uppercut to the jaw lifted my consciousness from its mortal cage. I floated skyward, watching my body waver back and forth like a pugilist whose brain hasn't processed the message that the last punch knocked him out. I drifted higher. A light opened above me. Was this a harbinger of the fabled afterlife all tribes dream of?

A female voice sang out, "Let him go!" Was it a high priestess come to bring down the temples? The mother goddess herself?

"No problem," Justin grunted, "I'm bored anyway." He shoved my carcass. I suddenly snapped back inside myself, eyes wide with fear. I fell like a cut redwood tree, momentum adding to my body's weight. I neglected to use my hands, so I smacked into the ground and shock waves coursed through my nervous system.

The Busybody Tribe surrounded us, shielding the crude ceremony from Groverly High's windows. Its affiliates goggled. Their eyes were large, their batlike ears stretched high to gather up every vibration and echo. When it became clear that I would do no more than moan, they vacated.

I blinked. Stared at an azure morning sky. Wisps of clouds floated in the air. Birds chirped. It could have been a nature documentary. I was relieved it was Friday.

A face appeared in my line of vision. Female. Blurry. Familiar. I batted my eyelids to clear my watering eyes. It was Elissa, my friend.

"Jesus, Percy! *What happened?*"

Several facial areas felt hot as coals. I rubbed my cranium. "I left my body."

"What?"

"I was floating and this light appeared, coming toward me. Maybe it was the afterlife."

"I think you have a concussion."

I tried to sit up. Not prudent. Pain fused seven lower vertebrae. "I am experiencing severe discomfort."

Elissa leaned over, blocking the morning sun. She was as tall and thin as me, her brown hair bobbed, her elfin face elegantly bisected by a slim nose. Her eyes grew wide and owl-like. They stared now, signaling concern and curiosity. She had epicanthic folds, though no obvious Asian ancestors. A sign that all humans share common traits.

Elissa had engaged in ritual body piercing, not for fashion, but in honor of ancient beliefs. Some African cultures believe that demon spirits fly up a person's nostrils and cause illness. To prevent this, she wore a nose ring. She had also situated one ring at the end of her right eyebrow, an ever-present silver tear flicked to the side.

Her fingertips brushed my cheek. "Ow!" I exclaimed.

"Why'd Justin do it?"

"It was my fault. I strayed into his territory." She helped me sit up; my back cracked with each movement. "He then spoke inciteful words to evoke a response."

"What?" Though Elissa has been my closest friend for years, anthropological vernacular can still escape her. "What did he say?"

"He asked whether you and I engage in sexual intimacy and what I thought of the experience. His exact words were: 'Hey, Percy, what's Freak Girl like in the sack?'"

"Freak Girl," she echoed quietly. "Freak Girl?"

"*His* moniker. Don't let it upset you. The gifted are often shunned by lesser intellects. Darwin himself experienced this throughout his lifetime. Besides, I struck back with a witticism. I likened Justin to a body orifice and he took offense."

"You called him an asshole?"

"Please! I was more specific. I implied he was the

mythical ape rectum that shat across the known universe. You should have seen the look on his face—well, once he figured out it was an insult, that is."

"Oh, Percy." She shook her head. Her earrings, two tiny spiders, swung back and forth.

"I know. Not wise. His machismo dictated he must respond in a physical manner. Obvious, now."

"What got into you? We ignore his type. They aren't our tribe. They don't matter."

Our tribe. Let me explain. Numerous tribes exist in friction at our school. The Logo Tribe exhibits name brands wherever and whenever possible. The Digerati Tribe worships bytes and silicon chips. The Lipstick/ Hairspray Tribe performs elaborate appearance alterations to attract mates. The Gee-the-Seventies-Were-Great-Even-Though-I-Wasn't-Born-Yet Tribe has predictable backward habits. The Hockey Tribe subdivides into Oilers, Canadiens, Rangers, and other assorted clans.

And finally there's us, the quasi-omniscient Observers.

We are a cohesive group of two—Elissa and I. We are privileged with a special disposition: We don't like the same music as everyone else, don't wear the same baggy clothes, can't always decode their dialects. We seem to have awakened from a Rip Van Winkle–like sleep to behold the ritualistic world called Grade Twelve. The natives fascinate us.

Justin's thumping was a primitive message: I'd trespassed his territory.

"How do my abrasions look?" I asked.

Elissa smiled. Her braces were removed three months ago, but I am amazed still at the white perfection of her teeth. I'm forever intrigued by mankind's ability to connive improvements on our evolution. "Not too bad," she said. "You'll have bruises for sure."

"He held back. If truly angry he would break at least one bone."

"C'mon, enough sitting around." She helped me to my feet. "We'll be late. You going to tell anyone about him?"

"No point. He reaffirmed he's the alpha male. If I'm careful he won't exhibit again before graduation."

We headed up to Groverly High: a hulking, ancient redbrick edifice centered with long stone steps leading to gigantic oak doors. Ascending the steps, you are forced to look directly up at the face of the school. Glorify the architect. See the vision of forefather Walter Groverly, who blessed the architect's design. See there is no escape—the moatlike river blocks off the rear, the street outlines the front. The building has a hundred windows, yet none at ground level. Escape impossible. A perfect plan.

Until Willard Spokes, that is. One year ago, he fell in love with Marcia Grady of the Lipstick/Hairspray Tribe. Willard was too shy to express his amorous feelings. Upon discovering that Marcia dated a basketball player, Willard picked the lock of the belfry and jumped from the tower. He smashed on the cement four stories below. This was after the morning bell rang, so only stragglers witnessed the event.

Willard didn't regain consciousness. After three days in the ICU, he passed to the next world while his mother held his hand. If not for that aerial misadventure, he'd have graduated this coming Thursday too.

He'd be grinning like a plump simian and cracking jokes. He was a leading member of the Smile Tribe.

Onward. When you step through Groverly's gigantic oak doors, you enter an über-hallway, standing on hardwood that creaks, suggesting that the building will momentarily collapse under the weight of teenagers and heavy angst.

After my father's untimely departure, money became scarce. My mother was forced to withdraw me from private school and I was sent here for Grade Ten. Groverly still constituted my habitat for six and a half hours a day, five days a week, unless I partook of any G.A.S.A.'s (Groverly After School Activities).

Elissa escorted me to my locker. En route she pointed to a bleached-blond girl. "Madonna Cult—I thought they were extinct." The female was called Karen, and she was the product of a Blue Collar–Lipstick/Hairspray Tribe union. A crucifix and a black pearl necklace hung between her net shirt–girded mammae.

"Definitely," I agreed. "Sad, isn't it? Clinging to the past. Not even Madonna's dance tracks could revive her cult. A tribe in decline—uh-oh." I bent down so my head wasn't visible through the masses, a reflex bequeathed by my hominid ancestors, who would crouch in marsh reeds to avoid predators.

Elissa also scrunched down. "Uh-oh what?"

I glanced over my shoulder. "Michael and Nicole sighting."

She giggled. "The Jesus Freaks."

"The Born-Again Tribe," I corrected. "I don't want their antievolution chant again. It's always so . . . circular."

Elissa stood and stretched her neck, ostrichlike.

"They're gone. Heading for homeroom. Punctual as Jesus commanded, I guess." She glanced at her portable chronometer, a Gucci. "Two minutes to the ritual sounding of the bell. You ready for algebra?"

I straightened my back. Major pain sparked from seven vertebrae. "Y-yes."

"Ah, the study of the incestuous breeding of numbers and letters. Invented by Professor Algebrady. Objective: to induce coma."

I smiled. Elissa invented fake histories for all our classes. She produced her reliable pen and printed the words *believe nothing* across her binder. She replaced the writing utensil in her shirt pocket and held up the notebook. "Today's motto! Did you know handwriting is a 'makework' invention? A monk liked its appearance, so he made his novices use it. Then civilizations worldwide mimicked the style. Printing is faster and clearer. Test it sometime."

"Yeah . . . okay."

Elissa's encyclopedic mind catalogued stacks of anecdotes about our societal fallacies. It was her *raison d'être*. Her parents are trial lawyers, so her house is home to constant allegation, rebuttal and proof. And expensive furniture no one sits on.

"So you're okay?" she asked.

"Yes. Just a hazard of my job."

"Maybe splash water on your face. At least clean the scratches; you know how bacteria love open wounds. Could contract the flesh-eating disease and expire before second period."

I smiled. The bell clanged like a fire alarm.

I must correct my observation. There was no bell,

only an electronic recording of one. It had the same effect, though.

"Assimilation time," I announced. We assumed our impartial anthro faces. Elissa amalgamated with the crowd, her head bobbing.

I headed into the field. Four steps later a deep voice commanded, "Percy Montmount, come here."

It was the leader of all the Groverly High strata. He-Whose-First-Name-Is-Too-Sacred-to-Speak.

Principal Michaels.

two

THE LUCK OF THE BEOTHUKS

Michaels waved me toward his office. He was adept at using his gargantuan hands to communicate. I obeyed. Justin sat in the outer waiting room, conducting a staredown with the floor—a sitzkrieg. He took time out to glower at me. I exhibited no antagonistic behaviors.

I hesitated at the door to the inner sanctum. What was protocol? Leave it open? Did Principal Michaels wish to display ascendancy to all? Or close the door, thereby inflaming plebeian wonder at the execution of his power?

Principal Michaels sat at his desk. His hand signaled *Close the door.*

I did so. He gestured to an adjacent wooden chair. I sat. His use of nonverbal signals was perhaps intended to intimidate me.

The office was spacious and clean, every book shelved, binding face out, and every spit-polished wall plaque hung squarely. The desk was exactly in the center of the room.

"Hello, Percy," he said carefully. "How. Are. You.

Today?" His slow elocution indicated that he assumed I was mentally challenged.

"Fine, I am," I answered, opting to mimic Dr. Seuss.

Principal Michaels cracked a crooked smile. Though a backward hominid, he was amiable. He was ruddy-faced and bald, heavyset, with amazingly thick eyebrows. They replicated two black, well-fed caterpillars clinging midbrow.

"Why are you smirking?" he asked.

"I—I'm sorry. I was preparing to sneeze." And I did. Lightly. Obviously fake.

His blue, serious eyes cooled. "There was a scuffle outside the schoolyard. What are those cuts on your face?"

I held myself rigid. "The result of a biking accident, sir."

"Did you ride your bike this morning?"

I paused. I had walked the three blocks from home. "No. Last night, sir."

"They look fresh. I was told you were in a fight with Justin Anverson."

I had overlooked the fleet-footed tribe of sneaks who lurk, awaiting the chance to insinuate themselves with the school patriarchy, intending to advance their grades and general status.

"First, sir, it was not a fight so much as an insightful interaction. Second, it was my fault. I transgressed the cultural boundaries between tribes, and this provoked him."

The principal's right caterpillar wiggled. "I don't understand. Did you start the fight?"

"It was not a fight. But take comfort: All is aright

15 ⭐

now. I know better. I knew all along—I just 'slipped up,' as they say. There will be no future altercations. Guaranteed."

Principal Michaels frowned. The caterpillars clung in place, then inched toward each other. "You're saying there won't be any more fights?"

"I will be mindful of the protocol. I won't trespass again."

Michaels examined me solemnly. "I'll be honest, Percy. I don't know if you're joking or serious. Neither pleases me. Your teachers have told me you've drifted away from your fellow students. And to be frank, some of your behavior is rather odd. Mr. Nicol said he caught you hiding in the dressing room, spying on the boys' soccer team at halftime."

"That incident was misinterpreted. I wasn't spying. I was curious about motivational speeches during athletic competitions. I attempt to be cordial to my peers, sir, but I must not influence their rituals. That's why I was hiding."

"Rituals?"

"Yes." I stopped. How to explain my whole project? "Their rituals," I repeated. "Their lingo, haircuts, special signals, all of that, sir."

His frown remained. "I want you to see Mr. Verplaz. You understand why, don't you?"

The school therapist. Again. He was a singularly valuable hominid. "Of course, sir. I will visit the shaman—I mean Mr. Verplaz."

"I get the feeling you're stressed, Percy. Are you worried about graduation?"

"No. Why?"

"It can be a tough time. Mr. Verplaz will help with coping strategies. I'll also talk to your parents."

I sucked air in sharply.

He had forgotten Dad was dead. Principal Michaels mixed me up with one of the hundreds under his authority, but in that instant I believed he *would* call my father, somehow communicate through the misty nebular spirals of the Netherworld and get a message to Dad.

Tell him . . . Tell him . . .

Tell him I'm trying. I'm trying very, very hard.

"Percy? What's wrong?"

Relief: He paused. I covered my eyes with my hands but quickly pulled them away. Wet palms. Salt stung my cut face. This was not to happen. Another error.

"Is there something . . . ?" Principal Michaels stood and took a hesitant step. "Did I . . . are you . . . all right?"

I stared at my hands. Tears. The universal symptom of emotional distress. "No," I said. "Yes. All right. Everything's all right." I rose, then turned and departed the sanctum.

The bathroom was empty. I must not display emotions to analysands.

I examined my hominid face in the mirror. Long and thin, with bulging chin muscles—a result of nightly tooth-grinding? Beneath short brown hair, a slanted forehead gleaming with a thin sheen. Sweat.

I look sad, lost, concluded the part of my brain that examined. *Poor little* Australo-Percy-ithecus . . . *can't find happiness. Can't control the physical manifestations of grief.*

The voice steeled me. I had made errors in the field. I

needed to concentrate on my task. It was time to perform my ritual. I retreated into a cubicle and closed the door.

I undid the top four buttons on my shirt, exposing a nearly hairless chest. I pushed my hand into my pocket for my container, opened it carefully and extracted a sharpened implement.

There was once a tribe in Newfoundland called the Beothuks. They were skilled canoeists who painted themselves and most everything they owned with red ochre. Don't bother looking for them. They're extinct. They were squeezed to death by Micmacs on one side and fish-hungry Europeans on the other. No longer able to fish their own waters, the shy Beothuks moved inland and starved. The last to be seen by outsiders was Nancy Shanawdithit, who died of TB in 1829. The rest disappeared. Few details of their customs are known.

But I imagined them. Before the final Beothuk died, he had grief to expel, so he traded a bone pendant with the Naskapi for three porcupine quills. He poked his flesh and his sadness leaked out.

I forced the pin through the pale skin around my left nipple. I felt a joyous pain and then . . . release.

I withdrew the pin and repeated the procedure.

I imagined I was the last abandoned, lonely, out-of-luck Beothuk, far away on my island, staring at the sea, longing for my tribe. My people. All gone. Forever. Dead.

I slowly closed the container and with keen deliberation refastened the four buttons.

I took control. I exited the cubicle and left the bathroom.

three

HOME IS A HABITAT

Mom expects the apocalypse daily. She watches for the grand event from Ninth Street, venturing out of our house only when the karma is right and there is no omen that the fabric of the universe will suddenly rip and suck humanity as a vacuum would dust. She admits to hoping doomsday will show the courtesy to wait until after my graduation.

I approached our house at 3:32 P.M., the same time I arrive home every day from school. I, like all humans, am a creature of habit.

I stood in the sun porch, collecting my surging, far-flung thoughts. With the door closed, the outside world was . . . outside. My muscles relaxed. I had survived another day of surveying. A night of cataloging awaited.

Our house hadn't changed since Dad went to the Congo. Its previous owners worshipped at the altar of the Beatles, and had splashed bright orange and red paints on each wall except those in the den, which they painted black. The resourceful decorators then tossed speckled stars into the paint to achieve the semblance of the starlit sky. Mom and Dad loved the house at first sight and changed nothing.

Except: the entranceway. Three years ago Mom installed stained-glass windows in the sun porch. They came from the Cypress Hills. She and Gray Eyes, her shaman, had sneaked out of their sweat lodge, stolen across the prairie grass, and liberated the windows from an abandoned Anglican church that had been converted into a grain bin. The stained glass lends an eerie kaleidoscopic effect to the porch. The light reveals a collection of seven impressionistic phallic paintings on the wall and twelve phallic statues lining the hardwood floor. Interspersed are various clay representations of the naked mother goddess, She-of-the-Mountainous-Bosom.

Even in the old days man was fixated on the size of mammae. We evolve, but some things never change.

I am convinced this exhibit offends the postman. I caught him peering like a priggish pontiff through the mail slot one morning. Mom hopes he peeks more, because the images will rouse his sleeping inner goddess.

She should know. Karmina, my mother, is a psychic. She does life readings (forty-five dollars), palms and tea leaves too (thirty dollars). She comforts worried clients, telling them existence continues after their carbon-based bodies expire. She prospers; everyone frets over the future.

Mother is also a body work specialist for a menagerie of clients. Even the mayor of Saskatoon, who asks for predictions midmassage, partakes of her services. The largest portion of her patrons are New Age *Homo sapiens,* bright-eyed and eternally optimistic. Their spiritual afterimages seem to float around the massage room.

Karmina is my mother's full name. When I was

young, she was Karmen Kristjanna Montmount, but she changed her name after the news about Dad. Karmina is in the yellow pages under *Psychic*—right before a world-famous Texan, Psychic to the Stars. She also appears under *Massage: Karmina, Massage Process, Body Work, Yoga and Colonics.*

"Is that you, Perk?" my mom called from the living room. It's the nickname my father gave me.

"The one and only," I answered, surprised at my peppiness.

"Can we talk?"

"Evolution gave us tongues—we might as well use them."

I pushed through the curtain, the plastic beads kissing and smacking behind me, faintly electrical. Pine and cedar incense fogged the room with forest scent, but a glazed window high in the far wall illuminated the haze. Before me was a jungle of lush green plants hanging from the ceiling.

Mom sat on her white hemp meditation pillow. It was stuffed with old rags because she refused to cushion herself on the plumage of deceased winged vertebrates. She also cringed whenever near a fried chicken restaurant. Her hair was unbound; her black-and-gray tresses flowed across her back. Her sallow skin was evidence that she suspected the ozone layer would no longer shield her from the feared ultraviolet.

I assumed the lotus position on a nearby pillow.

"What shall our topic be today?" I asked playfully. "Qi Gong breathing? Stocks and bonds? My report card?"

"Your principal phoned me," she said, her voice soft, calm.

"I expected that." Actually, I had forgotten his promise to call. "I'm sorry he interrupted your day."

"He's worried about you. . . . I'm worried." Silence. Mom stared out of clear blue eyes. "Were you in a fight?" she asked.

I nodded. She watched carefully, decoding my facial movements. A tic indicating unhappiness; a flicker, a lie. Perhaps she was reading the rainbow of colors around my head: my aura.

"Why?" she asked.

This was a multilayered question in Mom's world. She was inquiring: What karmic payments was I charged with? What negative energy compelled a situation that would harm my body? A past-life crime? She believed there were no accidents.

I had to protect her. She lived in a spirit world, easily disturbed.

"I bumped into this guy and he, like, flew off the handle," I said. Mom was more comfortable if I used teen vernacular. "He's, like, always doing this stuff. He's a bully, you know."

"And that was it?"

"He also said something rude about Elissa."

She nodded, digesting this information. "I know you're friends, but that's no reason to get into a fight. There are no good reasons."

Mom had listened to "Give Peace a Chance" far too many times.

"I didn't intend to get involved, Mom. It just happened."

"Things don't just happen. You know that. Did you respond to his rudeness?"

I let out my breath. "I may have said something back. But he deserved it."

"You could have chosen a dignified silence. Remained motionless and nonthreatening. Remember: 'Nonviolence is mightier than the mightiest weapon of destruction.' "

I recognized the quote. "Mom! Gandhi never went to Groverly High. I don't think he was ever a teenager."

"He faced down the British Empire. Your conflict is minor in comparison."

I sighed. How could I argue with that?

"I'm worried, Perk." Her voice was barely audible. "Mr. Michaels said you don't get along with your classmates."

I don't assimilate, was all he meant.

"I have friends, Mom. There's Elissa, and . . ." I strained my memory. A familiar plump face popped into my head. ". . . And Ms. Peters."

"Who?"

"The librarian." She was kind to me—at least she ordered the books I asked for—so she could be considered a friend. "Anyway, that's not the point. Principal Michaels expects me to act like all the homin—the keeners. He wants me to join the establishment." Mom grew up in the sixties, and I had long used words like *establishment* and *Woodstock* to convince her of the rightness of my argument. I stayed away from *free love*, though. A concept she didn't believe applied to teenagers.

She was impassive. "It won't happen again, will it?"

My jungle vibrated with aggressive tribes. Statistically, the chances of a repeat were amazingly high. "No," I said.

If it did happen, I'd ask Justin to only hit me in the gut to hide the bruises.

Mom nodded and closed her eyes, her face serene. I often wondered if she had only one emotion, calm, like an unbroken wave rolling peacefully across the ocean.

"Meditate with me," she said, reaching out. Blindly, unerringly, she found my hands. "Cold palms. Your energy levels are low. Unblock the Qi channels."

I closed my eyes. Her hands were hot. I concentrated on my breath, slowing it down, imagining energy coming in through my belly button, up my torso, across my shoulders and down my arms. I'd been doing this special breathing combined with yoga and Tai Chi since I was a child. After a few minutes my hands warmed.

I found my center. Calm. Still. Not bliss, but close enough. After a time, I slowly withdrew my hands.

A motorcycle passed the house, muffler growling. Groggy, I looked toward the sound. The trance was broken. I rubbed my burning palms together, massaged my temples.

Karmina "Gandhi" was at peace. She really did have amazing control over her body and emotions.

She suddenly lifted her head. Her eyelids snapped open. "I contacted your father about all this and reminded him that graduation is coming up. I don't know if he'll appear or not."

Typical Mom. She "spoke" to Dad regularly. With a Ouija board? Perhaps a three-way Ouija call, with Principal Michaels in there too.

Hello, Percival Montmount senior? Sorry to disturb your afterlife; it's about your son.

A pain grew in my chest, right next to my heart. My nipples ached. "I have to go to my room, okay?"

Mom examined me with all-seeing eyes. Several moments passed. "Yes, okay," she answered, "it's all okay."

four

PROM HOMINID

Corvus the crow stared as I entered my room. His eyes were two marbles. He was perched on top of the TV, his bone-wings spread as though about to fly. He had held that position for two years. Chessy, my skeletal cat, was curled around a clay human skull on my dresser. Scattered across various shelves were Mickus, a mouse; Boris, a bat; several pinned butterflies; a beetle display (labeled perfectly); a large dragonfly; a jarred calf fetus; three formaldehyded frogs; and five small blocks of petrified wood. I also possessed several wooden masks and two conical tribal dolls of cloth and beads from South Africa.

Segregated to one side was my collection of plastic *Star Trek* figurines (including my favorite, Dr. McCoy, a.k.a. Bones). They have no anthropological value but deserve a place of honor on my dresser. I spent many hours pretending to be on the U.S.S. *Enterprise* during my youth. I was the ship's anthropologist, a specialist in aliens.

Corvus was my first great taxidermy success. I had discovered his body in the backyard—no apparent cause of death. I brought him into my room and placed him in my aquarium (sans water), along with my dermestid beetle colony (I'd ordered the beetle kit from a company in Montana). These voracious chewers of decaying matter cleaned the flesh from Corvus within a few weeks. I then painstakingly reassembled him, all the time trying to picture his genetic connection to the dinosaurs.

I ran my finger across his furculum, the bone that absorbs the shock of flight. Without it, ol' Corvus would be cracking his hollow bones with every swoosh of his wings (when he was alive, that is). It's also called the wishbone because humans, after consuming a bird, like to take the furculum and pull it apart. Whoever gets the larger piece makes a wish to the heavens. This pagan Etruscan ritual survives to this day—they taught it to the Romans, the Romans brought it to Britain, the Brits brought it here. The past is always with us.

I sat at my desk, surrounded by shelves packed with anthropology books, including several editions of *The Origin of Species*, Darwin's little ditty about natural selection, which set the scientific world buzzing. I had nearly memorized it. Surrounding that were all the latest books on evolution, including one that presented the theory that evolution was the result of aliens fiddling with our DNA. It's a hilarious read.

In the very center of the desk was my field journal, a large scrapbook-sized tome with many hundreds of pages. It bore the title *The Origin of Species Revisited* by Percival Montmount, Jr. In it was every observation I had made about my environment for the past three years.

Normally, I would record the day's events immediately after school, but today I couldn't open it. There was too much to write down. I had to finish digesting the material. Instead, I opened a biography of Darwin.

About an hour later, I went to the kitchen and prepared a large wooden bowl of sprouts, seaweed, black olives, carrot sticks, butter lettuce and feta cheese. We had no specific mealtime. Mom believed you ate when your body informed you it was hungry.

I sat at our table. A second later Mom appeared, chewing on an apple, her reading glasses halfway down her nose. A massive historical novel was clutched in one hand—her only addiction, not counting yogurt-covered almonds.

"You getting enough to eat?" she asked. "There are rice cakes in the cupboard."

"I . . ." I swallowed a rather large chunk of seaweed. "I'm fine. You fruiting it today?"

She dropped the apple core into the compost pail. "Yep. Trying to cleanse myself. Having some intestinal discomfort."

"Oh." Thankfully, she spared me the details. "Hope it goes away."

"It will. You're looking thin. I should get some more beans. And goat's cheese. Would you like that?"

"Sure," I said, straining to sound enthusiastic. What I really wanted was a triple-patty burger. After my day, I needed animal protein. But Mom was haunted by the fearful clucks, bellows and gurgles of the animals she had consumed during her carnivorous years.

Herbivorousness is odd. Plants have the same two

goals as all species: survival and propagation. They can't vocalize, but perhaps they feel pain on a cellular level. When we pull them from the ground we strangle them. And where are the mite activists? Why don't we fret about the daily destruction of the two mite species that live on our faces, shuffling through hair follicles and sebaceous glands, munching dead skin cells? What about the masses of dust mites scuttling across our pillows? Crushed when we lay down our heads.

It's important to remember we are all ecosystems—never truly alone.

"What's on your mind, Perk?" Mom asked. "You're gazing into nothingness again."

I smiled. "I was just thinking that two bugs in the hand are better than one in the bush."

"You lost me."

"Well, I was reading about good ol' Charlie again—"

"Charles Darwin, you mean," she interjected.

"Of course!" I accidentally spat an errant sprout. "He was a bug nut! Totally avid! There was this time in the bush when he had two rare beetles, one in each hand. Every collector's dream. Just then another monster-sized beetle crawled into the open on a piece of bark. Even rarer than the others. 'How do I capture it?' he asked himself. Then the idea hit him. He popped one beetle into his mouth." I mimicked the popping motion. "He reached for the prize beetle. But the beetle in his mouth pooped out an acrid fluid that burned his tongue. He coughed, the beetle leapt to freedom and the other vanished. Funny, hey?"

"Yes, funny. He was just going to stick needles through them anyway, wasn't he?"

"Well, yeah, he was a collector."

Someone knocked. Mom took off her glasses and set them on the table, then answered the door.

Gray Eyes came in. Her shaman. Well, shaman to a number of people, actually. He was lanky and wide-shouldered, a direct descendant of the Vikings. His hair (once blond) was long and gray and thick enough to give a rock star envy. And his eyes really were a mysterious shade of gray. He'd been named by a native elder at a powwow in Banff.

"Hi, Percy," he said. "How's the universe unfolding?"

"The universe doesn't unfold, it expands," I said. "It isn't a sleeping bag. It is expanding at a greater rate every day, but don't be too concerned. That won't affect us for millennia."

Gray Eyes grinned. "You are so magnificently literal, Percy. I wish I could be half as literal as you."

"Thank you," I said. "That's the kindest compliment I've received today."

Mom had slipped her running shoes on. "I'm ready," she announced. She turned to me. "I won't be home until after eleven."

Friday, I thought. Most people would be going to a movie or a bar. But not Mom. "It's sweat lodge night, eh?"

She nodded. "You should go for a walk. Get some fresh air."

"I should," I said, but didn't elaborate. "Have a good time with your pagan ritual."

They both laughed, though I had been serious. I locked the door behind them.

I finished my meal but was still hungry. A mean case of hamburgeritis possessed me. To distract myself, I retired to my room to read *Discovering Archaeology*. The obsession soon subsided.

At 7:45, a finger tapped light as a sparrow on the glass. Elissa stood outside. Long ago she'd stopped using the front door, preferring to enter through my window. The grass below the sill had worn away. I'd placed a chair under the window so she could climb in easily.

I raised the window. In a motion reminiscent of our monkey ancestors, she grasped the bottom of the sill and pulled herself into my room, stepping to the chair, then the floor, and wiping her hands on her pants.

Beautiful. Her entrance, that is. All made possible by eons of evolution: mutations that gave her (and our species) opposable-thumbed hands uniquely qualified to grip the sill.

"What're you staring at?" she asked, with a lopsided smile.

"Nothing." I settled back on the bed.

Elissa plopped on the chair. She wore stylish fatigues and a T-shirt emblazoned with I DON'T KNOW. The shirt had been cut short and revealed a flat abdomen. Her belly button was an innie.

She rested her feet on the bed, saying, "Did you know a guy in Arizona was kicked out of school for wearing a Pepsi shirt on Coke day? Teachers felt he wanted to stir up trouble. Meanwhile students toddle around in shoes made by Third World children enslaved in factories and no one makes a peep. There's no logic to the educational system." She looked across at me, apparently finished. She needed to rant like this once a day. "What you up to?"

31 ⭐

"Reading about ancient Egyptians."

"Learn anything new?" she asked.

"Actually it's old. The old worlds. Ancient cultures were able to intuit more about the stars than we know today."

"Did they have weird ceremonies like, say, graduation?"

"No, theirs were advanced societies."

She ran both hands through her hair, making her shirt rise to expose her upper abdomen and lower ribcage. Her mammae were medium-sized. I note this only out of scientific curiosity.

"Have you thought about graduation?" she asked.

"The event itself or the future of the graduates?"

She began playing with a strand of her hair, twirling and untwirling. "The event. All the parties. Not to mention Grad itself. What will it mean? How will it change us?"

"I don't intend to change. It's my—*our*—job to observe the tribal actions."

"Have you thought about the specifics?"

"Like what? The gown? The scroll? The valedictorian address?"

"No, like who you'll take to Grad?"

I blinked. I'd been so wrapped up in anticipating the event, I'd forgotten that society expected me to pick a female partner. Whom would I take? Or, more to the point, who would go with me?

"You. We can study them together."

She grinned. "Are you asking me to Grad?"

"Yes. Isn't that what I said?" She was acting odd. Did she need a signed affidavit?

"Good. Everybody else had a date a month ago. I've turned several guys down while I waited for you."

Other guys had asked her? I tried to picture it but drew a blank. Then: Justin's face. Looming in my mind. No, he couldn't have, their tribes were so different.

Elissa crawled onto the bed and curled across the end. She had never reclined there before. But here she was, transgressing my territory, head propped on hand. Staring warmly.

She was acting . . . well, like she was attracted to me.

That couldn't be. And yet . . . My breath quickened.

This was one part of the human equation I knew little about. Well, nothing, actually. I'd never been on a date. I wondered what it would be like to hold her. She had inviting lips.

But we were professionals. Partners. Friends. It wouldn't be right.

Elissa touched my knee and I jerked. "Have you recovered from battling Goliath?"

"I wear the bruises proudly. Wounds from the field."

She gave me a flicker of a smile. Her large eyes were soft with emotion. Watching me. I was momentarily amazed by them; how did our cells decide to form eyes? What was it like when the first amphibian orbs opened to the world?

"I've been thinking about you a lot," she said.

"Oh?" Everyone was thinking of me today. Principal Michaels, Mom, Justin.

"Yeah, it's not like you to piss someone off. Even a reptile like Justin. You've been so uptight this last month."

Uptight? Emotional turmoil wasn't in my code.

"What set you off?" she asked.

I shook my head. "It was an unexpurgated outburst. It won't be repeated."

"Talk to me in your real voice, Percy."

Real voice? I only had one voice. "Pardon me?"

"Why did you get into that fight?"

I was tired of the same question. This was Elissa's second time in eleven hours. Her eyes wouldn't leave me. "I allowed myself to become involved in the situation," I slowly explained. "That's not good protocol."

"Why did you get into the fight?" Her smile was gone, her face tight, eyes squinting as if at a blinding light.

"It was an accident, Elissa. A miscalculation. I don't want to examine it anymore."

She nodded slowly. "I just wondered if it had to do with Willard."

I bit the inside of my cheek. "Willard," I said.

"Today's the anniversary of his death."

Why would she think I was connected to Willard? A bizarre leap of logic about the student who leapt off our school belfry. "I haven't even thought of him," I lied. I *had* thought of him as we walked toward the school this morning. "Why would this be about Willard?"

"He *was* your best friend, Percy. And mine. I can't stop thinking about him. And I don't know if anyone notices that he's gone."

Best friend? Yes, I had spent time with Willard. We had gone to movies. Exchanged books. Played video games (at his place). An image flashed in my mind: Willard standing outside my window in a downpour, smiling, looking like a drowned rodent. The memory Mesozoic old. He'd taught Elissa the habit of climbing in my window.

I *had* visited him in the hospital; that's how I knew his mother was holding his hand when he died. I'd sat in a chair in the corner waiting for him to wake. If I was there, then I was his friend. Maybe even his best friend.

Elissa cleared her throat. I couldn't find any words. Finally, I opened my mouth. "I overheard a teacher talking about lowering the flag to half-mast."

"Who?"

"Principal Michaels," I lied. Lying is immoral in our culture, but this "news" seemed to cheer her up.

"At least they're thinking of him," she said.

"Yes, they are."

We were silent for a very long time. Elissa repeatedly traced a pattern in my bedcover. Her circling finger entranced me.

"I'm happy we're going to Grad together," she said without looking up. I didn't answer. Her finger stopped.

"I, too, am pleased," I admitted. And I was: How many teens had spent angst-filled hours struggling to procure a prom date? I had avoided that pain.

I'd wear a suit, of course. To fit in. And Elissa would be in a long dress. Maybe something with a low-cut back. She had a beautiful spine. This also I note out of scientific curiosity.

"It's all coming to an end." She sounded almost sad. "Four years of Groverly's educational method: bore, bore, repeat, bore. Do you remember that first Halloween?"

"I still have the cavities." We'd dressed up and toured the neighborhood, ringing doorbells, then kneeling so that we looked like kids. No one was fooled, but they gave us loads of candy. Will was there too. We were chased by one brute who thought we'd egged his window. We hid by the river, snickering quietly, bonding and devouring caramels. "I can't believe we dressed like clowns."

"Clowns?" Elissa said. "We were aliens. Geez, nice memory you have."

I blinked. Aliens. Yet I clearly remembered clowns. One of us was wrong. But I wouldn't argue forcefully. The hippocampus is a notoriously poor recorder of memories. I wouldn't trust it as far as I could throw it.

"If you'd stayed in that private school you'd be ultra-stuffy by now," Elissa said. "Will and I really loosened you up."

"Gee, yeah," I answered. Stuffy? "I didn't want to leave St. Joseph's. But it ended up being a perfect new beginning. A rebirth. I wouldn't trade the experience for anything."

"Funny how things work out," she said.

We mused separately for a few moments. Then a familiar desire came over me. An *intellectual* desire.

"May I see your foot?" I asked.

Elissa looked up sharply as if I'd poked her with a pin. Then she rolled her eyes. "Not again."

"It is scientific curiosity, nothing else," I intoned. She didn't move. "Please," I added.

"You sure you don't have a fetish?"

"I'm certain."

She sat up and rolled down her right black sock, slowly displaying a typical human foot, complete with five toes, ascending in size. Her nails were painted a rainbow of colors. She swung her foot closer. There was nothing out of the ordinary.

"Please spread your toes."

"Whatever you command, kinky boy." She giggled.

I ignored her and waited patiently, though I admit my heart palpitated and my breathing became shallow. Slowly Elissa spread her toes. Thin webs of skin opened between them, joining her digits like a frog's. I sighed. Here it was. A webbed foot. A genetic leftover from our days as ocean-bound vertebrates. Or perhaps it was a recent mutation, the water beckoning us back home. After all, as embryos we humans do have gill pouches. One small step from becoming amphibians.

"That is the most spectacular foot I have ever seen," I whispered. Oddly enough, her other one was normal.

She wiggled her toes. "Try shoving it into sandals."

"Are you certain you don't swim any faster?"

"Not that I've noticed."

"Do you ever feel an urge to dive in the ocean?"

"What? Not really." She folded her arms. "My toes are tired of being on show."

"Thank you," I said, and I meant it. I owed her for showing me this wonder, and I thanked whatever lines of consequence had supplied a friend with a webbed foot.

"You're the weirdest person I've ever met, Percy junior." She laughed as she pulled on her sock, her eyes bright. "Weirdest to the utmost."

* * *

Later that night I opened my field journal.

I sketched the evolution of fins to feet and back again.

Then wrote an article titled *Codes of Violence: The Jock Tribe*.

When my hand cramped two and one third hours later I put down the pen. I went to bed and my thoughts turned to our greatest ancestor: *Australopithecus afarensis Lucy*. She was 3.2 million years old, the closest hominid to the missing link. Lucy and her relatives were likely the first to walk upright.

I wondered if Lucy's toes had been like Elissa's.

five

CARNIVORE

Like a gastronomical boomerang, my desire for
a hamburger returned and shadowed me all Saturday morning. By early afternoon I found myself on
Broadway, strolling past the restaurants and cafés, sali-
vating. Most, except the Taj Mahal, were *verboten*
to Mom.

But she had gone to Wanuskewin for a nature walk and
would be spending the night with friends in the traditional
teepees that were part of the park (this accommodation
was $79 per person, hallucinatory dreams not included).
This meant I was free to indulge. She'd never once told me
not to consume meat, but anytime I had she'd smelled it
on me or heard the ghostly moo of the cow. Then she'd
give me a look of absolute disappointment.

But today I had to explore my inner carnivore. I
slipped into the Broadway Café and ordered a triple
burger with fries and gravy. It arrived steaming hot, on a
platter-sized plate. I quickly devoured my meal.

Then: tears. Almost. I blinked them back. This used
to be my time with Dad. We'd sneak away from Mom
and what he called the "infernal sprouts" and come

here to gorge ourselves. He'd tell me about all the odd things he'd eaten while in the field (goats' eyeballs being his favorite). Then he'd slip me a stick of peppermint gum and say, "She'll never know." We'd slink back, keeping our distance from the matriarch.

I had swallowed a five-pound weight. My digestive system, trained on sprouts and celery, was at a loss. The hamburger seemed to be gaining mass by the second. The best action: walk it off.

I paid my bill, bought gum (peppermint) and proceeded toward the river, chewing. Soon I was strolling along the Meewasin Trail, staring across the river. This was a time to surrender the minutiae of my life and concentrate on the bigger picture. Where was evolution taking humanity?

I pictured Elissa's foot. Then her ankle. Her midriff. I shook my head. This wasn't the direction I'd intended.

I tried something different: the double helix. Encoded in our genes was almost every step of our evolution. Scientists had mapped the gene; now I had to find a way to follow that map to the beginning. Maybe there was information on the Internet that would help me.

The hair on the back of my neck suddenly tingled. A keen anthropologist develops a sixth sense. I looked up. A familiar broad-shouldered male lumbered around a corner.

I quickly inserted myself into nearby bushes, folded the greenery around me and crouched down. My heart thudded and a sheen of sweat coated my forehead. This attracted the attention of a fly, which tasted my perspiration with its feet. I tried not to think of the fly's previous explorations. A second fly descended. A third. I blinked, raised my eyebrows.

I willed: stillness. In the jungle I would have to deal with hordes of insects. I, Percy Montmount, Jr., could persevere.

Then: Thick trunklike legs became visible through the foliage. I looked up, moving only my eyeballs. Justin loomed. Could he scent me out?

"How're you doing, buddy?" he asked.

I made no response.

"Would you like some ice cream?"

Was this an attempt to bribe me out of my cover?

"You're pretty quiet today."

I held my breath. The legs moved down the paved path.

When I was sure Justin was a good distance away, I slipped into the open, nearly bumping into an ancient woman with a walker, a matriarch of the Denture Tribe. "You playing hide-and-seek, son?" she asked.

I shook my head.

Justin was slouching under the bridge, a little boy riding his massive shoulders. My eyes widened. I blinked, watched them disappear.

I followed, my right hand automatically reaching into my pants pocket, retrieving my field notebook. I wrote as I walked. Could this be a breakthrough? Justin displaying affection/protection in public. Was this a brother—a young Justin in the making? To be trained in the ways of the Jock Tribe? At what point did the rituals begin?

They stopped at a park bench and I stole under the bridge, using the shadows for cover.

Justin lowered his brother onto a bench, then sat beside him. They appeared to be talking. Justin tickled the young recruit. The boy giggle-shrieked. Justin wrapped him up in his arms.

I was stunned. I stepped into the open. Justin looked up, still hugging. His eyes narrowed.

I retreated, keeping the pillars between me and them. Then I scrambled up the hill on the other side of the bridge and headed for home, clutching my field notebook like a shield.

six

NAKED AND TIED TO A STICK

My father was always leaving. Most of my paternal memories are snapshots of him loading suitcases into the trunk of a taxi, a sun hat shielding his bald head. Or he'd be standing in line at the airport, backpack slung over one shoulder, flight tickets in hand. He'd perform a wiggly-fingered wave, then disappear through the departure gate. Mom would lead me to the window and we'd wave to his plane. Well, we'd wave to all the planes to be sure we got the right one. Whenever I see a jet bisecting the sky I think of Dad.

His destinations were glorious: the Australian outback, the Far East, Peru, the thick urban jungles of Hong Kong. Places where wondrous events occurred daily. Where dreams came to life. Sometimes we'd read about Dad in the back pages of one of the national papers, see a grainy photo of him standing beside an ancient statue or sitting among African tribesmen.

Invariably, two months, three months, even six months later, Dad would return and wrap me up in his arms, smelling of sweat and strange smoke. He'd give me a whisker rub. He'd kiss Mom. And we'd take him home. Glorious Dad, back in our little house.

That night, and many nights after, I would wait in my bed, vibrating with excitement. Story time. He'd open his mouth and spin tales long into the night.

My favorite was about how he'd outsmarted the RanRans, a cannibal tribe in the Roterwali Peninsula, near the Amazon River.

Dad was studying the peaceful Wanniwa. During the night the RanRans stormed the village, drove the men away and stole whichever women they could capture. When Dad poked his head out of his hut to check on the commotion, the invaders stopped and gawked at the first white man they had ever seen. He was in a typical anthro outfit: khaki shorts and shirt, unkempt hair (what there was of it) and a pen and pad of paper in hand.

The RanRans encircled him with bamboo spears, poked and prodded him through the jungle vines to their canoes, then paddled vigorously down an Amazonian tributary teeming with piranha. They stared the whole time. Even warriors in the other boats steered close to eyeball Dad.

At daybreak they arrived at their village. A wall of bamboo spikes crowned with impaled shrunken heads surrounded their homes, dome-shaped huts jutting from the earth. The cries of birds and wild monkeys filled the air.

There's a Bugs Bunny cartoon in which cannibals boil a large pot of water, slicing onions and carrots into it. Then they attempt to force Bugs in, managing only to steam his tail. This potboiling motif is a common misrepresentation. Cannibals tend to bash your head and slice and dice you on the spot. Then they boil you. It's similar to our treatment of cattle.

My father was fortunate because this tribe had strict traditions for food preparation: First the meat was sweated to cleanse it of evil spirits. So, they stripped Dad and tied him to a stake for three days, allowing him only a bowl of water and a handful of fat grubs. He ate the grubs happily because he recognized the nutritional value inside their slimy bodies. Still, he disliked how they wiggled down his throat and quivered in his stomach before succumbing to gastric acid.

The RanRans quizzed him nonstop. Where were you born? Did you come from a white-shelled egg? Were you birthed under a full moon so that the light whitened you?

My father remained silent, stoic. He knew enough of the RanRan language that he could have begged for freedom, but he chose to quietly endure the three-day torture, which left his balding head scorched and his eyes red and dry. Army ants crawled over his entire body, biting him. The tribe believed the ants would tenderize the meat and release the tiny demons trapped by the skin. Dad watched the sun and the stars, kept track of the days, so that even though he was naked and without a watch, he could have told you the time.

They finally untied him and marched him to the roasting pit. He was bound to a spit over a mound of kindling. The RanRans' custom was to cook their food alive because screaming would loosen the flesh from the bones. They began to make fire, spinning a piece of wood inside a wooden groove to create friction. Just as the smoke appeared, Dad said, *"Kewokee nok nig,"* which meant "Something bad will happen."

The RanRans were shocked. The chieftain said, *"Blegin blog,"* which translated to "Of course." They assumed Dad meant something bad would happen to him. They laughed uproariously, patting each other on the back and slapping their own cheeks, which was their jovial habit.

He repeated his warning and they guffawed and cheek-slapped again. Finally the chieftain approached with a flame. Dad uttered a third warning and the sky grew dark. The chief pulled back the torch and gawked up.

Above them, the sun was going out.

It was a total eclipse. Darkness rushed over the camp. Flocks of birds fled, confused by the sudden withdrawal of light. Only the corona of the sun was visible, burning like the eye of an angry fire god.

The chief RanRan dropped the torch and fled, followed by his tribesmen. The torch sputtered and died.

Within a few minutes Dad had wriggled out of his bonds and the eclipse had ended. The village was deserted.

"Remember, Perk," Dad would always say, announcing the end of the story, "even when you're naked and tied to a stick, there will always be a way out."

It's my motto.

seven

TRAPDOOR

Elissa had chosen a tiny skull and crossbones as her eyebrow ring. "It symbolizes the end," she explained, "the death of our high school personas. This is the final week before we become free."

"Clever," I said. We were in our usual position next to my locker. A cornucopia of humanity had disgorged before us, oddly active for a Monday morning. "They all look so invigorated."

"It's like a drug. Adrenaline rises as Grad approaches. They rush toward oblivion. So are you ready for the parties?"

"Ready?" I echoed. "I'm psychologically pumped. Test me. I dare you."

She laughed. "Okay, Darwin." She knew I loved it when she compared me to my hero. "Let's start with Tacky Party."

"A cross-tribal function. Dress: multicolored clothes. Drink: Yuk-a-flux, a concoction of alcohol and fruit juice. Music: loud. Time: tonight."

She whistled appreciation. A junior looked our way

and she winked at him. He blushed. I was momentarily jealous.

"Round two," she announced, "the High Tea."

"Easy! Time: tomorrow afternoon. Once a female-only ceremony; now both sexes serve their elders tea and edibles. Later it descends into a herbivore-roasting feast: a barbecue."

"Is your mom coming?"

I shook my head. "She couldn't handle the smell of burning meat. Plus she teaches yoga then."

"My parents can't make it either. Too busy. Guess we'll be each other's parents. The rest of the week's going to be a blast."

"Yes, the River Party, Neolithic to the extreme. And, finally, ritual of all rituals, the All-Night Grad Party."

"It's a casino this year."

"Ha!" I exclaimed. "We can bet on the odds of Justin evolving."

"Or making it through first-year university," Elissa quipped.

We smiled at each other and she touched my cheek. "Hardly a bruise. You've healed well." Her fingers were warm. *Healing hands,* I thought. *She has healing hands.* The bell rang.

"Take care of yourself," she said, lowering her hand.

"I will," I answered. "I—I'm happy you're going to Grad with me."

She blushed. "Me too, my anthropological angel. Me too."

I was overcome with the urge to hug her. I reached out, felt suddenly awkward and decided to pat her back. "Grad's gonna rock, I promise." We headed our separate ways.

Time passed with ease. Our teachers smiled, dispensing the last bits of their curriculum into our 1,350-cubic-centimeter brains. Some great witch doctor had greased the wheels of education, and they spun madly.

They stopped spinning at two o'clock, when I raised my hand in English 30. Ms. Nystrom, a kind teacher with a large birthmark on her left cheek, cocked her head and frowned. "Percy, you have something to say about Shakespeare?"

"Yes, I do." I stood up. The faces of my fellow students expressed a mild curiosity, as though a large insect had rested on my forehead. "Shakespeare was an amazing *Homo sapiens,* but his volumes of creative output can be reduced to one impulse: survival. His plays shouldn't be valued as works of art but as scientific proof of how complicated survival instincts have become. His creations were a means to secure food and shelter."

I continued. I cannot remember all I said, though I did trace the history of man's evolution from an anthropoid ancestor to clarify my point. The bell rang. The class immediately shuffled out. I paused in mid-oration. Enlightenment was not their goal. I glanced at Ms. Nystrom, but she was memorizing a spot on her desk.

I hadn't meant to go on at such length. It had just happened. I gathered my books and stumbled into the hall.

Where I ran into the past.

Delmar Brass stood there like a tree, an algebra book clutched in his hand. He was a tall First Nations

Saulteaux whose great-great-grandmother had been a member of Sitting Bull's tribe. They had fled to Canada after defeating an American army led by General George Armstrong Custer. They settled briefly in southern Saskatchewan. Most returned to their homeland, though Delmar's relatives chose to stay. I had once interviewed him for an article detailing the influence of cowboy movies on modern perceptions of natives. *Anthropology Today* never published it. In fact, no major scientific magazine expressed interest. My groundbreaking theories intimidated them.

Every time I saw Delmar I thought of the bison running over the plains, the grass growing tall and wild, no European-style cities darkening the land.

"Hear you were in a fight," Delmar said. "Need help?"

His eyes were dark, his hair black and tied back. He had developed an affection for me after the interview— that is, he occasionally nodded in my direction. Even once when he was with his friends.

"The situation is resolved. Thank you."

"Good. Take care." He continued down the hall, his tread surprisingly light.

I deposited my books, examined my watch: 2:35. Time for my appointment with Mr. Verplaz, the school shaman, He-Who-Lives-on-the-Top-Floor. A last-ditch attempt to correct the wayward.

At the very least, it would be a stimulating conversation. Plus he kept a jar of lollipops. I'd get a treat.

I walked slowly, deliberately. On the second flight of stairs, I became aware of the motion of my feet, pictured our ancient ancestors taking their first wobbly steps.

"Why you staring at your feet, Montmount? Afraid you're gonna trip?"

Justin loomed on the landing above me. Had he marked it and the soft-drink machine with his urine? Had I trespassed his territory?

"I was trying to figure out why we walk upright."

He shook his head. "You're retarded, aren't you? How's your face?"

His tone conveyed no concern, but I replied as if it had: "A scratch and a slight bruise. Thank you for the lesson in tribal interaction."

He glared. "What was that crap in English? Our last class and you barf up another lecture. I should give you a smack." He clenched his ham-sized fist, looked at it; then his eyes flicked back to me. "You followed me in the park, didn't you?"

"I was only there to clear my thoughts."

"Spying is more like it. Again."

"I don't spy. I observe."

"Whatever." He spat. The spittle landed near my feet. "We're sick of you."

We? Was he having a dual-personality problem?

"Everyone at school. *All* the students. You stare like we're freaks. But you're the freak."

I blinked. "I am not a freak. I'm not. I'm just trying to do my job. I didn't intend to disrupt your behavior."

A strange reaction followed: He looked genuinely sad. "You don't even speak English, do you? Just that quasi-science crap."

"I do speak English. It's the language of my culture."

He furrowed his brow, a look I imagined the Cro-Magnons got when they first saw something beyond their ken. "You and your weirdo friend are first-class losers."

I narrowed my eyes and clenched turnip-sized hands. "Did you ask Elissa to Grad, you . . . you big ape?" My heart pounded madly. I was shocked at my reaction and disappointed at the blandness of my insult. "No, wait . . ." I jabbed a finger in his direction. "Classifying you as an ape would be an insult to apes and all other simians." I sucked in a deep breath. "Did you ask her?"

Justin's brow furrowed even deeper. "Ask Freak Girl to Grad? I'm not desperate."

I glowered, silently.

He pointed. "Four days, Ugly, and we're done. Just be careful, Einstein." He turned and lumbered down the steps.

What interesting behavior, I thought. *What very, very interesting behavior.* I *was* slightly insulted. Calling me Einstein. *Hmmph.* Einstein was good, but he was no Darwin.

I walked up the next flight, letting my clenched hands relax.

The rooms on the top floor of Groverly High were mostly vacant. The fluorescent lights glowed dully; two of the bulbs were burned out and a third flickered madly.

A large abandoned art studio ran along one side. I plodded down the hall, passing under a trapdoor with an oversized padlock. This was probably where Willard had climbed to the roof.

"Percival," a voice whispered from the other side of

the trapdoor. I looked up, straining my sensory system. Something skittered across the wooden panels. My throat became dry.

Mice, I thought, picturing the beady-eyed rodents. They're always scampering around the school, foraging. It had to be mice.

I backed up. My brain adjusted my synapses so that I became two big ears, listening for another noise. Five steps away I heard a faint *"Percival."*

I turned the corner and leaned on the wall. There was a barred window at the top of the stairs, and I stared at the outside world, somewhat surprised to see daylight. The whisper had to have been my imagination. Or was it an echo of Will's voice? Forever trapped in the belfry.

Shapes moved at the edge of the schoolyard. The Smoker Tribe was gathered like a flock of crows, enjoying spring, their lungs filtering tar and nicotine. I held that position until my biorhythms steadied. I was not beyond superstition; the voice was a sign to avoid Mr. Verplaz.

Then the sound of squeaking hinges. A door?

Or: trapdoor?

I retreated down the stairs.

eight

A WINTER

Monday ended without any fanfare. Elissa and I exited Groverly's front doors. Three days until graduation, then summer holidays, followed by autumn. Which meant one glorious thing: first-year university. A swarming population from across the country and around the world. A hundred times the number of ritual events. My cerebral cortex vibrated with anticipation. I would have to purchase a new journal.

"Put this in your think box," Elissa said as we walked down the stone stairs. "If the highway speed limit were cut in half, most car accident deaths could be avoided. But our society chooses quick delivery of goods over safe travel. Illogical to the extreme! And did you know the majority of car accidents happen near home?"

"I was aware of that."

Her eyebrow ring glinted in the sun. "It's a misleading statistic. People spend more time driving around their neighborhood; it's only natural a greater number of accidents would happen there. Still, we should always be more careful. Especially you."

Was that supposed to be funny? Her words were

hard to follow. What had I been thinking about? Oh, yes, university. Anthropology 110: kindergarten. The professors would see my potential. My promise.

The second coming of Darwin, they would whisper. Just like Montmount senior.

"Something wrong?" she asked.

"No." I walked silently to the edge of the sidewalk.

"Look left before crossing," she warned. Another joke? I stepped off the curb. Car tires shrieked.

Time.

Slowed.

Down.

A car was coming at me. A teen with spiked hair glared through the windshield.

I froze. My survival instincts selected the wrong defense: *Stay still, the predator won't detect movement.* A prehistoric groan of the horn. The knee-high bumper hypnotized me.

I was yanked back and the wheels skidded just centimeters from my body. Air swished past, then another honk. The car didn't stop.

"Look left *and* right," Elissa said, releasing my shirt. "Do you need a crossing guard, Percy? Percy?"

No air. Lungs empty.

"What's wrong, Percy?" Elissa asked, squeezing my shoulder.

"Nothing. Just . . . need to . . . catch my breath." I sucked in. Oxygen! Sweet and pure.

Students on the school steps scowled. The drive-by had been planned. *He's the freak. We're sick of him.* Their common tribal mind spoke in chorus: *Cut him from the gene pool.*

That proved it. Justin was their chief.

I looked both ways, crossed the street. Elissa walked beside me, sneaking glances as if suspecting I might spontaneously combust. A block later Groverly was hidden behind an apartment complex. Students had vanished. I felt safer in this, my own territory.

"Is there something else wrong?" she asked. "You're shaking."

"I ran into Justin again," I admitted.

"What happened?"

"He said everyone hated me," I reported.

"That ugly Neanderthal!" Her vehemence was surprising.

"He's a Cro-Magnon. Neandertal is too evolved," I said. "The Neandertals had a larger cranium and perhaps weren't related to us. Justin has many human tendencies. Bad ones." I resisted correcting Elissa's pronunciation: she had said Neander*thal,* but the proper spelling is *Neandertal.* The word comes from the German and they now drop the silent *h.* "Please don't get upset. Cro-Magnon Boy is suffering brain envy. A common Jock Tribe sickness."

Her fists were white-knuckle tight. Her body vibrated. "I could punch him. I'm just so pissed off."

"Elissa, Elissa," I implored, "don't trouble yourself."

She stood still; then her shoulders sagged. "I suppose you're right." She released a deep breath. "Sticks and stones," she said, "just let it go." We carried on, and a few huffs later, she was back to her former mood. "You know, this is nearly the last time we'll walk home together from school. Do you think it'll be like this in university? Percy? Oh, Percy?"

"Yes." Luckily my cerebral cortex had noted her question. "We'll take the bus to university, so we likely won't walk each other home as often."

"How do you do that?"

"Do what?" I asked.

"Shut yourself off."

"I don't understand."

"Never mind. You're distracted. You worried about the party tonight?" We turned the corner to my house.

"The Tacky Party? It will be interesting. I'm not sure what to wear, though."

"Gee, you almost sound excited." She poked me in the ribs. I jerked away in surprise. "Maybe you don't have tacky clothes . . . actually, I take that back."

"What?" I examined my gray pants—two front pockets and a side pocket for field items, pencil and paper. "This is classic urban camouflage."

"You wear grays and blacks, you mean. You're two steps from Goth. Do you have anything with color? We do have to fit in. A T-shirt with flowers? Red pants? Flamingo beach shorts? I've never seen you in shorts."

I pictured the drawers in my dresser, rows of non-colors. She was right. "What will I do?"

She stopped, put one hand on her chest and extended the other as if she'd suddenly become royalty. "Allow *moi* to introduce *moi*-self. Baroness Eleeza Fashionoski. Kiss my proffered hand."

"Excuse me?"

"Kiss it!" she commanded.

I pressed my lips against her digits. Quickly. Caught a scent like strawberry bubble gum.

"You show da proper respect," she said, looking

down her nose. "I permit you to benefit from my fashion advice. We shall embark for my palace with haste."

"Your place?"

"Palace," she corrected. She lifted one eyebrow. "What da baroness vants she gets. Besides"—her accent disappeared—"you *never* walk me all the way home. You're so chronically self-centered." She winked. "It's your duty now. You *are* my prom date."

"I'm an ignoramus!" I admitted. "Let's go to your dwelling."

"Wow. My dwelling." Elissa tousled my hair. "The way you said that almost sounded romantic."

I straightened my locks. My skull tingled where she'd touched it.

We headed down the steep hill to Saskatchewan Crescent, a descent into the realm of the affluent. Houses were bigger here, sprouting from expansive lots alongside three-car garages, gazebos and crescent-shaped brick driveways.

"Columns are so passé," Elissa said, motioning toward a row of the architectural wonders on one house. "You'd think we were in Rome. *Invita Minerva*, baby!" She yelled.

Elissa also had an interest in an arcane language: Latin. "Which means?" I asked.

"Uninspired. Minerva didn't inspire them. She was the goddess of wisdom."

"I knew that," I lied. We turned a corner.

Among Saskatoonians, the closer you lived to water, the higher your status. Her parents had bought riverside property. The front was eighty percent glass: three levels blatantly exposed to the street, displaying their expensive possessions. I thought of Barbie and Ken's house.

Elissa's mom (Heather) and dad (Gregory) were each in their respective offices across the river. As hunters and gatherers of legal documents, they rarely returned to their nest. Elissa often prepared her own meals and once dressed two giant teddy bears in her parents' clothes and seated them at the dinner table. She served an expensive bottle of wine and discussed her allowance. Her parents didn't appreciate the joke or enjoy finding their sole offspring inebriated. Since then her dad has carried the liquor cabinet key on his key ring.

Inside, we were greeted by Fang. He immediately chomped down on my ankles and refused to let go, three kilos of unbridled toy poodle aggression. He was the second line of defense for the household, after the security system. Elissa's father had brought home this bundle of fluff the week after the wine-drinking episode. She swore she wouldn't be bought so easily, but her philosophical stand lasted about ten minutes.

I reached down, patted Fang's head. He rolled over and I scratched his belly. Thousands of years ago one of our ancestors took a wild wolf pup home and tamed it. Soon all the hunter-gatherers wanted one. Now here I was stroking a genetic parody of that wolf.

"Oh, little Fangy hungry!" Elissa exclaimed. Fang wagged his short tail (it had been clipped to impart visual balance to his body). He trotted after her into the kitchen. I trotted after them.

Fang immediately attacked his meal—a baked lamb specialty brand with a supplement that prevented rashes. If forced to live in the wild, Fang would fall apart in a week.

"Little Percy hungry?" Elissa asked. She motioned to a stainless steel fridge. "We have escargot. And peanut butter and jam."

"Do you have any royal jelly?" I asked, grinning.

She didn't get the joke. "What?"

"Royal jelly," I explained, containing my condescension. "When a queen bee dies another is elected by feeding this special jelly to a lucky larva. Royal jelly, get it? As in, I'm royalty."

"Hill-larry-us," she said flatly. "Maybe someday you'll evolve the ability to tell good jokes."

I put my hands on my hips.

"Wait, hold that pose." She lifted a pretend camera. "There! Perfect! *Homo sapiens poutitis,* a sad creature that wishes it had some good comebacks."

"I—I have comebacks. I choose not to lower myself to your level."

"Right," she said. "Now back to reality. Do you know what season you are?"

"What season? Like which is my favorite?"

"No, your season. Skin type, hair type—certain colors that accentuate your looks. Fall, winter, spring, summer. You're a winter, I bet. That means you look better in dark colors." Maybe there was a correlation between season and personality type. This could be the beginning of a groundbreaking thesis. "Don't look so worried. We'll find something completely tacky." Elissa pulled me out of the kitchen, up the stairs and into her room.

She positioned me next to the bed, which was

littered with stuffed mammals, mostly bears. Interesting how we choose the deadliest carnivores to render as playthings. A symbol of our dominance?

"You're actually kind of handsome," Elissa said, "Homo sapiens Don Juan."

My cheeks reddened. "Genetics," I mumbled.

She laughed and slid aside a mirrored door. "You look good in darks, so we'll forget about those." She searched, pulling aside sweaters and shirts, pushing back an entire rack of whites and beiges. Her clothes were color-coordinated with amazing precision—the browns went from dark to light brown, the reds and blues followed a similar pattern. She had enough to dress a small !Kung tribe.

Her movements amazed me. Especially her gluteus maximus. What was even more amazing was that she wasn't supposed to be here at all. On earth, that is. She was first formed when her father's semen was placed in a petri dish at a fertility clinic. One of those sixty million sperm united with an egg extracted from Elissa's mother.

You see, evolution had chosen not to continue her parents' genetic line: Her father had lazy sperm—they apparently preferred lounging about watching hockey. Her parents had cheated their biological destiny.

I watched Elissa, extremely happy that she had been able to become a living organism.

"Try these on," she said. A flashy red-and-green blur struck my chest. I closed my arms too late. "Nice catch!"

I looked down at a pair of large, baggy unisex shorts, designed to cover the knees.

"Get me a shirt, too, Miss Fashionoski," I said.

"As you command, Perky." She disappeared into the closet.

I slipped the shorts over my pants. They fit: two flamingo pillowcases on toothpick legs. A large oval mirror hung on the opposite wall. I examined *Australo-Percy-ithecus* in the shorts. I smiled. Elissa was one of the few who could make me feel truly happy.

Elissa. And Willard.

Will.

Willard was smallish and squat. Puberty had been cruel to him, planting an acne minefield under his face. He had a big smile, a high-pitched hyena laugh and a cowlick at the back of his hair that bobbed when he walked.

Once, the three of us went to a *Planet of the Apes* film festival. Grunting like simians, we monkey-walked to a nearby cafe and consumed several banana splits. Giddy with the sugar high, I told them my heart's dream was to be an anthropologist. To search for lost tribes in the jungle. Will said, "That's awesome!"

A year later he told me he loved Marcia Grady. That she was so beautiful he nearly wept when he saw her. It was one of our last conversations.

An ache the size of the La Brea Tar Pits filled me. He had been my friend. We'd shared secrets. Understood each other. And now I hardly remembered him. My brain was haphazardly erasing experiences, changing them.

Elissa emerged from the closet holding two shirts: bright yellow and a rainbow of colors. "Why'd you put the shorts on over your pants?"

"I couldn't very well undress in front of you."

She rolled her eyes. "I had my back turned. You worried I might see your Mickey Mouse briefs?"

"I—I'd never wear that commercialized rodent on my shorts!"

"Touched a nerve, did I?" She looked me over. "They fit, at least. Here, try this." She handed me the rainbow shirt, good camouflage if I had to hide in a parrot cage. "No, take off your T-shirt. Wear this one with a few buttons loose to show off your chest hairs. All two of them."

"I . . . I can't—"

"Don't be so anal. We're tribemates. Like two monkeys. C'mon."

"Yeah, but—"

"Hurry up!"

I undid my shirt, the air-conditioned chill forcing arm hairs to stand on end. She handed me a cotton rainbow; I stuck my arms through the holes. She attempted to button it but nearly choked me. "Too small! Your chest is bigger than I thought. You been working out?" She gave it another try.

"Hey," I said. "I need air."

Elissa let go. "Oops. Sorry. You . . ." She leaned forward, staring at my chest. "Wh-what are those scars?"

I looked down. A ring of white bumps circled my left nipple. My stomach filled with sand. "Ritual scarring. To release the pain."

Cool fingertips explored the marks. "Oh, Percy," she said softly, "oh, Percy."

"They're mine," I whispered. I stepped back and her hand fell away. She wore a look of absolute pity. I closed my eyes. "Mine. Mine."

"It's okay. Everything's so screwed up. Willard's gone. Your dad, too. You're . . . stressed. I understand."

She did? "Everyone. Leaves me. Like the Beothuks," I whispered. "Out of luck. One of them."

Her brow furrowed. "The what?"

I looked at her. Were we really from the same tribe?

I removed the shirt, grabbed my own from the floor and slipped it on. "This clothing, it—it—is not satisfactory," I said.

She still clutched the yellow shirt. "I've got more."

"No. I'll find something at home." I stepped out of the shorts; they fell to the floor. I backed away.

"We can talk, Percy."

"Talk?" Another step back. A third. "I. Must. Go. Home."

"Percy." A whisper. "We're friends. Don't shut me out."

I fled, taking the stairs two at a time, the sun shooting through the giant windows, lighting me up. Lighting the earth. Holding it inexorably in place. As it had for over four billion years.

nine

TRUNK

Within twenty minutes: relief. The skin around my left nipple ached brilliantly. My mind was clear. Copacetic. I cleansed my pin with rubbing alcohol and returned it to the container.

Silence. My mother was teaching a Qi Gong breathing class at the community hall. I sat on the meditation pillow in my room, assumed the lotus position and closed my eyes. Now, to order my thoughts. To analyze my reactions. To—

The phone buzzed. I remained still. The answering machine clicked on. Elissa's voice entered our house via the speaker. "Call me," she said, then coughed and hung up.

I breathed deeply, tightening my stomach muscles— a Tai Chi method I'd learned from Mom. I had a goal: to discover where all of this was leading. Evolution, that is. It pointed forward, indicating an obvious mission for us, a next logical step.

What was it?

I attempted to send my mind back through the millennia, to the source of all life. Somewhere in my brain was a link to the first organism with its orders to survive and replicate. Perhaps if I found the beginning, I could ascertain the end.

Green appeared in my mind, with a dark circle in the middle. I was envisioning mitosis—the nucleus dividing to form two nuclei. Chromosomes being copied. Life continuing. This was almost the beginning.

The phone buzzed again—a distant noise. The green faded to black. I concentrated on bringing the image back but failed. I uncrossed my legs, got up and rubbed my aching head. No contact with my primordial ancestors. No answer. Yet.

The light blinked on the answering machine. Automatic response: I pressed the button. *"Call me,"* Elissa's disembodied voice implored. Then: *"Percy, meet you at the party, okay?"*

I replayed the messages several times. I picked up the phone, punched in half her number, then clicked down the receiver. I repeated this procedure, then stood quietly listening to the monotone hum of the line. Soon the phone beeped loudly at me. A sign that I shouldn't call. I returned the phone to its cradle.

I concocted a meal of sprouts and seaweed. While masticating, I pondered Darwin's life. In 1831, at the age of twenty-two, he embarked on H.M.S. *Beagle.* For the next five years he studied animals, bugs, seeds and stones in South America, concentrating on the Galápagos Islands. From his observations he came up with the theory of natural selection. It took him twenty years to complete his first book on the topic.

I didn't have that kind of time. I wanted to understand now. To see the answer. To have that elusive eureka moment.

Time passed. I wandered from room to room, eventually ending up in the basement, where I was surrounded by rows of jarred peaches, pickled beans and bags of rice. The floor was a pad of concrete that supported an octopus furnace with large ducts running every which way across the ceiling. One light hovered in the center of the room like a giant firefly.

I bent under a duct and knelt before an old wooden trunk coated with dust. I opened it. On the top were several yellowed newspapers with headlines like *Local Anthropologist Identifies Mystical Zuni Object*, *My Life Among the !Kung* and *Montmount Mounts Mount Machu Picchu*. I skimmed the articles, then reached for the prize underneath.

My father's clothes in a neat, perfect pile. First: a canvas hat with a brim that flipped up. As a child I'd often donned the oversized headgear and pranced around the cluttered basement, imagining my father's adventures and shouting out: "Dr. Montmount, I presume!"

I slipped the hat on. It fit perfectly. I dug into the stack, discovering a multicolored shirt and a pair of khaki shorts. I stripped, not feeling the chill, then dressed in my father's outfit. Gently closing the trunk, I ascended the stairs.

I had a party to attend.

ten

THE DELUGE

I committed a fatal error at the Tacky Party.

The festive event was three blocks away at Sandra Woodrick's. I squeezed between several Jock Tribe members who congested the doorway, and helped myself to a pink lemonade–based punch. I sniffed gingerly. Conclusion: alcohol-free. I sipped nonchalantly, bobbing my head to the music. When in Namibia, do as the Namibians do, my father often said. Teens in colored shirts danced wildly through the living room; others sat on couches or the floor shouting to be heard.

I stood near the bathroom, jammed between a bookshelf and a life-sized reproduction of Rodin's *Thinker.* Hung behind him was a framed picture of card-playing canines dressed up like gangsters. I smiled. Anthropomorphism at its best. Mr. and Mrs. Woodrick must have a fabulous sense of humor, judging by the juxtaposition of those two works of art. Or no taste.

My smile faded as Michael and Nicole strode into the room. I ducked, but they veered in my direction like two lions stalking a lone antelope. And here was my fatal error. I broke a basic law of survival: Always have an escape route.

They approached, clad in matching garb: lime-green shorts and bright yellow T-shirts emblazoned with a red sun and a bird bearing a laurel branch. They absolutely *had* to talk to me: God's orders.

You see, they were from the Born-Again Tribe. They viewed me as a misguided mammal and were hell-bent on saving my soul.

"Percy," Michael said, "it's great to see you."

I straightened my back. "It is?"

"Of course." His light blue eyes were ethereal. His face flawless—smooth white skin and a glistening smile. His teeth had been artificially straightened.

"Are you having fun?" Nicole asked. She too had unnaturally perfect teeth; two large, friendly eyes. She tucked a curl of brown hair behind her ear.

"I experience a modicum of enjoyment."

"Modicum!" Michael echoed. "I like that. You have a real gift with words. It's a blessing."

"Thank you." I was flustered. I hadn't expected them to attend this function, had assumed it would be against their beliefs. But here they stood clutching cans of Canada Dry, looking . . .

. . . as if they belonged.

"Fun party!" Michael gushed as he watched the cavorting students. Did he see them as souls, some smudged with the darkness of sin, others shining bright as a thousand candles? "Drink?" He offered a can that dangled from a plastic six-pack holder.

"No, thank you." I raised my glass.

He moved a few centimeters closer. "I have a question for you."

My heart sank. "Not another Wilberforce," I whispered.

"Wilberforce?" Nicole asked.

"Bishop Wilberforce of Oxford," I huffed, annoyed that they didn't know their theological history. "Darwin's archenemy. He gave the *Origin* a bad review. Asked whether man was descended from monkeys on the paternal or maternal side. He knew nothing about science. He died when he fell off his horse and hit his thick head on a stone."

"Oh," Nicole offered. "Really."

Michael's smile hadn't faded. "That's interesting. But what I'm curious about is the fossils. I know you think we're crazy."

"No," I said emphatically, "religious beliefs are not an insanity. All societies consider it normal to believe in supernatural beings and forces."

"So you don't think we're crazy?" Nicole said.

"I just made that point."

"Good to hear." Michael lightly squeezed my shoulder. His hand was warm. I stared down at it until he removed it. "Anyway, about the fossils. You know how they date them and stuff. I asked our study leader why the scientists got it mixed up."

"Mixed up?" I asked. "Oh, that's right. You believe the world is only ten thousand years old."

"You don't have to yell, Percy," Michael said softly, "the music's not that loud. The earth is actually only six thousand years old. Adam was created in 3975 B.C."

Nicole edged closer. "And don't forget that lots of

scientists aren't sure carbon dating even works. Or that evolution is true. It's just another theory."

Michael used his opposable thumb to open the last can of ginger ale. It fizzed, so he brought it to his mouth. "Anyway, it's the fossils we want to talk about. They're real."

"They are?" I asked.

"Yes." Nicole was now face to face with me. They were a spiritual-philosophical tag team. "But you've been fooled by . . . well, you know . . . *him*." She pointed at the floor. "Evolution. Devilution. Soul pollution." It was a tribal chant. "*He* made you think that fossils are millions of years old. He does tell the truth but circles it with lies. You see, Percy, there *were* dinosaurs."

"There were?" I sensed a breakthrough. "In the Bible?"

Michael fielded this question. "On the ark. Two of each species is what God told Noah. And when the ark finally was caught on Mount Ararat, the dinosaurs stepped out into the new world. Rain had swept everything away. There were new diseases. All of the dinosaurs got sick, died, fell into the ocean and were compressed by the weight of the water, hardening their bones instantly into fossils. Do you see?"

"I understand," I answered, though the idea that the ark could hold enough animals to repopulate the world was ludicrous. A population cannot sustain itself with only two of its species: The gene pool would be too small. Not to mention that water pressure can't harden living flesh into stone.

Thankfully, I glimpsed Elissa across the room. She'd

chosen a flashy pink shirt and a giant gardening hat that could have doubled as an umbrella. When she looked at me, I waved. She removed her hat and held it like a shield against her bosom. She was trapped by overexcited dancers.

"You know," I said, turning my attention back to the Born-Again Tribe, "the age of the universe can be measured using the speed of light. Astronomists have devised a formula that proves light from distant stars began traveling toward Earth billions of years ago."

Put that in your philosophical pipe and smoke it, I thought.

"The speed of light has not been measured properly." Nicole spoke carefully, as though to a child. "Everyone knows that."

I slumped.

Michael drained his ginger ale. "You should meet our study leader. He'd like to talk to you. Our Bible study is fun, you know. Not like other churches."

Agitation saturated my nerves. A simple command to get out. *Out.* Elissa was still halfway across the room, surrounded by a chain of revelers doing the locomotion.

"You know, you're okay, Percy," Nicole said, briefly touching my wrist. "You're really okay."

I furrowed my brow. Okay? I was okay? My tear ducts welled up.

"Did I say something wrong?" she asked.

I shook my head. Elissa joined us at last, nodded at Michael and Nicole. They smiled back.

"I . . . I left my stuff in your car," I said to Elissa.

"What stuff?"

"Those . . . uh . . . field notes I took today. I must retrieve them. Now."

"Yes," she said, recognizing the crisis. "Right. You should."

I walked past Michael and Nicole, pulling Elissa along behind me. We wriggled through the sweaty, Yuk-a-flux–soaked congestion. Outside, I sucked in fresh air. Two teens lay gazing skyward. A tribe of skateboarders, heads shaved, some wearing ski hats, rolled again and again over a jump on the sidewalk, like mice endlessly repeating an experiment.

"What was that about?" Elissa asked.

"They—Michael and Nicole—they have all the answers. They're just so . . . happy."

"Yeah, freaky, eh? Sorry I didn't rescue you sooner. But you should have returned my call."

"Oh. I didn't get it." I breathed deeper. "Really, I didn't."

"You're lucky I came. I stopped by your house and your mom had no idea where you were. Why didn't you call me?"

"I—I just couldn't . . ."

Her look softened. "Are you upset that I saw your scars?"

"No, I'm not. I'm not."

"Don't . . . don't get worked up." She grabbed my hand, squeezed it gently between both of hers as if she'd caught a butterfly. "You take everything so seriously."

I had to take things seriously. How else would I get

my work done? "Elissa, I . . ." My thoughts were too random to express. "I'm sorry. I—I hurt. You. Your feelings, I mean. I didn't intend. To."

"Percy, it's . . . I think I understand. Well, not everything: Who in Hades were the Beothuks?" She grinned.

I laughed. I couldn't help it. "A tribe. In Newfoundland. They painted themselves with red ochre. They died out."

"I see," she said. "Now I do know everything." She squeezed my hands. "This'll all blow over soon. We'll spend the summer catching rays and drinking daiquiris. We'll survive Grad Week. Where there's a will there's a way."

It was one of Will's favorite sayings. A joke. I pulled back my hand. "I could have stopped him," I said. "Should have."

"Will, you mean?"

"He told me. About Marcia. He asked whether I thought he stood a chance with her. I—I was too forthright: I said it was unlikely. She wasn't from our tribe."

"You couldn't have done anything, Percy. Sometimes things just happen."

"Things never just happen," I said. "There's always a reason. I wish I'd lied."

"That wouldn't have changed a thing. It was more than just Marcia. He was—he just kept so much to himself. Who knows what he was thinking half the time?"

"Did he tell you about his crush on her?" I asked.

"Yes. I almost fell over backward to hear him talk about his own feelings. And not joke about them."

"What did you say when he told you?"

"I—I don't really remember. Something like it was good to fall in love. Something like that."

She'd been encouraging. Loving, not logical. "He was lucky to have you as a friend."

"He was lucky to have both of us," she said. "And we were lucky to know him."

I opened my mouth to say something else, but Elissa put a finger to my open lips. "Shhh," she whispered. "You're getting that dazed look. It always happens when you think too much." Her skin tasted salty. She pulled her finger away, put it to her lips. "Shhh. Just forget about everything for now."

I nodded. She grabbed my hand and led me onto the street. "Enough tribal interactions for tonight," she said. "One can only be tacky for so long."

We wandered along silently for several blocks. She didn't let go of my hand. I tried not to think about what this might mean, concentrated on enjoying the warmth of her skin. We walked onto Broadway, into the bright neon lights of the bars and restaurants. Cutting across the street, we took a dark lane instead.

"By the way," Elissa said finally, "I like your hat. It's very cool."

Pride swelled up, but then Dad's hat felt loose, as if a small wind might lift it from my head. Without thinking, I pulled my hand from hers and held the hat down. After several steps I realized my mistake.

Stupid. Stupid me.

Though we walked together for another twenty minutes, I never found the guts to reclaim her hand.

* * *

At midnight, Elissa and I hugged in front of my house. For a long time. Then I went inside, my legs all wobbly.

Mom was meditating in the living room, surrounded by candles and a haze of pine incense. *Ommmmmm* emanated from somewhere deep inside her throat. Her lips didn't move. She could *Ommm* for hours, contacting various internal organs, willing them to function in perfect harmony with the rest of her body and the universe.

I padded past her. Stopped. Changed my course and sat down.

She opened her eyes. Smiled. "You're home," she said. "Nice outfit."

I slipped off the hat. "I was at a party. A tacky dress-up party."

"So you went disguised as your father?"

"I was myself. I was pretending I was on safari."

"Was it fun?"

I shrugged. "It was . . . well . . . entertaining."

"Good."

A long silence followed. She continued to smile.

"Mom. Tell me again. What happens when we die?" I asked.

"We ascend to the next stage of existence. Shed our flesh. Become pure spiritual energy. We have so much more to do. To become."

"What if I don't believe that? What happens to me?"

"Your doubts are natural. All will unfold as it should."

I nodded. "That's good to know," I said.

I retired to my room. Everyone had an answer. But

I had none. I sighed. My lot, apparently, was to be an analyzer.

I went to my desk and recorded the day's events. Finally—arm tired, mind emptied—I collapsed on my bed and dreamed of jungles, tsetse flies and Elissa's warm hand.

eleven

SON OF THE NDEBELE

I was born in Saskatoon City Hospital at 11:05 P.M., August 19. My mother endured nine hours of labor and refused all medication. The attendees were a female doctor, two nurses, and Mom's midwife, Priscilla. I increased the population of the room, the city and the world by one.

I was also born at the same time fifteen thousand kilometers away in the district of Mpumalanga, South Africa. That's where my father was living with the Ndzundza, an Ndebele tribe. He had been there for six months, had heard of my mother's ever-swelling belly via letters.

Kgope, an old man of the tribe, burst into my father's conical mud house (there was also some dung mixed in as cement) and announced, "Unto you has son been born." It was 7:25 A.M. local time.

Dad was stunned. How did Kgope know? There were no phones. My father hadn't even spoken of the expected child.

Kgope explained: "My wife awoke. Shouted out 'Krep.' Then left our matrimonial bed and made this." He handed my father a Swazi tribal doll of cloth and beads. "It is gift. For you. It is called Krep. It is your son. Your son it is. He is Ndebele now. Protected by the ancestors."

He next presented Dad with a beer. Kgope was the best beer maker in the area. They drank and talked about the hopes my father had for me. When they were finished, Kgope stood, grabbed Dad's suitcase and began packing Dad's clothes.

"What are you doing?" Dad asked.

Kgope didn't stop. *"Ubaba makeze ekhaya,"* he said quietly.

It took Dad a moment to translate the words: *Father should come home.*

"Your son spoke to me. Through Krep. It is time for you to go."

And so he did. Dad came all the way home.

To see me.

His only son.

That was not the last of my connections with the Ndebele. Years later my father warned me about the cruelest physical stage all humans endure: puberty. He explained that manhood was a seed Mother Nature had planted inside me. When the time was right, it would grow out of my body. "It's nothing to be frightened of; we evolve. Never fear change."

I was ten. Holding a toy car in my hand, the metal cold against my palm.

Then he told me how the Ndebele take their pubescent males into the bush for two months, shave their heads, circumcise them and train them in the manly arts. This ritual is called the *wela*. When they return to the village, a celebration is held and they are admitted to the councils of men. As part of their training they learn a secret language in which words are spoken backward. This language may not be divulged to strangers, or even to their own women.

"It's a shame the West doesn't have any traditions like it," my father said. "Such an amazing sight, all those young men, their bald heads glistening in the sun. So proud." Dad promised to lead me through a Canadian version of the ritual upon his return. It would involve a trip to a northern lake, a fishing rod and sleeping bags. Luckily, I had already been circumcised.

"Even the most civilized mind needs rituals," Dad explained. "It soothes the primitive within."

He never got the chance to take me, but when puberty finally grew out of my body, I was unafraid. I knew I was an Ndebele youth taking that next inevitable step toward becoming a man.

About the same time, a doll arrived in the mail, from Kgope. Attached was a note in scribbled English: "Welcome to manhood, Krep."

Krep.

Perk.

A backward sign. A symbol.

I was a man now.

twelve

DREAM WORLD

At 7:50 A.M. our phone buzzed. Mom answered, talking in a hushed voice. A moment later, she padded into my room and presented a note. I read it groggily: *Session with Mr. Verplaz. 2:30 P.M.*

Mom's face was calm, except for the slightest downturn of her lips.

"I'll be there," I promised.

"I want to know why you weren't there yesterday."

"I—I forgot." Her demeanor indicated she needed more from me. "Mom, everything's so hectic at school. It's Grad Week. It's crazy! I honestly forgot."

"I would prefer if you didn't forget today."

I nodded. She didn't move. "You're too much like your father."

A chill skittered down my spine.

"You're in a dream world," she continued. "Not the real world. You've got to learn to stay grounded *and* dream. Let your spirit soar but remain in your body. Your father wandered too much in his own thoughts." She let out her breath. "You really should talk to him." Then she left.

I didn't move. She thought I was too much like Dad. I was worried I wasn't enough like him. I closed my eyes, pictured his face. I couldn't remember it perfectly, but I'd try to send him a message. Mom's orders. *Hey, Dad*, I thought. *Hello out there.* I wondered how long the message would take to reach him. *Ubaba makeze ekhaya. Pronto.*

Eventually, I got up. After a breakfast of oatmeal porridge soaked in soy milk, I marched toward my third-to-last day of school. The sun was in the east. Light that had traveled a hundred and fifty million kilometers in eight and a half minutes warmed my skin. A pleasant sensation.

Just as I caught sight of Groverly High, a wailing cacophony stopped me. The sound of thirty cats dying a slow death. Of the universe ripping apart.

Bagpipes. Somewhere nearby. The Scottish blood in my veins, from my mother's side, began to vibrate. My Celtic heart thudded with joy. I had no choice—I was genetically programmed to respond to that wailing. I followed the sound, heading toward the river.

The bagpiper was extremely good. He had to be part of a Highlander band. Or the army. I wondered if he'd be clad in full kilt, flame-red hair billowing in the breeze.

Dew dotted the grass. A few tails of mist curled around the edge of the river. A woman jogged past, weights attached to her wrists and ankles—her face set in a look of absolute determination. I strolled under the Victoria Bridge, turned. Froze.

There, above me on a knoll, was Delmar Brass. Clad in blue jeans and a black shirt, his long hair down, playing the pipes as if he'd just strolled off a Scottish ship. He was facing the river, blasting his song toward the high-rise buildings and hotels on the other side. The music stirred some ancient feeling in my body. Songs of my ancestors. A direct tonal connection to the past.

It tuned my biorhythms.

Watching Delmar, I was amazed at the revelation handed me. Two cultures exhibited in one person. Proof that we all came from the same tree.

There was also a lesson: Never make assumptions. Rely on observation, then make a conclusion.

I backed away and climbed up the hill. The bagpipes slowly faded, but I still heard them echo inside my mind's ear. Groverly swallowed me readily. I sleepwalked down the halls and with numb fingers opened my locker. *Click.*

I stepped back, books in hand. Someone tripped over my leg and fell.

Marcia Grady was on the floor, looking up at me, blond hair perfectly coifed, lipstick expertly applied, a trace of blue shadow accentuating her eyes.

A face to fall in love with.

Mom was right. I was living in a dream world.

"Sorry," Marcia said as she gracefully got up off the floor. She was taller than me. "I didn't see you there."

"I too am sorry."

She smiled, her automatic reaction to everything. I knew why Willard had fallen in love with her: such innocence and beauty. Unattainable.

She picked up my books and handed them to me. "How are things going?"

"They progress," I answered. "In a good way, I

mean. Fine. Really." No one had ever told her that Willard had been in love with her. I wanted to say: Remember those phone calls where someone kept hanging up? That was Willard. But I bit my tongue. Better for her not to know. Still, in my mind Marcia and Willard were forever linked.

"Well," she said, "gotta go."

"Wait," I said. "Do you remember Willard?"

"Willard?"

"Willard Spokes. Will."

Her face showed no recognition. Then: sadness. "Oh . . . yes. He was the one who . . . yes. I remember him. He was a friend of yours, wasn't he?"

"A good friend," I said. "I—I just wanted to be sure people remembered him."

"I do. He was a quiet guy. A nice quiet guy."

I nodded. "Yes. He was."

"Well, see you," she said, walking away.

"Yes, in the future," I answered, watching her until she was lost in the crowd.

Memory. Somewhere in the coils of her brain Willard still existed.

thirteen

READING MAMMOTH ENTRAILS

"**R**eady for your 'igh tea, Perky?" Elissa asked in a faux British accent.

"I certainly am," I said. We'd decided to stroll around the schoolyard during break. Stopping at a set of old swings, we performed our impressions of human pendulums.

"I did some reading about this weird tea thing," she continued. "We learned it from the Brits. But we're mixed up, as usual. A high tea isn't a high-and-mighty, hoity-toity event. It really means 'It's high time we had a spot o' tea and something to eat.' " She dug her feet into the sand, stopping herself. "You're daydreaming again," she accused.

"I'm in the zone," I admitted. "Attuned to the potential of the universe. Just waiting for a revelation to hit."

"Or a truck," she said.

"Don't you have days like that?" I asked. "Where the world feels . . . unreal?"

"I worry about you," she said. "Every day is real for me."

"Never mind," I said. "Obviously my brilliance astounds you."

"You *are* in a different world," she teased. "I hope you can still tell time. The High Tea starts at four-thirty. Why don't we meet outside the school?"

"Sure," I said absently. "I'll be there."

We soon returned to our classes, learning nothing new. At precisely 2:27 P.M. I climbed the stairs to Groverly High's top floor, passing the soft-drink machine where Justin had threatened me. My shoulders tensed. By the fourth floor the tightness had doubled and my palms were moist. I breathed using my stomach muscles, aiming to restore calmness. I entered the fluorescent glow and squinted down the long, shadowy hallway.

It took considerable willpower to move my legs. As I got closer to the trapdoor, spittle gathered in my throat. I stopped underneath, mesmerized. How had Willard climbed to the roof? Had he moved a chair to this very spot? Had he used his opposable-thumbed hands to pull himself up?

A scratching came from the other side of the door. The hinges rattled. Then I noticed that the padlock was open.

Perspiration gathered on my forehead. "I remember," I rasped. An ice age came and went. "I remember you, Will."

One final long scratch.

I hurried on to Mr. Verplaz's office. On the door hung a sign:

All words spoken inside this room
will remain here.

It was intended to inspire trust, but I felt grief for all those trapped words. I wiped the cold sweat from my forehead and knocked.

"Come in," Mr. Verplaz said gently, sounding as if he were waking from a potent dream.

I opened the door to a closet-sized office. Mr. Verplaz sat behind an antique wooden desk, his hands touching in a gesture of prayer. He was a forty-year-old ascetic with tanned skin, a hawk nose and small, round-lensed glasses. His eyes were spectacular, the over-sized orbs of a well-groomed lemur, evolved to soak up moonlight.

School shaman. Truth seeker. Witch doctor.

"I said *come in,* Percival."

I closed the door and stepped over a collection of scrunched-up papers by the garbage can. His office hadn't changed since Willard's death. A forty-watt bulb still hung from the ceiling. The shade was pulled. Light bad. Darkness good. Where dreams come from. Folders lay scattered across his desk. A half-empty jar of lollipops sat precariously close to the edge. Books were piled on the floor. All a symbol of the chaos of the universe.

Mr. Verplaz pierced me with his mystical eyes. "Please sit down. It's good to see you."

I sat on the leather chair, which suddenly reclined at a sharp angle; I became an astronaut waiting to test gravity's bonds. We had walked on the moon. Our footprints would be there for millennia.

Pencils were stuck in the ceiling. When would one fall?

Mr. Verplaz cleared his throat. "Now, I'm not upset, but I'd like to understand why you missed yesterday's session."

"I . . . I forgot." I knew at once the shaman would recognize my statement as a lie. He surprised me with nodding acceptance.

"You are an exceptionally intelligent young man," he said quietly, as if letting me in on a great secret. "Do you know why you're here?"

"I was in a fight, so Groverly's patriarch ordered me to attend."

Mr. Verplaz smiled. "Are you angry with Mr. Michaels?"

"No."

"Then tell me, what is the real reason you are here?" This was another tool of *Homo shaman therapist*—a skin bag stuffed with questions.

"Apparently, the Teacher Tribe is concerned about my behavior."

"Do you understand why?"

"They are hired to assimilate me. It's their duty. Even if it is the last week of school."

"What's your favorite color?"

It took me a moment to process the question. "Gray."

"Why?"

"It's the color of the volcanic sediment surrounding Lucy's remains."

"Lucy?" He scratched his head, confused. I lost some respect for him.

"Yes, Lucy. *Australopithecus afarensis,*" I explained.

"Do you mean the ape fossil?"

"She was *not* an ape but an ancestor of humans. You are confusing her with the 'missing link' between ape and man. She is on *our* side of the divide. I'm surprised you're not aware of that."

The corners of his mouth curled into a grin. "You know a lot about human history, don't you?"

I nodded.

"What's the worst thing that's ever happened?"

"Ever?" I repeated. "Through all time?"

"Sure, all time."

"Easy. When *Australopithecus* climbed down from the trees and walked upright."

His smile disappeared. "Why?"

"Hiroshima."

"Explain."

I gathered my thoughts. The walls of this office would not be able to contain these words, but I decided to release them anyway. "In 1945 a crew of hominids piloted the *Enola Gay,* a B-29 bomber constructed by hominids. It carried a four-hundred-and-eight-kilogram atomic device built by another group of scientist hominids. They called the device Little Boy. They dropped this bomb on Hiroshima, a city full of Japanese hominids. Ten square kilometers were flattened: a hundred thousand unsuspecting hominids perished immediately. Another hundred thousand later succumbed to burns and radiation sickness."

Mr. Verplaz was speechless. He leaned forward, as though trying to get a clearer picture of me.

I continued. "Why didn't they flatten Mount Fujiyama instead? Wouldn't that have conveyed the same message? But they targeted Hiroshima, a city founded in the sixteenth century, then returned three days later and flattened Nagasaki. Just think of all the genetic lines—the years of evolution it took to create those specific human beings—all gone in a flash that reduced their DNA strands to nothing."

Mr. Verplaz had crossed his arms and shifted slightly away. I slid my chair closer.

"Pretend we could go back to that lush jungle where *Australopithecus afarensis Lucy* sits in a tree, minding her own business. What if we told Lucy that when she climbed down and stood upright, she would begin a process in which her offspring's offspring would climb into the cockpit of the *Enola Gay?* Would she stand upright? Or decide to stay in that tree for another five million years, leaving the world to the apes and chimpanzees?"

Mr. Verplaz adjusted his glasses. "So mankind doesn't deserve to exist?"

"It's not my job to judge."

"What is your job?"

"To observe. To take notes."

"For whom?"

For my father. Verplaz had nearly dragged the words out of me.

"For future anthropologists," I said carefully. His luminous, hypnotic eyes stared. He saw secrets. He truly was a shaman, descended from the great shamans who guided our tribes through dream worlds. I sensed his spirit surrounding me. I was in his bear cave.

"You were about to say something else."

I shook my head.

"How's your relationship with your mother?"

"She's loving, understanding and nurturing. And

I . . ." I wanted to use the word *love* but it was too vague, its meaning slippery. Instead: "I try to be a good son."

He loomed closer, now peering directly at me. His ancestors had once read mammoth entrails. His magico-religious powers were fine-tuned to the point of omniscience. "What about your father?" he whispered.

"He died long ago."

This startled Mr. Verplaz: He blinked and squinted at a paper, presumably the profile of Percival Montmount, Jr.

"Your father's dead?" the shaman said with disbelief. "I'm sure I would have read about it in the papers."

"I assure you, he has passed on."

"Are you comfortable talking about it?"

"Of course. Death is part of the life cycle. My father was bitten by a beetle in the Congo and infected with black Azazel sickness."

"A beetle bit him? Do they carry infections?"

"Did I say beetle? I'm mixing him up with Darwin." My thoughts were jagged, broken. "It was a tsetse fly."

"When did he die?"

"Three years ago."

"What kind of man was he? Warm? Aloof?"

I tapped my foot on the floor. Stopped. "He traveled frequently."

"Did you like him?"

"Of course. He was my father, I . . . I loved him. He was an excellent storyteller."

"What kind of stories?"

"About adventures in the field."

"Can you give me an example?"

I nodded eagerly. "Once, when my father was in New Guinea exploring some ruins, he found an ancient emerald ax used for sacrifices, a priceless, one-of-a-kind artifact that belonged to a long-extinct tribe. He knew this one discovery would bring him fame.

"He couldn't escape the thoughts of glory: He saw himself in front of the cameras gripping the sacrificial weapon. He set out to bring it home. For two nights he was plagued by nightmares, and on the third day he discovered he'd come full circle and was back at the ruins again. He tried heading in the opposite direction. Same result. Finally he restored the ax to its sacred place and was able to find his way back to civilization. He never told anyone but me about the ax."

Mr. Verplaz leaned on his elbows; the desk creaked. "Were your father's stories true?"

"What?"

"Did he tell the truth?"

"Of course." Anger had crept into my voice. "Of course," I repeated quietly.

"Are you on any meds?"

"No." My foot tapped hard now. Bipedal motion. Heel. Toe. Heel. Toe.

"I think you should see Dr. Skein. She's a psychiatrist. I hope you aren't offended by this suggestion."

"I would thoroughly enjoy the opportunity." Skein was another variation of his tribe. Her territory was the coiled layers of the brain.

The bell rang, indicating the end of our session, but Mr. Verplaz held me with a look. I wasn't sure what he wanted. Finally he dismissed me with a nod. Partway out the door I stopped, realizing I had a spiritual question for him: "Have you ever heard a voice in the school attic?"

"What kind of voice?" he asked, clearly alarmed.

"Oh, nothing," I said, stepping out the door. I closed it behind me.

All words spoken inside this room will remain here.

The statement was false. The words Mr. Verplaz and I had shared buzzed around my head like dragonflies over some Mesozoic swamp. I walked quickly under the trapdoor and down the stairs. The school was deserted, but the students' pheromones and discarded skin cells clung to the walls. The buzzing words followed me home and into my room.

Then: I forced them out through my pen in perfect order. The day's events. Observations. Interpretations.

There was a knock at my window. I ignored it. It became more insistent. I carried on with my work. I missed the Graduation High Tea and the accompanying rituals. My article took precedence.

Later I grew vaguely aware that my mother was sitting on my bed in the lotus position.

"Perk?" she said.

I kept writing.

"Perk, what are you doing?"

"I'm trying to finish an article."

"Are you okay?"

"I am feeling incredibly self-actualized, Mom. Top-o'-the-world, in fact."

I jotted down another sentence.

"Will you please stop?"

"When I'm finished," I informed her.

I'm not certain when she left.

Sooner than I expected it, morning light brightened my room. It was important to keep writing. At last the words quit buzzing in my ears and I slept. After four hours I woke up, my mind precise. Focused. Omniscient.

fourteen

THE PRIMITIVE WITHIN

I waited for Elissa in the center of what used to be our front lawn, seated cross-legged on top of Ogo, a giant rock. Three years ago Mom had terra-formed this square space into a rock garden, ripping out the lawn, while feeling guilt over the death of every blade. She then brought home stones from her various spiritual trips, planting them alongside the rosebushes, vines and sunflowers. The stones had been infused with ancient spirits, so she'd asked each one its permission to bring it here.

Ogo was the biggest. And the most benevolent, according to Mom. He was the protector of our lawn, with a thousand years of wisdom in his igneous form. He also made a great chair.

The hair on my arms shot up. The streetlight began to hum, then flicked on, heralding the evening. Elissa's black VW bug pulled up and stopped. Synchronicity. Of course.

I couldn't see her through the darkened windows. The car had been a gift from her parents on her seventeenth birthday. She prized it second only to Fang, though she felt guilt about the carbon monoxide it produced.

I untangled my legs and walked over and tugged on

the door handle. It was locked. I knocked on the window. Nothing. Knocked again. *Click.* I opened the door, slid inside.

Elissa jammed on the gas and I slammed the door. She glared ahead as I struggled to fasten my seat belt.

"You're in a hurry," I commented.

She flicked a bit of fluff off her black baseball shirt. Her chest and back were decorated with a stylized ankh. The shirt was from Logoless—a company that designed clothing for modern activists. She'd ordered it online. "Where were you yesterday?" she finally said. "And today, for that matter?"

"I decided not to attend school," I answered, pressing a button that let my window down a crack; the effluvia of the traffic swept inside.

"You skipped the second-last day of Grade Twelve? What's the point of that?"

"I was working on my book."

She refused to even glance at me. Her mauve lipstick accentuated the thickness of her lips. Her favorite eyebrow ring with the tiny dragonfly glinted in the streetlight; sandalwood perfume drifted from her body. She smelled friendly but didn't look it.

We passed through the final set of lights before Saskatoon's outskirts. Vehicles of all descriptions stretched in front of us like giant manic crustaceans, speeding around the edge of the city and into the wilderness. We were navigating toward the River Party, the most primitive of all Grad celebrations.

A Mustang, its tires augmented to the point of parody, roared past, rear end swerving, horn blaring. Two males waved muscular arms out the window. The vehicle drove down the wrong side of the highway, then veered into the proper lane, dodging an oncoming truck.

The Highway Tribe. A short-lived species.

A kilometer later Elissa turned onto a gravel road, following the line of cars. "I knocked at your window. I saw you sitting at your desk."

"I don't remember that."

"That's funny. You looked up, then ignored me."

"Elissa, I didn't hear you. I was having an intense experience, writing an article about . . ." Now, what was the topic? "Well, I didn't mean to ignore you."

"You shut me out. That's the point."

"I am sorry. Very sorry. I just had to get my work done."

She nodded solemnly. We rattled along the road, trees forming a wall on either side. I leaned back in my seat, appreciating the insectlike elegantness of her VW bug; it was as though we were riding inside a hollowed-out bumblebee, engine buzzing.

A tiny plastic skeleton hung from the rearview mirror, jaws clacking with every bump. I gazed in awe at its bipedal feet, examined the opposable thumbs. What if we had evolved to the size of this toy? It would have been so much better for the planet. We'd inhabit one sixth of the space, our tiny anthill cities just dots across the world. Coyotes would control our population.

The VW bug glided over a rise and there it was: the river. An open view of black water, three giant bonfires along the edge, revelers dancing between them. A flashback to the primitive within; a return to the life-giving waters where our ancestors first built their tiny mud-hut communities. Tonight's celebration was about the most basic elements: fire, water, earth and air.

And beer. A cornucopia of brewed fermented barley. I wondered if it was to honor the memory of the two Groverly students killed while driving drunk last year. A libation to their hovering spirits.

The segmented line of cars disassembled, finding parking spots next to bushes along the road. Members of all tribes rushed exuberantly toward the bonfires.

Elissa guided the bug to the edge of the ditch and stopped. "We're here," she announced quietly, turning off the car. The dashboard lights went black. She let out a huff of air, indicating continuing emotional turmoil.

I glanced out the window as a swarm of teens streamed past. The riverbank teemed with life. Action. Interaction. There was so much to observe. I clutched the door latch, but Elissa wouldn't budge.

"When will you show me your field journal?" she asked.

"When it's *absolutely* ready."

"Don't bite my head off!"

Had I sounded that angry? "I—I want it to be perfect before I release it to the world," I explained. "You understand that, don't you? It's my life's work."

"Life's work?" She hugged herself. Her V collar displayed her clavicle. "You're seventeen, Percy. How can you have a life's work?"

I shrugged. Elissa pointed at the bonfires. "This is our final night as high school students. We should try to enjoy it."

She'd chosen a different topic, at least. "Yes, grad-

★ 98

uation," I agreed, "ascension to a higher order. To the next stage. We are pupae waiting for the end of chrysalis."

"What do we change into?"

"We?"

"Yes, you and I. What do we become?" she asked. The moonlight made her lips glisten.

"Nothing. It's the other tribes' task to change. Ours is to observe."

She went quiet again, ruminating heavily. "Don't you ever get sick of watching?"

"What?"

"It . . . well, it used to be a joke between us. All this anthro stuff."

"It's my . . . *our* job. Come on, Elissa. Let's observe—join the party. Have fun, like we did when Will was here."

Will's name had popped out. Just like that. Elissa's eyes teared up. "Do you think he's watching us now? From somewhere up there?"

This was not the time for me to get into my theories about the statistical chances of life after death. "Maybe he is. And he's giving us the thumbs-up. Doing his best *Planet of the Apes* impression."

She breathed in, steeled herself and opened her door. "Let's party, then."

But now I was frozen. This talk had resurrected the memory of Elissa holding me in my room after Will's funeral as tears slid down my face and she said again and again, "Everything will be fine."

"What are you waiting for?" Elissa had come around to my side of the car. "I thought you were ready for this."

"Thank you," I whispered.

"What?" she said. "Come on."

As we strolled to the river, flames from the fires licked the sky, lighting everyone's faces. Sparks scattered through the air as the wood crackled. Teens gyrated, hypnotized by the blaze. One Grunge Tribe member sucked in smoke from a joint and gazed at the moon with rapture. Was he a shaman divining the inner workings of the universe? About to announce the ultimate human dream quest? He coughed, releasing a smoggy cloud. Then he pressed one nostril closed and blew onto the ground, giggling.

"This *is* kind of amazing," Elissa said as we meandered through the crowd, the tribes dancing around us in a majestic celebration. All differences were forgotten, boundaries erased; tonight they were one, on the edge of their new lives.

Music pounded out of hidden speakers, rhythmic chanting against the beating of drums. My father had once penetrated the deepest, darkest heart of the jungle and discovered two tribes dancing and singing together. They had stopped their celebration to gape at him, believing he was a god.

So many stories. Night after night, by my bedside. Then he was gone, never to be seen again.

My eyes ached. I stumbled over a broken branch, nearly fell.

"You okay, Percy?" Elissa asked.

"The smoke. It stings."

She took my hand and led me away from the fire. There were other tribes occupying the hinterland, hiding from the light: the Necking Tribe, the Smoker Tribe, the Cool and Detached Tribe. We stepped around abandoned blankets and zigzagged between overturned lawn chairs and entwined bodies. We found a spot where we could be alone and stared back at the distant flames.

What was it like that first time a human saw fire? Were we mesmerized by the power inside that flickering?

"It's all too weird," Elissa said. "Like they're dancing while the world ends."

There was a clink. A pop. Then she pushed a cold bottle into my hand.

"What's this?" I asked.

"Beer. It was sitting right here. A gift from the gods, obviously."

"But I can't consume beer."

"Why?"

I squinted at the bottle. "It will affect my judgment."

"It'll loosen you up. Don't tell me you still haven't tried it."

"I won't."

She chuckled. "Not even a sip? Aren't you curious?"

"No."

"Think of it as a tribal potion," she whispered, so close her breath tickled my ear hairs. "You can't experience the tribe's inner world without this elixir. Just a swig. Besides, you need to relax."

She drank from hers, so I followed suit, feeling the cool glass on my lips and swallowing quickly. The beer was cold; the liquid entered my stomach with gusto. I had the momentary feeling it would all come gurgling back up my esophagus. Coughing, sputtering, I said, "People enjoy this? It's like ginger ale and vinegar."

"They adapt to it—that's what humans do. Adapt. It gets better."

Elissa swigged from her bottle; I mimicked her. The odor was putrid. Which tribesperson had mixed water with rotted grains and risked a sip? And then convinced other unsuspecting hominids to partake? I took another long gulp.

"You like it." She handed me another. "It's my new job to get you to loosen up. I'm the leopard queen of the Loosen-Up Tribe."

We sat on a big log, a good decision because I felt dizzy. The potion's essence was bringing out my inner Cro-Magnon. The pounding music. The smoke. I had established a link with my past. There was a driving force pushing all organisms forward, out of the water, always ahead, compelling us to survive, to become stronger, faster, better able to conquer our environment. I was channeling it now.

Elissa patted my knee. "You're pretty quiet. What are you thinking?"

"About everything." The words slid out. "About you. Me. Everything."

She took this as an invitation to move closer. I hadn't noticed how cool it had become. The heat of her body: comforting.

"I really do care about you," she said.

My arm was around her, though I couldn't recall positioning it there. My mind went blank. She turned toward me and I mirrored her. Her breath was tainted with beer, but it wasn't nauseating. We were from the same tribe, watching our ancestors dance.

She leaned forward and we pressed our lips together.

I had never kissed before. This seemed fated: From

the moment my cells formed, they'd been programmed to find her lips and kiss them.

She slid her tongue into my mouth. An ancient feeling: our tongues moving in a warm, moist place like the pool in which life first formed.

Elissa sighed. "That's nice," she whispered. I kissed her again and my hand explored her back, tracing each vertebra. It felt absolutely natural. To caress. Explore. I slid my hand under the front of her shirt and cupped my fingers over her left breast, using my opposable thumb to squeeze. She pressed closer.

I sighed, then spoke gently into her ear. "So this is what the female mammae feel like."

Elissa jerked as if she'd been stung. *"What?"*

My hand was frozen.

"What?" she repeated, sitting back. My hand slipped from her, fell onto my lap. "Is that all I am? An experiment? Another study?"

I opened my mouth: no words. My thoughts were caught in amber. Finally, I blurted out, "I was just remarking on the experience."

"Oh, Jesus!"

"Oh, Jesus what?" I asked.

"Is that what you were doing? Just observing my mammae? My mammae!" She crossed her arms, covering Mother Nature's gift. Her face was a pattern of shadows. The firelight glinted in her eyes. "You don't live, do you, Percy. You just record."

"I . . . I do my job."

"Your job? It was your job to feel me up?"

"I . . . I don't know."

"You don't live!"

"I do so!"

"You don't *live*. There's a big difference. God, I shouldn't have to explain it. I don't want you to touch me for the first time and just think how you'll write it in your stupid journal. I want you to *be* here."

"I . . . I was . . ."

"I'm tired of doing what we do. All the fake studies. The staring. It's not normal."

Elissa stood and looked down at me. "Your father didn't die in the Congo, Percy. Why can't you tell the truth?"

"I did tell the truth! A tsetse fly bit him. He died of black Azazel sickness."

"I don't believe you."

"He did. I swear it's the truth." I could remember the *National Geographic* reporter coming to our door bawling her eyes out, her long blond hair undone. Mom not letting her in. It had happened.

Elissa glared. "I'm going home." Her tone was cool. "I'll give you a ride."

I couldn't move. I couldn't speak. I shook my head.

"Fine, then. And I won't be going to Grad with you. I might not go at all." She paused for a microsecond. "Goodbye, Percy."

fifteen

SAME TREE

Temporal confusion.
Time had passed.
Amount: unknown.
One hour? Two?

I clutched a bottle. Empty. I opened my hand. The bottle floated down, crashed in slo-mo against its brothers. The bonfires raged, sparks shot into the sky—flaming moths. Dying galaxies. Shadows danced madly to a bass beat. Distorted guitars grinding like tectonic plates.

The fire beckoned. I stood, took a step, stumbled, fell. The contents of my stomach lurched, so I clamped my mouth shut, used a tree to pull myself up. What had happened to my feet? It felt as though I were walking through clay. Would future anthropologists gaze in wonder at my hardened footprints? I staggered past prone hominids, some with faces pressed together. Others sat cross-legged, mesmerized by the fire. The flames were higher than before, their heat making my cells dance.

I tried to enter the crowd that surrounded one of the

bonfires. I wanted to see the center of the circle of flames. The core. An evolutionary secret I had been denied was there. Maybe the teachings the Ndebele youth learned during their manhood rites.

I fell, putting my hands out too late. My jaw struck the ground. Time oozed. Then the pain hit; my eyes watered. I got up, wiping my face.

I tried to break through at a different place. A male pushed me away, his face blurry. The square jaw and short hair reminded me of Justin. It had to be him, or one of his brethren.

"*Gigantopithecus blacki,*" I slurred. "Species died out. They did."

"Bug off, Einstein!"

"I'm Darwin!" I insisted. "Darwin!"

"Okay, Darwin! Go puke somewhere else."

Vomiting? The mere mention of it awakened gastrointestinal turmoil. I stumbled, turned away from the flame and bent over a log, and my digestive system flowed backward.

"Hey, whazzat," the log said, despite its lack of a larynx. "Oh, Jesus, get away!" Something flew out of the dark, a foot, a fist, a bottle, striking me in the chest.

My eyes stung. I weaved toward the circle of bodies. They were hominids. I was a hominid. We had the same number of fingers, the same number of chromosomes. They would let me enter the inner circle. I wanted to see the flames close up.

I tripped and fell into a group of shadows.

"Aw, back off!" one said, shoving me away. "He's coated in puke." I was pushed again, so that I rolled over into a puddle of mud.

In the past now. Long ago.

Three First Nations males looked down at me. Two large. One bald and thin as a colt. Flickering flames sharpened their features.

Was this pre-Columbian times? Had I crossed the Bering Strait?

The thin one kicked the ground, and dirt clumps smacked the side of my face. "Get out of here—go on."

I held up my hands. "The buffalo are all gone—the bison, I mean."

"What?" a larger lump barked. "What did you say?"

"I didn't kill them," I explained quickly. "The slaughter wasn't my fault. And the Beothuks, I understand how they felt."

"Understand this!" the thin one hissed. "Shove off, whitey!" He stepped toward me.

"Wait," the third one said. He moved into the light. "That you, Percy?" A familiar visage. Young face. Ancient eyes. Delmar Brass.

"Yes. Yes. It is I."

"What are you doing?"

"Elissa left. She left. Left. Left."

They stared quizzically at me.

"You know this guy?" The thin one pointed.

"Yeah," Delmar answered, "I do."

I needed to explain the link between us. "We come from the same tree," I began. "All of us climbed down from the same tree. All skin colors are mutations of our original color. *Australopithecus* is inside everyone. Witness Lucy. We come from the same tree."

Delmar chuckled. "Yeah, we come from the same tree. That's right, buddy. Don't get yourself all riled up. I see."

"You see what?" the skinny one said. "He's drunk."

"How much did you drink?" Delmar asked.

"A vast quality. Quantity. Five beers."

"Five beers?" The thin one again. "That's all it took to get you to barf? What kind of . . ."

I blacked out. When I opened my eyes again, I was on my back, squinting up, and Delmar was hovering over me, laughing. I giggled. Maybe this was a vision quest. I'd need to find an animal spirit. I thought of an owl, but its large eyes only reminded me of Elissa.

"She went away," I announced. "She left. Left. Left me here. Flew away."

Oh, wait. I'd said that already.

"I'll give you a ride home," Delmar said.

"Just let him sleep it off here," whined the thin one. "He'll be fine."

"No. I have to." Delmar paused, scratched his chin and chuckled. "We come from the same tree."

He helped me up and guided my unresponsive body to an old, dented truck. The interior smelled of sweet grass. Or maybe the scent emanated from the Marilyn Monroe deodorizer on the rearview mirror. Her shape drew my attention, her dress blown up to reveal her famous limbs. So smooth. The engine roared. Delmar jammed the truck into gear. Marilyn wiggled.

Beauty. Beauty and evolution. A connection. Somehow.

I pressed my face against the window. The coolness felt good. The bonfires disappeared. Delmar cranked the radio and a rock song about love tumbled out.

"You play a mean bagpipe," I said.

"Thanks. Always did like the sound. Gets my heart pumping."

We are one, I thought. *We are all one.* I closed my eyes. When I opened them, we were home.

"You ever get that article published?" he asked.

"Still trying." Both words were a struggle. "*National Geographic* next. Or *Modern Science.* Someone will take it."

"Keep on keeping on."

I have to, I wanted to say. We all must keep on. Then I leaned on the heavy door and stumbled out, and he sped off. I slouched across the lawn and crawled through my window, shedding mud all over my bedroom.

sixteen

NDEBELE RETURN

My bladder was a giant, expanding zeppelin.

I woke up in the middle of the night with one desperate need. I blink-walked to the bathroom, relieved myself, then cranked open the sink tap. The first blast of H_2O was rust-stained, but I didn't hesitate. I drank deeply. A lost desert nomad at the oasis.

My brain expanded/contracted/expanded. Painfully. Some scientists say that if the spaces between everything were collapsed, the universe could be condensed into a cantaloupe-sized object. Not a grand watermelon or royal pumpkin: a measly cantaloupe. They suggest that was the dimension of the universe before the Big Bang. Well, another universe was inside my skull, rushing to obliterate the present.

I put my lips to the tap and gulped again. Looked into the mirror. Mud stained my face, a charcoal streak blackened my brow. *Australo-ugly-Percy-ithecus.* Sobering up stripped layers from my humanity. Desapienization. Soon I would be reduced to grunting.

Elissa didn't want to go to Grad with me.

We hate you, Percival.

I had clouded my anthropological eyes with alcohol and succumbed to imitating their behavior. I did not need a mate. I did not need them. I had to stay pure and prepare for the next great revelation. The Yanomamo call themselves *waiteri*. It means fierce. From now on I'd be *waiteri* in the pursuit of my goal.

I doused my face. My mind remained foggy. Embrangled. I needed something else. I thought of the Ndebele rite of passage. I dug in the drawer, grasped a pair of scissors. I clipped and cut, dropping hair into the sink.

I reached for the razor.

seventeen

REBORN

Mom examined me from her side of the break-fast table. When I'd first sat down she'd displayed shock, but like a stone dropped in the ocean, that shock sank below the surface. Placidity ruled.

She set down her tea. "So this is your last day as a high school student."

"Yes."

"And you've chosen rebirth?"

I spread almond butter across my toast. The pungent scent drifted up and my stomach tightened. I forced a bite. Masticated. "I am not sure what you mean, Mom."

"Why did you shave your head?"

I palmed my smooth skull. It was hot. The coils of my brain blazed and every razor nick tingled. My fingers were cool, which was comforting because my head ached. My first hangover; I would make notes later.

"I . . . uh . . ." The reasons had been lucid last night. Now: vague. Something to do with the Ndebele manhood rites. Krep. Krep. My thoughts conglomerated slowly. "It. Was. A. Dare," I said finally. "A dare."

"Who dared you?"

"Elissa."

A frown flickered across my mother's lips. Disbelief and anger nearly gained a foothold, but the placid look won.

She stared at me. I ate. A memory spilled out my lips. "Did Cindy Mozkowski come to our door?"

Mom turned pale. "When?"

"Three years ago. To tell us . . . about Dad. Was she here? Crying?"

"I've only seen *her* once. At the airport. Why are you asking this?"

"I. Just. I seem to have mixed up a memory of her. That's all. Nothing." I looked down at my toast.

"Your father is coming tonight."

I shivered. "Oh," I said. "Oh." I hadn't committed to an emotion. Then I felt it. Impossible. The genitor—father—would *not* be there. His body had been reduced to its basic elements. "Will he float down from heaven, Mom? Rise up from the Netherworld? Reincarnate as a butterfly and flip-flap through the ceremony? Will I wear him as a brooch?"

"Why are you so mad, Perk?"

A primordial anger soup boiled inside my skull. "We go back to the earth. That's the way of things."

"What are you talking about?"

I stood up. "Why do people keep asking that? No one ever knows what I'm talking about. What it means. No one! Stupid, stupid hominids."

"Percy, what is it?"

I shook my head. How could I explain everything from *Australopithecus afarensis* to modern man? "It's nothing. Absolutely nothing."

Then I pulled my backpack off its hook on the wall and banged the door shut behind me.

eighteen

LITTLE BANG

Let's begin at the beginning. The real beginning. The early universe had ten billion and one protons created for every ten billion antiprotons. What's the big deal about that extra proton? Simple. Without it, matter and antimatter would have destroyed each other and there wouldn't have been a universe.

After the Big Bang there had to be exactly enough matter to clump into planets and stars, but not so much that it would all be pulled back together by gravity into the cantaloupe. The sun had to burn at least three and a half billion years to aid the creation of life. The earth had to rotate the perfect number of degrees from the sun, have enough gravity to hold an atmosphere, and the proper conditions to produce water. Only then could life begin. Without any of these factors, you get *nada*. Nil. Zero. No sane sentient being would bet on life forming on the third planet.

Which made it a miracle that I was at the front doors of Groverly High for my final day of Grade Twelve. I strode inside, head erect, eyes darting back and forth, eager to capture every significant event. A few students stared at my new visage—a Back-to-Buddha look. Most ignored me, including Elissa, whom I twice glimpsed in the hallway. She didn't even glance in my direction.

There were no classes, only a final goodbye from each teacher. Some classmates exchanged gifts or cards with each other, but I didn't receive anything. I report this to keep the facts straight. I felt no envy.

After lunch my peers dressed for photographs. I declined since I didn't want my soul sucked into the camera. I would forever be remembered in the yearbook as "no picture available."

There was a break between school and the graduation banquet. I went home, retreated silently to my room and wrote in my field journal. I scrutinized my words until my stereoscopic eyes ached.

"You're here," Mom said, entering my room without knocking. "Did you go to the banquet?"

"I didn't have time."

"Time?" She paused. "I hope you're not mad because I decided not to go. I—I just couldn't be in the same room as all that roast beef. You know that."

"I'm not angry. I missed it for my own reasons."

"Are you feeling better? This morning you were so upset."

"I was tired. That's all. There's so much to do." I looked at my watch. "I have to get dressed; the ceremony's going to start soon."

"I'd better get ready too. I found the perfect outfit at Value Village." On her way out my door she added, "Your father will hate it, though."

Dad, again? I thought. *Just let it go, Mom.*

I clad myself in the gray suit she'd purchased at the Salvation Army. It was too small for my frame. Had I grown overnight? I clipped on my tie and slipped into a pair of black herbivore-hide dress shoes.

Mom met me at the door in a white robe that only a Vulcan would wear. She straightened the shoulders of my suit and let out a sigh. "You look beautiful, Percy. I can't believe you're graduating."

"Me either, Mom," I said, quickly kissing her cheek. Then I ran the three blocks to school.

The recently assembled Grad Tribe was in a hallway near the back of the stage. Various females had caked their features with makeup and preserved their hair with gel and spray. Males stood uncomfortably in their new suits, hands in pockets, tugging ties, inspecting their shoes as if trying to recall why they weren't wearing sneakers.

I approached the sign-in desk. Ms. Nystrom looked up, frowned.

"You're late, Percy."

"I am aware of my tardiness," I answered. "It was unavoidable. It won't happen again, I promise." I winked. Her face was blank. "Get it? School's finished so I won't be back, therefore I can't be late."

"Yes, that is funny," she replied flatly. "I'll miss your sense of humor."

I thought of all the times she'd indulged me in class when I'd expounded on my theories regarding literature and evolution. She deserved a final gift, so I offered, "A birthmark on the left cheek is a sign of intelligence and good luck in Thai culture."

She looked up, eyes guarded. Then: a slight smile, making her birthmark crease together. "Good luck to you, Mr. Montmount," she said, handing me a graduation gown. I slung it over my arm and joined the crowd, amused that the males would submit to such effeminate dress.

Clusters of visibly nervous students chatted hesitantly, straightening each other's gowns and fixing their tresses like monkeys hunting for head lice. I retrieved my field notebook and jotted notes.

No Elissa sightings. No surprise. We were packed in the hallway like lab rats in a cage. The masses parted for the walking monolith, Justin. He lumbered through the students, his robe draped over one shoulder, *Gigantopithecus blacki* on a mission. He paused to inspect me; his eyes revealed no warmth, no anger, just contentment—an odd expression on his square-jawed face. Graduation agreed with him; maybe he'd won a football scholarship.

"Bald is beautiful," he said. "You look like one of them Shaolin kung fu fighters. Pretty gutsy to shave your head for Grad."

I blinked. Was that a compliment? He waited for a reaction from me. I tried not to send signals of fear or antagonism.

"Do you have any plans for next year?" he asked. I was stunned; he wanted to converse. I remained silent, alert. At first he grimaced, then—a grin. "Happy graduation, Montmount," he said without a hint of malice, clapping me on the shoulder. Was graduation like the so-called afterlife in which forgiveness was offered to all? Or did the suit somehow make him transcend into maturity?

"Thank you," I said. "Same sentiments to you."

He gave me the thumbs-up and turned away. I stared after him until he was swallowed by the river of dark robes.

I found a corner and wrestled into my robe, a butterfly struggling to reenter a cocoon. As the gown slipped over my bare-skinned skull, something in me changed, as though each brain cell were suddenly imprinted with new understanding. I had accessed a secret layer of my corpus callosum, the site of intuition known to mystics and the greatest scientists. Eureka zone! My eyes focused perfectly. I looked down at the gown and saw the stitches a hominid had designed and bequeathed to mankind. A pattern within a pattern.

The graduates had coagulated into groups. Did an inner impulse draw them together like one-celled organisms? A genetic program passed to us by the amoebae?

I was on the edge of ascertaining this knowledge when the loudspeaker barked: "Ladies and gentlemen, please line up in the hall according to your last names."

Several teachers held up placards. I found M–P.

The line ahead of me had morphed. An apelike creature was at the beginning, followed by a slightly taller one. The next had wider shoulders, a straighter stance, then a fourth and fifth, each taller than the rest, still dressed in gowns. A vision. A reward. A teacher grunted and the line advanced. As each hairy graduate passed through the portal, we drew closer to the beginning of our own evolution. Step by inexorable step, I moved toward it too. What would be on the other side? I passed through, brain tingling.

The stage was lit like a football stadium. We shuffled across the gym floor, up the stairs and into the glare.

Several older tribes stared—fathers, mothers, grandparents, all witnesses to this ancient ceremony. We would be their replacements, the next batch of genetic material that superseded them. Our job would be to carry the human race forward for another generation.

Their eyes examined and measured. My naked skull buzzed, felt each molecule of air. We took our places, settling into seats set on risers. I spotted Elissa, her face hard as a Sphinx's.

The ritual began with Principal Michaels delivering a glorious oration to send us into the future. Time. Cut. Away. I snapped to attention for the valedictorian speech: our *über-teen*. A female who waxed on about how we would fulfill our biological destinies.

The principal returned to the mike, spoke solemnly, his words so deep they were garbled. But I caught the last few: ". . . a moment of silence for Willard Spokes."

I swallowed and glanced behind me at the *S* section. There was an empty chair for Willard. They had honored him. The silence lasted a lifetime. Then the spell was broken when a female yelled: "Willard rocked!"

Elissa. Everyone gawked at her, until someone began clapping: Marcia Grady. The graduates, then the audience joined in.

When the noise died down, Michaels spoke again. An invitation. One by one we descended to the stage to receive our totems. Justin was one of the first. He brandished his diploma as if he'd pulled a sword out of a stone. The crowd applauded. A few graduates later, another Jock Tribe member repeated the gesture and was met with half the response. Student after student accepted diploma after diploma. Delmar walked up smiling, hair tied back. Somewhere in the crowd his mother made a *hi-ni-ni* sound. Several others repeated it. Marcia Grady soon followed, looking absolutely beautiful. If only Willard could have experienced this moment. I glanced back at his empty chair.

Then: Elissa. She walked slowly across the stage, gown flowing around her. A priestess in a solemn ceremony, she wore no makeup, no jewelry, and her hair was tied back. When she took her diploma I expected some symbolic action, perhaps defiance. Instead, she joined the line.

Soon my name was announced.

The voice of Fate. I advanced to Principal Michaels, who guarded the triangular pile of rolled diplomas. Three steps led up to the platform. I climbed using a system of flesh, blood, reflexes and nerves that had taken millions of years to evolve.

Then it hit me. I was genetically programmed to die. Nature's tidy system: We expire so we don't compete with our children. The faster we produce offspring, the faster our species mutates into something better adapted to the environment. I was next in line. One day I would be sitting in that crowd, watching my replacements. Would their feet be webbed?

I stepped onto the platform. A spotlight nearly blinded me. I extended my opposable-thumbed right hand to receive the holy paper. *Australopithecus afarensis* reaching for a bone that would become a tool.

FLASH.

Neurons fired too rapidly to comprehend. Applause thundered as I grasped the scroll. And suddenly . . .

FLASH.

I saw all history. From the beginning of the universe to now, condensed into shining moments. The earth forming. The first movement of life. The rise of vertebrates. Dinosaurs. Mammals. Man painting his cave walls. Aztec priests cutting open the chests of prisoners of war and wrenching out their beating hearts, holding them to the sky. The Romans burning Carthage, gas flooding an Auschwitz chamber. Japanese hominids lifting their eyes, pupils dilated by a hydrogen flash, then my father leaving my mother for the woman with blond hair, leaving me for . . .

Wait.

That.

Was not.

A historical fact.

FLASH.

The crowd of hominids came into focus. Became individuals. There was my mother with her Mona Lisa smile. Beside her. Someone else. A hand raised in a half wave. A man.

My father.

Percival Montmount, Sr.

A glowing blue ghost. Waving.

I turned toward him. Stepped from the line of evolution into the brilliant light.

"*Dad,*" I whispered. Then I was falling, pushing aside a chair. Falling off the stage, down into darkness.

My body felt something (pain?) but maybe just a harsh jarring.

Voices. "Are you all right?"

My mother knelt beside me.

My father? Gazing at me? Light beginning to glow.

"Want your eyes back?" I whispered.

"Whu-what?"

"Taking? Your eyes back now?"

Then blackness.

nineteen

AWARENESS

The heat was unbearable. The smoke so thick my eyes watered, and the scent of burning sweet grass permeated every molecule of air. I was shirtless, sweating exponentially, my body quickly becoming a shell.

Gray Eyes sat across from me, the bucket of fire-heated rocks between us. He pulled out what looked like a bull's horn and sprinkled water across them. Steam rose, hissing. He sat back. He hadn't spoken for the last twenty minutes. He'd built the sweat lodge this morning, at my mother's request. She sat to my right, eyes closed. Clad in white, her hair stringy and wet, her legs crossed. She too had been silent, not even an *omm* to interrupt this afternoon sweat.

The door, covered by blankets and a tarp, faced east, toward the rising sun, the rising of wisdom. The Sioux, whom Mom sometimes emulated, saw the inside of the lodge as the womb of Mother Earth, the darkness as ignorance, the stones as the arrival of life and the hissing steam as the creative forces of the universe becoming active. The fire represented eternity.

They'd explained all this to me after I crawled inside, then told me to forget it. To dwell on the symbols would only lead to confusion. The sweat would purify me.

I closed my burning eyes, and that made them feel better. Behind them, vague memories. My arm ached. I'd fallen from the stage last night. My mother had guided me home to bed, where I'd slept deeply. When I awoke she dragged me to the table, fed me tofu soup, the best I'd ever had. A quintessential stomach heater. Then I was brought here to the sweat lodge. Willingly.

Wait. There was something else. I'd seen my father, too.

Alive.

"Percy," Mom whispered.

I opened my eyes. "Yes."

"Where are you?" she asked.

"Here. Right here."

She smiled. "Good. Gray Eyes and I will leave you alone now. It's time."

"Alone?"

"Yes. With your thoughts. With you. It will only be for twenty minutes. But it might seem longer."

I nodded.

They crawled out the front, lifting the flap to reveal a fire, just a few meters from the tent. Tiny tongues of flame licked red embers, and inside that heat were several rocks. Gray Eyes returned a moment later carrying two more rocks on a forked stick. He dropped them into the pail and handed me the water horn with a wink.

Then: alone. Me and my thoughts. But what was I

supposed to think about? The universe was too complex to comprehend. The last few days, months, years—even more complex. So I tried not to think of anything.

That worked for a microsecond.

Earlobes. That's what came to mind. Elissa's. The half-moon shape, the way she always wore some new, interesting earrings that jangled when she laughed.

Her laugh. High-pitched and from the belly. Her presence filled the lodge. I wept hard, struggling to muffle my sobs.

When I gained control of myself again, my mind's eye conjured an acne-scarred afterimage: Willard, smiling at me. It was as if I were staring at a cave painting, a message from an ancient time.

Where there's a Will, there's a way.

His voice. Speaking to me. The hissing of steam off the rocks. Then he was gone. Returned to sender.

I ached to talk with him again. And Elissa. The three of us together. But he was beyond us now, in his own universe.

I'd been still for too long. I had to move; I sprinkled the rocks and was enveloped in fresh steam. Time expanded inside this room. How long had it been since my mother had left?

The tribes had dispersed. Justin, Marcia, all the teachers: gone. Graduation was over and summer would swallow them. No longer would we walk the same hallways, breathe the same air, attend the same classes. Other students would fill Groverly, but I would have no connection with them.

Good. It was time to find new connections. New feelings.

An eon passed. My thoughts returned to the beginning.

I was suddenly at show-and-tell in Grade One, holding up a shrunken head, explaining to the class that it was from faraway Afreeka, a hot place. The head was from a white hunter whom the witch doctors had caught. I went into details: First they dismembered him, then severed his neck with cleavers. The teacher shooed me to my seat halfway through the story.

The plastic head had been a gift from my father, and I was only repeating a bedtime story he'd told me. Even then I was marked. His son.

Someone lifted the flap. My father crawled in, his glasses fogged with steam. Had I summoned him? He sat across from me and removed his specs. His eyes, so familiar, looked into mine. "It's hot in here, Perk," he said.

I sprinkled water and the steam rose. He wavered momentarily, then came into focus. Real. He was there.

"I hope I'm not disturbing you. Your mother said you'd be ready to talk now. How do you feel?"

"Disa . . . disassoc . . . crappy. And tired."

"You've done a good job of avoiding me," he said. "You ignored my phone calls. Always too busy to talk. Did you get my letters?"

"Yes."

"Did you read them?"

"No."

"Why, Perk? It's been hard to be in the field and to have lost all contact with my son. Three years without a word."

"You could have come back. Like you did when I was born."

He squinted. There were wrinkles around his eyes

and only a vestige of his hair remained. Time was creeping up on him. "It's not that easy. I was halfway across the world. It takes years to get the trust of a tribe. You can't just give it up."

"What about the trust of a son?"

He bit his lip. "Percy. Perhaps . . . perhaps I should have come home sooner."

"You can have your eyes back."

"What?"

"I can't look through them anymore. I need a break."

I held out my hand, palm up. "Take them."

He still didn't understand, but he moved closer and took my hand. I felt an ache in my eyes. I blinked. My sight sharpened.

"I . . . I . . . I pretended you were dead," I said. "I believed it, in fact."

He furrowed his brow, wrinkling up his forehead. "I—I see."

Time was stretching again. Between us. Sweat trickling down my forehead, down his, too. Like looking in a mirror.

"How was the field?" I asked.

"Long. Tiring. It was my last trip. I'm moving home. To Chicago."

He looked disappointed that he had to admit this. I half expected him to launch into a story the way he had when I was a child, about piranha-infested rivers, giant boas, ancient temples. That wasn't his world now. He would have tenure and an office with a window and a rusty air conditioner that dripped. A home with a green lawn, lawnmower and Cindy Mozkowski.

Things change. They evolve. One has to adapt to these changes.

"It is good to see you again, Dad," I said, "with my own eyes."

"Oh, Perk," he said, "Perk. I'll see you more often now. I promise."

A wisp of steam rose between us. "I hope so, Dad. I do."

epilogue

The next day my father flew home. I borrowed
Gray Eyes' car (an ancient Volvo) and drove Dad to
the airport. We chatted in the lobby, saying nothing
particularly significant to each other.

After he had boarded, I went to the window and
watched his plane take off. The airport was small,
so it wasn't hard to figure out which one it was.
I waved.

When I got home I was tempted to collapse into
my bed, but instead I picked up the phone and dialed
Elissa's number, my palms sweating. She answered,
and in a shaky voice I asked her to meet me at the
Broadway Roastery. She agreed.

I arrived early.

"Hi, Percy," she said, strolling in. Her hair was
tucked behind her ears. Two skulls dangled from her
earlobes. "How's your head?"

I had so many possible answers for that. "Bald but
still on my shoulders."

She smiled briefly, then went to the counter and

returned with a cappuccino. "You know, you shouldn't get so wrapped up in things," she said.

I sipped my tea. "Right now I don't want to be wrapped up in anything."

"Good."

An uncomfortable pause followed. It grew longer. We drank from our cups. I began to tell her about the sweat lodge, then stopped.

"I'm sorry I hurt you," I said finally.

She nodded. "Yeah, I know."

"I—I saw my dad."

"Knew that, too. Good."

"How long did you know? That . . . he wasn't dead?"

"Will and I figured it out. We made a pact that we wouldn't ask you. We'd hoped you'd eventually tell us. You must have been very angry with him."

"I was."

People walked by the window, heading to the stores up the street.

"So did the sweat help?" she asked.

"It cleared my sinuses."

She laughed. "Be serious."

"It centered me. I guess."

"Will that be enough?"

I shrugged. "I think I'll call up Mr. Verplaz. Have a talk with him. I'm sure he must get bored in the summer. It'll give him something to do."

"I'm glad to hear that."

Silence. Again. More watching through the window.

"Uh . . . ," I said, "if you have time in the next little while, call me. Maybe we could go to a movie."

"No, Percy."

My heart felt as though someone were squeezing it. Then she said, "You call me. Maybe I'll come." She stood up. "I have to go walk Fang."

We hugged, briefly; then she was gone.

I went home and life returned to normal. I avoided my field journal for the first week of summer. And the second. It loomed too large on my desk, heavy as an obelisk. I refused to turn my television on or open any books. I only used my room for sleeping. I went for walks along the river. My hair began poking out of my skull.

I visited Mr. Verplaz several times, engaging in long discussions about fathers, sons and dream worlds. He even gave me advice on a few university classes and loaned me a couple of jazz CDs, explaining that they'd calm me—they proved that something beautiful could emerge from chaos.

And eventually I convinced myself to phone Elissa.

"So, um, you want to go to a show?"

"Can't," she said. "Why didn't you call before?"

"I—I was busy." I decided to tell her the truth. "And I wasn't ready yet."

"Phone me again at the end of August. Ma and Pa decided to give me a surprise Grad gift. We're jetting off to Rome."

"When?"

"Tomorrow! They want us to have some quality time together. Might kill me. But I could always feed them to the lions in the Colosseum. See ya when I'm back, kiddo."

And so I was left with a lot of time to myself. I read fantasy novels and listened to jazz.

Weeks later a postcard arrived with a statue of Minerva on the front. On the back was written:

> *Hey. They have statues of me here.*
> *Carpe Diem, Perky!*
> *E.*

I laughed out loud.

Finally, on August 6, I opened the journal and flipped through it. There were over seven hundred pages of articles with hundreds of footnotes and a vast number of intricate drawings of skulls and apes and humans. Three years of work. I couldn't quite remember the person who'd written all this; he seemed to have had so much energy. I closed the book. It was still too heavy to move.

I went for a walk and found myself in front of Will's house. I hadn't been there for ages. The curtains in his room were open, and I grinned when I saw that his mother had left his *Planet of the Apes* posters up.

"You really do rock, Will," I said to the ether.

What had I learned? I asked myself as I made my way to the river. I found no clear answer. But I did know this—the sun produces over two hundred trillion trillion trillion neutrinos every second. These tiny particles pass unhindered through space, and through the planets, including Earth. Some are relic neutrinos, left over from the birth of the universe. Billions of neutrinos shoot through our bodies every second on their way back to outer space. For them, it's almost as if we didn't exist at all.

I thought about this as I strolled along the river, sat down on a patch of green grass and felt the sun's rays warm my skin.

So much passes through us without our ever noticing.

Arthur Slade (genus and species: *Homo sapiens*) was born in Moose Jaw and raised on a ranch in the Cypress Hills of southwest Saskatchewan, Canada. There he learned how to ride herbivores and drive mechanized farm implements. Early in his development, he began writing; he is the author of five novels for young adults and has won several prizes, including the Governor General's Award for Children's Literature. His current habitat is a house in the mythical city of Saskatoon. Arthur Slade can be visited virtually at www.arthurslade.com.